YOUR OWN ONES

YOUR OWN ONES

A NOVEL

SÍLE POST

GREEN WRITERS PRESS *Brattleboro, Vermont*

Green Writers Press is a Vermont-based publisher whose
mission is to spread a message of hope and renewal through
the words and images we publish. Throughout we will adhere
to our commitment to preserving and protecting the natural
resources of the earth. To that end, a percentage of our proceeds
will be donated to various environmental activist groups. Green
Writers Press gratefully acknowledges support from individual
donors, friends, and readers to help support the environment and
our publishing initiative.

Giving Voice to Writers & Artists Who Will Make the World a Better Place
Green Writers Press | Brattleboro, Vermont
www.greenwriterspress.com

ISBN: 978-0-9961357-3-3

PRINTED ON PAPER WITH PULP THAT COMES FROM FSC-CERTIFIED FORESTS, MANAGED FORESTS
THAT GUARANTEE RESPONSIBLE ENVIRONMENTAL, SOCIAL, AND ECONOMIC PRACTICES BY
LIGHTNING SOURCE. ALL WOOD PRODUCT COMPONENTS USED IN BLACK & WHITE, STANDARD
COLOR, OR SELECT COLOR PAPERBACK BOOKS, UTILIZING EITHER CREAM OR WHITE BOOKBLOCK
PAPER, THAT ARE MANUFACTURED IN THE LAVERGNE, TENNESSEE PRODUCTION CENTER ARE
SUSTAINABLE FORESTRY INITIATIVE® (SFI®) CERTIFIED SOURCING

FOR MY OWN ONES—
IAN,
MAIRE DE BRÚN POST
&
MY IRISH FAMILY
HERE AND OVER

I AM OF IRELAND—

W.B. YEATS

I'M GOING BACK,
TO MY OWN ONES . . .

FOR THE WORLD IS SO COLD,
DON'T CARE NOTHING
FOR THE SOUL
YOU SHARE
WITH
YOUR OWN ONES—

VAN MORRISON

I AM THE WIND
THAT BREATHES UPON THE SEA,
I AM THE WAVE OF THE OCEAN,
I AM THE MURMUR OF THE BILLOWS,
I AM A SALMON IN THE WATER . . .

AMERGIN

PRONUNCIATION GUIDE
FOR
IRISH GAELIC NAMES

ÁINE—[AWN-ya]

CÍARAN—[keyr-AWN]

CONOR—[CON-ur]

DA CHÍCH ANANN—[DAW CHEECH uh-NAWN]

DIARMUID—[DEER-mid]

EITHNE—[ETH-na]

FERGUS—FUR-gus]

FIONA—fee-OWN-a]

GEARÓID—GAY-RUD]

GRÁINNE—[GRAW-nya]

MAEVE/MEDB—MAVE]

MUIRÍS—MUR-ish]

NÍAMH—NEEV]

NA BRADÁIN FIÁIN—NA BRA-DAWN FI-AWN]

Part One

Away

IMITHE

CHAPTER ONE

SEA-CHANGE

CASADH NA TAOIDE

There are those who say that some things in life cannot be planned. But along the ancient coast of Ireland, they who understand the old ways know better.

"What's in a name?" the locals are known to proclaim, "Sure, both our past and our future. When we are named after the Old Ones, their passions, their traits, aye—their very lives—flow through us."

There among the waters and the wild of Dingle Peninsula, the Celtic past has an uncanny way of touching those in the present—however near or far away.

BEFORE THE SUN EMERGED along the horizon, wild salmon preservationist Áine O'Connor gently waded through the saltwater marsh in her Wellies, making her way to the point where the river opened to the sea. There, the wild salmon would return back home to their native streams on Prince Edward Island, after several years of swimming the northern seas. In the rivers of their birth, they would lay their eggs, and a new journey forward would begin.

As Áine set up her laser counter and camera, positioning them at the opening, she eagerly awaited the final numbers for her multi-year project on wild salmon re-population. She had spent the last several years in those waters preparing for this moment of homecoming.

As she waited, she glanced down at her rubber overalls, her daily attire for longer than she could remember. She grinned as it triggered memories of the refrain of her resolutely Canadian, though indisputably Irish, immigrant mother.

"Just look at the getup of you now. Sure, you're like a wild salmon yourself," Eithne had admonished. "Always fighting the currents of convention, you are, Áine." She sighed. "Can't you find a way just to *get along* like a good Canadian?"

Áine laughed. "Actually, Mum, I'm gaining a reputation in Government for being quite the *contrarian*—a trait I attribute to my Irish birth and heritage."

"Not all Irish are rebels, you know," her mother scoffed with an upward toss of her head.

"Don't they refer to the Irish as the '*fighting*' Irish in the States? Áine countered. That would be me, I suppose."

"Well, you're *here*, and you're meant to get along," Eithne scolded.

With a slight shrug of her shoulder, Áine said, "After all, I work in a decidedly male profession; I champion local food in a global economy, and I tend to look back— to traditional ways—as Grandma had always advised, for solutions to challenges in the present." With a sidelong glance at her mother, she added, "I remember how she would proclaim in her prophetic way, 'Sometimes, the journey *forward*, begins with a step *back*.'"

Eithne only scowled fiercely, as she did whenever Áine

expressed any interest in their Irish past. "Rubbish. Utter rubbish. Forget the past. Move *on*."

The exchange drifted away from Áine's thoughts as images of her Gaelic-speaking namesake swirled round her in the soft mist that floated about in the dawning light. The significance of her grandmother's prophetic claim rushed through her as she focussed her attention on the river's mouth, waiting for the salmon to return. Surely the journey of the salmon *back* to their birthplace, Áine reasoned, also represents their path *forward* into their future. Gently shaking her head, she gazed down into the river. "You are wise beyond human expectation," she exclaimed. "You have it all over us, salmon!"

An orange flame suddenly appeared in the dissipating mist as the dark sky faded into pastels of rose and heather. Daylight at the edge of the sea. "'Only that day dawns to which we are awake,'" Áine murmured, as she watched the majestic scene unfold. "Yet 'the sun is but a morning star.'" Now that her project was nearing completion, she wondered in which new direction her own journey in life would take.

The now clear waters transformed into sea-blue glass. Looking down into the translucent river, she could see the wild salmon swimming upstream, making their way determinedly against the current. Soon their eggs will hatch, and new generations of salmon will live on in these rivers, Áine thought, thrilled over the parade below her—*as long as we continue to protect them, that is.*

She had dedicated nearly a decade to the restoration project—her early twenties fizzled away in years of research, followed by several more in leading a team to create river habitats conducive to spawning. Her groundbreaking work on the merits of wild salmon over farmed and genetically engineered versions had caused a maelstrom among those Cabinet Ministers eager to grant sizable tax deductions, to attract investment along the virgin coastline surrounding the island province. Investors worldwide stood eagerly on the sidelines waiting for approval to set up their fish farms and genetic laboratories. Before deciding conclusively, the Government awaited from Áine and her team, the final numbers to assess whether to continue supporting the preservation project—or open the shoreline to multi-national investors. She counted the last of the salmon through the morning hours before packing up, confident that the numbers would convince the Ministers to endorse her preservation work.

And now, the moment had arrived after her years of hard work, she thought proudly, as she entered the door of her office building on the university campus in Charlottetown. *I'm reporting to the entire Provincial Cabinet!*

When Áine entered her office, she instinctively sensed a *sea-change* in the air. Scanning the room with an inquisitive gaze, she noticed a large packet on her desk waiting. *Something to do with Ireland.*

As she turned over the curious, legal-sized manila envelope, she heard the faint whisper of her grandmother's evocative words echoing from within the shadows of her memory. Although Áine *Críonna*, the "wise one," as she was called, had long forewarned her granddaughter of the power of the past to cast its spell on the present, Áine had chosen to overlook the old woman's warning until now—when she read the return address. FitzGerald, Solicitor, Dingle, Éire/Ireland. Looking away, she settled her gaze on the distant horizon. She then shook her head gently as if to dispel Áine *Críonna's* words ringing through her, before turning back to the envelope. As she started to open it, she dismissed her instincts, assuming instead, it was some matter related to the funeral in Ireland she was organizing for her Aunt Maeve. *Nothing more.*

Nonchalantly unsealing the packet, Áine read the solicitor's letter in disbelief, its effect transformational. The notice of the completely unexpected inheritance slipped from Áine's grasp like the last wave of the incoming tide clinging to the shore, before turning back out to sea. She felt the currents of the past, long submerged, suddenly sweep over her, flooding her with feelings now surging, rushing, swirling through her, before receding—leaving behind in their wake, pools of unshakeable, nostalgic yearning for a home she had never really known.

Closing her eyes, Áine could envision the ancestral cottage even still, sitting ever watchful along the mist-covered coast of Dingle Peninsula—an enchanting place, she recalled—where the Celtic past seemed to flow into the present, much like the rivers and mountains that tumbled into the sea.

In that instant when she read of her legacy, she heard the *calling* in the whisper of her grandmother's words now echoing in her head—felt it pulsating through her veins. Her duty, her grandmother had often reminded her, to return home, to carry on the family tradition.

She bent down to retrieve the papers, now scattered on the floor. "Ah, Grandma," she mentally called out, "I do protect the wild salmon, but *here*, in my home in Atlantic Canada. My historical legacy, with a twist—a literal *sea-change*." But now, she thought, as she rearranged the documents, decidedly a new twist of fate.

She tried to shake off the feeling of destiny that weighed her down. She didn't really believe in fate in the way Áine Críonna had always talked about. But why then, Áine wondered, had Aunt Maeve left *her* the ancestral property?

Áine felt her heart race as she continued to read through the entire notice. Ah, here we are, she noted, as she drew in her breath, *a catch*. She read it twice to make sure that she clearly understood the conditions. Her aunt had stipulated that before assuming ownership, Áine must reside in the old cottage for one year.

She leaned back, gently swirling in her chair, as she tried to decipher her aunt's motivation. Surely her mother had told Maeve about her important position with Government. She shook her head. *Did she think I would just pick up, leave, and go back?*

The condition made Áine sit up straight. One year on the remote coast of Dingle Peninsula—one of the last remaining vestiges of Celtic Ireland where they still spoke Gaelic. With a grin, she realized that she'd need to learn more than rudimentary expressions to get along, such as her standard response in the pubs when the lads got too fresh: "*Póg mo thóin*—Kiss me' arse!" The memory made her smile.

Áine returned to the notice. A few lines later, she gasped, "What?" *And* she was to write an account of Maeve's life.

She sat back stunned. Nothing had prepared her for the news—the utterly inexplicable legacy. She knew so little about the details of Maeve's past—aside from the flocks of husbands and properties she had accumulated. Áine paced back and forth in her office, trying to make sense of it all.

Instinctively checking her watch, she discovered she had just under an hour before the meeting started. *No time to think about this now!* Yanking off her wet, mud-encrusted Wellies, she flung them into the corner, usually reserved for her heels. "I must get out of this fishing get-up," she mumbled. "Can't meet the Provincial Cabinet looking like this!" She hastily replaced her waders with a black silk suit and a soft collarless cream blouse, knowing she had to sparkle for the Cabinet meeting. The thought triggered a favourite notion her Aunt Maeve was fond of saying, "Sure, there's nothing, Áine, like heels, to sway a man's thoughts." Áine smiled over the memory, wondering whether the theory applied to stodgy, old Cabinet Ministers—the very type she must persuade to protect the wild salmon.

After completing her final review, Áine stood up, and going over to the mirror, smoothed down imagined wrinkles in her suit, and fussed with her long red hair a bit, before walking over to the executive assistant's desk in the outer office. "Well, then I'm off," she announced to Margaret, her uncertain tone countering her assertion. She was convinced that surely, her nervousness was obvious to everyone looking at her.

Margaret looked up from her computer screen and sized up Áine in one sweeping glance. With a nod and a quick smile, she returned to her screen, though not before proclaiming, "Dazzling as usual."

Áine broke out in nervous laughter. "Do they pay you to say that?" She gazed down at her spiked heels. "You know how much I prefer my Wellies to these things. I'm always afraid while raising some incredibly important point, I'll fall flat on me' arse!" She sighed.

Laughing, Margaret reassured her. "Ah, you'll do just fine." She offered a warm smile of encouragement. "Just strut your stuff, and you'll dazzle them!"

Áine's eyes widened. "Odd saying, that. My Aunt Maeve used to say that often." She walked over to look out through the window. "She would use that expression when describing the mating games of the wild salmon in the rivers back in Ireland. I haven't heard it for *ages*." Turning back, she shook her head. "Odd you should say that, I mean."

Margaret shrugged. "A common expression in my own family."

Áine checked her watch. "Oh, I must go!" she exclaimed. "Wish me luck!"

"Luck has nothing to do with your achievements, Áine."

Áine looked away as she replied, "Ah, just a few wee splashes in the wide sea of change."

"If anything, I'd say it is your *fate* to chart new courses—as you have here."

"Fate, is it?" said Áine. "My grandmother in Ireland was always talking about fate."

As she started to leave the office, she turned back to look at Margaret. "Odd, that. She used to say it was my fate to take on the role of protecting the wild salmon as so many of my Irish ancestors had done." She smiled. "And look at me," she added, with a shrug, "following my destiny!"

Just as she was about to enter the Ministerial chamber, the Economics Minister called out to her. "Oh, Dr. O'Connor, just a moment, if you please."

Áine turned in surprise. "Yes, Minister?"

After finishing an exchange with a fellow Minister, he

swiftly walked over. With a brief nod, he said, "I need to have a word with you after the deliberations, so don't rush off to your salmon just yet."

She bit her lip. "Yes, of course, Minister." She shook her head slightly. "Is everything all right?"

He waved his hand. "Yes, yes. Just a few changes we're considering."

Startled, she said, "How fortuitous."

He peered at her from above his reading glasses. "Is that so?"

Trying to restrain an involuntary shudder, she said, "Actually, I was going to request a meeting. Em, something has come up I was hoping to discuss with you."

Nodding, he said, "Fortuitous, indeed. Precisely the reason I must speak with you immediately following the meeting. You'll wait around then?" He eyed her with a somber expression. "Our decision may take some time."

"Of course, Minister," she said in a soothing voice. "I'll just wait here until you and the others finish your deliberations." She offered a re-assuring smile.

"Right then," he said with a brusque nod. "Good luck with the presentation." As he turned to leave, he suddenly swung back. "Almost forgot the important bit. Did the numbers come in?"

She broke out in a radiant smile. "Indeed they did, Minister, and more so."

"Good, good," he said, before walking briskly into the chamber.

While the enthusiastic response from the Ministers to her presentation momentarily took her mind off the strange inheritance, Áine found herself unable to focus on her much-earned success. As she waited in the massive hall for the private Cabinet session to conclude, she sat with legs crossed, nervously swinging one foot rhythmically back and forth, much like an angler's fishing line across the surface of a river. The lure of the news of her inheritance seemed to reel her through currents of past memories, now rushing through her.

After the meeting concluded, the Economics Minister walked over. "I never thought I'd see the day when my fellow Ministers would vote for salmon preservation—over the lure of corporate profits!" He shook his head as he confessed, "We feared the issue over providing a ready supply of salmon was going to be a deal breaker for the EU seafood trade deal." He nodded at her, before adding, "While you demonstrated that indeed we *could* have provided them with wild salmon, based on the results of your project, you argued convincingly that we *should* reserve such special fish for local consumption only."

Áine beamed. "Well, that's a relief."

Nodding, he added, "We Islanders have certainly benefitted from your expertise in preservation, first, in protecting our historical cultivars—and now, the wild salmon." He smiled at her. "Perhaps the old ways *were* better for us as a province and a people."

"It makes sense, really," Áine said. "By bringing back the heirloom potatoes, wheat strains, and blueberries our ancestors once relied upon, as well as re-populating the endangered wild salmon, perhaps we are ensuring a sustainable future for ourselves. If we don't sell out our precious resources, that is. My grandmother was quite fond of saying that the journey *forward*, begins with a step *back*." She stopped, surprised by her sudden reference to Áine Críonna's favourite expression.

"Indeed," he said.

"After all," she added with a big smile, "we Islanders prefer to keep our wild salmon for ourselves!"

"Indeed we do," he affirmed. "That is precisely the matter I wished to discuss with you, Dr. O'Connor."

"About local food, is it?" She looked at him, waiting.

"Have you been reading about what's happening to the wild salmon in your part of the world?" he asked.

Áine arched her eyebrow. "My part of the world?" She studied him a moment. "But isn't that what I presented this afternoon—through my salmon research from North Lake?"

"No," he countered. "In Ireland." He looked at her. "You are Irish, aren't you?"

Her shoulders stiffened. "Well, yes, I was born there." Noting her diffident tone, she tried to diffuse it with humour. "Actually, I'm named after some mountains there—as well as the reigning Celtic goddess, of course." She rolled her eyes. "Quite a cultural legacy to live up to!"

"A mountain *and* a goddess?" he repeated, his eyes widening. "How are they connected?"

"Oh, it's a long story—several thousand years old!" She grinned, before adding pointedly, "but having lived *here* nearly all of my conscious life, just over three decades, mind you, I consider myself a local, an Islander." She met his gaze.

"Yes, yes, of course," he said, with a dismissive wave of his hand, "but since you are 'from away,' as we native Islanders say, I thought you might be following the intense debates in your country over allowing a series of salmon farms along the coastline there to meet increased EU demand."

She looked away, saying more to herself than to him, "Odd that you should mention the wild salmon in

Ireland. My grandmother actually used to say that being named after the goddess of the land, she and I had a 'calling' to protect the wild salmon—and here I am in PEI doing just that."

He glanced down at her from over the rim of his glasses. "Perhaps your own countrymen could use your expertise to help them think through the issues, as you have helped us here. Without your intervention, the wild salmon would have become yet another relic from the past—as they well may in Ireland."

"That would be awful," Áine said, "particularly since the wild salmon there hold such tremendous cultural significance."

"Is that right?" he said politely.

"Yes, actually, the salmon was sacred to the ancient Celts who believed that consuming it would provide insights into the next life." She smiled. "Quite mystical, really."

"You would know that more than most—being named after a goddess." He offered a rare smile.

"Ah, yes," she rejoined. "Anyway, what was it you wished to discuss with me, Minister?"

Turning back after a few steps, he stared at her. "As much as we would hate to see you leave our fair isle, we would like you to return home to help the salmon there."

Áine dropped her eyes. "But I am home—*here*—where I've lived all of my conscious life."

He shook his head. "No, no, your *actual* home in Ireland." Stopping, he looked at her directly. "And this brings me to the reason I had wished to speak with you."

"Yes, Minister?" She wondered whether he could hear in her voice the churning waves of anxiety pounding against her nerves.

"The EU contract comes with a stipulation that, after consulting with my fellow Ministers, we believe only you can provide, as project director for the wild salmon re-population initiative, coupled with your work on the local foods project here." His gaze was steady.

She recovered her composure. "Of course, Minister, however I might be of help."

"We need you to return to your home country," he peered at her, unsmiling, "Ireland, that is," he added with particular emphasis, "and work with the Irish government and its Council on Fisheries to help them assess whether to open up the coastline there, the western one, I believe, to fish farms, or whether, as in our case, promote only the wild salmon populations. I believe that somehow this question plays into their traditional foods initiative as well—on which I'm sure they will brief you." He nodded.

Áine was speechless. "Really? When?"

He stared at her through the readers. "Actually, immediately, as in right away." He shrugged. "Now that you have achieved the necessary numbers to justify continuing the re-population initiative, your team can take it from here, since your direct work is essentially completed." He must have noted her confused expression. "And well done, I might add."

The timing seemed perfect—*too perfect*. The thought crossed her mind that the Minister's request seemed beyond coincidence. Thoughts of her grandmother surfaced in the grey waters of confusion bobbing within her.

"Do you know where exactly along the western coast I might be working?"

Shrugging, he said, "I'll have my assistant email you the paperwork, but I believe it was along that peninsula made famous in an old film." He looked away a minute lost I thought. "Before your time, I'm afraid. Something about a daughter."

Áine's eyes widened to full moons. "You don't mean, *Ryan's Daughter*, do you?"

He snapped his fingers. "Yes, that's it. On that popular tourist route called the 'Ring of Kerry,' I believe."

Shaking her head, all she could utter was a weak, "Really?"

"Yes, you know the place?"

"Actually, I was born right there—on Dingle Peninsula."

He smiled briefly. "As I said, you're perfect for the role of consultant. After all, you're not only Irish, but you were born in the very location where the hotbed of acrimony rages over wild vs. farmed salmon." He nodded. "I told them you would go and straighten them all out," he said with a chuckle. "Now, I am certain, considering it is your own ancestral place." He stood with folded arms, signaling his impatience. "Now, what was it you wished to discuss with me?"

She shrugged her shoulders. "Actually, you have inadvertently solved my issue for me. Some complications have arisen regarding the memorial service I mentioned that I had organized for a family member in Ireland." She shook her head more in surprise than dismissal. "No need to discuss it any longer."

"Right then, Dr. O'Connor. Since you were going anyway, now you can just remain there and start your consulting project."

"When does that begin, exactly?" she inquired.

"I believe you're expected to report in a few weeks' time. I'll have the necessary paperwork for your new project emailed to you straight away."

"Yes, Minister," she said in a meek tone, unsure of what else to say.

He shook her hand. "Many thanks again for all of your hard work here. I'll look forward to hearing about your success in the 'old country.'" With a curt nod, he added, "I shall expect monthly reports," before turning away.

"Minister, how long is the project to last?" She wondered whether she looked as anxiety-ridden as she felt.

Briefly turning back, he explained, "One year at least, during which, of course, you'll not only retain your current salary here, but receive a sizeable stipend from the Irish government as well." With a perfunctory nod and a slight handshake, he said, "Good luck," before abruptly turning on his heels and walking briskly away down the hall.

"Of course, it's one year," Áine muttered in a cross tone, as she stared after him. Her thoughts and emotions seemed adrift at sea, tossing about in a series of waves. *Something fishy about all this.* Her pun didn't even make her smile. She couldn't quite decide whether to be grateful for the opportunity or angry that he considered her an outsider—after her years of hard work and dedication to the Province.

Áine remembered how her father used to say that one had to reside in Prince Edward Island for at least one hundred years, before being considered a "native" to the place. As she opened her office door, she walked over to the window with its view of the sea in the distance. She so loved living along the edge of the ocean.

"The sea flows through our blood, sure it does," her father used to say with a knowing nod, as he puffed on his pipe. "Once born in sight of the sea, ye can never shake off its effects."

She shook her head as a wave of sadness crashed through her. *He's gone forever.* She sighed over the realization that the older ones in the larger family were passing. And now Aunt Maeve, she thought, though well before her time. She stood up, trying to rise above the swells of melancholy that were threatening to engulf her.

That reminds me. She reeled around to her desk. In the excitement of her presentation, followed by the strange coincidence of her new project assignment, she had almost forgotten about the odd inheritance. She picked up the phone to ring her mother about the news.

"Hey, Mum. My presentation to the Cabinet went very well, but I need to talk to you about something monumental that just happened to me."

"You mean your report on counting fish, is it?"

"Well, it was a bit more encompassing than that." *Not this again.* She found that whenever she tried to discuss her work with her mother, she was forced to defend its importance. Changing the subject, Áine asked in as light a tone as she could muster, "Have you decided yet if you'll be coming to the Irish memorial service? It would be great—"

Her mother scolded, "Making us all traipse back to Ireland for yet *another* service for the woman." She huffed. "It's just a waste of time and money, as far as I'm concerned."

Áine inhaled deeply before responding. "But Mum," she began in a plaintive tone. *Stop it!* she admonished herself, knowing better than to wrangle with her implacable mother. Ignoring her inner voice, she continued, "Don't you think it's important to be buried in the family graveyard? It goes back hundreds and hundreds of years. All of the Ó'Suílleabháins have been buried there. I think it's a tradition worth preserving."

"O'Sullivan," her mother corrected. "We live in Canada—no need to romanticize the past with a dead language no one speaks here—or even there. Anyway," Eithne said, her voice rigid, "She lived over here—she should be buried here." A pause. "And don't you even *think* about doing the same with me when my time comes. I'll be buried *here*."

Áine decided to sidestep the reference to her mother's own demise, a topic she was quite fond of raising whenever the opportunity presented itself. "But Maeve was always going back every chance she had," Áine responded.

"No one needs to go back there—she doesn't, you don't, and I most certainly do not," she announced.

"Oh, Mum." Áine sighed. "Well, *I* have to go—now."

"And why is that?" her mother asked coldly.

"That's why I rang, to tell you about some truly incredible news related to Auntie Maeve, as well as to my position!"

"And what would that be?" she asked, her tone clipped.

"Mum! She's left me the family property back on Dingle!" When her statement was received in silence, she blurted, "Why me, Mum? Why on earth did she leave Grandma's—and her—house to *me,* when it should more properly go to one of my cousins?"

She waited for her mother to respond. Nothing. Not even her usual tirade. "Mum? Are you still there? Did we get cut off?"

"*No*, we did not." Her tone was pure acid.

"Well then, Mum. Did you convince her to leave it to me before she died?"

"I most certainly did *not*." She could visualize her mother's aggravated expression in her deep sigh. "Sure, you're the only one of the lot who endorses the *old ways* and would be willing to take on the old ramshackle of a farm. Besides, your cousins would just unload the place, which, despite my utter disinterest in ever returning there, would not be right." She sighed. "Sure, my mother would turn over in her grave if that were to happen."

"I suppose there's that all right," said Áine, all too eager for any explanation that fit. "I was the only one of the North American cousins, and most likely the Irish ones as well, who really enjoyed spending time on the farm." She stopped before adding, "But it does seem, well, I hate to say, rather uncharacteristically generous of Aunt Maeve."

Another pause. "She couldn't leave well enough alone."

Odd. Áine realized that she had significantly misjudged her mother's reaction to the inheritance. She had forgotten until now how much she despised looking *back*.

"Besides, Maeve had more than enough properties, which she wrested away from the rest of us, I might add," she said, her tone disdainful, "for her *own* children. I wish she'd leave *mine* out of her clutches altogether."

Áine decided she had better move the exchange along before her mother brought up the exhaustive list of injustices she had experienced at the hands of her sister, another favourite topic. "By the way, Mum, I didn't tell you about the conditions."

"Conditions?" Eithne retorted, her tone now openly bitter. "Of course, she never gave anything to anyone *freely.*"

"Well, they're curious conditions to say the least. Before assuming ownership, I am required to live for one year there—back on Dingle Peninsula, no less!"

"She's gone mad, altogether! For *God's* sake, you're not actually thinking of doing it, are you, of *living* there?" her mother asked, her voice rising in pitch to an incredulous shrill. "Surely, you wouldn't," she almost pleaded.

Áine responded more to herself than to her mother, "A whole year! What on earth made her stipulate that, I wonder?"

"She's still interfering in my life," Eithne muttered.

She said nothing, her thoughts a seething current. *Why is it always about her?* Áine was more than accustomed to her mother's almost exclusive focus upon herself—*but even now?* She couldn't figure out just how Eithne was victimized by *her* inheritance. Áine asked in as neutral a tone as she could muster, "What do you mean?"

"You do not belong there. You live *here*, in Prince Edward Island."

Áine decided to sidestep that issue as well, saying only, "Well, in order to fulfill the last condition of the inheritance, I will have to spend some time there. Besides, my boss, the Economics Minister, is sending me there on a diplomatic mission—to help the Irish decide what to do with their wild salmon."

"Oh, for Heaven's sake, if it weren't bad enough already," her mother exclaimed.

"Yes, he said it was because I was Irish."

"You're *not* Irish; you are Canadian." She could imagine her mother bristling, pursing her lips tightly, her blue eyes turning the color of cold, grey steel.

Áine shrugged into the phone. "Well, not according to him, I'm not. Besides, as I said, there's another condition to my inheritance."

"This just keeps getting worse," she muttered. "There's *more*?"

"I'm to write an account of her life as well."

"Oh, for *God's* sake," Eithne spitted. "The *strut* of her, the ego of her, to demand this from—*beyond*." She lapsed into a stony silence.

Undaunted, Áine continued. "I admit, it's rather odd. For Heaven's sake, I really don't know that much about her past—aside from the few occasions I spent time with her there and here, as well as her considerable collection of real estate, husbands, and children," she added dryly.

As Áine made the remark, she felt a wave of insight sweep through her thoughts. *Odd that.* She realized in that moment that her parents had never really referred to their pasts in Ireland. For reasons that remained unsaid, her family had left for Prince Edward Island soon after she was born. She shook her head. Not talking about the past, she surmised, *maybe it's an Irish cultural thing*. With a dismissive shrug, she waited for her mother to respond.

"Surely you wouldn't spend time digging up the rather sordid past of Maeve, would you?" Eithne retorted.

When Áine didn't respond, she added fiercely, "Leave it *buried*."

"Actually, Mum, I was thinking of a different kind of digging," Áine said with a chuckle. "You know, as part of my work there, I'm to advise on establishing a local foods initiative, like the one I collaborated on here, offering heritage vegetables and artisanal traditional foods for local markets. Maybe I could transform the old farmstead into such a venture myself, as a sort of educational model."

Silence. "You can't be serious."

"After all," Áine continued, unfazed by Eithne's resistance to the idea, "I was *born* there. It *was* my home once. And perhaps again."

Her mother exploded. "For *God's* sake, Áine, you can't go back! Your home is with me, here in Canada—on PEI," she sputtered.

"At least there," Áine said without thinking, "I am a *real* native." Stopping to soak in the profundity of that last insight, she suddenly realized that she *was* a "native"— though not to Prince Edward Island—of a place where, for countless generations, her ancestors had lived along the edge of the sea.

She sat gazing out the window at nothing in particular, her own thoughts pulsing through her. The phrase "countless generations" reverberated in her head, like the constant refrain of waves lapping the shore.

She then proceeded to relate her exchange with the Economics Minister.

"It doesn't matter how they think of you," Eithne retorted.

"It matters to me," she said sadly. "I want to feel as if I belong."

Eithne ignored her admission. "You belong to me, and we belong here—where we have lived for decades. Always look ahead, not behind."

"Odd you should say that. I was thinking of Grandma this morning while doing my final counts on the salmon. How she used to say that expression of hers that you detest, 'Sometimes, the journey forward, begins with a step back.'"

Her mother huffed. "Rubbish. Utter rubbish. Focussing on the past never got anyone anywhere." She added disdainfully, "Look where it got your father."

That was meant to hurt. Áine couldn't help but comment, "You have to admit it's a bit unusual for an Irish person to relinquish ties with the past. Isn't Ireland the very place where Joyce had proclaimed, 'History is a nightmare from which we never awaken'? It seemed to him, at least, that the past shapes the lives of the present."

Suddenly, an insight bubbled within her. It had never occurred to her that perhaps her parents had moved away from Ireland to *escape* the past. *Maybe that's what this resistance is all about.*

Eithne asserted with all the vehemence she could muster, "I am Canadian. I am no longer Irish. And neither are you!"

"I don't know Mum," Áine said slowly, "Can't you—and I—be both?"

"There's no need," Eithne sputtered, before adding with increased agitation, "And no, you *cannot.* Never mind what Maeve and my mother used to say. Living in the past got them nowhere."

Áine chose her words with care. "I don't think that's what Grandma meant by that expression. She only meant to say sometimes we must *return* to the past in order to move forward."

"Rubbish."

Ignoring her mother's response, Áine thought for a moment before responding. "Actually, like the wild salmon—and me—as it turns out," she said with a smile. "In order to move forward in my career, it looks like I must first take a step back—to Ireland."

"You could just say no," suggested Eithne, her tone hopeful.

Áine shook her head into the phone. "No one says no to the Provincial Ministers, Mum, and I am not about to test those shark-infested waters."

Realizing she was getting nowhere with her mother, Áine said she would think about it all. Before hanging up, she asked more as an afterthought than anything else, "By the way, do you know a Muirís FitzGerald?"

Eithne stammered, "No, no, not a *Muirís* FitzGerald, no." Then pulling herself together, she added, "Sure, the country is filled with FitzGeralds."

"I just wondered since he is the solicitor who sent me the paperwork—from Dingle town, I believe. He referred to the fact that I am organizing the funeral there. How would he know that I would have anything to do with it?"

Eithne just mumbled, "Must be some distant relation, so." Despite her reservations to the contrary, she added, "There's a whole slew of FitzGeralds from my mother's mother's side—quite a gossipy crowd, those FitzGeralds—always knowing everyone else's business. Quite high and mighty altogether, so they think, anyway." She sighed. "Now that's a group who lives buried in the past," she sniffed. "Imagine putting on airs because your ancestors came from *France* almost a thousand years ago. *Typical.*"

"Ah, well. I'll have to set up a meeting with him, however entitled he is," Áine said. "Okay, Mum, I'm off. Have lots to think about."

Her mother sighed heavily. "You're making a big mistake going there. Move *forward* with your life, Áine, not *back.*"

It was Áine's turn to sigh deeply as she turned off her phone. She looked around her office, wishing in that moment she could relate the news of her work on the wild salmon with her grandmother and Maeve. She smiled nostalgically over the memory of their shared passion for the "wee mystical creatures," as Maeve used to refer to them.

Her thoughts returned to her mother who remained relentless in her dismissive attitude toward her work. She recalled Eithne's typical response: "You want to preserve those smelly, slimy old things?" A huff. "I'd rather have lobster any day."

Áine made some tea, her thoughts racing along an endless strand. She thought of the Minister's comments regarding her "calling" to help protect the wild salmon in Ireland. *Odd coincidence, that.* And now, she was being sent back—to protect the wild salmon in her birthplace. She smiled to herself, realizing that she sounded like her grandmother. *Calling, indeed.*

She picked up the hefty packet of papers accompanying the inheritance notice to re-read them when, suddenly, a note fell out, landing face up on her desk. As she gazed down, she noted it was hand-written in the traditional Irish script. She smiled, deeming it some cultural attempt to remain tied to the *old ways*—even in modern Celtic Tiger Ireland. She picked up the note eagerly.

ÁINE A CHARA, (LEST YOU HAVE FORGOTTEN YOUR GAELIC, DEAREST ÁINE,)

I DO APOLOGIZE FOR THE FORMAL MANNER OF THE ENCLOSED PAPERWORK, AS WELL AS FOR MY OFFICIAL-SOUNDING LETTER TO YOU.

I WISH TO WELCOME YOU, "CÉAD MÍLE FÁILTE" AS WE SAY, BACK TO YOUR HOME & COMMUNITY HERE ON DINGLE.

WE EAGERLY AWAIT YOUR ARRIVAL—YOUR RETURN TO YOUR ANCESTRAL PLACE—HERE AMONG YOUR OWN ONES.

IT IS TIME NOW—YOUR TIME—TO RETURN HOME.

SLÁN LEAT,
YOURS,
MUIRÍS FITZGERALD

Áine sank into her chair, trying to sort through all of the abrupt changes in her life. She found her eyes returning to the phrase, "your own ones." Leaning back with her eyes closed, she tried to recall where she had heard that expression before. As her thoughts drifted inevitably back to Ireland, she suddenly opened her eyes in recognition. Áine Críonna used to refer to her "own ones" when talking about the wild salmon, as well as to the features of the land around her, as if she were part of the land and seascapes herself. Áine smiled, realizing that her grandmother—and she too, after all—had good reason to think so, being named after the mountains protecting their ancestral homestead.

With a sudden burst of enthusiasm, Áine felt her imminent move to protect the wild salmon in Ireland—*her own ones*—irresistibly enticing. Whether the subtle winds of fate, the desire to belong, or her *calling* to protect the salmon ushered the *sea-change* in her life, Áine felt her memories, feelings, and hopes reeling her through rushing water, now flowing in a new direction—oddly *back*, to the place of her birth.

CHAPTER TWO

ÁINE'S PEOPLE

TUATHA DÉ DANANN

ESPITE A SLEEPLESS OVERNIGHT FLIGHT, Áine decided to head down along the rugged coast of County Kerry straight for Dingle Peninsula. Now that she had landed back in Ireland, her keen sense of anticipation outweighed the sheer exhaustion she was feeling. As she sped along the Dingle road leading to the family farm, she could see the Atlantic shimmering in the distance. With rising excitement, she realized it wouldn't be long. At last, arriving at the property, Áine jumped out of the car and whirled around to take in the enticing landscape about her—mountains, fields, and the shining waters below.

She followed the line of the ancient mountains trailing down to the sea. *It's no wonder*, she thought, that her ancestors had identified so deeply with the place. She stood gazing around her, trying to recall the exact expression Áine Críonna used to say when claiming her place among the rocks and hills. Suddenly, it seemed as if she could hear her grandmother's words whispering in the wind:

I am who I am by being Here among me' own ones.
Take me away from these mountains and fields, the
salmon and the sea, and I am nothing more than a
poor, old woman—a sean bhan bocht—just the Mrs.
to Himself. But Here on me' own bit of turf? I am
the indomitable mountains above, the fertile fields
around, and the endless waves below.

The poignantly mystical sentiments flowed through
her in a rush like the river that swept by the land. Was it
only her family, she wondered, who identified with the
natural features of the land and sea? She glanced up at
the mountains surrounding the ancestral farm, before
shifting her gaze to the glistening green fields lined in
stonewalls, that stretched down to the water's edge. In
that moment, she felt closer to her namesake than ever
before, as she realized that the place affected her as well
in some fundamentally *soulful* way.

"Aptly named," murmured Áine, as she read the sign
posted on the entrance gate announcing the name of the
property. *Tuatha dé Danann*—"Áine's people"—named
after the original Áine, the great Celtic goddess, legend-
ary first settler of their part of Ireland. Áine reflected on
her long family history as she passed through the gate
and walked along the pathway leading to the cottage.
Although she tried to add up all of the Áines in the larger
family, she soon lost count. The family was nothing if
not consistent, she thought—*at least with names*. She
laughed aloud.

She gazed up at the twin summits that towered above
the farm. The goddess's sumptuous bodily form, it was
said, became forever memorialized in the womanly shape

of the rounded mountains overhead. They were dazzling—if not slightly erotic—to behold, she noted. The Paps of Áine. *How is it in Gaelic?* Suddenly, it came to her. *Dá Chích Anann,* named for the goddess Áine, the great Protectress of the fertile land and its people—*my cultural ancestors.* She shook her head with a smile, over the realization that it didn't take long feeling part of the place, before believing in the old Celtic views of the world.

Áine turned to gaze at the family house tucked under the *Dá Chích.* It was a small cottage of ancient origins, built in the traditional style, once washed in a coat of white milk paint, now chipping in the salt air. Two long, low windows adorned both sides of the wooden half-door in the middle. Weathered boxes of purple and white heather flowered below each window, while tufts of mounted hay lined the roof in the thatched style.

It's so charming, she thought, as she admired her new abode—*even if it does need a lot of work.* She shrugged her shoulders. What can one expect of a dwelling, she reasoned, parts of which had existed for hundreds of years, and those, built on the even older remains of the ancient beehive stone structures of her Celtic ancestors? For thousands of years, the ocean farm had sat sheltered at the base of the mountains near the edge of *Corca Dhuibhne*—Dingle Peninsula—an ancient projection of land and rock that stretched out into the Atlantic.

A long historic line it was, and now she, Áine, had returned to the land of the *Ciarrige*—the people of Kerry, children of the *Tuatha dé Danann,* to carry on the legacy. A daunting challenge, she thought to herself.

She tried the front door, but as it was locked, she decided to try round back. Locked. She shook her head, assuming the caretaker would have already opened up the place. She checked her watch. She had forgotten how relaxed people were regarding matters of time.

Feeling the need for a quick stroll along the beach to revive her sagging energy, Áine walked down the lane that lead to the strand below. While she remembered the mountains overlooking the far side of the bay as usually shrouded in mist, the morning revealed a bright orange orb skimming along deep-blue summits. She could see the gently folding waves of the Atlantic below virtually glimmering in the golden rays of the early morning sun, leaving behind a trail of illuminated white foam along the edge of the five-mile strand that stretched out into the bay. As she stepped onto the sand, she felt its powerful magnetism. She had forgotten how much the beach, with its tufted sand hills and meandering strand, affected her.

As she followed the water's edge, Áine thought about her unexpected inheritance. Since no explanation welled up within her, she turned with an instinctive glance toward the open ocean, as if to find a reason riding among the waves rolling into shore.

Instead, she discovered there a simple profundity. She was walking the very sands her ancestors had done for so many countless generations before her—and most recently, Maeve—who, it was reported, had spent her last summer pacing the strand, before returning to Canada to succumb to her tragic fate.

The reflection brought Áine to a grinding halt. With all the talk about fate in her family, she wondered whether it was fate that had summoned her back. She gave a firm shake of her head, instantly dismissing the idea. She felt certain that it was up to her to create her destiny. Despite her belief, she did find it oddly synchronous that she was carrying out her grandmother's words, through creating her future by returning to her past. She chanted in rhythm with the waves lapping the shoreline: "'The journey forward, begins with a step back.'" She laughed and addressed the waves before her. "But you already know that, being waves that travel back, then forward, now, don't you?"

She continued along the length of the beach, until she reached the place where the Bradáin River joined the sea—the same Salmon River, as it was called, that meandered along the farm from its source high up in the mountains. Memories poured from her, not unlike the rush of the river's current flowing into the sea. Even now, Áine could recall the touch of the older woman's hand on her own, as she would relate the history of the river's origin when she used to visit:

When at the time of her passing, as the Goddess Áine lay down to rest forever along the mountaintops and turned her face toward the sea, her tears of gratitude for this lovely land transformed into bradáin fiáin, wild salmon, you know, the fish sacred to our ancient Celtic ancestors for their spiritual wisdom. From that day to now, our ancestors have found the river that flows here alongside us, teeming with wild salmon. As her namesakes, we have inherited the duty to protect them.

As Áine felt her long, red hair whip about her as it caught in the wind, she recalled the wild salmon that she used to see each evening during summer visits. She'd come to watch the fishermen vainly trying to catch them in their nets—only to have most of them jump out and continue their dance along the waters upstream into the sunset. And now, she thought, *they want to incarcerate the salmon here.*

She shook her head as she gazed into the river. It felt almost as if the practice of reigning in the once wild salmon—the long-time symbol of mystical Celtic Ireland—would result in the loss of the traditional culture, if the Irish didn't free themselves from the shackles of economic "success." But that'll be my job, she realized, to convince the powers that be, that *all good things are wild and free.* She grinned over her poetic formulation of a Thoreauvian maxim.

As Áine searched the translucent waters of the river's mouth for any wild salmon, she suddenly noticed not too far upstream, through waves of mist, a lone figure standing in the river with a net in his hand. She stared transfixed, as if something about the scene—or the fellow—struck her inner core.

Her discovery of his presence in the river triggered another favourite bit of wisdom from Áine Críonna:

You must look deeply inside, then out to the mountains and water around you to find your other half. 'Tis only the lucky few, who combine such traits with another person—someone part of the land and sea as much as we.

Áine smiled, thinking that the fellow sure seemed like he was connected to the natural world. She watched him with heightened curiosity as he bent down over the water in the morning light. She found herself wondering whether he was an advocate of fish farms, or a champion like herself of the wild ones. She studied his movements some more. *Something about him makes me think he's for the wild ones.* The thought made her heart beat a bit more quickly.

Suddenly, the fellow stood straight up—as if he could feel someone watching him, and turning around, noticed Áine downstream. Dropping his net, he just stood gazing at her with his arms folded across his chest, the water rushing past him. She quickly dropped her own gaze, embarrassed to be caught observing him. The effect of his stare rooted her to the sand. Despite her embarrassment, she looked back at him, waiting—for what, she didn't know.

The two stood staring at one another for a few minutes, before he waved and shouted out to her the traditional greeting in Gaelic, "*Dia Dhuit*! Good day!"

Flustered, she instinctively shouted back the traditional response, "*Dia's Muire Dhuit*! Good day to you!"

Unsure of what to do next, she waved back and turned away. She decided to figure out at some later time, the fellow's relation to the wild salmon. In the meantime, she slowly forced herself to walk back along the strand, wondering whether he shared her attitudes about the wild salmon.

Impulsively, she stopped to glance back over her shoulder at where the fellow had been standing. She was astonished to discover that he was still there—watching her through the waves of mist, now rising slowly above the river. *Must have made a good first impression,* she thought as she grinned. *Life could get very interesting out here on old Dingle Peninsula!*

With a start, Áine realized then that he was shouting out to her again. She turned around to listen, trying to catch what he was saying. She retraced her steps a bit so she could hear him better. Then she made out his words, "*Fáilte! Fáilte, Áine, Fáilte!* Welcome!"

She stopped abruptly, when she realized he knew her name. *How is that possible?* She stood still, staring at him in astonishment. Suddenly, she smiled. Of course, he knew her, she realized. She was likely the only newcomer there, and given what she remembered of everyone knowing everyone else's comings and goings, he must have known she was Maeve's niece. Smiling serenely, she gazed at him, thinking how charming it was that he remembered her name. He seemed like a nice fellow, she decided—that is, *if he's protecting the wild salmon out there.*

She threw out her most authentic sounding "thanks" in Gaelic, "*Go raibh maith agat!*" and waving one last time, turned to walk back, musing over the interesting encounter.

The fellow stood watching Áine as she made her way back along the edge of the sea. "*Fáilte*, Áine! You've finally come! I've been waiting a long time to meet you," he called out quietly to her. He shook his head as he muttered, "Sure, I only hope you're as wonderful as Maeve had claimed you were." His eyes followed her until she disappeared into the mist down the strand.

Áine was so tired by the time she returned to the cottage that all she could think about was getting some much-needed sleep. When she found the doors still locked, and no way to get in, she decided to find a comfortable spot to wait for the caretaker. Gathering her anorak and down coat from her bag, she soon nestled in a soft spot of moss on the ground near the door. Within minutes, she was fast asleep.

Some time later, the caretaker arrived, laden with groceries. Discovering Áine curled up in a deep sleep, he stood and gazed at her. "Ah, doesn't she look angelic there all soft and sleepy-like," he murmured, as he tossed his head to the side. Bending down over her, he whispered, "From what Maeve told me, you're quite the handful when awake. Best to enjoy these moments of tranquility before rousing you, so." Quietly unlocking the door, he went into the house to light the fire and make her a pot of tea.

Soon after, he returned and knelt down beside her. He touched her gently, not wanting to frighten her. "Áine," he said, trying to rouse her, "Áine."

Stirring from her deep sleep, Áine half-opened her eyes. Looking up, she found a rugged, salmon-haired fellow with his hand on her shoulder. She squinted at him through half-closed eyelids that tried to close again. She said, her voice groggy, "I seem to know you but—" She stopped, her eyes shutting firmly.

He chuckled. "Ah, sure, you and I, Girleen, go way back, we do."

"Oh, right," she mumbled. "You're that fellow from the river—a friend or foe to my salmon."

"*Your* salmon, is it," he said, with a toss of his head.

Seeing that she was again fast asleep, and not wanting to wake her, he retrieved a duvet from the house and tucked her in as he whispered, "I'm here to protect your salmon—and perhaps, you—if you'll let me."

Chapter Three

WILD SALMON

NA BRADÁIN FIÁIN

Á INE WOKE TO DROPLETS OF RAIN falling on her face. Stretching, she looked around in surprise to find herself outside, underneath a fluffy down comforter. She wondered how long she had been sleeping. Sitting up and hugging her raised knees, she gazed in awe at the mountains, now shrouded in mist, while the emerald fields glistened in the soft rain. The beauty of the place filled her with joy over living there—*again*, she had to remind herself. She had lived there, she realized—*once upon a time.*

"Awfully thoughtful caretaker, whoever he is," Áine remarked to herself as she removed the duvet. Upon entering the now unlocked cottage, she found an inviting fire and a pot of tea simmering on the Aga cookstove. She smiled, thinking he was definitely a keeper.

She hadn't been back to the family home for years—almost a decade, she figured. After walking through the various rooms, she returned to the kitchen—half expecting to see her grandmother emerge from the garden, laden with herbs that she would prepare into medicinal tonics for people around the peninsula.

It seemed as if time had changed nothing, preserving everything just as she remembered, with the notable exception of the absence of her grandmother—and Maeve—sitting at the table talking spiritedly. She reflected on how the past possessed an uncanny ability to conflate with the present, making it feel as powerful and as real as the current moment. She looked around again. Áine could sense Maeve's presence, almost smell her scent of lavender and rose she used to call the fragrances of passion. Overcome by the trigger of memory and the palpable images it conjured, Áine felt a sharp tug of remorse spread throughout her senses.

Trying to change the atmosphere, she poured a cup of tea and cut a slice of brown bread she found waiting on the counter alongside a crock of butter. Hoping against hope, she opened the refrigerator. "Don't tell me!" she exclaimed, "a bottle of fresh milk with the cream on top!" She shook her head, realizing she hadn't seen that in years. And what's this? she wondered, as she opened a wax papered packet, *smoked salmon*! She scrutinized it carefully and declared aloud, "Yep, it's the wild kind!" She couldn't wait to meet the considerate fellow, hoping he wasn't some old old geezer who hung around, pining for Maeve.

She munched on some bread and salmon. Oh, my God, she thought, scrumptious—utterly delectable! She tried to remember what made the smoky flavour so special here in Dingle. Then it came to her. Peat, of course, the traditional choice for heating houses and smoking foods. To Áine, nothing tasted quite as savoury as peat-smoked wild salmon, a long-standing delicacy available only during the angling seasons.

That reminds me. Before focussing on her new position there, she thought, as she looked around, *first things first.* She took out her notebook and started to plan the menu for Maeve's memorial service. She realized that she'd better see about getting some wild salmon for the funeral meal, feeling that it wouldn't be a true commemoration without serving Maeve's favourite food. Thankfully, it was in season. *No illegally poached or farmed salmon for Maeve's send-off.* After finishing her meal, she gathered a few shopping bags and went off in search of some wild salmon.

In Dingle town, she stopped in front of a shop called FitzGerald's, written in the old script. She figured that the large wooden salmon placard, gently swaying in the breeze, served as an indication she could find the *real* thing inside. She wondered whether the fishmonger might be related to the FitzGerald who had sent her the letter about the inheritance, but smiling, remembered her mother's claim regarding an entire clan of FitzGeralds about the place.

"*Dia Dhuit*—Good day to you," greeted a dignified-looking gentleman behind the counter, as she entered the small fishmonger's shop.

"*Dia's Muire dhuit*," she responded with a smile. It had been such a long time since she was greeted in the Gaelic language—*with the intriguing exception of that interesting-looking fellow down by the river.*

She changed to English after they exchanged the traditional exchange. "Have you any wild salmon?" she inquired.

"Sure, ye can't get the wild kind anymore in the shops," the fellow told her. "Gone are those days forever, it seems," he muttered, as he wiped his hands on a linen towel.

"Ah, but someone around must fish them straight from the river. Aren't they in season now?" Áine pressed. "I really must have the wild kind," she added, her tone firm. "I believe it should be in season—however short that might be these days."

"I'm sorry, Miss." He turned away from her.

"Please, Sir," she pleaded.

"I'm sorry," he repeated, though a bit softer this time.

Áine thought a moment, before asking him again. This time, she repeated her request in Gaelic, "*Lé de thoil. Mas e de thoil. An bhfuil aon bradáin fiáin, na feirmeithe, agat?*"

Silence. Then without turning around, the shopkeeper asked quietly in the old tongue, "*An feidir leat Gaeilge a labhairt?* Have you the Irish on you?" He reeled around to look at her squarely in the eyes.

"*Bheagán, fíos bheagán,*" she admitted with a slight shrug. "Very little." Switching to English, she said, "We moved to Canada soon after I was born."

"*Sin é trua,*" the man responded in Gaelic. "Too bad, that." He shook his head slowly. "What a pity," he repeated.

"What's too bad?" Áine asked him, bewildered by his response.

"You had to live Over," he said, nodding in the direction of the water. "Sure, 'tis a wonderful place right here," he asserted triumphantly, as he tipped his cap, folded his arms over his chest, and facing her with a broad grin, offered an utterly charming smile.

Áine smiled in return. Trying hard to smother a giggle

that welled up inside her, she teased, "Sure, don't I know that, Sir? Isn't that why I've returned at all?"

The shopkeeper peered at her again. "And where would ye be returning to, is it, if I might be so bold as to inquire, Lass?"

Áine gazed at him with a wide smile. "Well, right here, of course, don't you know! Is there anywhere else?"

The fellow tossed his head to the side and smiled at her. "Ah, sure, you're most definitely from one of the families here, that I'm now sure of, now." He nodded knowingly, tipping his cap as he scrutinized her features. "Question, is, which one, now?"

Áine responded in Gaelic, "Ó'Suílleabháin."

The man stared at her. "Ó'Suílleabháin, is it?" before slapping his hand on the counter. "Sure, of course, you are, Lass! Wouldn't I know those cheekbones anywhere? Those Ó'Suílleabháin women have always had the most *lovely* high cheekbones around the peninsula, entirely."

He winked at her, as he tilted his head in the traditional manner. "Sure, you're one of us, ye are, so!" he spurted out with clear pride in his voice, as he turned to her. "Why did ye not say so, Lass, from the start?" Shaking his head, he wagged his finger. "I was a bit put off by the Yank accent."

"It's not a Yank accent," she countered primly.

Seeming to ignore her last remark, he thought for a minute before nodding. "Sure, ye can't help it if your parents absconded with you as a wee helpless babe to live in the wilds Over." He grinned at her. "But, sure, now that ye've come Home, you're one of us again—and sure, won't you be losing that awful twang, once you're around your own ones again." He leaned over and added, with a wink and a toss of the head, "Might even pick up more of the ancient language."

"I didn't know my pedigree and linguistic patterns were required to purchase some wild salmon," Áine replied, her tone diffident.

The fellow scoffed. "Indeed, they are, Lass. Do ye think, now, I would waste my precious bit of wild salmon, me darlin' *bradáin fiáin*—which is illegal now, to catch, most of the year, mind you—on one of those *immigrants* from Eastern Europe that's trying to take over our country?"

"No, I suppose not," she said in a hesitant voice, unsure of how exactly to respond.

He groaned, before lapsing into a tirade. "Sure, didn't we spend eight hundred years," he declared, his voice rising in anger. Shaking his finger, he continued, "Eight hundred years, Lass, mind you, fighting against the tyranny of the Brits—only to willingly give in to the tyranny of the *European Union!* Union, me' arse! And now they want to tell us—Kerrymen, of all people— how to fish and even package the salmon once they're caught—by keeping the poor craythurs in nets all day and night. Sure, that's not fishing a t'all!" He spat in disgust. "It's bloody oppression of our cultural traditions!"

"Ah, yes, so I've heard," she murmured.

Turning to Áine, followed by toss of his head, he boasted, "Ah, but we fought off the English, and we'll fight off those buggers in *Brussels*—trying to make rules for us Kerry fishermen!"

"And how will you do that, Mr. FitzGerald?" Áine asked, wondering how his actions might assist her in her own struggle to sustain the sovereignty of the wild salmon.

He leaned over the counter, and after looking around to make sure they were alone, whispered, "Sure, haven't we organized a *Resistance* movement already—just like in the old days when our ancestors—God rest their souls—

fought and died for this country. Your own granduncles who died at the hands of the Black and Tans would be proud!" He stood up, and tilting his head swiftly from side to side, admitted, "Aren't we ready to help free the wild salmon from those fish farms the *blackguards* up in Dublin are planning. Ha! That we are, indeed." With a fully formed scowl, he growled, "Just let them try."

"Indeed," she said, realizing with alarm that the wild salmon debate was rapidly turning volatile.

He gazed furtively around, as if expecting the *Gardái* to come rushing in to arrest him, before admonishing her in a whisper, "But, hush now, on that particular subject!"

Áine responded in a plaintive tone. "My aunt was a great advocate of the wild salmon. I'm at my wit's end, really. I need to serve some wild salmon, if just as a symbolic gesture, for her funeral meal. Her soul just couldn't bear any other kind to be served in her memory."

Mr. FitzGerald reeled around and squinted at her, followed by eyeing her up and down. Pushing up his spectacles that had remained low on the bridge of his nose, he peered at her again, before exclaiming in unrestrained excitement, "You wouldn't be talking about *Queenie* Ó'Suílleabháin's family, now, would ye, Lass? Sure, you're not one of *those* O'Sullivans now, are ye?"

"I am, indeed, Sir," Áine replied with a wave of pride in her voice.

The shopkeeper leaned well over the edge of the counter to stare at her. "Of course, you are! Actually, you're the spitting image of *Herself,* you are." Looking away, he added as much to himself as to Áine, "Ah, sure, 'twas a pure tragedy what happened to her, 'twas, indeed, God rest her poor soul. Tragedy, it was. A pure tragedy, now—and she a great advocate of the wild salmon."

He shook his head slowly from side to side, before turning to squint at Áine again. "Sure, you must be one of Maeve's lasses yourself. You share her great beauty," he said with undisguised admiration. "Isn't looking at you, almost like looking at Herself, it is." He gazed at her silently. "And now, here you are yourself, watching after the wild salmon, so I've heard."

"Have you, now?" she asked, arching her eyebrow. His statement reminded her how much everyone knew about everyone else and their business, even those who had just arrived on the scene.

"Heard as much from me' son," he replied.

Áine shook her head. "I am Maeve's niece. I'm her sister, Eithne's daughter," she explained. "But I'm organizing the funeral and the meal for the family, and my poor aunt would be so distressed if we didn't commemorate her passing with her favourite food."

Upon hearing her explanation, the old man opened a refrigerator from under the counter, and pulling out a sizable packet of wild salmon, scolded, "Sure, why didn't ye say so in the first place, Lass? You are one of our own ones, you are? And aren't I one of your cousins—second or third, surely, or is it fourth?" He shook his head. "Ah well, sure, never mind about that, now."

He stopped talking, when he found himself choking in remorse. "Wasn't Maeve one of my dearest customers, entirely?" He brushed a tear from his eye. Turning toward Áine, he admitted, "Ah, sure, she and I go way back, we do."

The fellow stood quietly for a few moments, lost in reminiscence. Áine remained silent, waiting for him to return to the present. "Ah, Queen Maeve could be as seductive and as fierce as her Connaught namesake, she could, indeed," he said as he shook his head. Suddenly, he leaned over the counter and confessed, "Didn't I ask for her hand, but she turned me down to go off to Dublin?" He sounded shocked—as if he still couldn't believe it. He abruptly turned to package up some wild salmon and possibly wipe off more tears that Áine was almost sure had resurfaced in his eyes.

"Oh, I didn't know," she said, startled by the admission.

"And how much would ye be wanting for the family?" he inquired, only to explode in a hearty guffaw. "Ah, sure, if the entire family comes Home, you'll be needing a lot more than this." He thought a moment, before snapping his fingers. "I'll tell you what! I'll have more brought round to ye, I will," he said in a reassuring tone. "I'll see to it ye have enough to feed the entire family!"

Áine gave an audible sigh of relief. "Thanks a million!" but remembering who she was thanking, repeated in Gaelic, "*Go raibh míle maith agat.*" She opened her wallet. "How much do I owe you, Mr. FitzGerald?"

The man silenced her with a firm wave of his hand. "Call me Gearóid—Gerard. Sure, not a thing. Not a thing a t'all. It's on me," he said, as he brushed another tear from his eye. "Sure, haven't I yearned for that woman me' whole life?"

Áine arched her eyebrow. "Indeed?" Life was getting quite heated on the peninsula, she concluded, between the wild salmon and family legacies.

He leaned over to her. "Even with the Mrs. I was fortunate to have gained the hand of," he admitted in a whisper. "Ah, sure, didn't Queenie steal the heart of every man she cast those wily eyes of hers upon?" He tilted his head in agreement with his own statement. "Aye, that she did. And now—she's gone."

Swept away by the old man's emotions, Áine choked back her own grief. "Awful. Just awful."

Thumping at his heart, he proclaimed, "But we'll always hold her memory *here* in our hearts, won't we, Lass? That we will, ay."

She now felt tears trickling down her cheeks. "Yes, indeed, we will, Gearóid."

He gazed out through the window to the mountains above before turning away. "Good Luck, *Slán Leat*, Lass. I'll have me' lad bring the salmon round to you by and by," he said, as he walked behind the curtain separating him from the counter.

"*Slán, agus go raibh maith agat!*" Responding in Gaelic, ever so grateful for this old man's kindness, Áine left the shop.

As she hurried back to prepare for the arrival of her family, she thought with relief that the wild salmon were still considered sacred to the locals. "Well, perhaps some of *old* Ireland still thrives," she said to herself, "even amidst the grand European *Union*."

CHAPTER FOUR

THE SALMON WELL

TOBAR NA BHRADÁIN

As she waited for the coveted salmon to arrive, Áine spent the afternoon preparing for the commemorative meal. She loved using the old wood-fired Aga cookstove that had occupied the centre of the kitchen for as long as she could remember. She baked loaves of traditional brown bread in the baking oven to accompany tureens of potato leek soup she would serve as a first course, both dishes emitting a deliciously enticing aroma throughout the cottage. Since she could not pre-cook the main course of wild salmon, boiled potatoes, and roasted carrots with parsnips, Áine moved on to layering Waterford glass bowls with sherry trifle, which would serve as the dessert.

She had decided upon this very simple luncheon, including only her aunt's favourite dishes. Maeve was famous for picking at her food, consuming little more than a bite here and there, preferring, what seemed to others, as near starvation—over the risk of losing her inordinately slender figure. In keeping with her aunt's food preferences, Áine decided there wouldn't be much superfluous fare at the dinner. What lacked in food, however, would be most certainly made up for in drink, she was sure—even at mid-day, since it was, after all, an Ó'Suílleabháin gathering.

After completing those preparations, Áine pulled on her Wellies and an old, torn, wool sweater she had found hanging on a wooden peg and went outside. She walked through the reeds and the gorse to the side of the house, where she had discovered a sizeable kitchen garden that had been kept while Maeve had resided there that last summer.

Although it looked as if it had been irregularly cared for since Maeve's passing, the garden still sported a significant variety of root vegetables, growing in among the weeds that had sprouted up in between the once tidy rows. After pulling up some carrots and leeks, and digging out some parsnips, she noticed the remnants of dried-up potato stalks. Digging underneath into the mounds, she discovered a bevy of potatoes that had successfully overwintered, most likely a result of the weeds, which had served as mulch. *Always room for more spuds!* She smiled, knowing that her relatives would require at least several each. Finding a spade in the garden shed, Áine proceeded to dig up the potatoes she would need for the meal.

Before long, she was streaked in dirt—all over the sleeves of her sweater, her cheeks, and even in her hair. She had given up the spade and simply dropped down on her hands and knees to release the potatoes—the *prátaí*—recalling the Irish word—from the embrace of the earth, and when that didn't work, she sat down right in the soil and unearthed them from all around her, covering her legs in dirt in the process, much like she did as a young girl, playing in the sand.

It was so enjoyable that Áine decided to feel the full pleasure of rolling around in the soil. She stretched out on one side to peer up at the great feminine shapes of the mountains rising up behind the farm. She felt so at peace and one with the verdant land around her.

"Well, isn't that a unique way, now, for digging up the spuds, then," came a deep, though lilting voice from behind her. "Guess you'd call that the bottoms-up approach, is it?"

Áine looked up in astonishment, only to discover a fellow leaning down over her with a most bemused expression. He simply stood there observing, a grin spreading across his face.

"Being an *earthy* sort, I prefer my hands to spades," she replied without missing a beat, though she was feeling more than a bit embarrassed at being caught in such a compromising position. "My grandmother always did say I was named for the goddess of the land whose form is embedded in the mountains around us here, so I was simply connecting to the earthy part of my ancestry."

The man gazed up at the rounded Paps of Áine towering overhead before turning to admire the shapely form of the woman before him. "Yes," he quipped, looking her up and down. "A most definite resemblance, indeed! Goddess, may I help you up, so?"

Áine jumped to her feet. "You'd be amazed at how self-sufficient we goddesses are," she retorted, evading his extended hand, but noting her tone, added more softly, "though, thanks very much, anyway!"

The fellow surveyed the scene of potatoes strewn about the ground, while clumps of carrots and parsnips sat thrown in heaps wherever she had pulled them up. "I can see how self-sufficient you are, indeed, though if you don't mind me saying, you might be wanting a helping hand to manage this farm," he said with a toss of his head.

Without noticing what he had observed, Áine turned away before responding. "Not to worry, I can manage myself."

"I can see that now, can see that now, indeed," he said in a soothing tone. "Of course you can, Girleen, of course you can, now, with such fiery Ó'Suílleabháin blood stirring in your veins, as well as your direct ancestry from the goddess above," he added with a wink, as he flicked his finger up towards the Paps. "But in the meantime, I'll be getting the basket for the spuds." Before she could refuse his kind gesture, he took off for the garden shed, soon returning with a fine wicker basket.

"And how did you know where to find the basket, might I ask?" asked Áine, her voice cracking.

"Where else would you be keeping baskets, now, truly?" he retorted. "I had everything nice and neat here before you started digging! What a mess altogether you're making of me' garden." He folded his arms over his chest as he stared at her with a wide grin.

Áine placed her two arms on each hip. "*Your* garden, is it? And how exactly is it *your* garden?"

The stranger looked at her. "I planted it, of course."

Thinking she detected more than a hint of indignation at her question, she peered at him through narrorwed eyes. "I seem to think we have met before—ages ago— and yet . . ." Studying the features of his face, she added, "And yet, recently, as well, but I can't quite place you." She continued to gaze at him. "If I didn't know any better, I'd say . . ." She countered, "No, I must have been dreaming."

He offered a broad smile. "Maybe in a previous life, so."

She quickly looked away, before suddenly turning back to him, realizing whom he might be. "So are *you* the caretaker who opened the doors for me when I arrived?"

He took a deep bow before her, saying gallantly, "The very fellow—at your service, Goddess."

She scrutinized the features of his face. "But did we actually meet?" She looked away, trying to remember. "I seem to half remember you, but it's all so hazy." She offered a sheepish smile.

"'Tis no wonder. Sure, you were more asleep than awake, so. Didn't I find you nestled on a bed of moss?" He grinned coyly.

"Well, I was so excited to arrive here that I didn't sleep a wink on the plane. Guess the time difference caught up with me," she said with a shrug. "So it was you who covered me, then?"

"The very same," he said with a nod, before adding with a cavalier flourish, "Don't I see it me' duty to protect the innocent?"

She laughed. "I'm not as innocent as I may have looked!" Remembering her manners, she added, "It was so thoughtful of you to bring me such wonderful food. I particularly loved the salmon. It was simply amazing." Suddenly, she stared at him in alarm. "It was wild, wasn't it?"

"Of course," he said with a smile. "We never touch the farmed stuff. Sure, 'tis not real salmon a t'all."

"Yes, yes, I know." She looked at him as she inadvertently twisted her mouth, wondering how much he actually knew about wild salmon.

He bowed graciously. "Smoked it myself, I did. One of my specialities."

"*One* of your specialities?" She arched her eyebrow.

"Ah, sure, I have a few more rolled up me' sleeve." He erupted in laughter, long and hearty. "Of course, you don't know a thing about me, do you, since you have only just arrived and Maeve—well, not long gone, God rest her soul. I don't suppose she mentioned me to you Over, did she?"

Áine stopped to think a moment about the implications of what he had just said, and as her thoughts raced to make sense of his statement, she became increasingly more embarrassed. Turning away from him with now enflamed cheeks, she said softly, "You're not saying, are you, that you, em . . . and . . . and . . . and Maeve . . ." She faltered, unable to proceed with her question.

The fellow roared with laughter. "Are you asking me, Lass, if Maeve and I, if we were 'together' as it were? Sure, I'm half her age, Girleen!" He added with a toss of his head, "You Yanks have some odd thoughts, altogether."

Áine could not contain her sharp tone. "I'm not a Yank. I am Canadian—and Irish." She shrugged. "You wouldn't be the first younger man to show an avid interest in her."

"God, no!" he shuddered. "Such an interest was reserved for me' da' who possessed a mad passion for her in their younger days."

"Your father?" she stared at him, waiting for his explanation, before a look of understanding suddenly crossed her face. "Of course, you are the son of the fishmonger, then."

He erupted in laughter at the categorization. "Well, that's one of my—and his—many claims to fame, I suppose," the stranger responded. "It's time I introduced myself." With that, he said simply, though proudly, "I am Muirís—Muirís FitzGerald. Lovely to finally meet you."

She studied him through widening eyes. "So, you're the fellow who wrote to me, then." She studied his features carefully. She dismissed him at once, deciding on the spot that he was as arrogant as he was good-looking.

"I am, indeed." He stared at her through sparkling eyes.

Áine walked towards him, before stopping abruptly. "But what did you mean by saying this was *your* garden?" Her green eyes flashed red. "I was under the impression that *I* had inherited Maeve's house and lands. You said as much in your letter to me," she said, before adding with a smile, "among a few other curious statements."

Muirís smiled down at her. "Ah, so you remember my words, then." He winked at her. "I must have impressed you with my poetic writing style."

She eyed him intently before speaking. "And how, exactly, did you become Maeve's executor?"

He gazed down at her. "She trusted me."

"And why was that, exactly?" She placed her hands on each hip as she waited for his response.

He turned away from Áine's penetrating gaze. "She had her reasons." He crossed his arms across his chest before explaining. "I understood Maeve in ways you may not—at least, not right now."

"Well, I'll get to the bottom of the matter, as I'll be researching her time here."

He turned away abruptly, bending over to pick up the stray potatoes. As he tossed them into the basket, he muttered to himself, "An elusive wild salmon herself, she is. Maeve was certainly right about her."

Áine followed his lead, collecting spuds. "What was that?'

"Ah, don't mind me—I think aloud," he said, turning to her. "Let me set the record straight, now, on the gardens here. You have indeed inherited them, though they are mine, in a manner of speaking, as well. Sure, didn't I take care of them for Maeve—when she could no longer? I planted those beds of carrots and parsnips, you're after making a right mess of," he admonished.

Bewildered by his admission, Áine exclaimed, "Were you expecting an army, or was Maeve going into business? There's more than enough here to feed the entire family for the funeral supper!"

He gazed steadily at her. "Sure, it was all planned, don't you know, for that very purpose."

Áine looked at him with a stupefied expression. With hands on her hips, she exclaimed, "Are you telling me that Maeve had expected these vegetables to be served for the commemorative meal?"

Muirís offered a sad smile. "Ah, she did, indeed. Instructed me before she left to plant extras—as you'd be wanting them in preparation for her great meal, so." Gazing down at her, he gave a quick toss of the head, "She also said you'd be wanting me help with things."

"Is that so?" she replied, her tone as haughty as the sharply arched eyebrow she cast in his direction.

He laughed. "I repeat what I said earlier, you'll be needing some help with this farm—if this is any indication of your gardening abilities." Muirís tossed his head to the side. "Ah, sure, I shouldn't be so hard on you. Ye probably grew up in some large city Over. I suppose you bought everything from some immense supermart, rather than grew it yourself." He shot a sidelong glance at her to assess his effect.

Áine countered. "Actually, I did grow my own vegetables, and I was not reared in some urban metropolis, but in rural Price Edward Island—in Canada," she said, emphasizing the country, assuming he didn't know the location of her tiny island home. "Not so different from here, really—well, except there are no mountains—and not as many rocks, as here." She flashed her eyes at him. "And the fellows there aren't as sure of themselves as here, either."

Tossing his head to the side, Muirís roared with laughter.

"And what is so funny, might I ask?" said Áine archly.

"I'm just imagining the state of your gardens, not to mention the poor lads whose hearts you surely trampled on," he said with a wink.

She raised one eyebrow at such an angle to resemble geese flying. "With all these mighty assumptions about my terribly deprived and incompetent life 'Over,' as you would say, not to mention some highly inaccurate theories about my social life," said Áine, her words dripping in sarcasm, "I have forgotten my manners—not that you would notice. Would you like a cup of tea?"

Muirís smiled. "Well, now, what kind of tea would you be offering?" he asked with a twinkle in his eye. "I never turn down a good cup of tea, as long as it isn't a tea bag—though given the fact that you're a Yank, and due to this inclement weather, I suppose I'll make an exception."

Áine let the insinuation go for the moment regarding her nationality and corresponding tea-brewing abilities.

"Pick your battles," she reminded herself. "This weather?" she asked. "I don't understand. It's dry and sunny."

"Not for long," Muirís responded, as he pointed down to the beach. "Look at that squall coming in there off the sea—quickly, now, grab the carrots and the parsnips, and I'll bring in the spuds and the leeks." Scurrying to their respective tasks, they made it the kitchen door—just as the wind kicked up, and the rain descended in horizontal sheets.

"Well, now, it smells awfully enticing in here. So you can bake then," Muirís commented. He gazed in admiration over the loaves of bread cooling on the table.

Áine poured out some tea from the teapot that had been simmering on the hob. "Will you have a slice of bread to go with your—loose—tea?" she asked somewhat primly—though proudly. "I just baked them."

"I would, indeed," Muirís responded. His enthusiasm for eating revealed no polite restraints. "We'll have to see now, whether it tastes the same made from Canadian hands . . . "

"It really is amazing to me the amount of ethnic typecasting I'm hearing from you," Áine interjected. "One would think you deem Canadians a useless nationality, altogether. Besides, I *am* Irish, you know. I hold an Irish passport—it's just that I was reared 'Over,' as you say. I'm as Irish, as I am Canadian." She abruptly turned on her heels—though not before shooting him a glance that revealed her rising indignation.

"Well, now, I assumed you were your mother's daughter, considering that she couldn't boil water, as the saying goes, though she did love the wild salmon—I have to say that for her. Even left money to support the wild salmon project here."

"Oh?" she said slowly, not knowing that bit of information before now. "We can chat about that later, but first, let's clear the air a bit, shall we?" said Áine in as caustic a tone as she could muster. "First, she was not my mother—but my aunt. And second, speaking of salmon, where is the salmon your father promised me? I don't see it with you."

"Ah, sure, isn't that why I'm here—to give you the full *bradáin fiáin*—wild salmon—experience?" he said, with a gleam in his eyes, followed by a mischievous smile.

"What do you mean?"

"Being the wild salmon preservationist that you are, sure, you wouldn't want to have any salmon that you didn't catch yourself now, would you?" He looked at her with a smile. "Sure, wouldn't you want to ensure they were caught properly—and in season?"

"Actually, I eat very little salmon, as I prefer to conserve them." She stared at him. "How do you know about my wild salmon project?"

"Sure, Maeve told me all about it. Wasn't that one of the reasons for her generous legacy to our preservation project?" He added with a big smile, "Besides, I promised her."

"Promised Maeve what?" she asked in a tone betraying her increasing discomfort with the tenor of the exchange.

"That I would take you to *Tobar na Bhradáin.*"

"I've got the *Bhradáin* part—salmon—but what does *Tobar* mean?"

"Have you no Irish Gaelic on you?" He peered down at her, and without waiting for her response, added in a tone of remorse, "Ah, sure, you Yanks speak only the Queen's English."

She glared at him. "*Bheagán. Fíos bheagán.* A little." She shook her head sadly. "I deeply regret that I know only the odd expression, really. I hope to remedy that, while living here." With eyes blazing, she added, "However, we *Canadians* are also largely fluent in French, and some, in various languages of the First Nations."

"Pity that," he said.

She looked at him through wary eyes. "Your father said something similar. What's a pity?'

He gazed at her evenly. "'Tis a pity that all the other Yanks, but the Irish speak the ancient language of their ancestors. What's wrong with the Irish Over? Ashamed of their language, is it?"

Knowing she wasn't going to win this battle, she sighed. "It's a long, tragic, story. Shall we save that for another occasion? Now, what is a *Tobar*?"

"'Tis a holy well, *of course*. Named after the holy wellspring where the sacred salmon spawn—the salmon of knowledge, that is. Afterwards, we'll get our salmon where the river meets the sea."

"I'd love to, really, I would. You know, my father was a fisherman, and I enjoyed accompanying him on some of his fishing trips," Áine said in a somewhat hesitant tone, not wanting to disclose her suspicion that the fellow thought of her aunt's funeral dinner as something more like a treasure hunt than a solemn commemoration. She looked at him through plaintive eyes. "But I must prepare the food for the meal."

Muirís glanced around the kitchen. "Seems that you're prepared enough, now, except for the poaching of the salmon and the boiling up of the spuds that you can't do until the morning of the meal—and until you have caught some wild salmon," he said with a sly grin. "Sure, 'tis an essential part of the preparations. Besides, didn't I promise Maeve—"

"Promised Maeve what?" Áine interjected in an exasperated tone. "After all," she added, "do you really expect me to believe that Maeve planned her own funeral to this degree of detail—if at all?"

He looked through steely blue eyes before responding. "Sure, I had to promise Maeve that I would bring her daughter when she arrived to the sacred wellspring, before any salmon were served at her funeral supper."

"But that's just it," said Áine, exploding with impatience. "I'm not one of her daughters—I'm her niece." She gazed over at him uncertainly. She decided then and there that the fellow was utterly daft.

He tossed his head to the side. "Well, now, I admit that there's a bit of a discrepancy here, but Maeve was very keen on saying that Áine, her *daughter*," he added emphatically, "would arrive soon after her death, and that I was to see to it that you blessed yourself at the sacred *Tobar*." He shot a look of pity at her. "Wellspring—before drawing in some salmon for her funeral meal."

"Surely, you must be mistaken. It's very odd, altogether. Maybe she was confused there at the end, mixing me up with her mother, Áine. She didn't use the names Faife, Cainder, or Bair? They're her actual daughters."

"No, she was very clear. Áine. She repeated it again and again," his voice firm.

"Well, I can't explain it at all. And why she thought *I* would oversee the preparations and not her daughters is another mystery, considering we haven't seen one another in several years. I was sure she had long forgotten about my existence."

Muirís shook his head. "Not a t'all. She spoke of you frequently and knew all about you. Sure, didn't I know that you lived in Canada—in Prince Edward Island?" He shook his head again. "Though I must say, that's a terribly British-sounding name for a Celtic island."

Áine stared at him. "But how? And why?" she sputtered, then proceeded to scold, "And if you knew all along that I lived in Canada, why do you keep insisting on labelling me a Yank? Canadians are not Americans, you know. For more than a few of us, that's like calling the Irish, well, *Brits!*" She glared at him. "Judging by your comment regarding the name of my island province, I sense how you feel about *them.*"

He laughed, amused by the vehemence of her response. "Don't get me started on that topic. Ah, sure, I was having a bit of sport with you. Indeed, 'tis easy to get a rise out of you. Well now, those other anomalies will need solving another day," he said, draining the last sip from his teacup. Helping himself to a few slices of bread, he explained, "Might need these for the great journey, so." He quickly squirreled them away in his jacket before she had a chance to respond. "It's getting late now. We must rush, so, to get in our salmon by nightfall." He stood up, and indicating that he would not take no for an answer, said in an authoritative voice, "Right so, we're off, then."

"And am I to believe you about all this?" Áine asked Muirís. She seriously questioned his motivations.

Opening the door, Muirís said, "You'll have to accept it on faith, I suppose. Since the dead can't speak to us except through the living, I suppose you'll have to assume I didn't make it up."

Heaving a big, audibly discernible sigh, Áine gave in and submitted to his seemingly crazy plan of action. Just as she was closing the door to the cottage, Muirís pushed it open again. "Jaysus. Didn't I almost forget the important part."

"What's that?" asked Áine, surprised by his outburst.

He looked around the kitchen. "You'll be needing to bring the urn," he said.

"The urn? You mean my Aunt's *ashes*?" she asked. She looked at him wide-eyed.

Muirís nodded. "That's right. We'll be needing some of them for the well. We're to spread some of the ashes in and around the *Tobar*, as well as in the river as we catch the fish."

"What? You can't be serious—are you mad, altogether, man?" Áine asked, her two hands on each hip. She became openly defiant. "I need this urn to bury in the family graveyard." She stopped and peered at him suspiciously through slitted eyes. "Just how do you know this, exactly?"

He responded in a serious tone. "Maeve gave me very strict instructions before her death. She made me repeat them several times to make sure I had the steps right. Said something about her soul needing to be released." He gazed down at her with a wide smile Áine reluctantly found charming. "I am a solicitor, you know."

"Good God!" exclaimed Áine. "Did she turn into a pagan Druid or something before her death, or are these typical acts you engage in as a solicitor?"

"Not really," Muirís responded carefully. He gazed at Áine through sad eyes. "Sure, didn't she think you would cop on to the Celtic significance of these actions—despite your years in Canada. Do ye not know of the Brehon Laws on your Gaelic island Over? Besides, she intended for part of her remains to be planted in the family plot."

He looked at her with disappointment. "I pictured you differently based on Maeve's account of you. I'd say you are more American than you think—and she thought."

Áine decided to ignore—yet again—the barb about being an ignorant Yank. Turning to look up at him, she asked, as if baiting him, "And how, exactly, would you know this? She died Over."

"Maeve told me all this the summer she was home from America before returning—when we drew up all the legacy paperwork."

Áine thought about it for some minutes. "This doesn't make sense."

Muirís took her arm and guided her with urn in hand to his car. "I'll explain all I know, now, to you as we drive, so."

As they sped along the winding roads, Áine thought about their exchange. As he drove, she stole a few side-long glances at Muirís to try to determine whether he was sane or not, cautiously concluding that he looked like he was telling the truth.

Turning to him, she said slowly, "The trouble with this story is that my Aunt didn't even know she was ill until it was too late. We only found out late last autumn, when she called one of her sons in a panic, saying she didn't know where she was and had forgotten her way home."

Muirís offered a sympathetic glance before explaining. "Well, she knew something that summer for that's when she made all these preparations."

"It's all very mysterious," commented Áine, for lack of any better term to describe the untoward circumstances, as they headed for the wellspring.

As the sun neared the western horizon, Áine scooped a handful of ashes of her aunt's remains and tossed them into the well. "This reminds me of an old Irish poem—do you know the one about the well?" Peering at him, she added, "but then again, you probably don't read much poetry with all your legal work—and gardening."

Muirís smiled at her with a mischievous grin. "Ah, well now, you'd be surprised at how literate-like we fishermen can be in these parts." He stood and chanted in a singsong voice the words to the poem to which Áine referred—as she listened in stunned silence. When he finished, he winked, and said, with a toss of his head, "Now, if you're a good lass, you just may discover some more of me' hidden talents. But now, we must hurry, so."

As the sun sunk slowly into the horizon, they drew the net from one side of the river to the other as Muirís waded through to the other side. "Now lift!" he commanded. Inside the net were well over a dozen salmon, some quite large.

They folded the net over onto itself, and Muirís brought his side back to Áine. "Right, so. Now we must take the most beautiful one—and give her back."

She turned to him in disbelief. "What do you mean?"

"Maeve said we must return the loveliest one back to its wild state—and toss some of the ashes in with it as it returns."

"Good God, we'll have no ashes left for the ceremony if this keeps up," muttered Áine. "This is the most intricate set of funeral directions I have ever heard of," she added in a tone of complete bewilderment.

Muirís wasted no time. "Right, then—which one will we pick?"

Though Áine surveyed the lot of them, she immediately spotted one among those in the middle—all colours of salmon, streaked with green, brown, and gold—and pointing in its direction, declared, "That one, there, without a doubt."

Together Muirís and Áine lifted it from the net and tossed it back into the river. Áine followed by tossing some of the ashes into the radiant waters, now illuminated by the golden light.

It seemed as if the salmon had waited for that act to occur. As Áine tossed in some of her aunt's remains, the salmon jumped out of the water, straight into the spray of ashes, before diving below and swimming out to sea— *wild and free*—forever.

Muirís and Áine stood looking out, each lost in thought. Standing there at the ocean's edge in the twilight, Áine couldn't help but feel as if somehow she were freeing her aunt's soul from the suffering it had incurred through the tragic way that she had died.

Both seemed relieved that the salmon took to the sea. They watched in awe as the last rays of light cast hues of salmon and gold upon the waves, when suddenly, the salmon made one last jump high into the air, before descending into the currents of the sea.

"Something mystical in that," murmured Áine.

Muirís gazed down on her in admiration. "Perhaps you are beginning to understand what we here in the Gaeltacht have long experienced," he said slowly.

Áine's response did not disappoint him. "Odd thing, that. I keep repeating that expression since returning here," Áine said, looking up at Murís. "I keep finding myself discovering the mystical in the natural surroundings about us here. It's a bit unnerving, and yet consoling, all at the same time." She stood lost in thought a moment. "Although the landscape was wild and beautiful in Prince Edward Island where I was reared, it didn't have this mystical quality I keep feeling here."

Muirís nodded in empathy. "That's the essence of our Celtic Irish culture, the very thing that the EU is trying to wrest away from us," he said bitterly, "in getting us to think we need to live like the Yanks—no insult to present company intended," he added in a rush, lest he hurt Áine's feelings. "We're to exchange our old ways for cell phones, extra holiday homes, and of course, fish that we can locate down to the very fish farms from which they were generated."

She shuddered. "I detest fish farms. That's one of the reasons I am here," she said with a sidelong glance at Muirís, "to ensure that the salmon remain wild, not farmed."

He stopped a moment to gaze out to sea. "Give me the ancient wellsprings and wild salmon any day," he said gallantly, "and I'll die fighting to retain our ancient ways, EU or no EU."

Áine peered at him. "You sound a bit like my grandfather did whenever he spoke of the 'Bloody Brits,' as he called them."

"Sure, haven't we exchanged one form of servitude for another?" asked Muirís. He continued with deep passion in his voice. "We might have more money, but we have a poorer quality of life now, since we no longer buy carrots covered in soil, having just been plucked, but rather, uniform looking, pre-skinned carrots rinsed with chemicals for our ease. Aren't they trying to introduce spuds from new seed strains made from GMO origins, rather than handed down from one generation to the next? Sure, it's as if Ireland has declared a holiday from all traditional ways and sold out—in order to work for big computer companies and to eat food nicely packaged from the large Continental supermarts, which are tragically, replacing the local shops in our villages and towns."

Áine nodded. "I completely understand. That's another reason I'm here, actually, besides the inheritance, of course. I'm to consult with Government on the fate of the wild salmon—as well as on the merits of creating a local food campaign based on traditional foods."

He turned to her in surprise. "Is that right, now?"

She smiled at him. "Indeed, it is. My goal in coming here—*returning* here," she corrected herself, "besides my governmental work, was to explore the idea of starting up an heirloom vegetable business—and perhaps traditional foods here—after my contract ends."

He smiled down at her and said with a wink, "A woman after me' own heart, you are."

Sidestepping his remark, Áine tried to turn the exchange back. "You have touched on issues directly related to my projects in Prince Edward Island. I worked there on creating local food economies and wild salmon protection—all based on the old ways of doing things."

"Someone must step in and save our ways before it's too late. Who will save us if we don't save ourselves? *Sinn féin*—ourselves alone. Something right about that notion." Muirís's tone sounded determined, unwavering, resolute.

Áine studied him before speaking. "And how are you attempting to accomplish such a tremendous, though noble, task, Muirís?"

With a toss of his head, he said obliquely, "Well, now, we may be able to coordinate our efforts." He leaned down studying her, before shifting his gaze to the river and sea beyond. "Ah, well now, we have our ways. We have our ways, indeed."

With that, Muirís turned away from Áine, and hoisting the net on his back, said it was time to prepare the fish for her meal. The two left the water's edge both deep in thought—thoughts they did not share with one another. But the last lingering rays of light seemed to sense the subtle bonds that had formed through the shared experience of releasing the salmon and freeing the soul of Maeve—for as they ambled back to the car, the long shadows cast by their separate forms became intertwined by the now setting sun.

CHAPTER FIVE

THE PASSING OF MAEVE

BÁS MEDB

THE NEXT MORNING, Áine and her guest, who had just arrived from Dublin, were seated around a small table set for tea in the traditional cottage kitchen. "I'm so glad you could come to the memorial service for my aunt," said Áine to the genteel woman across from her.

"I cannot believe she's gone," Elizabeth said, her voice immeasurably sad. "She was so young." With tears in her eyes, she reached out to touch Áine's arm. "Will you tell me all about it?"

"Of course," said Áine with a gentle pat on the older woman's hand. "Will I put on the kettle? We'll be needing an entire pot for what I'm about to tell you." Elizabeth shifted in her chair as if to ready herself.

"The story of the passing of my aunt Maeve is both tragic and dramatic." She shook her head. "My grandmother used to say that she named her for Queen Medb of Connaught, for even as a newborn, her fiery eyes conveyed the unbridled passion that fed her soul."

"She was well-named, I'll say that for her," agreed Elizabeth, before forcing a smile.

Áine chuckled as she poured out the tea. "But wasn't that her way? Passionate and dramatic to the end and beyond, most likely—into the next life!"

Elizabeth visibly relaxed as Áine recounted, "Wasn't it even one of her own sons, Ciarán, who proclaimed at her memorial service in Nova Scotia, 'One funeral wasn't enough for her. Only Maeve would manage to have two funerals—and in two different countries, no less.'" They both smiled, knowing how closely the proclamation reflected Maeve's personality.

Elizabeth leaned over and pressed her hand lightly over Áine's as she asked gently, "Were you there, Áine, at the end?"

A bit surprised by the question, Áine explained that she hadn't been living in Nova Scotia at all, but in Prince Edward Island where she had grown up.

Elizabeth looked away. "I thought perhaps that you might have gone to see her before she, she . . . "

Áine continued the woman's train of thought with a sigh. "It all happened so quickly, Elizabeth. I don't think Maeve lasted more than a week or so after we all realized the seriousness of her illness. I had arranged to take some time off from work, so I could drive over from PEI to Nova Scotia to see her, but she suddenly died from one day to the next."

She was silent for a few moments before saying more to herself than to her guest, "Quite the moving account about her last moments."

Elizabeth leaned over again toward Áine and said in a consoling tone, "If it's not too difficult for you, my dear, I would so love to hear it."

Áine launched her story. "For some reason, that remained inexplicable to me really, beyond the sheer *insult* of the corporate scam most likely underlying the cause of Maeve's demise, I took the news of her impending death very hard—very hard, indeed."

Elizabeth patted her hand in a soothing gesture of empathy. "I am sure you did, dear."

Áine gazed at the woman, wondering how she could understand how she had felt. "No, it wasn't that she was simply my aunt, Elizabeth," Áine explained. "We were not that close, really, however deeply I admired her." She gazed into the distance for a moment before continuing. "I think it was more that Maeve always appeared so *strong*, implacable, actually, like a rock face on a stony mountain—an example of such invincible strength and fortitude that getting the best of her would be like trekking to the summit of the world's most formidable mountain range in one's stockings." She looked away, before gently shaking her head. "I always revered that in her."

Elizabeth smiled at the apt characterization of her friend. "Indeed, I saw that in her myself," she admitted, "and loved her for it." Looking away for a moment in silent reverie, she then prodded, "Pray, do continue, my dear."

Áine tried to explain. "It was that I found myself feeling just infuriated over the cause of her illness—that something as sinister as corporate greed could disintegrate the mountain of strength within her. Up to that point, no one could restrain her, and no problem she encountered was insolvable. She always seemed to succeed—until . . ."

Áine had stopped, finding it difficult to continue—for

reasons she didn't understand. Finally, she spoke. "In fact, I remained convinced that she would pull a 'Finnegan's Wake' on us all and rise from the dead."

Elizabeth chortled in her quiet way. "Indeed, she most certainly evinced a wall of strength, fuelled by her passion, through everything." She glanced over at Áine. "I have interrupted you—you were recounting your anger over . . . "

Unfalteringly, Áine took up where she had left off. "Upon finding out the news from my mother, I searched the internet rather obsessively for any cure—alternative therapies, even emailing the world's expert in mad cow disease at Oxford."

She stopped, lost in thought. "I have a few theories I'm investigating about the particular cause of her death," she said with a grimace, before shifting her gaze out the window to the sea below. "And I'm not happy with what I am discovering—but that's another story." Some minutes passed before she continued.

Elizabeth smiled over how inextricably linked she found Áine's response and the passionate nature of her old friend. "I'm listening, Áine," Elizabeth said gently, in an effort to bring her back to the present tale.

"Right," said Áine. "I listened in absolute disbelief as my mother telephoned to provide daily updates on the rapidly deteriorating condition of Auntie Maeve, who from one day to the next, had transformed from her highly spirited, determined—some might say, *calculating*—self, to a confused woman with little memory in a matter of what seemed like days."

"My God!" exclaimed Elizabeth in horror.

"If that weren't enough," Áine added, "she rapidly degenerated from not remembering her family to absolute, complete physical incapacity within the short span of just over a week."

Áine stopped to take a sip of tea. "It was simply unbelievable that this strong, clever, fierce—often cunning—woman could fall so hard."

"Ah, the poor dear," exclaimed Elizabeth with a deep sigh.

"Exactly," said Áine. "The very woman who, according to her ex-husband, Conor, possessed the ability to charm the snakes back to Ireland, who rather cleverly sought out the most incredible real estate bargains—buying ocean-front mansions about to go into foreclosure, and turning them around to make hundreds of thousands by flipping them—suddenly couldn't find her way home one day."

They both shook their heads in silent horror.

Áine continued, the account now pouring from her. "At that point, she apparently still had the druthers to ring up her son, Ciarán, who was away studying at St. FX in Antigonish." She glanced over at Elizabeth. "It's a university in northern Nova Scotia."

"Yes, yes, pray, do continue," urged Elizabeth.

Áine leaned toward her listener. "Apparently, she said to her son, 'Ciarán, ah, Ciarán, my boy, ah, ah …' Maeve's voice then faltered, as if aware there was no stepping back into yesterday.

"'Yes, Mum. Are you all right? You don't sound well,' he responded concerned.

"'I seem to have lost my way,' said she.

"'What do you mean, Mum? Where are you?' he asked with rising concern, since he couldn't recount any phone calls from her that *ever* indicated a need for help.

"'Well, that's just it, Ciarán, now, isn't it? I don't really know where I am actually, or where I'm going.'

"There was a momentary silence on the phone as Ciarán processed this exchange.

"'Are you speaking metaphorically, now, Mum? Are you having a philosophical crisis?'

"'Ah, don't confuse me now, son,' she sobbed into the phone. 'I haven't a clue what you mean. I just came from . . . well, actually now, I'm not sure where I was coming from, I think one shop or other, and have forgotten how to get to my home from here. Can you just direct me now, whilst I stay on the phone?' she pleaded. 'There are so many cars . . .'

"And her voice faded away."

Poor Elizabeth broke down over hearing about the devastating state into which her friend had descended.

"Will I go on, Elizabeth?" inquired Áine tenderly, "or is it too hard on you?"

"No, dear," said Elizabeth between sobs, "I must hear what happened to poor Maeve."

Áine proceeded with the tragic account. "Well, by this time, Ciarán was highly alarmed. While used to such phone calls from his father, who loved to drive about the Maritimes, even though he was almost legally blind—never had his proud mother ever, *ever*, indicated the slightest hesitation from proceeding on her chosen path."

"Indeed," proclaimed Elizabeth. "That was the Maeve I knew and loved."

"Yes, I understand completely," said Áine, with a nod. "We were all in awe of her amazing, unfaltering sense of resolve." She shook her head sadly.

She continued with the story. "So, Ciarán realized something was terribly wrong and fortunately took control of the situation.

"'Where are you now, Mum?' he asked.

"'Well, that's just it, now, Ciarán. I don't exactly know,' she said in a weary tone.

"'Just have a look at the street sign on the nearest corner and tell me what it says,' he said.

"'Right so. It says Upper Water Street,' her voice trailing off, as if she were trying to remember where that was.

"'Right, Mum, so you are still in the city centre. I think Mac must be down there at the harbour—just down the road from you. I'll give him a call and have him come get you,' said Ciarán.

"His mother didn't respond.

"'Mum?' he asked, 'are you there?'

"'Can't you come collect me?' she asked weakly. 'Who is Mac?'

"Ciarán thought his mother didn't hear him properly.

"'Mac?'" he repeated, 'Mum, Mac, *Mac*. He's your new husband!' he nearly yelled into the phone—as a great boulder of absolute dread seemed to crash down upon him.

"'How will I recognize him? Do I know him?' Maeve asked timidly.

"Ciarán was almost speechless as the new reality engulfed him.

"'Not to worry, Mum. He'll know you. I'll stay on the phone with you the entire time.'

"And with that, he placed a call on the land line to Mac, and telling him it was a dire emergency, instructed him to go find Maeve."

Elizabeth broke down again, this time allowing the tears to flow freely. "My God, how absolutely awful!" she cried.

Áine leaned toward Elizabeth. "Well, now, Elizabeth,

I cannot explain to you, exactly what came over me, but when I was told this account of poor Maeve, something gushed to the surface from deep inside. I was simply resolved, utterly *determined* to save her." She looked off into the distance as she recounted her desperate efforts.

"As I mentioned before, I spent endless hours researching—looking for alternative treatments. I pleaded with my uncle Conor—who had now abandoned his *Táin Bó Cuailgne*—*The Cattle Raid of Cooley*—in which he had been engaged with Maeve, to oversee her care—to try to persuade the physician there to use the alternative cures I had found—if only to give them a try."

Áine stopped a moment as tears pooled in her eyes. Wiping them away, she said softly, "The doctors there would have none of it—even knowing that the woman would die." She waited a moment, before adding, "It was so exasperating, to know that some people had stopped the disease in its tracks, and one of the North America's most renowned research hospitals refused to even try." She stifled a sob. "My poor aunt."

"So, it was the mad cow, then, was it?" asked Elizabeth in horror.

Áine's facial expression darkened measurably. "Or something even more sinister. As I said, the next corporate scam in food '*production*.'" With a vigorous shake of her head, she snapped, "All they're doing, as far as I can see, is producing untimely deaths of the consumers." With a grimace, she added, "Though until I have my facts all lined up, I don't want to even talk about it."

They both sipped their tea in silence, each grappling with memories of the once seemingly unstoppable Maeve.

As if a flash of lightning ignited her, Áine suddenly turned to Elizabeth. "But wait 'til I tell you how she passed. It is simply the most *extraordinary* story."

"Do," urged Elizabeth, "Do tell me. Surely, our poor Maeve did not simply fade away into the good night."

Áine smiled. "Not our Maeve. She was indeed dramatic to the end—if not downright mystical!"

She lapsed into the tale of Maeve's last moments:

"It was a cold, damp, drab afternoon in November, when the last rays of yellow light lingered in the room where the family had gathered round Aunt Maeve's hospital bed. She lay half inclined—though more by the mountain of pillows supporting her, than by her own will power, which had significantly ebbed in the last few days.

"The children—my cousins—had been summoned by their brother to their mother's bed, as he feared the worst, wanting his mother to have at least the empathy of her family around her—even if she didn't seem to recognize any of them at all.

"Even Maeve's sister, Eithne, my mother—with whom she had spent her life sparring, sat by her sister's bedside, trying hard not to betray any inner emotions that surely rocked waves of anguish within her, as she watched her younger sister slip into death. Instead, she focussed on the bereaving children, trying to get them to buck up and remain strong in front of their mother.

"'Now tears won't be needed at all here,' she admonished in her bristling tone. 'There'll be plenty of time for that *after*. We need to be strong now and be joyful around your Mam,' she insisted.

"'Joyful, Auntie Eithne?' Bair repeated with a sneer. 'Look at her!'

"As if on cue, Auntie Maeve moved her hand toward her sister.

"'She wants you to sit next to her,' urged Ciarán.

"Somewhat hesitantly, my mother sat down next to her sister and whispered, 'What is it, Maeve?' Maeve again moved her hand, as if trying to touch her sister's face.

"'What is it she wants?' asked Ciarán, as he watched his mother who hadn't moved in a few days, vainly attempt to touch his aunt's mouth. 'Is she trying to get you to say something?'

"Just then, Eithne laughed. 'Vain to the end!' she cried out triumphantly, as she interpreted her sister's gestures. 'She'd like some lipstick!'

"They all roared with laughter as Eithne gently dabbed her sister's lips with a dark red lipstick, while one of the girls brought over a brush and fixed up their mother's hair.

"'Of course, she wants to look her best,' exclaimed my mother to them all. 'It's in her nature to be so. Thank God, that hasn't changed! She's still in there!'

"And indeed, it seemed as if Maeve perked up somewhat with the bit of lipstick. Although she could no longer move her head, she shifted her eyes from side to side, gazing intently at them all.

"'Yes, Maeve, dear. You're still the centre of attention. We're all here, gazing at you with the same dazed admiration we always have shown to you,' said my mother.

"Maeve looked about her at her children and sister. From her red lips came two words,

'Áine. Salmon.'

"Everyone looked at one another and at her in confusion. Eithne leaned over Maeve and gushed, 'Áine? Our mother, Áine, is it, you mean? Are you seeing our mother in Heaven, then? And salmon, Maeve? Are you wanting some salmon to eat? Dear God, you haven't eaten any-thing in a week! What is she on about at all?'

"Suddenly, Eithne nodded in understanding. 'She's seeing the Heavenly Light, surely.'

"Maeve seemed not to understand the words of her sister. At that moment, the door opened, and in walked my uncle Conor—the very man with whom Maeve for years had been locked in a vicious battle over every pos-session they had once owned jointly—including the children."

Áine stopped to sip her tea. "As I alluded to before, surely the famed *Cattle Raid of Cooley* was not as vicious as the battle that ensued between those two warriors!" With a twist of her mouth, she remarked, "Which is the main reason I avoided being around at all."

She looked over at Elizabeth and said with a sly grin, "Believe me, Prince Edward Island way up in the Gulf of St. Lawrence wasn't far away enough when those two got started!"

Elizabeth quietly nodded in assent. "So I have heard. But do, continue—to the very end."

Áine complied with the woman's request. "Well, then, approaching the bed slowly with a bit of unsteadiness in his walk, Conor said only, 'I thought I should be here.' He then actually broke down in tears and admitted, 'Truth is, I couldn't stay away. Sure, the woman holds an uncanny power to draw me in.'

"They all made way for him around the bedside. All eyes switched to Maeve, who seemed to be watching her former husband as he approached the bed. There appeared to be a struggle within her, as she vainly tried to sit up straighter to receive him. Her eyes seemed to shift from a clear, vacant stare to almost a sparkle, as if the sun had emerged from behind a cloud—to warm up the cold seas below.

"'Well now, if that isn't something, altogether,' muttered Eithne. 'Leave it to a man to make her feel special. That woman hasn't changed a bit—even on her bloody deathbed.'

"They all watched in amazement as Conor stood next to his wife of old, and leaning down over her, gently kissed her lips. Maeve looked at him for a moment and suddenly managed to move her hand to his. As he clasped her hand, Maeve, ever so unexpectedly, smiled—a broad smile that transformed her pale face to a shade of her former radiance. They all looked on in awe.

"She looked over one last time at her family gathered round her, and shifting her gaze to the sorrowful face of her former lover, who clasped her hand now tightly and shed tears of sorrow from his glistening eyes and heaving body, Maeve slowly closed her eyes forever."

Áine stopped for a moment to collect herself, feeling waves of anguish raging inside. With a long gulp, and a dab at the now flowing tears, she concluded by recounting the mystical events that transpired upon the passing of Maeve.

"And here is the incredible ending of the tale, Elizabeth. The more spiritual members of the family who witnessed the passing, still claim that as the last embers of light flickered throughout the room when Maeve's soul left her body, the image of a salmon dancing up through the air appeared—just before the room turned dark."

Áine arched her eyebrow as she looked at Elizabeth. "No one can explain it."

"Poor, poor Maeve." Elizabeth stared at Áine for some moments, unsure of how to respond. Finally, she spoke. "That was quite the account. You tell a tale wonderfully—even one as difficult as Maeve's tragic passing."

She stopped to sip some tea before starting up again. "And that brings me round to the subject of why I am here, my dear," Elizabeth began softly. "As you know," she continued, "I have been one of your aunt's closest friends through the years, ever since I met her at university in Dublin."

"Yes," said Áine absently, her thoughts still immersed in her story. "So good of you to come all this way."

She then leaned over to Áine, and softly touching the younger woman's hand, she explained, "And that's why I'm here, Áine, dear. Maeve was quite specific in her will that she wanted me to ensure that her instructions were carried out."

"And why me, Elizabeth," Áine asked with a twist of her mouth. "We hadn't even seen or spoken to one another in several years."

"Well, now, Áine, being the writer in the family—" she began.

Áine, taken aback by the characterization, interrupted her. "I'm no writer, Elizabeth. It's true, I've written some academic articles, but—"

"Well, that is how Maeve referred to you," interjected Elizabeth. "Perhaps she was thinking about the depth of passion it took to do such research," she said in a soothing tone, "and that's why she chose you above her other children—children—I mean, to inherit the family property."

"I don't understand," said Áine.

"She was hoping that if you came here and spent

some time, you would be able to write her story—from her point of view."

"And why did she think that?" Áine countered. "As I said, I haven't even laid eyes on the woman for several years, nor do I know her 'story'—as you called it—except for what other members of the family have related, together with my old childhood memories."

Elizabeth nodded. "That's precisely why, Áine. You haven't been tied to her emotionally, since you've been busy making your own way in the world—away from Ireland." She nodded as she waved her hand in the air. "She felt that, while your own experiences differ in detail, you have been searching for things in life she herself had done so determinedly—and defiantly—at one time," she recounted with a mysterious air.

"It still defies comprehension," said Áine, with a shake of her head.

"Ah, Áine," the older woman continued, her voice full of plaintive emotion, "Maeve's tale, as she used to say to me, is the story of all the women around you here—and their mothers before them." Elizabeth paused before continuing. "And I do think she was utterly correct. Didn't I spend my life as an anthropologist studying the lives of women in Ireland?"

"So why didn't she choose you to represent her viewpoint?" asked Áine, arching her eyebrow in an overtly suspicious glance.

Elizabeth leaned forward to touch Áine's hand again. "I was her friend, Áine, and I have a friend's loyalty, but you are one of her own ones, a member of the family, and as such, have an insight unknown to me, but through her admissions," she said. "After hearing for years about your own dauntless courage to take on challenges Over, Áine," Elizabeth said in a rather pointed manner, "with the wild salmon, and that traditional foods project you initiated, she was sure you would find the motivation, shall we say," she said, briefly looking away from Áine, as if she knew things about the younger woman she shouldn't, "as well as the requisite experience and skill to consider and assess the complete picture."

"Well," exclaimed Áine, as she sat back in her chair, "I'm not sure what to make of it all—my childhood memories of her are so fleeting, and my distance rather great to the larger family. You know, I've been away from Ireland for so long." She shifted her gaze, from her guest to the view from the window of the sea in the distance.

"Time is a fluid concept here, Áine, don't you know." Elizabeth silently sipped her tea, giving Áine a moment to soak in the implications of their discussion. She offered, "I think Maeve felt that in re-discovering your place here in Kerry—and in Ireland—you would find the story that needs to be written about your family—and her. Perhaps, even, Dearie, I dare say, about yourself."

Áine was amazed at these revelations and suggestions. "I'll think on it all," she said after a moment's reflection. "I'm not quite sure what to make of it yet."

"Right so, Áine," finished Elizabeth as she got up from her seat. "I'll leave you now to prepare the last bits for the funeral supper. I'm off up to Dublin after the ceremony."

"You're not planning to stay for the meal, Elizabeth?" asked Áine, staring at her in surprise. "Surely, you must."

"It's for your family," she said. "It will be the first time you'll all be together after so many years, will it not?"

"That's right!" exclaimed Áine. "I hadn't quite thought of it that way." She looked at Elizabeth and scolded, "but

Maeve would be very upset knowing that her closest friend didn't attend the supper. You must stay."

"I suppose you're right," she agreed with a slight nod. "If you don't think it's too imposing."

Reaching out to touch her arm, Áine said with a bright smile, "Not at all, Elizabeth. The family would be delighted to meet the oldest friend of dear Maeve. I'm quite sure of it."

As Elizabeth turned to leave the room, she suddenly stopped before turning back. "Oh, and Áine, one more thing. Maeve made a point of asking me repeatedly to make sure you continued your salmon preservation work from Canada—here. I believe she left money to ensure the continuation of the Kerry project overseen by some local bloke. She asked that you pay particular attention to protecting *your* salmon, as she put it." She gazed at her through questioning eyes. "She said you'd know what she meant."

With a twist of her mouth, Áine asked, "His name wouldn't be Muirís FitzGerald, now, would it?" She arched her eyebrow.

"Ah, yes, that was it, indeed," proclaimed Elizabeth. "He's that fellow who wrote to me regarding my designated responsibilities to carry out the directions in the will."

"Yes," said Áine with a sigh. "He seems to have his hands in everything." Shaking her head, she added, "I didn't know that he was directing a wild salmon preservation project." She gazed at Elizabeth. "Odd coincidence, that, given my own work. Wonder if Maeve knew."

Elizabeth offered a definitive nod. "Yes, of course. It is his project to which she has allocated a good portion of her legacy, assuming when you returned, you would collaborate." She said nothing for a moment, before remarking to Áine, "You know, dear, about that account of yours. Maeve's last two words, well, do they not seem to point to you? 'Áine. Salmon.' Asking me to instruct you to look in after the salmon. Not sure what to make of it, but then, she assumed you would know—or find out." With those elliptical words, Elizabeth left the room.

Áine gazed out a side window that overlooked the Bradáin River. *Áine. Salmon.* It seemed to odd to her that Maeve chose those last two words before submitting to her death. She thought back to the highly successful salmon restoration project in Prince Edward Island she had initiated. It had been so exciting to see the return of wild salmon spawning in their historical streams and rivers, in locations they had been rapidly abandoning due to overfishing. And now, she had been sent to Ireland to continue her work with wild salmon for the Irish government. Thoughts of her grandmother's words emerged: "*Tis our family legacy to protect them.*" With a toss of her head, Áine couldn't quite help but wonder whether it was all coincidence—or some mystical fate.

As her thoughts switched to Maeve, she walked over to the side window and gazed out over the river. It was she who had introduced Áine as a girl to the wild salmon. One evening when they were both back visiting, Áine heard what sounded like pounding rain. Looking out the window, she saw the sun low in the western sky and marvelled at how it could pour with the sun out. Maeve laughed and told her that the wild salmon were gathering for their mating games. She described how the males struggle to "strut their stuff," as she used to say, in front of the females, who would then proceed to choose their mates. Maeve would say they were the souls of ancient Irish women—the Celts—who had the freedom to decide their mates and live a wild, completely unfettered life—guided by their passions.

While standing on the bridge over the river, Maeve and Áine used to watch them together congregate below. There were so many salmon that the river would be filled with hundreds, maybe even thousands, of them playing about in the dark water below. "They're the symbol of all that Ireland stands for," Maeve told her.

"How so?" Áine asked.

"Well, now, Áine, the ancient Celts used to say the salmon was the wisest of all the ancient animals," she said. "She was the messenger to the human world of the wisdom of the spiritual world, and thus the source of inspiration and vision for poets and wisdom seekers. To eat of the sacred salmon is to gain insights about life."

Turning to Áine, Maeve continued, "The salmon represents our passionate natures—look there, now, and you'll see what I mean." She pointed below to the amorous moves of the salmon swimming around one another.

Talking more to herself than to Áine, she added, "Ah, sure, don't I have a yearning, just like those salmon, to be free to express my passion, to love and be loved so passionately that we would be able to swim up even the wildest waterfalls to make it back Home again, right here to the site of my birth—only to celebrate our passion and to live a life free of restraints." With the briefest of glances at Áine, she turned to gaze out over the river. "Ah, to be able to swim down river to the sea and back—to swim wherever our passions took us, yet always be free to return Home again—to dance and love again in these sacred waters." With that, she leaned over the bridge, lost in her dreams.

After a while, she turned and said in a consoling tone, "Ah, never mind my wanderings, now Áine, I've always come here to dream about my future, and well, now I'm living it, I suppose."

"And did it turn out as you had once dreamt, Auntie Maeve?" Áine said, though hesitant, fearing the response—knowing some of the challenges her aunt had faced, living according to her passions.

"Well, now, Áine," she said, her tone betraying her remorse, "I followed my passions all right, but I don't think I gained much in the wisdom department." She laughed again, and as they walked slowly away, she offered, "Perhaps that *is* the lesson of the salmon—the wisdom to live one's life passionately, going out into the world in search of it, but having the freedom and wisdom—there it is again, Áine—to know *how* and *when* to return Home. Haven't they survived and thrived for thousands and thousands of years? We'd do well to heed their message, we would." No more was said on the subject, as they returned home for their evening tea.

Áine continued to gaze out at the river, once brimming with wild salmon. It felt odd to her to be back again in Dingle, years and years later, taking up residence in the home of her ancestors, and preparing for the memorial service for Maeve. Soon, with her extended family who were coming from both far and wide, they would all bury Maeve's remains in the family plot, just as the family had done for one another for hundreds and hun-

dreds of years. As Áine looked out the window, she wondered what it would be like to see her larger family, many
of whom she hadn't seen in almost ten years. With that
thought firmly embedded in her mind, she finalized her
preparations for the meal.

PART TWO

AMONG

I MEASC

CHAPTER SIX

THE FUNERAL MEAL

AN BÉILE SOCHRAID

THE FUNERAL TOOK PLACE in a small, stone church in an ancient hamlet outside Dingle town. It had been the setting for the funerals of Maeve's parents before her, and most likely, their parents before them as well—as far back and as widely spread throughout the family as any could remember. Here they celebrated the baptisms and weddings, and now, the passing of their most fearless—and feared—relative.

Maeve had returned to Ireland the summer before, simply driving through Dingle—without even stopping in to see anyone. That last summer she had apparently kept to herself, even refusing visits from the few who made an effort to inquire after her. They had all assumed that she was holed up with a new love passion and required privacy. Little did they know, Maeve was planning her own death.

Queen Maeve, they all called her after her historical namesake—the haughty, passionate Queen Medb of Connaught. "All in a name," they would proclaim with a fateful shrug when referring to her. A few even whispered that the full attendance was more the result of an innate curiosity to confirm that the powerful, willful queen of the family clan had at last been defeated by a force more powerful than her own wants and desires.

The sons and daughters of Maeve entered first, who sat in the front row. Cousins of the elder generation entered, followed by the younger, with the throng of extended family filling in behind. All told, the church was almost completely filled with family, with the exception of a handful of villagers who had been praying there.

After a bit of carrying on with people talking to one another, the church fell silent. The overhead lights went out, with only a host of candles on each side of the altar for illumination. The priest emerged on the altar, and coming to the edge, stood and instructed the crowd to kneel, many of them obeying either from respect or fear—though the daughters and a few of Maeve's seven sons remained seated. Raising his head to look above, Father O'Garvey folded his hands in prayer:

"God, have mercy," he bellowed, with the God-fearing among the family responding,

"Christ, have mercy."

"God have mercy on the departed soul of Maeve Ní Ó'Suílleabháin O'Connor, and upon all of you," the priest intoned, as he gazed purposefully at those still seated, which sent some of them scurrying to their knees. He then stood and held out his hands.

From the back of the church, the wail of the uilleann pipes broke the silence with a shrill note—everyone stood and turned around toward the source. Conor, dressed in the full traditional regalia of the bagpiper, complete with kilt, hat, and wool knee socks with tassels flinging from side to side, started the funeral procession down the aisle by playing the traditional song, "The Lament of Queen Medb," accompanied by the soft keening and mourning of the village churchgoers off to the side.

As Conor marched down toward the altar, a ripple of suppressed giggles and soft laughter followed, upon hearing the musician let out the occasional "Shite!" whenever he tripped over his own feet, adorned in flipflops. The unknowing Father showed signs of anger at the levity he was observing among this unruly family. As Conor moved to the side to let Maeve's sister, Eithne, deliver the urn, the priest glanced down to discover the bagpiper regaled in beach sandals. He sighed heavily and decided in that moment, that despite what he had agreed upon with the daughters, this was his only opportunity to save their lost souls. Announcing to the crowd in a solemn, authoritative tone, he declared a full Mass would follow.

Since he delivered the Mass in Gaelic, only the linguistically fluent and devout among them could respond, but the ceremony held a sense of awe among all but the most hard-hearted. As the priest delivered the urn for blessings of the Almighty, the keeners intoned a mournful tune, accompanied by the piping that augmented the effect of the heart-wrenching service on the family.

The impact culminated with the ceremonial shaking of the hands, when the local villagers attending Mass there, each slowly walked by the front row softly keening, as was the tradition. Shaking the hands of various family members, they offered their condolences through the traditional way, "Welcome Home. I'm sorry for your troubles," both in English and in Gaelic.

One the older women among them sought out Áine, grasping her hand in hers. "Ah, I remember your Mam, I do. She was a terrible beauty—just like yourself." Before Áine could respond, the older woman had passed by, resuming her song of mourning.

The utter warmth and sincerity of these gestures spurred in Áine a gripping sense of belonging, as she felt the powerful draw of community and *place* there on the ancient peninsula of mountains and rock. She looked around, awestruck by the realization that she formed part of a large family that had its place in the traditional community for hundreds, if not thousands, of years.

These feelings expanded as the funeral procession moved from the church to the graveyard. Áine gazed at the myriad of tombstones where members of the Ó'Suílleabháin clan had been buried for centuries— their stone Celtic crosses a testimony to tradition. She shook her head gently as she asked herself if she even had any choice but to champion the traditional—with such blood pulsating through her veins. *Fate, indeed.*

As they placed the remains of Maeve into the grave, Áine watched through tear-brimmed eyes. *Good-bye, Auntie Maeve. And thank you. Thank you for bringing me back Home. I promise to carry on your legacy and look after the salmon.* Leaning over the grave, she placed a branch of wild heather alongside the urn. She slowly walked away, knowing Maeve had returned Home at last.

The family emerged from the burial ground, soon gathering in various groups. Feeling as if they needed to explain away their deep-felt emotions over the ceremony, several of them exchanged quick one-liners: "'Twas grand," "Quite moving," and the occasional "Wow!" from the Canadian side. Laughter quickly resurfaced, as they shifted their focus to one another.

Áine stood apart, silently observing her extended

family laughing and carrying on. She felt as if she were the only one despondent over her passing. The loss of Maeve felt to her as if she had been robbed, but of what precious possession beyond her aunt, she was not sure.

Stifling sobs that rhythmically broke through her like waves breaking upon the shore, Áine lowered her eyes, hoping no one would notice. Following the family motto not to make a pathetic spectacle of oneself, she admonished herself. She repeated her mantra, "Keep it together, Girl! There's still the meal to oversee."

But one person did notice. Suddenly, Áine felt a comforting arm around her shoulders, which she leaned in towards instinctively, grateful for a sturdy shoulder upon which to cry. She sobbed softly into the chest now offered.

"There, there now, Áine. 'Twill be all right."

As she recognized the voice, she looked up surprised—into a pair of blue eyes translucent from grief. It was Muirís. Gazing at him through her own eyes glistening with tears, she whispered to him, "Are we the only two here mourning the loss of Maeve?"

He tightened his grip around her. "Ah, they have an odd way of showing it, is all." Releasing her, he looked down at her and smiled. "Stiff upper lip, you know—the Irish way!"

Áine gazed at him in wonderment. "Odd that, I was just thinking something along those lines before you came over to me." She looked around, as she stifled a sob welling up to the surface. "Guess I didn't inherit that particular family gene."

Removing a handkerchief from his pocket, he dabbed at the tears streaming down her face. "I am truly sorry for your loss, Áine." He looked out over the different groups milling around. "And for my loss—and theirs, as well. Sure, she was the Queen of the clan, Maeve was."

Suddenly, music pierced the air. Conor had started up again with his bagpipes, strutting around through the crowds standing here and there.

"Conor, what happened to your shoes, man?" shouted one of the extended relations, while the group around him laughed as they pointed to the flipflops.

"Haven't I started a new fad in the fashion of piping," he quipped, before continuing up again, making his way among the various groups.

Áine turned back to Muirís—only to see him slipping away into the crowd, which inevitably enveloped him. Her thoughts lingered on him even after she could no longer see him. She noted how considerate it was of him to offer his condolences when he must be suffering from as much a sense of loss as she, given all the time he had spent with Maeve in her final months. A wave of sadness spread out within her. She was particularly struck by how deeply Muirís affected her, as if some subterranean stream rushed through her whenever in his presence. She forced herself to stop searching for glimpses of him through the throngs of family. *I must get on with this funeral!*

As Áine stood at the edge drying her tears, she spotted Elizabeth making her way through the crowds toward her. "Such a moving ceremony," exclaimed Elizabeth. "Maeve would have loved it."

Áine sniffled. "I still can't believe she is gone."

"A terrible, untimely tragedy, her death." Elizabeth dabbed a tear from her eye with her linen handkerchief. Suddenly, she caught sight of the departed piper.

"Though we could have done without the theatrics of that musician. Who on earth is he?"

"That my dear, is my uncle Conor, Maeve's ex, over whom my Auntie must have commiserated with you on more than one occasion. Though we younger set adore him, mostly for his 'in your face' approach to things—like his flipflops—the elder, and perhaps wiser, among us, find him terribly disrespectful."

Elizabeth nodded. "He's quite the character, all right."

She walked over with Áine to the church hall where the family was adjourning. Since Áine had already delivered the food she had prepared, she was free to mingle. She realized that Elizabeth relied on her to make introductions.

The two stood together, each sipping a cup of tea, as the extended family slowly made their way inside, though not, of course, without first quenching their thirst at the bar that had been set up for that purpose. And thirsty they were all, indeed, as the drinking area soon became filled with cousins and more cousins, followed by aunts and uncles once, twice, and thrice removed.

Elizabeth scanned the scene and remarked in her prim voice, "Though Irish funerals are known for their conviviality, nothing in my experience quite compares to this, this *spectacle* of boisterous frivolity," she said, as she raised her shoulders and twisted her head.

Áine observed her changing facial expression with amusement. "This event must appear to you as more a party, than the commemoration of a fellow family member's passing," she remarked dryly. She nodded. "Not unlike any pub scene on a Saturday evening across the country, I should say."

Elizabeth smirked. "Actually," she admitted, with an air of the highbrow proclivity to which she was inclined, "I assumed this was a typical country funeral, something to be tolerated, but certainly not condoned." She looked around with pursed lips, releasing them only to lean over to whisper in Áine's ear. "If you don't mind me saying so, I think it's no wonder poor Maeve took off for Dublin." She tossed her head, as she shrugged her shoulders.

"Well, now, Elizabeth, if this gathering isn't a perfect opportunity for you to do a little anthropological field research, I don't know what is," Áine said, with a grin. "I think you might find it highly entertaining to approach them all from your professional perspective as an anthropologist."

"Indeed," said Elizabeth.

Áine laughed. "Too bad, really, that you're not a psychologist—this group could well benefit from that sort of analysis."

Elizabeth smiled tightly. "There is hope for you yet. You're quite on the mark with that particular insight."

She looked at Elizabeth, who appeared rather out of place. "Do let me get you a glass of your choice," with the intention of relaxing the poor woman before the meal began, since she knew full well what could transpire as the group unwound.

"That sounds lovely," agreed Elizabeth, a little too eagerly. "Sherry, please. Before you go fetch them, tell me why that man," she said as she thrust her thumb in the direction of Conor, "doesn't seem very disconsolate as the bereaved husband."

"Ex," Áine reminded her.

With a slight shrug of her shoulder, Elizabeth said

in a dismissive tone, "That doesn't excuse him in the least." She watched Conor suspiciously as Áine left for the drinks.

Áine soon returned, regaling Elizabeth with family tales.

"Tell me more," Elizabeth giggled. "I'm quite enjoying these accounts. I can see why Maeve delegated the telling of her story to you!"

Áine beamed with the positive response to her tale, but dismissed it, saying only, "Ah, go on. I'm no story-teller. I much prefer to listen."

"Indeed you are, Áine, and quite accomplished at it, I might add."

"Well, then, perhaps I'll finish up another time the account of this 'different'—as we say in Prince Edward Island—family of mine," said Áine.

Elizabeth leaned over to Áine. "But what of Maeve's sisters? I understand they were close."

Áine responded carefully, "Well, now, perhaps from time to time." Sipping her wine, Áine continued with great animation. "But it was truly Aunt Maeve who reigned supreme in the family. Both the queen of fashion and real estate, God rest her soul, she reigned unequalled in the area of romance, and we girls all were enthralled by her tales. Wasn't she engaged—and married—it seemed, more often that the rest of us put together?"

"Indeed, she was," she assented. "I can attest to that from personal experience. She never tired from having men hanging off her arm."

As tears started to form in Elizabeth's eyes, Áine, sensing she had said enough, changed the focus by adopting a lighter tone. "I'm surprised Maeve didn't tell you about the family."

Straightening herself up, Elizabeth wiped the last remaining tear away. "These tales of, shall we say, *peculiar* personalities of a country family—from *Kerry*, no less—would hardly have gone over well with the Dublin crowd, of which she had attempted to be part," scoffed Elizabeth. "She tried hard to rid herself of her Kerry accent, which is why everyone thought she was British—since she could speak the Queen's English quite flawlessly, I must say."

Áine nodded. "Indeed, she did. Everyone in America, and later in Nova Scotia, where she lived with Mac—you know the fellow she had met in Chester—thought of her as British, a perception she did little to dispel instead, playing it to her advantage." She laughed, before adding, "I'm sure one or two of her husbands were convinced they were marrying a dignified English woman!"

Elizabeth smiled, but asked, "Was it necessary for her to do that in America and Canada as well, in order to be accepted by elite social circles?"

"Not at all," countered Áine. "It's more fashionable to be Irish, actually." She glanced around the table. "Shall we continue this reminiscence of Maeve later? You might enjoy meeting some of her children."

Leaning over to some of the cousins who were involved in an animated discussion, Áine said, "Hi everyone! This was one of your mother's closest friends here in Ireland. She'd love to talk with you, while I see to some details as well as greet the others." She made introductions with her cousins, who greeted Elizabeth with much enthusiasm, before leaving to make sure the meal preparations were progressing smoothly.

After checking in on the volunteer servers for the meal to make sure that the food had turned out just as she had hoped, Áine went round to the various tables to chat with family she hadn't seen since her last trip to Ireland, some ten years before.

"Where on earth did they keep you hidden?" asked Áine with sparkling eyes, to a fellow she had never met from the larger family.

"Ah, sure didn't they keep us Kerry lads away from you Yanks in the family, thinking ye might steal our hearts, altogether?"

Áine grinned. "Though I'm not a Yank, darlin', wasn't it a good thing they did, for surely we would have tried!"

He laughed, as his wife just raised her eyes up to the heavens, unsure of how to respond.

Áine added with a twinkle in her eyes, "I wouldn't have minded meeting you when we were teenagers."

Putting her arm around her cousin Níamh's shoulder, she added, "But, sure, you stole the heart of our most beautiful Irish cousin truly," to which she felt her cousin visibly relax with the compliment.

"Are there any more of you around that I should meet?" Áine asked with a tease. "Any brothers you might send my way?"

Fergus laughed, and tossing his head to one side, quipped, "Sure, now that I know you're available, I'll be keeping a good eye out for you!"

His wife added with a tinge of sarcasm, "Well, now, any mate to Áine here will have to be a farmer or a fisher, since she spends more time digging in the soil Over in Spudland and fishing for salmon than anything else, isn't that right, Áine?" She arched her eyebrows in the classic family V formation.

Her husband leaned forward and asked with great enthusiasm, "Do you now, Áine, in America, is it?"

Áine smiled patiently at the incessant way her Irish side of her family lumped the Canadian relatives with the American. "Actually, it was in Prince Edward Island, in Canada, and yes, quite well known for their spuds!" She laughed.

He stood up and held out his seat to her. "Come on now, have a seat, and tell us all about it. Sure, I didn't know we had any Canadian farmers in the family."

His wife smirked. "'Tis a shame you two didn't meet years ago. Fergus here grew up on a farm—actually Grand Uncle Owen's farm, and after all these years living in the city, he still can't get the straw out of his ears!" The comment met with laughter all round.

Áine jumped in and said without thinking, "I understand completely. I can't seem to get rid of all of the dirt from underneath my nails!"

Groans of revulsion sounded from her stylish female cousins around the table, each with her own set of perfectly polished nails.

"At least, since our soil in Prince Edward Island is all red, it looks like I'm sporting a unique nail style with red tips!" They all roared with laughter. She continued in a passionate tone. "Actually, I was very involved in a resurgence in growing organic vegetables, the old varieties which have not been fiddled with, once revered for their flavour, and since returning, I've taken over Auntie Maeve's plots."

"Have you, now?" Fergus inquired with a bit of awe. He leaned over to his wife and urged, "Now, love, wouldn't you like to do that yourself in the garden or conservatory?"

Áine didn't wait for her response before jumping in. "Níamh, you have a conservatory? That means you could grow tomatoes and salad greens all winter long!"

Her cousin turned to her in horror, as the other cousins laughed. "Good God, Girl! Have you gone mad, altogether? Grow *tomatoes* in my conservatory and other vegetables? Never!" She tossed her head in disdain. "I grow only rare orchids! Vegetables, indeed. We'll leave that to you, Darlin', though you're daft, altogether, as you can well afford—with that high-profile government position of yours—to buy carrots and spuds!" The rest around the table laughed.

Áine turned to them, her expression somber. "I don't know if you have been reading deeply into the economy, but there's a real plunge coming, so the more we all can do to be economically self-sufficient, like producing our own food, the better." She gazed round at them. "Never mind the advantages to the land itself when we grow our own the way our ancestors once did—organically."

"Sure, Ireland has one of the best economies in all of Europe!" someone retorted in protest.

"Indeed, it does," agreed a few voices around the table, as a few of them checked their cell phones.

Áine persisted. "Well, there's a large real estate bubble, which is about to burst, both in North America and most likely, here. Those who understand what's about to happen have paid off their mortgages and any other debts, have cashed in their retirement accounts, and have deliberately simplified their lives—by downsizing their homes and lifestyles considerably, selling off vacation homes, extra cars, and the like, and maximizing their food self-sufficiency."

This news was greeted by peals of laughter. Níamh's sister, Nuala retorted, "My God, Girl, first you want us to turn our lovely flower gardens into spud plots,"

"And don't forget the carrots," jested another cousin.

"Then you want us to sell off our holiday homes, forego our trips to the islands and Spain, and live as frugally as our grandmother did?"

She turned to the other cousins, and pointing to Áine, dismissed her. "You're mad, altogether!"

One of the husbands piped in. "Ah, sure, you're all *gloom and doom*, like your cousin Diarmuid, you are," he said, as a few nodded in agreement and added, "Whenever he comes Home, he rants on and on about the very same topic."

They all nodded, while Níamh leaned over, studying her with a wary look, "Have you been speaking with Diarmuid, Áine? It is a bit odd that you both speak the same language about the downfall of Ireland and the world!"

At the reference to her cousin, Áine responded, "No, not at all. Haven't spoken to or even heard about him in years and years." She looked around, noticing he was not among the crowd. "Speaking of Diarmuid, where is he? I haven't seen him here at all."

His sister Nora explained. "Ah, he couldn't make it. He's having some troubles of his own."

The husband added, "'Tis a shame you two couldn't commiserate together about the imminent downfall of the world, while we drink and plan our next holidays to Spain!" He turned to some of the others around the table. "Speaking of holidays, where are you going this summer?"

The talk moved to the holiday plans of everyone around the table, and knowing that there was no more to be said, Áine stood up. "Well, lovely talking with you all. If you ever change your mind about growing spuds, come see me up on the farm!"

They all laughed, while one cousin, speaking the minds of all said, "Indeed we will—if we lose our funds!"

Áine returned to the immediate family's table to make sure that the toasting glasses had been filled all around. She turned to her cousins, mother, and Uncle Conor and asked, "It's about time to do the welcome as a start to the meal. Who would like to offer the toast to Maeve?"

Conor replied, "I've prepared something to say," at which Cíarán interrupted and said, with obvious annoyance, "Conor, I hope it is appropriate to the occasion."

Conor turned to him in mock horror over the insinuation and said in a tone a bit too loud and too shrill, "Well, of *course, it's appropriate.* Wasn't I her husband?"

"One of them," said one of the sons.

"And not the last one, either," added another.

"Well, I'm the only one who's *here,*" he said, casting a smug glance at each of them.

One of the sons responded with a brusque scold. "You know that's because we all knew you were coming, and we didn't want to overwhelm Father O'Garvey with more than one bereaved husband. Unlike you, Mac graciously agreed to remain at home."

"Well, I was her first," Conor retorted, now visibly pouting.

Cíarán sighed. "Okay, Conor. If you can behave and not make a spectacle of yourself, you can speak after I do."

"Great," said Áine. "I'll just start things off." Everyone nodded in agreement.

Standing up, she tapped her fork against her glass until the room was silent. "*Fáilte,* Welcome, everyone, to the commemorative meal for our cousin, aunt, sister, mother, Maeve."

"And don't forget husband!" injected Conor.

Laughter rose throughout the room. Someone called out from the corner, "Sure, how could we forget you, Conor," while someone else added,

"Though we're sure Maeve certainly *tried*!"

Cíarán couldn't resist adding, "Don't you mean, *Ex*, Conor!"

Gales of laughter rang out among the tables.

Conor stood up and sputtered, as he gazed around the room for full effect. "Once married, always married—sure that's what we believe in the Catholic Church!"

One of the more sarcastic daughters spoke up. "Gee, we don't remember you feeling that way when you fought with her over all the *assets*!"

Conor retaliated. "Sure, she was the mother of my darling children, like you, my dear!"

His daughter only smirked at him, not responding.

Exploding, Ciarán stood up, and pushing his step-father down on his chair, admoznished, "Sit down, for God's sake, Conor! Will you stop making a damn spectacle of yourself! Let Áine start the bloody meal!"

Everyone roared with laughter.

Áine addressed the crowd with a shrug, "We can't take the man anywhere!" Turning to Conor, she said in a soothing tone, "Now Conor, don't be pouting, you'll have your moment of glory in just a few minutes."

Turning back to address the tables, she started again. "*Céad Míle Fáilte*, a hundred thousand welcomes, everyone! It was so good of all of you to come to commemorate the passing of our Maeve, whose untimely death came as a shock to all of us, I'm sure." There was a sea of nodding heads, along with murmurs of agreement.

She continued. "As a young girl, I spent time with Aunt Maeve who spoke to me often of the beauty of the wild salmon, *na bradáin fiáin*, which she used to point out to me on the bridge near the family homestead, so in honour of her favourite food, we are serving the highly prized wild salmon, courtesy of Gearóid and his son, Muirís FitzGerald. Are you out there, Gearóid?"

Everyone clapped, as he stood up with head bowed shyly.

"Will you say a word, Gearóid?" asked Áine.

Brushing a tear from his eye, he proclaimed, "Sure, we all will miss our Queenie, I, as much as the others who hold her most dear in our hearts . . . " before abruptly sitting down.

Conor leaned over to his sister-in-law and asked in a querulous tone, "Who's that fella laying claim to my Maeve?"

Ciarán just snubbed him. "*Your* Maeve. She was *his* well before you, old man!"

He just turned away and drank down some more Guinness.

Áine, taking a long sip of wine to bolster her courage, looked around to see if Muirís was at Gearóid's table, and called out, "And of course, Gearóid's son, Muirís, not only helped catch some of the salmon for this meal, but he tended to and helped our Maeve through much of her last summer here in Dingle."

"*Tended*, did he?" retorted one of the men. "And what was it exactly you helped yourself to, there, Lad, while staying with Maeve?"

Some people laughed nervously as they looked around for Muirís.

Another added, "Ah, she was a beauty to behold. No man could resist her."

Ciarán shouted out, "Would you hold your filthy thoughts to yourself, you drunken lout! This is a funeral dinner, and it's my mother you're talking about." He stood up with eyes blazing. "Will we take this talk outside?"

Áine quickly diffused the heightened tension by putting both her hands on the shoulders of her cousin, and pushed him gently back down into his seat. "There's no need." Then turning to look for Muirís, called out to him again to ask if he'd like to say something about Maeve.

Muirís stood up from his table and said in a solemn voice, "Maeve must be looking down at this lovely meal prepared by Áine and feeling forever grateful that you all came to remember her. She loved the wild salmon. Me' da' and I are only happy that we could provide her favourite food for her funeral meal."

Áine continued again. "Thank you, Muirís, and Gearóid, for your generosity." She gave Muirís a stiff nod as he sat down again and received a kiss from a woman next to him. Áine gulped and continued, "Along with the wild salmon, which, thank God, is still untouched by big agri-business, which brings me back here to Ireland—"

"Sure, we'll be keeling over next from those farmed fish and GMO potatoes they want to foist on us if we don't stop them!" one of the men shouted out.

"That's right!" exclaimed another.

"Jaysus, don't urge her on!" shouted Nuala's husband, Séamus, to which his wife quipped,

"Watch out for the likes of Herself, for she's after urging us all to grow tomatoes in our conservatories!"

"And spuds among the flower beds!" added another cousin.

Laughter erupted around the room.

Áine chuckled. "I'll stop trying to convert you all, but don't say you weren't warned!" She wagged her finger at the table of her Irish first cousins. "Right so," she continued. "All of the vegetables, which are organic and heirloom, are from Maeve's garden," she said somewhat proudly, "and represent her favourite vegetables, roast potatoes—*prataí*—together with carrots and parsnips."

Someone shouted out. "Did you say, Áine, that Maeve *grew* spuds? That doesn't sound like the Maeve we all knew!"

Laughter rang throughout the tables.

Someone else retorted, "Sure, you're putting us on, Áine. It's not yourself you're speaking of, Girl, it's *Maeve*, who was always dressed to the hilt."

Everyone roared with laughter as the speaker went on to question the very idea that Maeve, who was always perfectly attired, would ever condescend to placing her perfect fingernails in dirt or dress in anything that was not high fashion.

Áine retorted, "I didn't say how she was dressed!"

Someone added, to peals of laughter, "I'm sure she set a new fashion for the Kerry farmers!" to which Áine good-humorously concurred, "I'm sure she did. She always looked beautiful," to which most of the listeners nodded in silent agreement.

Áine added, "Unfortunately, her fashion trends haven't rubbed off on me, unless she dressed in faded jeans with holes in each of the knees!"

"That's highly doubtful!" interjected someone in the crowd, as the rest chuckled over the very idea.

Áine went on to recount that during her last summer in Ireland, Maeve had turned to growing vegetables in the family fields. "Seems Auntie Maeve took up the life of a grower, at least, close to her passing." She stole a glance over to Muirís who, with arm slung easily around the back of his companion's chair, was smiling up at her with a bemused expression on his face. She added dryly, "From what I understand, she was aided by the ever accommodating Muirís."

"Ah, the Red Knight helping out yet another damsel in distress," chimed in a woman unknown to Áine.

"Sure, haven't some of us benefitted from his helpful ways?" another added coyly.

Áine looked over at Muirís to see how he was taking the insinuations.

He snorted and shouted out, "Sure, you know, Darlin', I'm always available to help you!"

A male voice piped in. "And how many have you *helped* out by now, Muirís?"

The crowd laughed.

"Sure, I've lost count! But there's always room to rescue more ladies in distress!" he bantered.

Fergus interjected, calling out to Áine, "Now, there's a lad for you, Áine, who shares your passion for farming and fish—among other things!"

Without missing a beat, Muirís tossed his head to the side and added, "Sure, haven't I already offered me' services to the lovely lass?" He turned to Áine. "Didn't I say, now, I was always ready to lend you a *helping* hand?"

Áine, glaring at him and the woman beside him, retorted, "And I've explained the wonders of self-sufficiency to Himself over there in the corner."

"If ye call digging the spuds with your hands effi-cient," he volleyed back.

"Sufficient, not efficient, as in *self-sufficient*," she responded, while her eyes flashed red.

Ciarán exploded. "Sounds like you two could use a boxing ring to duke it out."

"Or a room to kiss and make up," shouted out some-one among gales of laughter.

"But in the meantime, could we please return to the subject at hand, and get on with the bloody toast to Maeve?" shouted Conor.

Fuming, Áine said, as she sat down, "Well, then, I'll leave the toast to Conor." She glanced over at Muirís, who, erupting in laugher, lifted his glass and toasted her. She nodded curtly and turned away to listen to Conor.

With that, Conor stood up and took over. "Ah, my Maeve, she was, to borrow from W.B., '*a terrible beauty*' she was!"

Various individuals murmured in agreement. However, inclined as he was to utter sharp barbs dressed as humour, Conor didn't stop there. "Ah, sure, even in our darkest moments, when we were fighting away in the courts, I used to look at her admiringly—she was so stunning and regale! Didn't she use her beauty to turn the judgments to her favour."

"Jesus, Conor, would you give it a rest!" roared Ciarán from his seat.

Conor stopped for the moment, before asking all pres-ent to raise their glasses. Taking up his own, he started to intone, "Sure, it was her stunning, queenly beauty that stole me' heart so long ago." He actually stopped and choked back a sob, causing his children to gaze at their usually comic father in surprise.

A dead silence filled the room.

Regaining his equilibrium, Conor continued, "Of course, the reason that Maeve continued through a host of men like her ancestral namesake was that she required four things of a man: a husband without avarice, without jealousy, without fear." He stopped to let the import of his words sink in, before adding solemnly, "As you know, I was all these things to her."

"And what about the fourth?" asked one of the cousins.

"Great wealth, of course!" retorted Ciarán, as the room exploded in laughter.

"Which she definitely extracted from me!" quipped Conor. He stood waiting for the mirth to end, and as it died down, he said with a dramatic wave of his hand, "Ah sure, she was my Queen Maeve, the Goddess of Intoxication, and I, her Conor mac Nessa, for I was smitten by her from the first second I laid me' eyes upon her. So in honour of her intoxicating effect on everyone around her, let us toast with this special glass of mead, the drink of her ancestor, Queen Medb, and say, "*Slán Leat*, Good Luck, Maeve, wherever you are."

Everyone toasted and drank down their mead.

Conor then called for another glass. "Right so, for round two. While you're eating this special meal, I thought I would recite some lines from Maeve's and my historical tale: the *Táin Bó Cuailgne*—to you non-Irish speakers, *The Cattle Raid of Cooley*."

At the primary family table, someone moaned in disgust. "Must he be the centre of attention—even at his own wife's funeral supper?"

The more sensitive among the sons and daughters

rationalized his behaviour by saying, "Well, at least, he'll be entertaining while we eat. Anything's better than the bloody bagpipes!"

Towards the end of the dinner, Conor picked up his glass of mead, and asked everyone to offer one last toast to the memory of Maeve. "She was, indeed, a terrible beauty—a force to be reckoned with!"

"*Sláinte*! To Maeve!"

Murmurs of sláinte could be heard throughout the room, followed by a return to conversation.

When everyone had finished their meals and started to leave, Ciarán stood up and addressed the larger family. "Well, now, if you brought your tin whistles and fiddles, we'll be moving on to FitzGerald's *Traditions* Pub for a wee *seisiún*."

As Áine gathered her things in preparation to join the others at the pub, she felt an arm firmly clasp her own. She looked up to see Muirís. She scowled fiercely at him.

When he observed the expression on her face, he broke out in laughter. "I see you're still put out, you are." He smiled at her with a bemused expression. "Sure, I've just come over to compliment you on the lovely meal you put together."

Áine softened a bit at the praise, managing a terse, "Thank you."

"It was just what Maeve had envisioned." He touched her arm again. "Didn't she say you were the only one of the lot who could pull it all together."

Áine dropped her guard momentarily. "Why me?"

Muirís looked away, unable to meet her inquisitive eyes. He said quietly, "She said something about you and she having interests not shared by the others." He looked back at her again. "You were the two 'traditionalists' is how she put it, I believe." He gave her a quick glance. "She was so proud of your work with the wild salmon Over."

"Really?" She studied him between narrowed eyes. "You two had quite the *tête à tête*—or was it, perhaps more of a *heart to heart*?"

He broke out in a wide smile. "Sure, just performing me' knightly duties." He tossed his head.

Áine scoffed. "Hmpf! Nightly indeed—as in under the moonlight, I would think."

"Do you really think me so cavalier, now, Áine?" He gazed at her through stern, steely grey eyes. "And with a dying woman, no less?"

"Doesn't it go along with your *knightly* persona?" She turned away—just as he reached out for her arm.

As he turned her around back facing him, he said, "Ah, that's harsh, now, Áine. Didn't I feel your glare piercing me from the back of the room?" He smiled at her. "Sure, if I didn't know any better—you being the self-sufficient goddess that you are, I'd say you're just a wee bit irritated over the presence of my, em, 'previous engagement.'"

"Not at all." She turned away from him, just before he spun her back around.

Tossing his head, he said with a chuckle, "Had I known we would have got on so well, I would have come alone."

"Absolutely no need." Áine disengaged his arm as a shout rang out.

"Come on, then, Muirís!"

Áine turned to see a—*much too pretty*—girl calling out to him.

"I'll be right there, so," he said to her.

"Jesus, they're crawling out of the woodwork," Áine mumbled.

Muirís's eyes twinkled. "What was that? Having another conversation with yourself, is it?"

She glared at him. "I was just remarking on how well you get one with the local ladies—both young and old."

"Always on the lookout for a new 'local'—as we say," chuckled over his pun.

"Oh, is there room for more?"

He flashed a charming smile. "Sure, there's always room—unless one particular 'local' fills me."

Turning away, she retorted, "Oh, I'd say you're one of those insatiable types." She watched the girl make her way toward them.

"Persistent little thing," Áine muttered.

"Come on, then." The girl tugged at Muirís's arm.

"Right, so." He turned back to Áine and whispered in her ear, "Sorry, Áine. As I said, a previous engagement."

"Indeed."

She watched them leave before walking out slowly by herself and down the lane. Her feeling of sadness remained when she entered the pub, despite the scene. An assembly of various musical cousins, uncles, and aunts were gathered around two large tables overflowing with pints. While some played tunes, the others chatted away. Áine quietly joined a table where a rousing exchange about Maeve was transpiring.

"Ah, but, poor woman, didn't she die an awful death? Bad luck, it was. Ah, the craythur," mourned one of the older women. "'Twas a real tragedy, it was."

Another, a second cousin to Maeve, retorted, "*Karma*, I tell ye." Taking a slug of her pint, she elaborated, "'Twas *karma*. If she hadn't been so greedy, going after everyone else's property and money, she wouldn't have died in such a horrid way."

"Jaysus," exclaimed another. "That's harsh, now. Sure, that's like saying we each deserve whatever bad things happen to us." Some nodded in agreement.

"And don't we?" challenged the second cousin. "What goes around, comes around," she droned. "Sure, we all know that."

Áine scanned the faces around the table, looking for any gesture of sympathy for the departed. "Regardless of what she did in life, it was surely a terrible way to go. I'm sure we'd all agree with that."

Ciarán added, "Even though I had a few battles myself with the woman, I think it's terribly bad luck to wish not her well into the next life."

"Here, here," chimed in one of the older men. "Let's drink to that. *Sláinte!*"

"*Sláinte! Sláinte!*" added others, as they all emptied their pints and a new round was ordered. Soon, conversation flowed as copiously as the pints.

"Was it the Alzheimer's, that got her in the end?" asked one of the more distant relations.

Áine responded with a vehement shake of her head. "No, actually, though her disease mimicked it in a general sort of way, she died within half a year from the onset of her symptoms—quite unlike the years, even decades long, degeneration of Alzheimer's."

Another distant relation jumped in. "Sure, didn't the same thing overtake over me' own da'?" He nodded solemnly.

"And what was his ailment, then?" asked another.

"'Twas the Mad Cow, to be sure," he said, with a solemn shake of his head.

Fergus leaned over towards Áine, and with wide eyes asked, "Have ye the Mad Cow Over?"

Ciarán stepped in. "Now, we don't know what she really died from. The neurologist called it 'respiratory complications,'" he said with a shrug.

One of the distant cousins chimed in. "Ah, sure, that's what they said about my own brother, who, as ye all know, actually died from the Aids." She gazed around at the crowd. "Couldn't bear to break the news to me' ma. Would have broken her heart, though she died anyway, they say, from a broken heart over his death, just the same."

With a deep scowl, Ciarán snapped. "Well, I won't have it said that my mother died from Aids."

"No, she certainly did not," offered another.

"Well, then, what was it exactly? Was it the Mad Cow, then?" With a shake of her head, Nuala said, "Sure, I didn't know ye had it Over in America."

With an impatient roll of her eyes, Áine stepped in. "Actually, Nuala, Maeve lived in Canada, where yes, there has been the odd outbreak of Mad Cow." She shook her head. "But the doctors there didn't think she had gotten that—despite the overlapping symptoms."

Ciarán tossed his head in Áine's direction. "She thinks it had something to do with the farmed salmon Maeve used to eat when she couldn't get the wild ones." He snorted. "It's still anyone's guess what the poor woman died from," he said with a glance over at Áine. "She's researching it."

"Well, then," said Níamh lightly, as if she hadn't heard a word of the previous discussion, "Anyone going to the islands, this summer, or Spain, is it?"

The exchange made Áine feel inconsolably sad. With a brief nod, she stood up. "I think I'll go for my daily stroll along the strand. I'll catch up with you all later."

"Right so, Áine," said a few.

"*Slán!*"

She left the family sitting around the table, happy to ignore the import of her words. She sighed as she closed the door behind her.

As she walked towards the beach, she felt an overwhelming sense of loneliness engulf her. For the first time since she had arrived, she felt so alone, without anyone to rely on, or simply to connect with, someone who shared her sense of things—of what was important. She loved her larger family, but none of them seemed to grasp the importance of protecting their traditions.

"Too taken up with holiday home in Spain, rare orchids in their growing spaces," she muttered. She stepped up her pace, hoping the waves of the sea, dancing in the early evening sunlight, would improve her outlook.

CHAPTER SEVEN

THE STRAND

AN TRÁ

ÁINE WALKED AIMLESSLY along the strand, deep in thought. Memories of her family floated about within, as so many small waves bobbing along, here and there, occasionally, even colliding—collapsing upon one another into one endless, flowing stream. At last, she reached the point where the Bradáin River swept into the sea. Like the river alongside her, Áine felt carried away by currents of memories and visions of Maeve. Overwhelmed by grief she could not fathom, she sat down among the sandhills to let it flow through, around, and perhaps away, from her with the now outgoing tide.

She recalled those rare evenings when her aunt and she would by chance be on holidays there at the same time, Maeve insisting on wild salmon for supper. They, together with her older cousin, Diarmuid, would go off in the early evening, walking along the strand together to the point where the Bradáin River met the ocean's edge, to buy a salmon from one of the fishermen. She looked around, thinking how odd it was to be at the very scene of her memory, which only yesterday, she had revisited with Muirís. She gradually sank back into her memories of the past, all inextricably woven into the waters around her.

Áine had never tired of watching the nightly ritual during angling season, of placing the nets carefully in the river, where they were slowly dragged across the water to the other side. The fishermen would perform the same duties as their fathers and grandfathers had before them, just as the day started to slip into evening—a gauze of golden light streaming onto the river and the sea beyond.

The scene had always appeared mystical to her, as if it were an image caught and re-played at special moments throughout time. Here she was, back again. Áine felt overwhelmed by the raw ability of her memories to rekindle smouldering emotions. They felt like a wave gathering momentum as it transformed into a gigantic swell of white turbulent energy, sweeping everything along in its cyclonic path—before quietly receding to shore.

Soon immersed in the past, she sat oblivious to the present moment. Áine closed her eyes, as the waves of things past flowed through her. Her thoughts turned to Maeve, whose images pierced her heart. "I'll get to the bottom of what happened to you," she whispered. "And I am determined to save your wild salmon, whatever it takes."

Waiting for a moment to leave quietly, Muirís, not finding Áine among the gathering in the pub when he arrived, slipped away after a pint, unnoticed. He headed instinctively for the water, knowing that she must be on the strand. He walked the length of the five-mile spit, feeling the sea breezes sweep about him. With each gust, he thought of the first time she saw her, her red hair riding the wind. So caught up in acting upon the feelings he had stored deeply inside ever since Maeve had begun talking about her, he headed for the place among the sandhills where he first saw her—without even stopping to think about whether she might be there at all.

And suddenly, he spotted her—her long, salmon-coloured hair streaming in the wind that swept past her as she gazed into the water. With a slight thrust of his head, he marvelled at the idea that Áine found the place special, wondering whether she would sense his presence. With that question in mind, he stood and watched her, taking in all of her gestures, her every move. He had never seen anyone else blend so much into the landscape around her. He chuckled to himself. No one else would sit there gazing with such concentration, gently swaying with the wind, hoping each gust would carry her grief out to sea.

He slowly walked up behind her, and bending down, touched her shoulder with his hand. A spark of energy instantaneously pounded through him.

Áine was so deep in thought that she hadn't even heard the rustling until he was just behind her. Only one other person—now forever lost to her—knew her favourite spot there on the strand. It was the only place where she could feel the ancient energy spring from the water, the place where scores of wild salmon once swept by in motion with the memories in her heart whenever she went there. As she took in the scene before her, she felt a spark inside spur rivers of energy rushing through her veins, just as Muirís touched her shoulder.

As she started to turn round in complete surprise, she cautioned herself that it must be the energy of the sacred spot carrying her away to a place elsewhere in time, rather than someone who had come all the way to find her sitting among the sand hills and the rushes along the river bank—to ease her pang of loneliness. She stopped midway in her turn, not wanting to lose again that surge of energy and deeply intense feelings that had completely overcome her in that touch. She now stood, not moving, half turned in hopeful expectation, and half in fear of being utterly disappointed.

Muirís took both her shoulders in his hands and slowly turned her around to face him. "I thought I'd find you here."

"Oh, Muirís," she exclaimed, holding back a spontaneous sob. "I had to get away—I just couldn't take the lack of grief over Maeve's passing."

"Well, now, I am here to grieve—as well as to console you." As he drew Áine upright and held her closely to him, the wind swept past and a soft rain fell upon them.

Áine folded into his arms as the waves crashed to shore, and the wind of the sea swept round them in powerful gusts, as if the ocean rose to embrace the sudden sea-change in the air.

And then all was quiet. The storm abated, the winds and the water, as well as the racing heartbeats rolled to gentle swells of emotion.

They sat together, their shoulders touching, silently looking out over the sea. Finally, Áine spoke. "I've been away so long that everything seems completely different now," she said with a glance over at him. "Particularly, the family."

With a toss of his head, he said, "The 'tiger' economy has turned them into predators themselves, greedy for things they shouldn't even want—like sterile packaged foods and engineered fish." With a wave of his hand in the direction of the river, he said, "Don't I remember how we used to come collect the salmon here—before you could buy the farmed kind, imported from Norway and the like, in fancy packaging from the superstores."

Áine stared at him. "That's just what I was thinking before you came up to me," she said. "We used to come here to get salmon from the fishermen. There was always more than enough to feed the locals, as well as to ensure their spawning." She gave a shrug. "But now, no one even seems to care about that."

He gave a thoughtful nod. "Aye, I understand completely," he said, "Isn't that why I have been initiating some projects to preserve our cultural traditions." He smiled at her. "I took care to name our family pub 'Traditions,' for a reason, don't you know."

She arched her eyebrow as she looked at him. "Oh, it's not named after the traditional music, then?"

Nodding, he said, "That and more." With a toss of his head, he said, "I'm thinking to add an entire traditional pub grub menu, made from local ingredients and based on the old recipes."

Áine turned to him in excitement. "What a great idea! Maybe there's something I can do to help. I am supposed to be consulting with Government over some traditional foods campaign they are planning, as I had mentioned to you before."

He gazed at her curiously. "If Government's involved, I wouldn't be so positive about the outcomes." With a shrug, he added, "Isn't that why I have gone out on my own to do what I can—through our family businesses?"

"Really?" she asked. "I'm surprised. We managed quite well on Prince Edward Island to initiate a local and traditional foods campaign that took the island by storm—

re-introducing heritage strains of vegetables, fruits, and grains."

Muirís shook his head. "Really, now?"

"Indeed, we did," she said. "Not to mention our amazingly successful wild salmon re-population project." She met his glance. "Didn't Maeve tell you that I'm here to consult with Government on how to introduce the very same here?"

He gazed at her with a sympathetic glance. "No, no, she didn't actually, Áine."

With a gulp, she said softly, "Oh, of course not. My new appointment happened after . . . " She let the sentence complete itself in the reality of the situation.

"You'll have your hands full, trying to convince this lot," he sneered. "All they see is a treasure chests of tax revenues upon allowing the Norwegians to farm the salmon along our coasts."

Áine offered her own sympathetic glance. "Exactly what they tried to do on our island—though it was a crowd from the States."

He shook his head with an adamant shake. "They'll kill off all the wild ones, only to replace them with those genetically engineered ones, before killing us all off into the bargain."

"Yes, I know," she said with a deep sigh. "I'm looking into the health repercussions of consuming such types." She glanced over at him, as tears pooled in her eyes. "I can't help but think they have something to do with Maeve's untimely demise." Wiping away a tear, she added, "But we can discuss that another time."

"Ah, sure, we have all the time in the world—and then some," he said with a knowing look. "For your daunting project."

She placed her hand on his arm. "Well, we did beat them there, and we can here, as well. I am just sure of it." She looked away. "Besides, I've promised my aunt Maeve that I would continue her legacy, as well as my grand-mother's, of protecting the wild salmon here."

He gazed at her in surprise. "Did you now? And when did you do that?"

With a shy glance, she admitted, "Well, actually, just before you arrived on the scene." With a shrug and a smile, she said, "I figured she led you here—to me."

"Ah, she did, indeed, Girleen," he said easily. "She led me right to you. Didn't she tell me as she and I used to walk here of all the times ye came to this very place." With a nod, he added, "Sure, that is how I knew where to find you."

She looked at him with questioning eyes. "Oh? And not because this is where we first met?"

"That as well, of course."

She bowed her head, hoping he wouldn't see the tears welling in her eyes.

Noticing, he leaned over and wiped away a stream trickling down her face. "Ah, I miss her as well, you know, Áine. But perhaps we can join forces against the pow-ers that be to convince them of their disasterous way of thinking—before it's too late."

"Yes, maybe." She gazed up at him through glistening tears. "I don't feel so alone anymore."

Lifting her chin up, he gazed into her eyes. "Sure, you're not alone at all. Didn't Maeve see to that?"

Arching her eyebrow, she asked, "What do you mean?"

"Besides funding our wild salmon preservation project, that is," he said evasively. Letting go, he gently raised her to her feet, and placing his arm under hers, they leisurely strolled along the edge of the water. "Ah, sure, it's just a matter of time, really."

She gave him a furtive glance. "You're a bit mysterious, Muirís FitzGerald."

He looked down at her. "Ah, not really," he said amiably. "What was it that Yank writer said—'tis not what you look at that matters, but what you *see.*'"

Frowning, she said, "And what is it I am supposed to see?"

With a grin and a toss of his head, "I should think everything, actually. Haven't you inherited the visionary genes of the great goddess herself?"

Áine looked over at him. "My grandmother used to say that—when she spoke of my 'calling' to protect the salmon."

Leaning into her, their shoulders brushing, he said lightly, "Ah, it's our Celtic spirit that inspires us to protect our own ones—from the wild salmon and their river homes, to the old ways."

She stopped and thought a moment before speaking. "Maybe that's what my grandmother meant by saying *'The journey forward, begins with a step back.'*"

"Indeed, indeed," Muirís said, as he squeezed her arm. "Sure, you're already beginning to *see* the way *before* you."

Áine chuckled. "Very clever—the way *before* you." With a shake of her head, "You sound like my mystical grandmother."

They walked slowly back along the strand lost in thought.

CHAPTER EIGHT

THE PAPS

DÁ CHÍCH ANANN

INSPIRED BY THE EXCHANGE WITH MUIRÍS, and realizing there wasn't a moment to lose in the battle to save the wild salmon from extinction, Áine decided to focus on setting up her consultation work project with the government. After considerable time on the phone, being shuffled between the offices of the Minister of Fisheries and Economics, she finally managed to secure a meeting in Dublin. "Three weeks away," she muttered, as she hung up the phone, "so much for 'pressing needs' requiring my immediate attention." As she looked out the window overlooking the Bradáin River rushing down the mountainside to meet the ocean below, she realized with delight that the salmon would be free to continue their spawning. Maybe there was some merit in delay— at least for the salmon, she concluded, with a sly smile.

After cleaning up the last of the dishes and food from the commemorative meal, she decided, with a glance out over the vegetable plots, now in disarray after harvesting them, it was a great time to start up a new season of produce.

Going out to the shed, she found a hoe she could use for cultivating the soil. Starting at the edge of the garden, she dug right in, enjoying the feeling of working the earth. Unlike the soil in Prince Edward Island, with its bricklike reddish hues, the soil was jet black. Previous growers had obviously taken great care in nurturing it. Her thoughts shifted from her grandmother to Maeve, before focussing in on Muirís's hand in maintaining the garden.

Just then, she heard a voice behind her.

"And what are you planning to do with me' garden?"

Reeling around, she discovered Muirís standing there, with a large sack slung over his shoulder. "I was just thinking of you," she admitted with a shy smile. "Though the thought that this was *your* garden wasn't one of them—my thoughts, that is." She looked at him before turning back to continue her work. "I'm going to plant a new garden."

"We must be on the same wavelength, so," he said with a grin, as he placed the sack on the ground. "I've brought you just the thing to get the garden going."

"What's that?" she asked, turning to face him.

Opening the bag, he reached in, and taking hold of it contents, opened up his hand to her. "Seaweed, of course. Best fertilizer there is," he said with a nod.

"Yes, we use that back home as well," she said. "I had planned to go down to the beach among the rocks to find some after I finished here."

"Thinking as much, I thought to save you the trouble, as I have other plans to occupy your time."

Leaning against her implement, she arched her eyebrow. "And what would that be?"

With a shake of her head, she said, "I'm only doing this now because I'm unable to meet with the government people for three more weeks."

"I'm not surprised," he said with a scowl. "They'll push you off if they think you're for the wild ones, while sliding in their fish farms right under your nose—if you aren't careful."

"Yes, that's why I contacted them first thing this morning," she said, her tone terse. Glancing at him, she added, "After our chat yesterday about the salmon, I decided—now that Aunt Maeve's funeral has come and gone—to do something about the salmon, and from what you implied, the sooner the better."

"You'll need to keep on them," he said "but in the meantime, how about a wee hike—to experience some of your ancestors?"

Áine shot him an inquisitive look. "My ancestors?" she asked. "Which ones?"

With a flick of his thumb up, he said, "Those up there. We're taking a wee hike to the site of your ancestress's burial place."

She looked from him to the towering mountains behind the farm. "You want to hike up there? Which one?" she asked. He pointed up toward one of the Paps. "That one," he said solemnly.

"You call that a 'wee' hike?" She stood gazing up, not moving. "That'll take us all day."

"Yes, indeed," he said firmly. "If we hurry so, we can make a great day of it." He smiled at her. "Tomorrow, we can finish up the garden work," he said with a toss of his head. "Besides, you'll be needing more seaweed."

"Well, all right, then," Áine said, intrigued by the idea of seeing the tops of the famous mountains. She had actually never climbed them in all of the times she had visited her grandmother and Maeve.

He stood observing her, waiting.

"I've always wanted to do so," she said with a smile, "so why not now?" Looking at her hands covered in dirt, she said, "I'll just go in to clean up a bit and be right with you."

"Right so," he said agreeably, and walking over to take the tool from her, he stored it back neatly in the shed, along with his bag of seaweed.

Minutes later, Áine returned dressed in jeans, a flannel shirt, and an Aran sweater. "Is there anything else I might need?"

"Perfect." He eyed her up and down. As she walked past him, he murmured more to himself than to her, "Doesn't matter what you wear—or don't."

She turned to him, arching her eyebrow. "What was that last bit?"

He gazed down at her smiling. "I said, 'Doesn't matter what you wear as long as you have some sturdy hiking boots and some raingear.'"

"Hmm, that's not quite what I heard." She eyed him warily. "But thanks—almost forgot the anorak."

"Never you mind, there, Girleen," he said, patting her arm. "You're still a bit droopy from yesterday's drama."

"Drama?" she asked, as she turned to him, while arching her eyebrow. "Did we engage in a bit of drama of which I'm not aware?"

"Not a t'all, not a t'all, Girleen. Off with you now."

"This way," he said, as he led the way up behind the barn toward the mountains. And with that, he turned away and trotted up the incline.

Soon they made their way along the winding, old sheep path, up through the progressively higher hills.

"Let's stop a moment and take in the sea, so," said Muirís. "Look behind you. Isn't it grand, altogether?"

"Oh, my God! It's so beautiful!"

They gazed down over the lower hills at the maze of green fields surrounded in stonewalls that cascaded down to the sea. While in one direction, they could see the ocean glistening beyond the steep cliffs farther out on the peninsula, directly below them, they looked out to the five-mile strand rocked by an endless series of waves.

"I always say this scene makes it well worth the effort to climb up here," Muirís said.

Áine nodded in agreement. "We don't have such hills and mountains on Prince Edward Island—just fields and sea. As pretty as it is back home, this is really spectacular!"

Muirís cocked his head to the side in wonderment. "I can't imagine living in a place without the mountains tumbling into the sea," he commented. "Seeing you agree, I guess you'll just have to remain here!" He threw her a wide smile. "Surely, you aren't planning to return Over, are you? Isn't *this* place your home?"

"Like you had claimed in your note to me you included with the inheritance letter?" She gazed at him with a quizzical smile. "I had wondered how you knew— that is, before I learned of your connection to my aunt." She cast a sly glance in his direction.

Side stepping the insinuation, he turned to smile at her. "Exactly so." Tossing his head to the side, he added, "Ah, Áine. This place has been your home for so much longer than you even realize."

"What do you mean?" she asked perplexed. "I know I was born here—"

"It is said here on the peninsula, that we inherit the fate of those who came before us, don't you know?" He smiled broadly at her. "Sure, you have the spirits of all your family namesakes, particularly the goddess Áine, living through you, you do." He touched her chin. "Isn't that the reason why this land, this very *place*, resonates so deeply within you? The spirit of this place lives within you, it does, surely."

"Hmm. Never thought of it like that—a sort of 'collective consciousness,' as it were." She looked off into the distance. "Very intriguing notion. My grandmother—another Áine, as you know—used to say something similar to me. My 'calling,' she would say."

"One which I hope to explore with you," he said, before he turned abruptly and took off climbing again. Áine stood and gazed after him, wondering about his intentions.

He turned back to look at her as she just stood there muttering to herself. "Are you having words with yourself there, Girleen?"

She looked up at him and shouted, "I was just wondering what your intentions were—your 'calling,' as it were."

"I'm to cure you!" he retorted.

"Curing me of what?" she called out.

"Of your desire to return Over, replacing it with a passion for *this* place."

"Oh, really? And why would you want that to happen?" she called out to his fleeting back.

Stopping, he turned to gaze down at her. "Well now, once you develop an insatiable hunger for me, I'm going to marry you, of course, and take care of your gardens and fields, and help you in your calling to protect the salmon and the lands around, don't you know?" he retorted with a charming smile.

"You're *what*? So you think that's to be my fate, is it? You can stop right there, Muirís FitzGerald!" she scolded, wagging her finger. "I'm not—"

"Sure, I'm way ahead of you, Girleen! Have you not copped on to that reality yet?" With that, he took off running up the incline.

Soon they left the world of villages and farms behind. Trees and cultivated fields remained below as they slowly climbed ever higher up along the mountain. Navigating through seas of purple heather and bracken, they slowly made their way along an ancient path, past a lough, to the summit. Waves of mist swept by them, obscuring the view and transforming it into an inscrutable landscape.

Áine shivered. "It feels so ancient here!"

Muirís nodded in agreement. "Sure, isn't it one of the few places left in Kerry, altogether, that seems to have maintained its primeval character." He looked around him. "It's easy to imagine our ancient Celtic ancestors paying homage to the land and to the mountains here that stood as they do today—providing protection to the fields below."

Áine shared with him tales her grandmother, in turn, had told her about the Old Ones. "I'm really delighted to come up here to see for myself the embodiment of the landscape after whom I was named." She laughed and added, "I always remember the quizzical looks I would get from fellow islanders over on PEI whenever I told them I hail from a long line of women named after two mountain tops!"

Muirís laughed and tossed his head. "Sure, I bet you didn't tell them what *kind* of mountain tops, did you now, Áine?"

"Not exactly," she admitted with a sly grin.

They had arrived just north of the two summits, at the place where they would move to scale the eastern Pap, before crossing over to the western one. Muirís pointed towards the south. "Look now, Áine, and you can see from here the shape and particular forms of the two Paps—the breasts of Áine."

Áine gazed at the spectacle before them. "It's a bit racy, actually, isn't it?"

Muirís smiled in his beguiling way, while tossing his head to the side. "Ah, sure, we're a sensual bunch, we Celts," he said easily. "Imagine creating the nipples there out of stone so you could see them for miles in any direction," he said in awe. "Quite sexy, actually!"

Áine grinned, agreeing she had never seen any topographical formations quite like them. "It's a real tribute to the female form," she said, "almost pornographic."

Muirís interjected. "Ah, no, not pornographic in the least. Actually, they are a tribute to the power of female sensuality, something that the ancient Celts revered," and glancing over at Áine, added seductively, "as we descendents still do to this day." He said more to himself than to her, "Amazing that they still stand erect, so to speak, as they have for thousands of years."

Áine looked over at him in surprise at his bluntness. "I suppose they were more forthright in their sensuality than we, who have been shaped by the dictates of Catholicism."

He nodded, as he lightly brushed his hand through her hair. "Ah, sure, now, you are about to discover how sensual we Celts really are out here in the *whest* of Kerry. Sure, we haven't lost our fascination for the female form a t'all, a t'all!"

A current of sensation swept through her at his words

and touch. "Well, we'll see about that," she said diffidently, trying to diffuse the effect he had on her.

"Indeed we will, then!" he countered, smiling coyly, sensing full well that she was receptive to him. "We're off to explore those luscious rounded forms!"

This is the most sensual hike I've ever experienced. Her heart pounded, as she wondered about the outcome. They slowly climbed through the dense stands of heather until they arrived at the vegetationless, rocky summit. Mountain top after mountain radiated around the Paps in almost concentric circles, spreading out in shades of lavender and deep blue. It felt as if they stood alone at the top of an ancient world.

They circled round the stone cairns that formed the top of the eastern Pap, while gazing up at the rounded tip that reached firmly into the sky. "You know," said Muirís, "They say these are burial chambers. Will we see if we can find the opening?"

As they made their way around, they arrived at a small opening on the eastern end. "Aha!" he proclaimed. "This must be where the sun shines inside there at the summer solstice. We're sure to find something equivalent on the western Pap that lets the rising sun enter at winter solstice—much like Newgrange up North, or Stonehenge over in England."

Áine thought a moment. "Rather than acting as an astronomical observatory, like those other places you mentioned, maybe it's more like the sun shines here, right into the heart behind the breasts, symbolizing both sensuality and love—the essence of being female. I know my grandmother always said that the fertile form of Áine/Anu served as the source of all growth for the fields around."

"Ah, sure, aren't you thinking like a Celtic goddess yourself?" he said with a grin. "'Tis truly an extraordinary culture we come from, isn't it now, Áine?" Muirís exclaimed with deep pride.

Happy that he was finally regarding her as a fellow Celt, rather than as some displaced *Yank* from Over, she responded, "I am very proud to be descended from a culture that worshipped women, nature, and love, instead of power and riches, and I'm even prouder to be named after the one whose form is embodied here as a testimony to such values."

Muirís put his arm around her. "Yes, I most definitely see the resemblance—and hope to benefit from any sensuality you may direct my way!"

She slapped him gently on the arm, as she slowly disentangled herself from his partial embrace, saying in playful astonishment, "Muirís!"

As they walked towards the western Pap, Áine summarized for Muirís the cultural history surrounding her name and said, "I'm sure you know that it is said that Áine, whether goddess or human, was the first of the *Tuatha dé Danann*, Áine's people, to settle here. Even as late as the end of the nineteenth century, local farmers used to pay homage to Áine, by lighting sticks on fire on the eve of *Beltaine*, the first day of summer in the Celtic calendar, to thank her for protecting the land and making it fertile. No wonder Áine meant '*bright*' in the old language."

"Ah, sure, we all know about Áine," replied Muirís easily. "Is she not the goddess of all we hold dear? Agriculture, crops, animals, and," leaning over very close to Áine, "fertility and sensuality."

An involuntary shiver shimmered through her. She smiled at him as he continued.

"These mountaintops forever look after us and protect us from the evils of mankind." He was silent for a moment, before adding, "Sure, isn't that why our little peninsula of the world here still reflects our Celtic heritage, even while much of the rest of the country has sold out to 'economic' success and a global identity?" Grimacing, he added, "Here we still speak the ancient language and follow the ways of our elders before us. God pity the poor bugger who tries to stand in our way!"

Áine found his passion over protecting the culture a welcome respite from the sneers of her cousins, who considered her attachment to the old ways crazed at best. "You're a bit like old Áine yourself, Muirís, in wanting to protect the land and the old ways," she remarked.

He gazed down at her. "Indeed, I am, Áine," he said solemnly, "and Time will tell if her namesake is the same."

Áine laughed softly. "Well, I'm afraid my family thinks me daft for even thinking about living out here in the old cottage, let alone bake bread from a wood-fired oven, grow spuds, and spend time protecting the wild salmon!" She smiled at him and added, "As much as I have wanted to feel close to them all, I suppose my interests and philosophies do not coincide with their more metropolitan attitudes."

Muirís stood still as he gazed searchingly at her. "So, you think you could embrace life as it has been lived for thousands of years on the peninsula?"

She did not hesitate. "If that's how life was, then most assuredly."

He asked her gently, "You surprise me, Áine, for all Maeve told me of your ways. Sure, I didn't think anyone in America would endorse the old ways—don't ye all rely on microwaves and eat food from tins, and the like? How did you come to be so, well, *traditional*, living Over?"

Áine laughed at his characterization. "Now, Muirís, let's have a bit of a geography lesson, shall we?" she said archly. "Can you get it through your thick noggin that I am NOT American? I don't live in some city that extends for hundreds of miles in any direction, and I do not think globally at all." She shook her head vehemently. "Quite the opposite."

"Well, tell me then, Áine. Sure, Maeve told me all about the glorious life in the city you all enjoy," he replied.

"Maeve lived in the very affluent town of Chester, Nova Scotia." She looked over at him, interjecting, "that's south of Halifax on the eastern coast—before she met some yachting fellow named Mac, who sailed her here and there—down to the North Shore of Chicago where he had some lakefront mansion, and then on to Florida to some island home—before returning her back to Chester, to his heritage oceanfront estate."

She looked over at him. "Are you with me so far on the geography lesson?"

He smiled and nodded. "Aside from not exactly figuring out the waterways they used to sail around like that, I have a general understanding of the locations of the places you mentioned."

With a chuckle, she continued. "I, on the other hand, come from an island off the northwestern coast of Nova Scotia. The Province of Prince Edward Island is very small. Though the physical size may be of Ireland as a whole, we only have 1/20 the population—no more than 130,000 people."

"Is that so, Áine?" he exclaimed in surprise.

"And may I remind you, you thick-skulled Irishman,

that I am *Canadian*. We are a separate country from America, and we do not like to be lumped in with them at all!"

"Is it like the North and the South, so?" he asked.

"Not at all," she responded firmly, "more like Germany and, say, Austria. Though we are physical neighbours, speak the same language—if we're not Quebecois, that is—and share overlapping histories, and to some degree, cultures, we are distinctly Canadian."

Now that she was finally making sense to him, she continued, "On my little island, we are steeped in Scottish, and to a lesser extent, Irish cultural traditions and are very proud of those legacies. We even have Céilidhs more frequently than you all do here!" she said smugly. "We also grow potatoes as the main staple, besides blueberries, that is, and like you, we fish for a living."

Áine stopped a moment and sighed. "Although some of the traditional ways are being replaced by big business, many of us fight hard to protect them in an effort to keep the island the way it has been for the last hundred years or so. That's what I did there, essentially."

Muirís took all this in, and after a few moments of reflection, said, "We're not so different, you and I." He studied a moment silently. "Maeve was right, so."

The reference to her aunt in the middle of this earthy exchange surprised Áine, particularly since she never thought such topics interested her. "Maeve was right about what?" she asked, bewildered.

"She said we were very similar—almost '*like two peas in a pod*,' I think is how she put it," he said quietly.

"How would she know?" replied Áine, her tone diffident. "She knew little about how I thought since we rarely communicated."

He looked over at her in surprise. "Well, now Áine, it seems she knew much more about your comings and goings than you may have thought."

"Must have been my mother who kept her up to date—during those rare moments when they were on speaking terms, that is," she clarified.

"Umm," he said in a non-committal tone. "Hard to know."

They each had been so engrossed in their exchange that they hadn't noticed that they had reached the western Pap. "Look where we are now," murmured Muirís, as he gazed out over the ring of mountains.

"It's phenomenal!" exclaimed Áine. "I am amazed by how primitively beautiful it is up here," she added. "This wildness is such a contrast to the charming landscape of fields and cottages below. I almost feel as if we were climbing the mountains in the wilds of Western Canada somewhere."

Muirís was enjoying her enthusiasm for the untamed mountains surrounding them. "Ah, sure, we're a wild lot, altogether, here in the *whest* of Kerry," he bragged. "Sure, aren't these wild mountains an extension of our Celtic spirit—natural, untameable, and forever resilient." He then added with a wink, "and let's not forget, sensual, judging by the shape of this particular Pap!"

"You don't let up, do you? You are certainly taken with these Paps."

"Well, now, I would say I am deeply taken with the essence of the Celtic woman, as embodied here," he said, while tossing his head to the side.

"I'm sure you are," she said with all of the cynicism she could muster. "From what I have observed and inferred, you must be quite the ladies' man." She twisted her mouth downward.

"Ah, sure, I've had me fill," he said easily, "but I'm only truly interested in one lady."

Áine didn't respond, biting her lips together, instead. She didn't quite know how to take his comment. *Could it be me,* she wondered. He certainly *seems* attentive. She sighed. She found herself enjoying the time with Muirís so much that she didn't want to break the spell, lest she wasn't the one. And she certainly wasn't interested in hearing from his lips about another. Dreading any additional details, she averted her glance, changed the subject, and declared she was getting hungry.

"Will we break, so, for a bite to eat?" asked Muirís. "I packed us a bit of a meal." He pulled out from his backpack an enticing lunch for them of wild salmon with brown bread and cheese, together with a canteen of hot tea.

Áine drooled in admiration. "You're amazing!" she exclaimed. "I hadn't even thought to bring anything."

He downplayed the compliment. "Ah sure, I couldn't haul your sorry self all the way up here without feeding you, now could I?" he said. "You need nourishment—of all kinds!" he added with a wink and a quick toss of his head.

He gazed over at her with a pensive expression but said nothing. They both sat in silence eating their lunch and taking in the rugged beauty around them.

After some time, Áine broke the silence. "Tell me about Maeve."

"Why did you ask me that just now?" he looked at her with a suspicious glance.

"What do you mean?" asked Áine, not understanding his tone.

"It was like you were reading my thoughts is all. I was just thinking that you're a bit like Herself—all passionate and fiery, terribly impetuous, yet amazingly capable." He gazed at Áine. "And beautiful of course, just like she was."

"Really? I never thought I was like her at all. Actually, that would be considered a bit of an insult to members of my family—my more immediate family, that is, since she was seen as conniving and willful."

"What's wrong with being willful?" he pressed. "How is one to get anywhere in life if ye haven't determination?"

Áine thought a moment and admitted, "I've never thought of it that way."

His usual clear blue eyes clouded over, as he darted a look of chagrin at what must have sounded like an irreverent attitude toward Maeve, but being ever the tactician, he apparently decided to overlook it for the moment. "Anyway, she was an extraordinary woman, really she was. She had such a way about her."

"What do you mean, exactly?" Áine asked, immediately regretting the archness to her voice. She looked away, hoping not to betray her suspicions that he had been more than taken with her aunt.

"What do you want to know?"

Áine rolled her eyes. She figured he was resorting to the classic Kerry technique of answering a question with another, when asked for direct information. She shook her head, assuming the rhetorical strategy resulted from age-long political oppression. "Well," she began slowly, "You seem to have spent a great deal of time with my aunt that last summer before her passing."

"'Tis so," he said, his tone soft.

Áine decided to press him, although he seemed reluctant to offer details. "Tell me about that last summer, about your interaction with her."

"What, exactly, would you like to know?" he countered.

Áine decided to be direct. "From the little you've told me," she said, glancing at him out of the corner of her eyes, "from the way that you described her planning her funeral, she seemed to know that she was dying."

"She did, indeed," he responded. "She told me she didn't expect to live very long a t'all." He leaned over towards her. "I'm sure she is very grateful for the wonderful commemoration you put on in her name."

"Thanks," she said absently. Áine found his response perplexing and pressed, "But she didn't tell any of her family back in Canada and America."

"Didn't she, now?" he exclaimed, with a toss of his head.

"No, she did not," Áine added firmly. "She just got lost one day and had enough presence of mind to call her son, Ciarán, on the phone and ask for the way home. We were all flabbergasted." She reflected a moment before continuing. "She went quickly downhill after that—with none of us knowing what was wrong with her."

Muirís gazed at her a moment before speaking. "Maybe she didn't want to worry you."

"Maeve? She loved having people fuss over her!" huffed Áine.

"Maybe it's different when you are facing death, so," Muirís countered.

"Hmm, maybe," she acknowledged.

He added, "Well, now, she knew something was wrong with her last summer, but she just didn't know quite what it was. I remember her saying she thought maybe she had Alzheimer's, because she kept forgetting things. She had moments of complete forgetfulness, followed by clear lucidity."

Áine was surprised by this admission. "I don't think anyone even knew that," she said. "How did she spend the summer—if you don't mind my asking," She arched her eyebrow, expecting to hear the worst.

"Well," Muirís began, ignoring her tone, "She spent the mornings with an early stroll down the strand, much as you are wont to do." He smiled at her. "Then, she would pick a weed here and there in the garden—and leave the rest to me," he said, chuckling.

"I can't imagine my beautiful aunt weeding," she said with a grin.

He glanced over at her in surprise. "Did you not know Maeve a t'all?" he asked. "She loved the garden."

Áine gazed at him with wide eyes. "I'm almost wondering whether we are referring to the same person! I can't imagine her spending time in any garden."

"Actually, she liked to gather a bouquet of flowers for her desk—since she spent the spent the mornings writing," he replied.

"*Writing*?" Áine repeated. as she arched her eyebrow. "I never thought of my aunt as literary in any way." She shook her head. "In fact, I don't remember *ever* seeing her read anything but real estate and fashion magazines."

Muirís looked away, not meeting her disbelieving gaze. "She said she had some things to explain before her time came."

"Hmm, I wonder what she did with that writing? I haven't seen any evidence of it in the house," said Áine.

He could feel her eyes staring into him. He finally

turned back to meet her gaze. "She asked me to hold onto it for her," he said, his tone measured.

"Really?" Her eyes widened even farther. "How interesting! She really came to rely on you, didn't she?"

"She did," he said quietly, again averting her penetrating gaze.

Aha! thought Áine. *Here it comes—the admission.* She really wanted to know. She inhaled deeply before speaking. "And why was that?" she pressed.

He didn't respond. Áine sat staring intently at him. "Why, Muirís?" she asked again, this time a bit more gently.

Muirís said simply, "She said she needed someone to give her the space and support she required to get some writing done—before it was too *late*."

"What did she write about?"

Avoiding her stare, he responded, "She said she had some unresolved matters in her life to clear up."

"Really? Like what?" asked Áine, now visibly intrigued.

"I couldn't say for sure," he said, looking away from her, "but I think it had to do with the family—as well as her own past."

"Well, I would really like to read it. Where did you put it?" She looked at him. "As her executor, you might recall that I am to write an account of her life, so her writing would be very helpful to me."

He didn't say anything for a few moments. "I have it, actually." He studied her face.

Áine was visibly astonished. "You *still* have it?" she asked. "Why so?"

He tried to explain. "She gave it to me and said to hold onto it for safekeeping—until the right time."

"What right time?" asked Áine, her voice arching in tandem with her eyebrow.

"When the time was right for me to show it to others."

"And how will you know that?"

"She said I would know when I read it."

"And have you read it?" she pressed.

"No, not completely," he replied. "But I'm going to finish it now."

Áine countered, "Why don't you let me read it first, then?"

Muirís shook his head and looked over at Áine. "I can't do that, Áine," he said somewhat sadly. "I promised Maeve I would read it first, then act on what I had read when the right time comes."

"Hmm, all very mysterious," remarked Áine, her tone dry. "I just can't make sense of it."

"Well, Áine, she said that I should read it and give it to her *daughter,* the one who would come to live in the house," he said, avoiding her direct gaze.

Áine squinted at him. "But that can't be the same person, since she left the farm to me, and I'm not her daughter," she said. Wrapping her arms around her bent legs, she thought about the new information for a bit before responding. "Maybe she thought that one of my cousins would come to live with me here, or perhaps that I would give it to one of them eventually," she considered. "I'm mystified. Was she in her right mind when she told you such things?" She gazed at Muirís.

"She was, she was, indeed. As clear as the day," said Muirís. "Though she had her moments of sheer confusion, she was quite lucid at other times. Said she had a lot to do before her time came."

Áine's curiosity got the better of her, and she asked again, "So will you let me read it since I'm the one in her house?"

"Can't," he said, smiling down at her. "Sure, you're not her daughter. Haven't you said so yourself on many the occasion?"

Áine retorted, "She must have been confused, as I said before."

Muirís leaned over towards her. "Right so, we'll do this. Once I've finished it, I'll let you know what I am able do for you, all right? Since I don't know how it ends, I can't commit to you right now."

Áine reached over, playfully swatted his arm. "You Irish men! Never willing to commit!"

Muirís wasted no time in responding. Grabbing her by both shoulders and pulling her towards him, Muirís gazed down at her. "Well, now, I can commit to this!"

And then he kissed her—a soft, yet tingling, kiss that Áine felt she could receive indefinitely.

CHAPTER NINE

POTATOES

PRÁTAÍ

THE MORNING SUN broke through a mountainous bank of rain clouds, casting bright rays along the water's edge, as Áine looked out from her kitchen window. Must be a sign, she thought, as she sat swirling her tea round and round in her cup. She had been going over the events of yesterday in her mind, culminating in that completely unexpected kiss. Rousing herself from her daydreaming, she decided she'd better get back to the garden planting.

As she watched the sun move across the fields around the house, she burst out in triumphant song, "It's now or never." She continued on in a gleeful tone. "If I can't have you, I can at least be free, from the EU—and its lousy food!" With that, she donned her Wellies as well as an old hole-filled woollen jumper she found and headed out to the front.

She stood among the reeds and wildflowers growing in thick batches here and there, assessing the amount of work it would take to bring back her aunt's kitchen garden. Once neatly ordered rows lined with cabbages, carrots, and potatoes—*prátaí*, she corrected herself, it now produced more weeds than vegetables. *Guess ol' Muirís gave up on the place when Maeve left.* She smiled, imagining how impressed he would be upon discovering her gardening abilities. With one determined push, she heaved the spade into the black earth and started the process of taking back the garden from the wild that encompassed it.

As Áine began to harvest the remainder of the overwintered vegetables, she marvelled over Muirís's claims regarding Maeve. It seemed so unlike the Maeve she and the rest of the Canadian family knew to have deliberately planned an extra-large harvest, assuming that it would be used for her funeral meal. They didn't even know she had enjoyed gardening.

Using the spade as a staff, she stood gazing out over the fields, trying to figure out how Maeve could have predicted her own death—and even more bizarre, her funeral meal down to the last vegetable. She shook her head. The hardest bit for Áine to understand, though, was whether Maeve actually knew her death was imminent, and if so, why she didn't share that news with anyone back in Canada. She dug and dug, hoping to unearth an explanation for the inexplicable actions of her aunt. As Áine pulled the parsnips and leeks Maeve had planned for her to harvest so many months ago, she deemed the entire situation as utterly surreal.

As she unearthed the carrots in large clumps, a deliciously sweet fragrance filled the air. She knelt down among the rows of carrots, breathing in the enticing aroma of *fresh*. She shook her head in awe. Absolutely nothing compared with the fresh scents of nature.

Wiping off some of the soil that had adhered to them, she bit into one, savouring its succulent, sweet crispness. She grinned over the discovery that nothing tasted quite as good as fresh nature, either.

Slowly chewing one carrot, then another, Áine sat and gazed at the sea below, the mountains behind, and the fields all around. Convenience aside, she just couldn't fathom how anyone would trade such a sumptuous, nearly mystical, epicurean experience for the bleached, tasteless, lemming-like packaged variety, aerated with chemically-laden chlorinated water in some cavernous, stultifying supermart.

"Convenience me arse!" she said dismissively to the air, as she thought about some of her convenience-seeking cousins. "What'll they do when life gets decidedly *in*convenient for them," she muttered.

Had this generation of Irish lost the agricultural wisdom of countless generations of ancestors before them, who knew how to work and nurture the soil? Had they really traded such life-affirming experiences for the luxury of driving—and owing on—she qualified with a smirk, extra large autos for driving to their second homes along the coast? Do they even *see* the landscape around them—*see* what their ancestors had worshipped at the foot of those mighty mountains—along the shores of those wild seas?

Finishing her carrots, Áine stood up, stretched, and gazed heavenward to the summits of the Paps, where only the day before, she had gazed *down* at the very field in which she now stood. She remembered how charming she found it from above—the tufts of reeds here and there, gently swaying in the breezes, the impressive, if overgrown, rows of vegetables standing tall in the sunlight, carpets of spring flowers cascading down the slopes—and now, standing there, she, too, was part of that landscape. A gentle current of tranquillity oozed through her, melding her into the very earth Herself.

This was how it felt to be truly rooted in *place*. To feel so close to the earth, the sky, and the sea—understanding the very life force that animates their essence, flows through humans as well, uniting all creation. Isn't this the reason to live close to the Earth, she thought. To nurture Her, and She us. To experience this life force pulsing through our veins, invigorating us to feel, to see, to love—real love.

She hoped that she would feel that someday, praying it would be as sweeping as the wave of Oneness she felt right there, right at that very moment as she stood in the dirt, lovingly protected by the mountains above and the sea below, with Her in the middle. *My own ones.*

Her thoughts flew from the earth into the breeze about. She was sure such feelings had animated her ancestors—her grandmother, and hers before her—as they dug into the soil. She hoped that Maeve had experienced such deep ties to the land that last summer. She mulled over those musings as she used the old scythe she had found in the shed to cut away the weeds. Luckily, she was well adept at using the implement, having relied on one in back on Prince Edward Island.

As she rhythmically swung it from one side to another, she tried to imagine her ancestors, using that very tool for preparing the same beds year after year. The regularity of it all—the continuity of it all—back six thousand years or so. Áine found it transformative to participate in an act as natural as carrying on family traditions. It was so—grounded—in history and in the very place itself.

As she completed cutting down the weeds and the remains of the vegetable tops, she gathered the cuttings with a pitchfork, placing them in a large heap at the end of the rows. She looked around trying to determine what to do next. Harvest. Feed. Plant. *The gardening mantra.*

Discovering a hand tiller in the barn, Áine next tilled the soil, turning in whatever remained from her cutting. She grabbed some of the thick, black soil, to let it slip through her fingers. Assuming it had decades of inlaid and blended compost, she was impressed that it was not as rocky as she had expected. She surmised that the superior condition of the soil was a testament to the care her ancestors had invested in the soil. And now it was her turn to take on the roles of Protectress and nurturer. She turned back to gaze up at the Paps. The name had such a pagan, Celtic ring to it. She wondered whether she, too, had inherited that bloodline.

Looking around, she realized she needed a load of seaweed to top dress the soil before planting. Although Muirís had promised her more, she didn't know when to expect it. As she thought of ways she could haul it herself from the beach, her thoughts were suddenly interrupted by the sound of an auto making its way up the hill to the farm. As she recognized the lorry—with a colourfully painted salmon adorning its side, she chuckled, before mumbling, "That man sure has an uncanny sense of timing! Maybe we should add *mind-reader* to his long list of professions!"

Áine went over to greet Muirís, who came laden with the very thing she sought—kelp and dulse! "You always seem to know what I need, when I need it," she remarked dryly.

Muirís jumped down from the truck. "Thought you

might need something else to focus on, now that you've spent the better part of the morning day-dreaming about our kiss."

"What—seaweed?" She crinkled her nose.

He gave her a huge smile and a toss of the head. Before she started to scold him for being so vain, he added, "Sure, there's nothing like tossing a little seaweed here and there to re-establish your link to your ancestral legacy from the goddess above." He nodded in the direction of the Paps. "Re-grounding you in your *real* place in the universe will displace any false assumptions regarding moves back Over," he added in a husky tone. "Besides," he said, smiling, "it's planting time."

"And you thought I would be sitting on me' duff, pining away for you, was it?" she asked, arching her eyebrow. "Are you always so sure of your effect on women?"

"Normally, normally," he responded, offering a sheepish shrug of his shoulders, "but in this case, well, now, one never knows with you Yanks . . . " His wide grin told her he was playing with her.

He lifted down some of the baskets from the back of the lorry and carried them to the garden. "We'll start here, so."

"Ah, sure, I'm way ahead of you!" With a proud smile, she watched him look round in utter astonishment at the prepared beds.

"You never cease to amaze, me, Girleen!" he said with clear admiration in his voice. "You have more of a green thumb than I gave you credit for, then."

He picked up a handful of seaweed. "Shall we?" He tossed some along the top of one of the rows. Áine followed his lead, and soon, the two were busy covering the soil with the seaweed. They worked for well over an hour without even talking—though each stole glances in the other's direction from time to time.

Muirís felt a sense of great lightness in watching Áine attend to her task. He had truly wondered whether she was capable of all the abilities Maeve had assured him existed in her. He thought of Maeve and how some of her mating choices had shaped the contours of her life in a way that she had come to regret. She had shared that much with him. "If only I could relive that part of my life," Maeve had said one day. That resolve had motivated her in those last months as she sickened before his grief-stricken eyes.

And now here was Áine, assuming the role of managing the family homestead in an essentially foreign country to her. He bolted upright from his task and glanced over at her. Jaysus, couldn't say *that* to her, even though intended sympathetically. Sure, she'd castigate me, altogether, he thought. He watched her as she scattered the seaweed on the beds, knowing how touchy she was about her identity.

He gazed out to the sea below. He figured with a grimace that transplanted Celts Over lose the very essence of their Celtic souls, forever cast into the nether reaches of fog-enshrouded doubt. No part of life Over appealed to him. He tossed his head again to the side. I like it well enough right *here*, he declared mentally, where we still live the old ways and speak the ancient language. With eyes wandering back again to Áine, he added, *particularly right here—with Herself by me' side.*

He stood watching Áine, who, apparently focussing on her work, seemed oblivious to his attentive gaze. He noted with contentment that she seemed to blend in quite well there herself. To be around her, she gave the impression that she had always been part of the landscape, although she tended to be a bit more idealized in her outlook than most of the rest round the peninsula, he thought with a chuckle. He liked that about her—always taking on the near impossible with a seemingly endless supply of enthusiasm. He cast a long, sombre glance at her, as she bent over tossing about dulse and kelp. She was so proud—like Maeve. Must be a family trait, he figured—on the *other* side of the family line. And so determined to make a go of it there—quite a distinctive romantic streak in her. If only she would direct her romantic inclinations toward him—full force. He sighed and returned to the task.

When they had finished spreading the compost and digging it into the soil, Muirís announced to Áine that he had some gifts for her—something he was sure she would relish. Her curiosity piqued, she did not even respond with a caustic retort, as had been her inclination around him. She wanted him to see her in control, sharp, witty, even though she didn't particularly feel that way. She shrugged, realizing she just wished to appear attractive to him—not yet another pathetic creature, hanging on to his big, strong arm for dear life.

"I can't wait to see," she responded. "No need, you know, to arrive bearing gifts."

He removed some brown burlap bags from his lorry and brought them over to her. "Best to open these at the table," he suggested, and with a big wink, "along with a nice cuppa' to wash the surprise down." He grinned at her with an utterly charming smile.

"Of course," she responded. "Will I help you bring in one of those sacks?"

"Not a t'all. You'll be guessing at the gift, then," he admonished. "These are very special gifts altogether. Very rare. Very rare, indeed," he added with an air of mystery, "for a unique lass."

"I can't imagine," she said, with a timid shake of her head.

When seated around the table, Muirís asked Áine to close her eyes, while he laid out the first of the gifts in her hand. "What is it?"

She opened her eyes and gazing from the object in her hand to his face, she said, bewildered by the item in her hand, "A *potato*?"

With an energetic toss of his head, Muirís smiled, the light in his face almost casting a haloed glow all about him. "Ah, Áine, love, sure, that's no ordinary potato. No, indeed," he announced with tremendous pride in his voice.

"That potato there sitting nice and snug in your lovely hand is a true heirloom spud, from me' own family's agricultural holdings."

Áine turned the potato round in her hand as she studied its every feature. "It's very interesting looking—I've never seen one quite like it with its deep blue eyes, yet pinkish skin. How old is old, I wonder?" she asked.

Clear pride radiated from his translucent eyes. "That spud cultivar has been saved in my family now for many generations. Some even believe it to be a pre-Famine type that survived the infamous blight."

"Can you tell me more about it?" she asked, truly intrigued.

He smiled, enjoying her interest. "We in the family call it *Geáry Blue*—after several of my great grandfathers who cultivated it on the farm—"

Suddenly realizing something, she interrupted him. "I've been meaning to ask, Muirís, just where is your family farm? I think this is the first you have even mentioned it. And why do you call them 'holdings'? You make it sound like a vast track of land."

He smiled at her. "Well, now, sure, didn't it used to be much larger? Well, never mind that now. 'Tis not every lass I bring home, don't you know. All in good time." He gave her a wink.

"I didn't mean it that way," she said dryly.

He continued with his story. "There are versions out there called *Kerry* and *Skerry Blues*, hence the pun on me' father's name. Sure, it has a lovely creamy flesh, much like your own," he said, with a toss of his head

"I have always admired the idea of saving seeds from one generation to the next—even if I have never been part of a family who has done so. My parents didn't bother, having been immigrants to Canada."

Muirís leaned forward, and placing his hand over hers, retorted, "Indeed, you have, Girleen. Why your root cellar beyond is filled with heritage seeds saved by your grandmother, and hers before that, I should say. Saw and used them meself. Sure, weren't those vegetables you harvested from those very seeds of your grandmother?" He nodded slowly. "Ah, sure, they are the real antique thing they are, heritage carrots, parsnips, and leeks." He leaned over to her and said, "We'll go have a look after, so."

"I didn't know," Áine said softly.

He looked at her with a sombre expression. "Sure, you just haven't personally been involved—your family was doing it all for you while you lived Over," he said, his tone overtly consoling, lest he hurt her feelings about being left out of the family tradition. "Your namesake, wise old Áine Críonna, was well-known round the peninsula for her ancient herbals and remedies, don't you know, and they all came from her own gardens of seeds she had carefully saved from one season to the next."

"Really?" asked Áine in awe. "Of course, I do remember her giving me various remedies whenever she felt I needed them and making them up for some people when they'd come to the door asking. But how surprising to hear of my grandmother—from you," she said slowly, not sure exactly what she meant by that, but felt compelled to say anyway. "It's well, as if you are a family member sharing something interesting about one of our common relations."

He chuckled. "Well, actually, love, I *am* a family member—though quite distant," he qualified hastily. He stopped a moment then added, "Wasn't your Grandmother, Áine, my, my, well now, what was she exactly to me?" He scratched his head. "It can get very convoluted, keeping track of this family history."

"Anyway," Áine interrupted, "You were saying about your potato."

"As I understand it from me' grandfather," he began, "whose own father before him had cultivated and grown different types of potatoes that were exhibited at the Royal Hibernian Botanical Society—"

Áine held up her hand. "Wait. I thought you were all fishermen. I'm confused."

Muirís laughed. "My family was, shall we say, fond of cultivating the land. Angling was part of the lifestyle, together with a host of other pursuits. But we have never been fishermen, per say, more like, men who fished—if you get my gist. If you'll excuse the term, my ancestors lived as 'gentleman farmers'—cultivators of the soil."

"How interesting," she said with a pensive look. Áine was startled by the revelation. She had made assumptions about the fellow that apparently didn't hold up. Just when she thought she had him sized up, he always seemed to surprise her.

"Can you tell me more about the heirloom potatoes that your family has grown?"

"Well, ever since the Famine—" He looked over at her. "You do know about that, don't you?"

"Of course, I do," Áine retorted crossly. "I'm not completely culturally impoverished—even if I am a *Yank,* for the lack of a better word for those of us who hail from the Northern Territories of North America." She scowled at him.

He patted her arm. "Sure, I meant no harm—no harm, a t'all. Never mind, then." He exhaled deeply. "Right so." He nodded. "Ever since the Famine, certain families with the means to do so, have been attempting to create a cultivar that would be blight free, while remaining true to types that grow the best in our particular soils and serve our culinary predilections for boiled potatoes."

Muirís stopped, gazed over at her, and asked somewhat timidly, "If you don't mind me asking, now, Áine, you do know that certain potatoes are better boiled and mashed than baked?"

Áine smirked at him. "For *God's* sake, Muirís, learn some cultural history outside of your own. I did grow up on *Spud Island,* the common name for Prince Edward Island, as we grow and export more potatoes than any other location—including *Ireland,* I might add." She rolled her eyes. "And as a conservation economist directly involved in a traditional foods resurgence on the island, I helped promote historical cultivars there over the GMO types, so I know a thing or two about potatoes. I just haven't seen this particular cultivar."

She stopped, realizing she must sound too indignant. Deliberately softening her tone, she added, "I am just really interested in knowing about Irish heirlooms, since they differ from the Canadian ones. Ours historically originated in Scotland."

Muirís launched into an historical overview of the history of the Irish potato as well as his family endeavours to grow traditional, yet pathogenically resistant varieties. Opening up the bags he brought with him, Muirís showed her five different cultivars that had been in his family, explaining for each, its culinary uses, as well as its flowering characteristics.

Áine was overjoyed by the windfall of such highly prized heirlooms. "Shall we plant them now, Muirís?" Her voice flowed with excitement. "The ones from this sack look all nice and sprouted."

"Sure, why not?" he responded with a smile and a toss of his head. "I prepared them a while back." He rustled through his bags, before pulling out a smaller sack filled with a special cultivar. Removing it from the larger sack, he handed it to her, saying tenderly, "I had especially prepared these to plant in the garden here."

Áine looked at him in surprise. "But, why?"

He shook his head and said hurriedly, "Sure, 'twas before you came on the scene. I had promised me' father I would plant these in honour of Maeve."

"What do you mean?"

He smiled at her. "It's a cultivar me' da' had developed, oh, God, years and years ago, from seeds taken from his father's collection. It's called the *Queen Medb* cultivar."

"Don't tell me—named after . . . " exclaimed Áine, completely amazed by all this knowledge and intertwined history.

"'Tis a small world round these parts, Áine," he said, sensing her bewilderment. "'Tis a real lovely one, this one, with fiery red flowers surrounded in vivid blue-violet tips—much like our Maeve."

He stopped to finish the remainder of his tea. In a reverent tone, he said, "Sure, there's nothing quite like seeing a field filled with the delicate blooms of these historical cultivars. Each one flowers differently in truly exquisite variations, don't you know, as I have explained."

"Spoken like a true botanist!" Áine declared, revealing her ever-deepening admiration for him. The extent of the man's knowledge seemed endless—from traditional foods to wild salmon, to fertilizers, and now to heritage cultivars. *Impressive. Very impressive.* She looked up at him through contemplative eyes.

Carrying the sacks out to the garden, Áine and Muirís spent the afternoon planting the seeds in hillocks they had devised. Although they rarely spoke to one another, each felt the ever-tightening bond that grew between them as they shared in the cultural ritual of planting the prátaí, just as their namesakes had each done before them, for hundreds and hundreds of seasons.

While Muirís felt especially invigorated over the planting, as he knew more about their shared ancestral history than she, and thus saw their joint efforts as carrying out their legacies, Áine discovered that sense of tranquillity oozing through her again, as she felt entirely *one* with everything around her, including him. It all seemed so utterly natural, simple, yet incredibly meaningful on so many levels.

She stood up and gazed round at their work. The sun was now shifting over the mountains, casting its light farther west. So this is how it feels, she thought, to sow the seeds of history, of culture, of shared passion. This is how it feels to belong to family, to *Place*, and, with a glance over at the bended form of Muirís, *to another.* She sighed. *If even for just a moment in time.* She dared to wonder whether it might it be possible to extend that moment in time, forward into the future. Could it become her ritual—*their* annual ritual?

The prátaí of our collective cultural past, thought Áine, as she placed the last of the seeds into the soil. Looking up at the Paps above her, she prayed. *May this last seed sow for us a common future—if the Fates would have it so.*

CHAPTER TEN

LEGACIES

NA OIDHREACHT

SOME MORNINGS LATER, Áine decided to go for a swim, as the weather had become unusually warm. Taking off her sundress, she ran into the waves, bobbing up and down as she floated along. She then rode the length of one wave, while diving under another, each one taking her slightly farther out to sea. The cool salt water refreshed her spirits, making her feel keenly alive.

As she enjoyed herself floating along the waves, Muirís entered the strand looking for her, when he had not found her at home. He looked up and down the beach, but seeing no sign of her, started walking along the sand dunes in case she had gone down the length of the strand to the river. After a time, he came across the purple dress he had seen her wear. It was the historical icon for which he had been waiting.

Taking the dress with him, he took off toward the water's edge, when he heard a voice hailing to him. Looking out over the water, he saw her, diving under the breaking waves and calling out, when she saw what he was after doing.

"Hey!" she yelled. "You're taking my dress! How am I to come out of the water?"

He laughed. "Come out in your birth clothes!" Holding up her dress, he shouted, "I don't suppose you know this is a sign that we were meant to be together?"

She continued to demand her dress, before asking, "And how does our common fate relate to your taking my dress?" She swam in towards him, keeping her body submerged.

"Well, now, if you come out, I'll tell you all about our common history and future."

"Likely story," she scoffed. "You just want to see me naked." Áine stood neck high in the water while her long, red hair floated around her like a cloak. She started to swim away, ducking under each wave that rolled in.

Muirís shouted after her. "Áine, come back! Don't go too far out there! There's an undertow here that's too strong for you!"

She ignored him, swimming farther and farther out, riding each wave that came swirling around her.

He waved her dress out in front of him. "Right so, you win! Here is your dress! Come collect it!" he shouted.

Áine shouted back, "I'm swimming back over to Canada! I've had it with you Irish men!" With that, she turned on her back and floated over the waves.

Muirís now grew seriously worried. He shouted again over the ever-increasing distance between the two of them, "Áine, you must come in now—sure, you're out too far!"

Not sensing the heightened danger, she countered, "Not to worry. I'm half-mermaid!"

"Prove it to me, then!" shouted Muirís. "Swim towards me a wee bit and prove to me you can do it!"

He could hear Áine's laugh over the sound of the waves gently crashing to shore. "Stop your worrying!" she shouted.

Muirís, knowing the sea as well as he did, realized with alarm that she was too far out to get back through the undertow. He looked up and down the strand for any sort of boat, and seeing a curragh lying beside the oceanside pub down the way, decided to run for it, but not before he shouted out instructions in a voice of utter desperation:

"Now, Áine, listen to me, Girleen! Swim along the length of the wave—not over or through it. I'm coming for you!" With that, he ran for the curragh, and before she knew it, he was paddling urgently towards her.

Realizing that he may know something more about the water there than she, Áine tried to swim over the waves and return to shore, but she quickly discovered the truth of Muirís' warnings. She couldn't get in any closer to shore. She tried not to panic, knowing that he was coming after her. Thank God, he's so seasmart, she thought. She just kept treading the length of wave, hoping that she wouldn't travel out any farther out to sea.

In a matter of minutes, though it seemed like hours to Áine, Muirís reached her with the boat. Stripping off his shirt, he reached down, pulled her from the water, and wrapped her in his clothes.

"Sure, you almost sealed our common fate before it had a chance to unfold," he murmured, as he held her closely to help reduce the shivering she was now experiencing. Rubbing her back and arms, he tried to increase her circulation enough to start warming her.

"Is this another one of your '*knightly*' tricks?" she asked, as he rubbed her up and down.

He looked down at her sternly with the steely blue eyes he occasionally flashed, admonishing her, "You could have been drowned, don't you know, Lass. This is a very rough sea here, one not to be taken lightly." He withdrew his hands. "I don't resort to tricks to be close to a lady." Then he abruptly turned, quickly rowing back to shore muttering, "Surely, this experience has been a 'twist' of fate."

Áine looked at him in surprise. "What do you mean by all these references to fate?"

He glanced over at her for a moment, before looking away. "Maybe someday the Fates will have it that I'll tell you. Then again, maybe it will never come to be." He rowed back to the strand in stony silence.

"Will you come over for a cup of tea?" Áine asked him lightly when they reached the shore.

Muirís looked down at her with steel blue eyes. "You're just *toying* with me, Girleen." Lifting her chin in his hand, he added, "As I've said to you before, I don't waste my time with lasses more interested in playing with their prey, than in women actively interested in reeling in a mate." With that, he strode off in the opposite direction.

CHAPTER ELEVEN

THE TROUBLES

NÁ TRIOBLÓIDÍ

From seemingly out of nowhere, a tidal wave crashed over the western shores of Ireland, voraciously devouring each strand, field, and cottage along its path. While shining in its glory as the world's strongest small country economy only yesterday, suddenly, the Emerald Isle glistened from tears of lament heard all over the small, but populous island nation.

The economy had crashed. No one was spared from its ravage. No sochraid—funeral procession—ever experienced the depths of grief as the keening that befell the country on the day that the pensions disappeared, and the shops closed down. 'The Troubles'—thought long buried in the Irish past, had returned—with a vengeance.

Á INE, unaware of the new waves of national troubles that had unexpectedly swept over the country on that Friday morning, drove to the local market down in the village. Arriving in front of the shop, she peered in at the closed door, bewildered by the sign that read, *"Shop Closed."*

Consulting her watch, she noted that it was after eleven, the time most shops would be open before closing for the noon dinner hour. "Ah, well," she sighed, "Afternoon is a better time to get my errands done here. I'll have to remember that the next time I come to town."

She then drove down the road to see whether she might get her shopping list filled at an even smaller local shop just at the edge of town. Though she did notice small groups of men and women dotting the pavements throughout the village, she attributed the unusual scene at this time of day to the cultural propensity toward, as they would say, "putting off today, what you can do tomorrow." Something nicely quaint about not needing to be in a hurry, she thought. Parking in front of the next shop, she tried to open the front door, but it was locked. "Hmm," she wondered, "maybe it's a holyday I've forgotten about." She checked her mental calendar to see whether it could be the Ascension—perhaps the Assumption? When she dismissed those two events, she couldn't figure out any other reason for the closures. Perplexed, though unruffled, she decided to break down and drive to the large supermart centre over in Killarney. She preferred the tiny village shops that, while not having much in the way of variety, did adhere to time-honoured tradition of selling in-season produce from the surrounding farms.

As she drove to Killarney along the winding, twisted backroads, which she greatly preferred over the new highway system—created primarily for the new wave of second home owners, always rushing to get from the cities to their "country" homes and back—Áine recalled the summers during her teenage years during which she spent helping out one of her aunts in her shop. There she sold everything from new potatoes to freshly roasted rotisserie chickens, and Áine, always anticipating the next meal or snack with relish, revelled in her role as shop assistant.

How odd it seemed that the shop didn't carry grapes, or tomatoes, or watermelons—the vegetables and fruits she identified with summer. Instead, she found dirty carrots in clumps with the tops still on (not like the pre-cut carrots in the Atlantic Megamarts), piles of big cabbages, and crates of potatoes still brown with soil.

When she asked why there weren't any fruits and vegetables she recognized as summer ones, her aunt gazed at her with a queer look in her eye.

"But, Áine, dear, those don't grow here at all. We only eat what we can grow." It seemed like such an odd concept at the time.

Now, though, after having come to understand the host of economic, cultural, and even personal implications of choosing to buy locally over globally, Áine dismissed the idea that summer fruits could—or should—be bought in the midst of winter. She was also very uncomfortable with the practice of buying foods—mixed veggies, for example, imported from India, China, and South America—when carrots and beans, for example, grew right in the fields of Kerry. Although the traditional selling practices in her aunt's shop seemed less glamorous— boring, even—at the time, the food was certainly fresh, with maximum nutrition and its origin precisely known. She now realized that the traditional ways of selling only local food in season was so much better all round, than shopping at the glossy stores filled with global fruits.

Áine left the village, heading for Killarney. Not long after, she came upon a woman walking along the road who appeared to be crying out to anyone who would listen as they passed by.

Slowing down, Áine heard her thunder, "Those murderous thieves have stolen our money, our pensions, our country yet again!" She then added, "We've been sold out again!"

Perplexed by the outcry, Áine turned on the radio, only to hear waves of despair being reported. With a firm push of the button, she shut it off. As she drove, she wondered what was to become of the wild salmon amid such economic devastation.

Immediately upon entering the cottage, she checked her phone and her email, only to discover a message from one of the Economics Minister's staff, cancelling their meeting until "further notice." Áine shook her head, realizing now how dire the situation was—for both the citizenry and the salmon. She felt certain that the government would be forced into supporting the fish farms. The thought made her cringe.

Later that stormy evening as she sat reading by the fire, she heard someone knocking on her door, followed by it creaking open. "Who's there? Is it you, Muirís?" she called out. "I'm coming." Walking out to the hallway, she stood in astonishment as she gazed at her visitor. It was her cousin Diarmuid, soaking wet and shivering.

He glared at her. "Muirís?" He raised his voice. "Not surely Muirís *FitzGerald*, is it, you were expecting?" He approached her with a disapproving blue stare and spitted out in a menacing voice, "Surely you're not keeping company with the likes of that fella, now, are you?"

Áine was utterly taken aback, not only by his unexpected arrival, but also by his impudent tone and overall demeanour. She shot back, "Diarmuid! What do you mean by just showing up and hurling accusations at me the moment you walk in!" Glaring at him, she added, "We didn't even get a chance to speak at the funeral, and before that—" she crossed her arms, "years."

He came over to her, and putting his arms around her tightly, he drew her close to him. "I've come to live with you." He tried to kiss her, but missed, as she turned her head in an attempt to pull away. He reeked of beer and whiskey. Diarmuid tightened his grip, not letting her go.

"What? *Live* with me?" Áine struggled to release herself from his hold.

"To take up our old feelings for one another," he said, tightening his hold.

"Diarmuid, let go of me this instant!" she demanded. "What are you talking about?" She tried to push him off her. "Have you gone completely mad?"

Just as she had decided to kick him in a place he wouldn't easily forget, the front door suddenly swung open. In one fell swoop, Muirís pulled Diarmuid off Áine, and with one great punch in the gut, sent him flying across the foyer into the wall where he fell in a slump on the floor, moaning, "I'm ill; I'm ill; sure, you can't hit a sick man."

Placing a booted foot on Diarmuid's arm to subdue him, Muirís threatened, "You're about to get sicker, you gobshite! While I may be tempting your fate, you'll not be doing so with mine! You lay another unwanted hand on that lass, and it will be your last day on this earth, I can guarantee you that!"

"Jesus!" exploded Áine. "What's going on here?"

Scowling at Diarmuid, she demanded, "Where did you come from?" and turning to Muirís, asked, "And how did you know he was here? Can someone explain what is going on?" She glared from one man to another, as she waited impatiently for someone to explain the untoward circumstances.

Muirís glanced over at Áine. "I'll explain what I know, so, just as soon as I am assured this rake is no longer a threat to you." Turning back round and leaning down over Diarmuid, Muirís asked, "If I let you up now, you drunken shite, will you behave, or will I have to take you outside?"

Releasing his foothold on Diarmuid, Muirís turned to explain the situation to Áine, when Diarmuid, now standing unsteadily on his feet, immediately swung at Muirís, shouting, "You're nothing more than a bloody Blackguard pushing his *pedigree* around—*Red Knight*, me arse!"

"Look out!" Áine alerted Muirís.

"Why you little shite!" roared Muirís, swinging round to Diarmuid. "I warned you!"

Grabbing a piece of rope hanging from a hook inside the doorway, he tied Diarmuid's hands together behind his back while the latter bellowed out a string of threats. "Ah shut up! You drunken sod!" thundered Muirís, as he pushed Diarmuid down into a chair, and taking off his belt, tied the man's arms to the back of the chair. "Now, you'll stay put until we decide what to do with your sorry arse!" growled Muirís.

Áine gazed in disbelief from one man to another, then broke out in tears. "I don't understand what is happening!"

Muirís patted her on the back. "Ah, 'twill be all right, now Áine. Not to worry. This drunken lout was mouthing off in my pub about his new life with you, how you will be tending to his needs—*all* of them—and the drunker he got, the more concerned I became for you, as you hadn't mentioned to me of his arrival to take up residing with you, now, had you, Áine?" His expression looked soulful, though quizzical. He stared into her eyes, as if trying to locate the answer in her expression.

Áine sat speechless. First, she glared at Muirís. "I wasn't aware I needed to consult with you about my house guests." Turning to Diarmuid, she asked in a tone dripping in sarcasm, "Would you care to explain the meaning behind all of this?"

Diarmuid slumped in his chair as Áine stared at him. "Ah now, Áine, if anyone has ever suffered, 'tis me. I'm after finding out that I've lost my house, my position, and now, I'm losing years due to my liver disease. Sure, you can't turn me away, Áine," he pleaded. With a side-long glance, he added, "Is this not the family homestead? Besides, haven't we a deep bond between us?"

Muirís snorted in defiance. "Ah, now, that's not quite the version of this tale he was after telling, all high and mighty-like, in the pub, it wasn't a t'all."

Áine looked in despair from Diarmuid to Muirís. "Jesus, will you two stop now?"

She stood up and glared down at Diarmuid. "Diarmuid, if we let you loose, will you behave? If you don't, I'm having Muirís here throw you out of my house. Do I have your word?" she demanded.

Averting his eyes, he nodded.

"I'm going to make some tea, now, and we'll sit down and get to the bottom of this." She went over to the cooker to put on the kettle, while an uneasy silence filled the room, each quietly smoldering.

With the tea made, Áine poured out cups for each and sat down. Turning to Muirís, she placed her arm on his. "I'm sorry for my tone. I've been taken aback by this whole unfortunate situation. I really do appreciate your coming to look out for me." He continued to look down, crestfallen. "Really I do," she repeated.

He looked over at her, and she smiled back at him with that sweet smile that had claimed his heart from the first time he had witnessed it. "Right, so," he said gruffly.

She turned to Diarmuid, but remembering something she had wanted to ask Muirís, turned back to him. "Why did Diarmuid call you the 'Red Knight' just now, Muirís? What does that mean—a nickname from school, is it?"

When Diarmuid started to respond, "He's a Fitz—"

Áine interjected with a curt, "You, hush. I didn't ask you."

She turned back to Muirís, waiting. Deciding this wasn't the time to discuss family history in her highly agitated state, he brushed the question off with a toss of his head. "Ah, sure, I'm known for me' *protective* ways."

She chuckled. "Well, I certainly appreciate them." Turning to Diarmuid, she demanded, "Now Diarmuid," with eyes flashing, "What are you doing here? What has happened to you? And where do you get off mishandling me in that completely unacceptable, ill-bred manner?" She arched her eyebrow. "Apparently, you have forgotten we are cousins—first cousins."

"I thought I was special to you!" In a whining voice, Diarmuid continued, "Aren't I all rattled in my brain — after the beating I got from the likes of him!" Glaring at Muirís, he muttered, "The *blackguard*."

"Enough!" exclaimed Áine sharply. "You leave Muirís out of this and explain to me what you are doing here." Then softening, she asked in a more tender voice, "What is this about you being ill, Diarmuid?"

Sensing his moment, Diarmuid coughed and took a sip of tea, before beginning. "How I have been suffering, Áine! Didn't they find a spot on my liver," he related in a sorrowful voice. Turning to glare at Muirís, he blurted, "And you after punching a sick man in the liver."

Muirís grumbled. "Sure, if we all carried on drinking ourselves silly as he's wont to, we'd all have damaged livers!"

Áine glared over at Muirís, imploring him with her facial expression to refrain. He sat there glumly, looking quite despondent, knowing full well that the woman's good nature would be taken in by the miscreant. He only hoped that her emotional generosity wouldn't be her downfall—and thus his.

Ignoring his competitor's remark, Diarmuid continued to work on Áine. "Didn't we take you in to live with us whenever you returned home to Ireland?" asked Diarmuid, whose shaky voice sounded unusually sharp.

She looked down at her teacup. "Yes, Diarmuid, your family—as well as Grandma—did indeed do that, and I am forever grateful," she replied.

"Well, isn't it your turn to show your gratitude by returning the favour, then," he said. "Take me in, now, Áine," he pleaded. "Sure, everyone knows in the family you're the responsible one." He shook his head. "You're responsible for me, now."

"You want to live here—with *me*?" she asked bewildered, not knowing how to interpret this request.

"I was hoping you'd look after me," he said, his voice brimming in sorrow. "I thought maybe you might have some folk remedies to cure me from the disease plaguing me."

"And aren't you married?" she asked archly. "Why isn't your wife tending to you?"

"Ah, the poor craythur, she can barely take care of herself, let alone me. I can't add to her already heavy burden. You must know," he implored, "she suffers terribly."

"Poor dear," said Áine absently, trying to make sense of the scene being played out before her.

Muirís who had been shifting around in his chair, couldn't help but interject, "Sure, it seems an *uncanny* amount of suffering goes on in your household, so."

"Shush, Muirís!" said Áine, eyeing him sharply, though barely suppressing a smile.

Diarmuid pressed on, ignoring Muirís altogether. "Didn't I lose my position due to my illness, and as a result, even my house, when I couldn't make the payments?"

Áine softened over learning of the string of misfortune. "That's terrible!"

Muirís chimed in. "How was it, then, you could afford to pay for all the rounds of drink you and the boys there poured down, so? Sure, the amount you washed down your gullet would have made a nice gesture toward a monthly payment, it would."

Grimacing, Diarmuid ignored the remark, launching a defence. "Ah, sure, Áine, I wanted to take the edge off—before I came on bended knee to you!"

Muirís stood up abruptly as he exploded in disdain. "Bended knee, me arse! You came trying to have your way with the woman!"

Áine turned to Muirís and pleaded with him to stop, though she took up the point he was making with Diarmuid. "Well, Diarmuid, how *do* you explain your behaviour to me when you arrived?" she snapped. "You seemed more intent on bending my will—than in bending your knees to me in supplication."

Muirís chuckled before muttering, "Ah, sure, there's hope for the girl yet. Surely, she sees through this freeloader."

Diarmuid glared at Muirís, before stumbling over to touch Áine's face. "Sure, it was only my lifelong affection for you, Áine, that I wanted to express."

Muirís jumped up from his chair to overtake Diarmuid, as Áine stretched out her arm and pushed him back down in his chair. "Sit down, Diarmuid," she said wearily. "Enough with the moves." Turning to Muirís, she said in a strained voice, "I am fine, Muirís, thank you."

She stood up and addressed both of them. "All right, Diarmuid. You may stay the night, and once you've recuperated from your drunken stupor, we'll talk about all this." Then wagging her finger in his face, she added, "But if you even attempt to lay another hand on me, I'll boot you out of here more quickly than you attacked me."

Although he slumped in his seat, Diarmuid agreed. "Does that mean you'll have me?"

Áine retorted sharply. "Have you?" She twisted her mouth into a tight grimace. "That means you'll be sleeping in the guest room—by yourself—with no more moves in my direction. Understood?"

A bloodshot, blank stare was his only response.

She then turned to Muirís, who was now standing with his arms crossed firmly across his chest. She started to speak to him, when he interrupted her. "I'll not be leaving this house until I am convinced that *he*," glaring over at Diarmuid before continuing, "has learned his manners."

Though exhausted from the tumult, she felt a surge of relief over hearing Muirís insist on protecting her.

Good sign, she thought. *Red Knight, indeed.* "All right, then, Muirís," she said agreeably, "Do you mind sleeping on the couch?"

Glaring at Diarmuid, he said, "Not a t'all, not a t'all, Áine. I prefer it, actually, so I can keep an eye out for any *sleepwalker* who might think he can make his way to your bed in the middle of the night. I'll be right there in the middle between the two bedrooms."

He shot a sharp look of dire warning at Diarmuid.

"Right, then," said Áine. "I'll go round up a duvet for you, Muirís." When she left the room, Muirís stood and staring down at the slumped Diarmuid, shook his fist at him as he threatened, "I'm on to you, boy. I'm on to you. You make any unwanted move in her direction, and I'll take you to the woodshed—liver or no liver."

They both left Diarmuid to stumble by himself to his room.

Muirís walked into the living room where Áine was making up a bed for him. "Thanks very much, Áine, I can do that. You go off now and get some much-needed sleep, so."

He leaned down and lightly kissed her forehead before she had a chance to respond. "Not to worry, Áine. 'Twill be all right."

Looking up at him, she lightly touched his arm before moving away. "Thanks so much, Muirís, for looking out for me. I appreciate it more than I can say right now."

"Ah, sure, it's me *knightly* responsibility. And any time you'd like me to make it a *daily* task, you just let me know, so," chuckling over his pun.

"Ah, very clever," she said, offering a coy smile, as she wagged her finger at him.

Taking her finger in his hand, he lightly kissed it. "Good

night m'Lady." Calling out to her again, he repeated it in Gaelic, "*Oíche maith agat*, Áine," as she climbed the stairs.

She turned and responded sweetly, "*Agus oíche mhaith agat*, Muirís."

He stood with arms folded after she left. "I won't let anyone hurt you, me' darlin' Áine," he vowed to himself. Ah, sure, there's hope for her, thought Muirís, with a toss of the head. There's surely hope for her, there is. Surely, she won't be taken in by this freeloader so, however pitifully he presents himself to her. Surely, she won't. He settled down to sleep upon that re-assuring thought, but only after he heard Áine turn the lock to the door of her room above.

Áine awoke early the next morning just after dawn to the sound of an insistent knock on the front door. Racing down to the door in her nightgown, she opened it to another unannounced visitor, Fiona, who strode in with a suitcase and looked around.

"Where is he? I knew he would come to you!" she thundered. "He calls you his Gráinne for some historic reason."

Áine was dumbfounded by the revelation. "Actually, if you are referring to Diarmuid, he is—"

Fiona wagged her finger in Áine's face and said with a sneer, "Don't bother making up excuses—I know about your old romance!" Pushing past the astonished girl, she stomped into the kitchen. She stopped with a jolt when she saw Muirís making a pot of tea.

Muirís held up his hand to the blistering woman and commanded, "Whoa, whoa, there woman. Whist. 'Tis much too early in the day for so many insults. Sure, you don't have to throw them out all at once, like. Haven't you the entire day to spread them out."

He poured out a cup of tea for her. "Sit there now, like a good girl, and drink down some tea. Maybe it will soothe the raging *cougar* inside you."

Leaning over Áine, and with a toss of his head, muttered, "Now, if any two people were made for each other, 'tis those two!" In spite of the situation, Áine smiled at his insinuation.

"Indeed," she whispered back. She gratefully took the cup he offered her.

Fiona glared at him. "And what are you two on about there? I'll not have you insulting me or my poor husband." She looked around the kitchen. "Where is Himself a t'all?"

Áine looked coldly at the woman and said evenly, "You'll find your husband in the guest room, more than hung over. Feel free to take him away at your earliest convenience. Now is more than convenient for me."

Surprised by the information, Fiona didn't comment. "I don't suppose you'll be making a bite to eat. I'm famished."

Áine stood up and started to collect ingredients for the refrigerator. "Tell you what," she said to Fiona. "I'll make a fry for everyone while you go raise Diarmuid. We can all hash out the purpose of your visit over breakfast."

Fiona started to leave the kitchen, only to suddenly turn back to face Áine. "Will you be making some of those American fried potatoes?"

Surprised by the question, Áine replied, saying pointedly, "If you'd like—we eat those regularly in *Canada*."

With a toss of her head, Fiona replied diffidently, "Well, now, I'll take mine without skins. I don't like how you Yanks prepare them with the skins. Skin mine first so." She left the room.

Muirís turned in disbelief to Áine before exploding, "The *strut* of her! Sure, I've never heard such rudeness!"

Turning to Áine in disbelief, he couldn't decide which troubled him more—her sad countenance or her passive admission. She looked down and said, "Oh, Muirís, I'm used to it. Just another enduring family *trait*."

The astounded man snapped back, "Not on *my* side of the family, it isn't, then."

As tears welled up in her eyes, which she tried to wipe away, she added, "Though I never seem to avoid being hurt whenever such rudeness rears its ugly head." She then turned round and with an audible sniffle, started to fry up potatoes and rashers—although she pointedly did *not* skin any of them first.

Diarmuid arrived in the kitchen, barely able to walk straight even after eight hours' sleep. Clearly hung over, he mumbled a quick "mornin'" and asked for tea, with Fiona following close behind.

"This should be good," murmured Muirís to himself, rubbing his hands with glee.

Fiona entered the room and sat down as directed by Áine to the assigned seat. Although everyone else had begun eating, Fiona simply stared down at her plate. Diarmuid turned to her and demanded, "Why aren't you eating, woman?"

Fiona responded with a whine, "I told her that I don't like them with skins." She glared at Áine. "Sure, with my intestinal problems, I can't digest them properly."

Áine looked away in shame, regretting not preparing them as the woman had instructed, despite her great rudeness. "So sorry, Fiona, I'll make you up some now," she said, as she rose from the table.

Diarmuid grabbed her arm, stopping her, as he growled, "You'll do no such thing." Turning to Fiona, he thundered, "Nonsense, woman! I've seen you devour them Yank style."

Fiona twisted in her seat as if to raise herself higher in the chair. "Sure, when we were growing up, didn't me' da' give the skins to the pigs? No one would *lower* themselves to eat the skins." She cast a sidelong glance over at Áine. "Besides Yanks, of course."

Muirís groaned and glared at the woman, while Áine replied quietly, "Isn't it a shame that the pigs in Ireland received more nutrition than the people? It's the skins that contain the best nutrients in the potato."

A burst of laughter emerged from Muirís, as Fiona sat icily in her chair and started to eat her rashers and eggs. "Have you any soda bread, ah, but you wouldn't, would you?" she asked primly.

Áine got up and removed a pan of hot scones from the oven. "Actually, I whipped up some scones for breakfast," she said, as she wrapped them in a cloth napkin and placed them in a bowl on the table. Trying hard to be gracious despite the situation, she smiled over at Fiona, as she offered them. "They're an Atlantic Province specialty, *Canadian*, that is," she added.

"No!" Fiona exclaimed, turning away.

"You wouldn't like a scone?" asked Áine, incredulous over Fiona's response.

"*No!*" She continued in a curt tone of pure ice. "I prefer my scones *cold,* and I don't like your butter. It's tasteless. No salt."

"But it's freshly whipped organic dairy butter from

locally pasture-fed cows—it's the best there is," responded Áine weakly.

Fiona shot her a dagger look that sliced through Áine's heart. "*No!* I said. I won't have any." In the two fingers usually reserved for wagging when scolding various people, she picked up one of the scones Áine had made and exclaimed, "I don't like the looks of them at all." She spoke in the disapproving tone that a main chef in an *haute culture* French restaurant might use for the unacceptable efforts of some fledgling *sous chef* underling.

Muirís jumped up from the table and started to take away Fiona's plate. "I think you're just about finished here."

Áine put out her arm to stop him. "Please, Muirís," she pleaded, "Just let her be."

Muirís exclaimed, "Jaysus! 'Tis too early in the day for this civil war!" He turned to Áine and said, "Unless you'll be needing me to referee, I'll be leaving you, now, to duke it out with the two of them." He tossed his head to the side as he left the table. "I can take no more of this rot!"

Diarmuid looked up and glared at the departing man. "We'd like that!"

Áine placed her hand on Diarmuid's arm. "Don't start, Diarmuid, please!"

Watching Áine trying to soothe things over, rather than stand up for herself was more than Muirís could take. Thanking Áine for breakfast, he stormed out of the kitchen before the disconcerted woman could stop him.

Going after him, Áine caught up with him at the front door. "I'm really sorry, Muirís, about all this."

He looked down at her and touched her shoulder. "Áine, you do not have to take their shite, even if they are family."

She sighed. "I know, I know. Let me work it out with them and find a solution."

"Right so," he said in a clipped voice, and as he went outside, added, "You're much too nice, Áine."

"I thought you liked me for that trait," she replied, her tone both defensive and despondent.

As he walked away briskly, he turned suddenly, shouting out, "For God's sake, Áine, don't let them take advantage of your good nature."

She watched him leave through tear-drenched eyes, before reluctantly turning back into her house. A deep feeling of loss and dread overcame her as she walked into the kitchen to deal with her cousin and his wife.

Diarmuid smiled smugly at her as she entered. "We'll not be needing the likes of him," he said, "pushing his weight around here. Aren't I still reeling from his punches?" He glanced at both women before moaning, "Ah, the pain I'm in."

He got up and looked around the kitchen, saying in a decidedly more cheerful voice, "Sure, a wee *dram* would go a long way towards taking away the pain, now, Áine."

Áine stared at him in amazement. "It's not even nine o'clock in the morning, Diarmuid! Surely, you don't mean you'd like some drink?"

"Ah, sure, it's the only thing that keeps the pain at bay," he moaned.

She sidestepped the remark, saying dryly, "You just have some more tea—I hear it contains marvellous pain-quenching abilities."

A moan was his only response.

Áine poured him some more tea and sat down. "Can we focus on discussing the reasons why you are both here?" Turning to Diarmuid, she continued, "So,

Diarmuid, please explain to me what's wrong with you, and what you were thinking in coming here."

Casting his eyes downward, he said, "I have no one to turn to, Áine, but you."

Before she could interject, he glared at her through bleary eyes. "Besides, doesn't everyone know in the family there's the unwritten rule that anyone who needs shelter can come here to stay. Sure, you haven't been so selfish as to change that family *understanding*, now that you've managed to get your hands on the ancestral house and lands, have you, Áine?" She could only stare at him in disbelief, too stunned to respond.

Fiona sat up and wagged her finger at her. "That's right," she added icily. "Did you not come to stay here with your grandfather when you had nowhere else to go?"

Stunned by the accusation, Áine started to explain. "That wasn't the reason I came here to stay. My grandfather—"

Fiona cut her off. "Save us the explanation. I suppose you're going to say that it was your *responsibility* to tend to your grandfather."

"I had promised my grandmother that I—"

Again, Fiona interrupted her, sneering, "Well, have you not a *responsibility* to your cousin here to take him in when he needs you?"

"It's not that I don't want to help Diarmuid," Áine replied, frustrated by the exchange, and turning to face Diarmuid, asked, "Would you please tell me, exactly, what is wrong with you?"

Fiona exploded. "He's bloody well *dying* and leaving me to fend for myself!" She then continued, "Ah, sure, how do you think I feel, Áine, with him all sick now.

Sure, I can only stand by helpless with no one to help me as he did."

Áine turned to Fiona and said quietly, but firmly, "Fiona, please. We'll attend to your needs in a moment. First, I need to speak with Diarmuid directly."

"Of course you do, of course you do," she sneered. "It's Himself you care about. I'll just go unpack my things in the guest room," and before Áine could say anything, Fiona left the room.

"Ah leave her be, poor ducky," implored Diarmuid. "How is this to work if you keep on after her? Just let her have her say."

"How is *what* to work?" Áine asked, arching her eyebrow.

"Our living here with you, of course, Áine." He took her hand in his own shaking ones. "Sure you wouldn't throw me out on the road, now would you, Áine, with my illness and all? Aren't you the one in the family who protects the needy—or is it only salmon you care about?"

Áine pulled her hand away, though gently. "No, of course not, Diarmuid," she said quietly, "though I don't know how the three of us can live under the same roof together."

He said with a whine, "Do it for my sake, Áine."

Áine gazed at him, her facial expression revealing her increased irritation with the situation. When did he transform into such an ungodly presumptuous and arrogant creature, she wondered. Sighing, she sat up and sipped some tea. "Tell me about this illness of yours."

"Well, the long and the short of it is that I have cancer of the liver."

Áine's heart thundered to a halt at the news. Though very angry with him for his terrible behaviour, she felt devastated over the news, feeling sick herself over the prospects of his deteriorating illness. She faltered over her words. "How, how, long . . . have you?"

He studied her through glazed eyes, assessing the effect the news was having on her. He feared her ambivalence over taking in both Fiona and him. Studying the sorrowful expression on her face, he decided there was no harm in speeding up the prognosis. She may be more apt to take me in, he figured, only to be grateful to discover that I linger on longer than predicted. He shook his head. "A few months," he said, looking down. Waiting a minute to let the information sink in, he then added, "You'll need to look after me." Meeting her sorrowful stare, he pleaded, "Sure, no one else can do it but you, Áine."

Áine didn't know how to respond. The news of his impending death was so sudden, so unpredicted, so—final—she thought. She was just getting over the passing of Maeve with whom she hadn't even been that close, yet over whose death she felt a terrible, though largely inexplicable sense of loss, made all the more palpable by living among her things in her house.

But *Diarmuid?* How would she come to feel about his passing? She couldn't bring herself to utter the word "death"—even in her thoughts. Here was the fellow who as a younger lad had watched out for her whenever she visited, and now he needed her, to help him, console him, nurse him, ease his pain, watch him die. Her heart felt wrenched in two. Tears streamed from her eyes.

When he observed her tears, he kept up the pressure. "Ah Áine, sure, you're the only one who would be willing and ready to see me into the next life. No one cares like you."

Her heart welled up with empathy for him and his situation. "Of course, Diarmuid, I'll help in any way I can. We'll work out the details in a day or so, all right?"

She looked at him as she reviewed their exchange. Something inside was telling her that this new crisis could prove as disastrous as the economic troubles sweeping through the country.

After Diarmuid left the room, Áine sat down with a sigh, wondering what had she gotten herself into. She sat swirling her teacup as she remembered Muirís' warning. She realized that if she didn't watch it, they would walk all over her—particularly Diarmuid.

She shook her head sadly, as she wondered with the new set of responsibilities assuming front stage, what she was to do about the salmon. She looked out the window down to the sea below. She felt herself alone, cast into a rigid net of responsibility, not unlike the watery dungeons waiting to constrain the wild salmon.

CHAPTER THIRTEEN

FATE

CINNIÚINT

FTER SEVERAL WEEKS OF MISERY, Muirís decided to contact Áine—Diarmuid or no Diarmuid—to see how she was faring. He reasoned that he couldn't let his feelings toward Diarmuid sway his attitude toward Áine. "Sure, I can't just leave her to deal with that lout on her own," he muttered. He apologized for not getting round to see her, but the thought of encountering the *poacher*, as he referred to Diarmuid, was too much to take. "Besides," he whispered into the phone, "I miss you more than I thought possible."

Áine readily agreed to meet for a late night supper at The Sandbar, which overlooked the sea at the edge of the strand. Attempting to steer the conversation away from the subject of Diarmuid, Muirís inquired, "And how are the wild salmon getting along—now that you've come Home to protect them?" He gazed at her green eyes.

Áine shook her head. "Well, I suppose there's one positive outcome from the economic crisis."

"How so?" Muirís leaned forward to hear more details about the ambivalent news.

"The government," she said, as she sipped a bit of wine, "now broke, of course, has stopped the EU trade deal, not knowing whether there will be a food shortage here in Ireland, as a result of the crisis."

He tossed his head to the side. "At least, they won't be feeding others when our own are going hungry, as they have done in the past."

She twisted her mouth into a faint smile. "Wasn't that the British, more precisely?"

"Ah, well, don't mind me," he said, with a forward toss of his head, "Sure, I'm always looking for conspiracies."

She chuckled. "Well, there may be a conspiracy in the offing if the banks have their way, as they are secretly negotiating for a bailout for their poor investments."

He straightened up. "Ah, for God's sake, those bloody blackguards."

She nodded. "Exactly, but the implications are profound for me, for you—for all of us, really."

He briefly reached out to touch her hand. "What about your position, then?"

She shrugged her shoulders. "At the moment, it's all been put on hold, though for how long, I couldn't say, with the Norwegians waiting to throw fistfuls of money at the government in exchange for our wild salmon."

He shook his head. "I've read that they are destroying their own coastlines with their bloody fish farms, and now they want to claim ours, is it?" He drank some wine. "We won't let that happen here in Kerry, I can tell you."

She studied his fierce expression, the way his jaw set into a rigid position, his eyes of now steely grey. "Well, I wouldn't mess with you," she said with a chuckle.

He leaned toward her, clasping both his hands around hers. "Sure, I would hope, Áine, that we'd always be on the same side of any battle."

She nodded at him, letting her hand remain ensconced in his. How warm it felt not to be shouldering all the responsibility alone. "On the issue of the protecting the wild salmon, we certainly share the same view." She smiled. "And, it seems, traditional foods."

"Ah, sure, I hope in many more areas." Releasing her hand, Muirís asked, "But what are you doing for work, then, if you're not collecting your income?"

"Oh, the PEI government is still paying me, since I have a contract with them." She smiled. "No contingency for national economic crises, I guess."

"Well, the government here certainly didn't expect it to happen."

"Anyway," she said, as she leaned forward in obvious excitement, "The delay is giving me the time I need to work up my culinary initiative. You know, my traditional foods and heritage idea," she said. Only too eager for a positive exchange, she launched into a highly animated account of her plots since Muirís had helped her get started.

"You found the heirloom seeds left by your grandmother and Maeve, then?" he asked.

"I did, indeed." Her voice brimmed with enthusiasm. "All nicely sealed in the root cellar." She leaned toward him. "Some had dates back to cultivars from the 1920s!" She gazed over at him and stopped. "But I suppose you knew that, having sown those seeds yourself."

He nodded in the affirmative. Noting her slight disappointment, he added, "But isn't it grand discovering them for yourself?" They proceeded to discuss which cultivars of root vegetables he had found the tastiest producers.

"And how are the spuds coming along?" he asked.

"They're just great!" Her voice was radiant. "I can't wait to see them in flower, particularly after you described to me the different variations of colour they display," she added. "I have been adding a seaweed 'tea' I made from the leftover dulse and kelp, like we used to do on Prince Edward Island."

"I'll bring round another load for you, straight away, so, to lay out on the beds," he said, nodding. He then leaned over, took her hand, and asked unsmiling, "Now that we have reviewed the state of the gardens, how is life *inside* the house, so?"

She took a sip of wine before responding. "Ah, that tastes great—haven't had a drop these past few weeks, as I was modelling healthy living!" With a wry grin, she added, "Not sure, though, how well my lesson went over." She then provided him with an account of her efforts to help restore Diarmuid to health, concluding, "Though I can't be sure, I believe Diarmuid is on the mend."

Muirís cocked his eyebrow in disbelief. "Is that so, now? From liver cancer?"

She smiled. "I'm not so sure about that, mind you, but I believe he is over wanting to rely on me."

"Impossible," he retorted, leaning toward her. He rested his hand over hers briefly, before removing it. She could read the ambivalence on his face.

"Well, now, you'd be surprised how quickly one can get over another, who, assuming the role of *taskmaster*, insists on the recuperative value of *weeding*!"

Muirís erupted in a hearty laugh over the very thought

of Diarmuid and his old lady weeding. "You mean you're not waiting on the two of them hand in foot?"

She chuckled. "Not a *t'all*, as you would say," though she qualified her general mirth over the topic. "Once the results came back that he did not actually have a tumour, but only some considerable irritation as the result of copious amounts of alcohol, I moved into the perfect cure—hard work, no alcohol, and poor-tasting herbal remedies to rid his liver of the toxins he so happily placed there, through his excessive drinking."

She took another large sip of wine, and leaned forward in her seat, laughing. "Not to mention the odd bowel cleansing regime thrown in!"

Muirís tossed his head to the side, chuckling away. "I can only imagine how they went over, then."

Aine offered a mischievous grin. "There were no end to the complaints of the tinctures and teas! I even threw in some for Herself for good measure, lest she thought she was being ignored." Wth a laugh, she said, "I might admit in present company that I made my remedies, hmm, shall we say, less *sweet* than usual?"

Muirís threw his head back and laughed heartily, almost choking in his mirth. "I'm just imagining the two drinking down some horribly tasting tinctures, muttering, 'Be Jaysus, we must be out of here—before the lass kills us, altogether!'"

"But they definitely did the trick," she countered. Gazing at Muirís, she asserted in a solemn tone, "Despite my humour here over the situation, I was determined to cure him. I gave him the full cancer alternative diet—only alkaline foods—all of which he hated, mind you, soaked him daily in a mixture of dmso, baking soda, and hydrogen peroxide to penetrate any cancer cells that might be mutating, and fed him bitter herbals. After a month or so, he looked one hundred percent better."

"And the weeding?" asked Muirís, smiling.

"Ah, that, well, I explained the benefits of physical activity—which extended beyond walking to the nearest pub and stretching out on the barstool," she said with a smirk. "Every day, the two of them had to go out to work the garden, pulling up weeds and the like, harvesting some early season greens, and general maintenance."

"They must have complained so," commented Muirís.

Áine smiled. "Relentlessly. I just put on my headphones and went about my chores," she said, chuckling. "But it did them both a world of good."

She sat looking away lost in thought for a few minutes. "Funnily enough, after about three weeks of my health spa treatment, Diarmuid said he felt so improved that he and Fiona would move on, and not trouble me further."

Muirís leaned forward eagerly. "And who are they sponging off now?"

Áine frowned at him. "Muirís, they weren't—"

"Never mind," he interrupted, not being able to bear his dear Áine defending the lout. "I misspoke, so."

Áine looked down at the table. "Well, it seems they found a bit of money, after all," she said, arching her eyebrow, "and decided that both of their health conditions necessitated a trip to the French Riviera." She smiled up at him. "Apparently, our Kerry wind and rain were just *awful* for their health. Nothing but sun and heat—"

"And French wine—" interjected Muirís.

"would suffice," she finished.

Muirís picked up his glass, and smiled broadly at Áine. "A toast, then! To their continued health! *Sláinte!*"

She laughed as she toasted him back. "You really are *incorrigible!*"

"Only trying to protect you!" he retorted.

"Ah, the *Red Knight* has returned, has he, watching over damsels in distress?" she quipped.

"'Tis my nature to do so," he said, with a slight bow. "I am only relieved for you that you stood up for yourself, so. I was worried that you wouldn't be able."

She looked up at him. "Actually, it was less standing up for myself, than assuming the responsibility of helping him learn to heal himself. I only hope I succeeded," she said as her voice faded.

"I'm sure you were grand," he said, in a soothing tone. "Sure, you can only go so far in helping him. He must do the rest with maintaining the new lifestyle changes you modelled for him—for his own sake. Only time will tell. Well, never mind, now, you've helped him recover, and he's gone on to sunnier climes."

She looked away, before saying in a tentative, faint voice, "He may be back, and I would feel compelled to take them in again."

"Ah, I wouldn't count on it!" He laughed. "Herbal tinctures and hard work don't seem like their preferred cup of tea," he said. "I'd bet my last pence on it, and I'm not a betting man."

He leaned back, taking her in. Before waiting for her response, he admitted, "Ah, 'tis grand to spend time with you again, Áine."

Their conversation moved away from Áine's emotional challenges with Diarmuid to the various initiatives she was trying to implement on the farm. Over supper, they both discussed the importance of growing historical cultivars, as well as the necessity for preserving the land, through relying on traditional techniques. She described some of the work in which she had been involved in Prince Edward Island, to reintroduce traditional methods. There, she explained, they adopted a more holistic approach than what had been practised, including the act of creating a closed loop of re-using composted food waste, as well as composted animal manures and green cover crops to nourish the soils. "This way," she smiled at him, "we ensured that we growers fulfilled our duty to protect the land."

Muirís sat back in his chair, smiling back at her with an amused expression covering his face. "When I first laid eyes on you—'nurturing the soil'—little did I realize that you would assume your historical legacy. Sure, it's as if your namesake Áine has herself returned from the days of old to revitalize the land once again, as she places her nurturing hands in the soil to fertilize the earth, and casts her protective gaze on all the fields about her."

Áine smiled at his characterization of her as a fertility goddess. Maybe he was finally abandoning those awful stereotypes he had expressed of Canadians and Yanks—and beginning to understand my inner nature, she thought hopefully.

"It is a daunting legacy to inherit, being responsible for the fertility of the land," she said, "but I am hoping to spread the word about the success of these traditional ways. I remain convinced they are our salvation, particularly now, in this economic crisis."

Muirís leaned over the table toward Áine. Gazing at her, he asked in a hesitant tone, "I don't suppose you know about your other historical legacy, do you, Áine?"

She slumped in her seat. "My God, haven't I enough legacies to live up to now, Muirís?"

"This one is really serious," he said in his quiet, serious tone, as he placed his hand over hers.

"What is it?" she asked, feeling open to any suggestion—as long as he would continue to be part.

"It involves me, as well. How do you feel about that, Áine?" he asked in a somber tone, searching her face for an indication of anything less than complete openness.

It was as if she could read his thoughts. Gazing back at him, she could feel him reminding himself that he couldn't give himself to someone who was less than willing. He needed someone to open her heart to him— secretly harbouring the hope that Áine was *the one.*

Áine replied, her voice soft, "I hope you know how I feel about you, Muirís." She hesitated a moment, and to quell the deafening silence as he waited for her to continue, she sipped some wine slowly and deliberately. She continued, her voice wavering, "It's just that . . . "

Muirís gazed at her with saddened eyes. Noticing, she could feel the depths of his disappointment, hoping she would want to be with him, despite all obstacles. And there was something about their common fate.

And then she said the unexpected. "I just need more time to think through what my place here may mean."

He gazed into her eyes and squeezed her hand. "Ah, Áine, this is your place, as you'll understand once you realize that you and I are more intertwined than you even know."

She pulled back her hand involuntarily and asked in a hesitant voice, betraying her ambivalence over knowing the details of this new admission. "What do you mean?"

"Have you not heard the story of our ancestors?" he asked.

"Our common ancestors?" she gazed at him. "No, actually, since I barely knew you FitzGeralds were distant cousins."

"Ah, love, we're more related than you know—*Fate* has offered us a chance to continue what was created before in our common history."

"What on earth do you mean?" she asked bewildered over his statement. A look of horror crossed her face. "We're not really *first* cousins, are we?"

Muirís laughed and took a sip of wine. "Not to worry, Girleen, we're not first, second, or even third cousins—well, perhaps third, depending on how one counts." He smiled at her. "Let's say distant enough in that way."

Áine visibly relaxed under this assertion. She peeked at him from under lowered lids. She wanted nothing more than to reciprocate. But she needed to know that Diarmuid was truly out of the weather before she could get on with her life—unimpeded by her sense of responsibility to him should he need her.

Muirís watched Áine as these thoughts passed through her. He felt as if he could read her mind. Ah, sure, she's struggling with her sense of responsibility to that bugger, he surmised angrily. This was more a sign of her innate goodness and warmth of heart, he reminded himself, than of her inability to stop others from taking advantage. *She is so decent and pure-hearted.* My right to be with her lay only in our mutual willingness and desire, nothing more—well, he qualified, perhaps with a touch of historical precedent thrown in. *Has it not been fated through our ancestral namesakes?*

Would he tell her tonight about this link between them? What if she laughs it off, dismissing it completely out of hand? Although it had come to mind whenever he asked a new intrigue her name, hoping it would be Áine, he dismissed it as nothing more than a fairy tale, a touching story of romance between two historical—even mythical—figures.

But his curiosity intensified as he spent that summer listening to Maeve talk about her Áine. From the moment he heard the name of this girl who seemed a counterpart to him, he felt a thrill of deep recognition, of connection to her that went beyond time and place. Although he tried to shake it off, he wondered whether he would know in meeting her.

And indeed, he did. When he finally saw Áine for the first time, he felt a deep current of connection between them, even though it may have gone unnoticed by her. That morning as he cast his net over the river to gauge how many wild salmon were left in the stream, he had noticed in the dawning light, the lone lass slowly walking along the strand, stopping here and there to gaze at a shell or a piece of kelp along the water's edge. There was something about her that caught his eye. He could perceive in her movements that she appreciated the natural forms around her. She was most definitely a daughter of Nature.

Unlike the majority of others who absently walk the strand, lost in the distraction of their thoughts, this woman seemed to be taking in everything around her— the way the first rays of sun caught the top of the waves, how the very grains of sand glittered in the golden light. She seemed to notice, as well, the school of dolphins that made their journey back from the sea. He watched her as she stopped and gazed back at the Paps behind her, observing them radiate blue, then, as the light increased, a bright orange. Finally, she focussed on the river where he was standing. For a moment, though obscured by distance and waxing light, they stood locked in a mutual gaze. He wondered whether in that glance she could feel a bond of connection between them. He certainly did. He looked over at her quizzical expression, wondering whether he was reading too much into her. He hoped not.

Muirís finished his glass of wine and suggested that they go for a walk along the strand, before calling it an evening. Áine didn't move, protesting, "But you haven't yet told me about our historical, how did you put it, *legacy*, between us?" She gazed at him intently and pressed, "I'd really like to know." He smiled at her, gladdened by her interest. He said he would tell her on the way back.

They walked along a beach riddled in stars. Neither said anything as they made their way down the strand, both taking in the stillness of the night and feeling the warmth of their companionship.

"'Tis unusual to have such a night sky teeming with stars," noted Muirís, breaking what had been a comfortable silence between them. "'Tis wondrous, surely."

Áine smiled at him. "Maybe it's a sign."

He looked at her with questioning eyes. "And what kind of sign would that be, now, Áine?"

She grinned at him. "Not sure, really, Muirís, but I like to think of unique natural events, such as this starry night, as a sign of something—greater clarity, perhaps, symbolized by the starlight?"

"'Tis Nature speaking to us, so?" he offered.

"Something like that. I've always believed that if we listen closely, we can hear Nature speak."

He put his arm around her shoulder and brought her close to him as they walked side-by-side, saying,

"Ah, you're a real mystical one, you are, Áine of Old. Completely in keeping with your ancestral heritage."

She leaned into him, enjoying their closeness. "Speaking of heritage, what was it you were going to tell me about some common history we share? You've piqued my curiosity." She added with a tease, "I don't suppose you're going to tell me that we met in a past life or something like that, are you? A good Catholic boy like yourself? I wouldn't have taken you for a Buddhist, or the like!"

Muirís chuckled. "Well, now, your instincts are good, but a wee bit off. Let's just call it a common legacy from our Celtic heritage." He stopped and looked down at her. "The question, Áine, is, now, or actually, will be, whether we do have a legacy, or perhaps a shared fate written and sealed by the pattern of the very stars above us."

Áine gazed up at him. "A shared fate?" she asked, as if repeating the words would shed insight into their meaning.

He took her arm and continued their stroll by the water's edge. "Yes, indeed, a fate that we share with our ancestral namesakes, perhaps." He stopped suddenly, choosing his words carefully. "As well as a fate we both share together, as a result of each of our own historical legacies."

Áine squinted at him. "You're a bit mystical yourself, Muirís, and sound like you're talking in riddles. Explain it to me," she implored.

"Let's sit here on the sand," he suggested, "and I'll tell you a story that might explain my allusions." Muirís reached out and brought her closer to him, and he took her hand as he started.

"I don't suppose you know that we were meant to be together?"

Áine looked at him in wonderment. "I would have never taken you for a hopeless romantic, but now, I'm convinced!" She laughed lightly, the sound like pebbles jingling in a soft undertow.

He protested. "It's not a matter of my romantic inclinations, of which, I fear, I do indeed possess more than an abundance," he admitted. "I'm referring to pure history."

"What of it?" she asked. "What happened in the past that makes you say that?" She arched her eyebrow.

"Do you remember when I took your dress whilst you went swimming?"

"I do, indeed," Áine replied, with a shake of her head. "That was a unique way of trying to get under my clothes." She swatted him playfully on the arm.

He smiled tenderly. "And do you remember how I referred to our common fate—by taking your dress?"

"Yes, I do," she said dryly. "Your act of boldness almost drowned me!"

"It wasn't supposed to go quite like that."

"What do you mean?" she asked.

"Well, now, I tried to carry out our fate, but it got a bit jumbled with your travelling out to sea, rather than into my arms," he said. "Will I tell you, now? Are you ready to hear of our common fate?"

His earnest tone surprised her. She said nothing for a moment, before urging him, "Bring it on, lad!"

"Well, then, Áine, your namesake—a mighty beauty, she was—as is her direct descendent, I might add," he said, as he stroked her hair, "spent her days taking care that the land remained watered and nurtured, that the wild salmon mated, and the cows provided sweet milk and butter for her people."

Áine chuckled at the characterization of her name-sake. "She was quite a loving creature."

"Indeed she was, and the people adored her for her gentle, kind, protective ways." He leaned into Áine, their shoulders touching.

"But one man loved her even more for her beauty."

"Indeed," huffed Áine, "I don't suppose he was a handsome prince."

Muirís laughed heartily, saying, "Well, now he wasn't a prince to be sure, but he was of nobility, owning vast tracts of land—"

She interrupted with a snide, "That he most likely *stole* from the Irish natives."

"Well, now, I'll concede you that point," he said in his good-natured manner, "but this lord was quite protective of the lands he had, hmm, *inherited* so, to put it politely, so he dedicated his life to nurturing the land in similar ways, though not supernatural ones, like those deployed by the goddess, Áine."

"At least they both shared a common passion for the land," she said.

"Indeed, and that common passion, coupled with the goddess' overwhelmingly enticing beauty—as forever embodied in those racy Paps overhead, prompted the dashing young man—"

"Oh, dashing, was he?" interrupted Áine. "Not some ugly old frog?"

"Not a t'all—much like present company, if I may say so myself," retorted Muirís in a tone of complete bravado.

"Hmmm. The story is getting more interesting," she said, her tone now openly coy. "Pray, do continue. Just

what did this handsome nobleman do with all his rugged, good looks?"

"He watched, and he waited for the goddess. Knowing
that she was very fond of bathing in the sea, he waited
for one spectacular morning when the sun had cast her
golden glow over the waves, knowing full well that Áine,
in one of her personas as Sun goddess, would celebrate
the sun-filled dawn with her ritual bath."

Áine laughed. "It must have been one of those *rare*
dawns, as the sun isn't likely to shine until almost the
sunset around here."

"Sure, it 'twas, truly," said Muirís with a nod. "Do you
remember yourself that wondrous sunrise we had when
you first arrived? You walked the strand over to the river's mouth, where the salmon are drawn."

Áine was silent for some moments before responding.
"So it *was* you," she said. "I have often wondered about
that. What were you doing there? I've been afraid to ask."

"I was looking in after the salmon," he said.

"Which ones?" she asked, her tone betraying her
suspicion.

"The wild, of course," he said, smiling. "I noticed you
that morning."

"I noticed you, as well," she responded easily. "I was
wondering whether you were an advocate of the wild
salmon or not."

"Now you know, love," he said, as he placed his hand
on her shoulder. "There should never be any doubt that I
would side with *na fiáin*—the wild ones." He then mumbled more to himself than to her, "The more we can do
to maintain their wildness, far from cages, the better off
we all are."

"What was that, Muirís?"

"Ah, never mind, now, Áine. We can discuss our efforts to free the salmon another time, so."

Áine stared at him, before asking, "I don't suppose you were trying to free any penned-up salmon."

"Actually, I was. I was trying to see whether the wild salmon had 'escaped' from the nets some of those corporate boys have already been creating—even though they haven't any permission yet to do so. 'Experimental,' they call it. It's something me' da' and I do quite frequently—all on the quiet, mind you," he admitted.

"Escaped? How do they escape, Muirís?" she asked, arching her eyebrow, as she anticipated the answer.

With a toss of his head, he whispered, "Ah, sure, as the boys sang, '*with a little help from their friends.*'"

"Ah, I see, you and your da'—and God knows how many other Kerrymen, have continued waging economic resistance against the invaders, is it? Something along the lines of our IRA great-grandfathers?" she surmised. "I thought *you* were part of the *invaders*, from what you told me earlier."

He smiled at her. "Something like that. We'd like to make those detestable fish farms they are planning, economically unfeasible for them." He looked over at her. "And, no, Áine, it was not quite like that. Our history is much more complicated, so. I hail from a family line that was originally Norman French. We were *never* English. Indeed, we fought them off, so we did."

Áine sighed. "And still *are*, I guess, though now the invaders are more likely multi-nationals. God help us. Just when I was falling for you, you'll end up incarcerated yourself—like our poor wild salmon."

His voice was quiet, divested of bravado, though nonetheless proud. "Sure, it's in me' blood. Didn't my ancestors take on the Bloody Brits in the famous Munster rebellions? Actually, we FitzGeralds teamed up with your clans—the Ó'Suílleabháins and the Ó'Conchobars."

She leaned over and touched his arm tenderly. "In this day and age, it's better to fight them with the research and proven evidence. That's where I come in. I have indisputable proof to support the wild salmon. Besides," she said, wagging her finger at him, "you aren't helping the wild salmon one bit by allowing any farmed ones in among them to share their diseases." She shook her head. "That's the really sad part. Once they are penned up and fed those carcinogenic foods and antibiotics, they must remain separated from the wild—for the sake of the wild ones."

He leaned over to her. "Are you with me, then, on fighting off—however we must—the *invaders* from incarcerating our salmon, our sacred *bradáin fiáin*?"

She offered a warm smile. "Of course. Now onto the rest of the tale."

Spellbound, she listened to the tale of how Muirís's ancestor had waited until that rare dawn to follow the goddess Áine to the strand. "Averting his eyes, as she removed her cloak from around her,"

"Oh, *really* now," Áine interjected. "You had me until that moment."

Muirís chuckled, admitting, "Well, with such a form, she wasn't one to ignore, I suppose. Right so, we'll alter that wee bit of the tale, so," and continued, "He watched spellbound as the beautiful young woman removed her cloak and swam into the waves."

He stopped, saying no more.

"Well? What happened next?" Áine asked impatiently.

Muirís responded with a far-away look in his eyes. "I

was just thinking what he must have thought—seeing that absolutely heavenly naked form standing there in the dawning light. She must have been nothing short of utter perfection."

"I see you're a man who deeply appreciates the female form," she said, her tone pointed. "You must get plenty of practice, gazing at the lovely young things that frequent your pub."

"Indeed, I've to look no farther than your own incarnation of that ancient beauty to witness utter *perfection*," he countered in his beguiling way.

"But it's dark." Her protest weak, she betrayed her delight in his interest in her.

"Sure, isn't the night for *feeling* that which we cannot *see*?" he murmured, his tone seducing her.

"Ah, you're a real sweet talker, you are, Muirís," she countered, "on with the tale."

"Ah, right so. I was just warming up to the *feeling* part," he admitted, "so once the lovely apparition had entered the water, Muirís—"

"Muirís? What do you mean—Muirís?" she interrupted. "Surely, that was not his name."

"Pure historical facts, love. Indeed, his name was Muirís, Muirís FitzGerald, like meself. In fact, he was my Great—thirty times over or so, grandfather."

Áine was stunned by the revelation. "This *really* happened?"

"So say the history books," he affirmed. "Early thirteenth century, it was."

Now Áine was nothing short of spellbound by the tale, listening in rapt attention. Urging him on, she said, "On with it, Muirís, what happened? How does the tale end?"

"It ends—and begins again—with two people, named Muirís and Áine, sitting on the strand under a sea of stars."

Áine lightly swatted him on the arm. "Don't be talking in circles, now, Muirís, on with it." Then she stopped, sighed, and added, "Unless, there is an unhappy ending."

"Not a t'all," he countered, "Quite the opposite. Right so." He related how Muirís took the cloak of the goddess into his arms and hid it behind him, so that when she emerged from the water, she would be his.

"And how did she become his?" she asked, looking over at him with a suspicious glance.

"When she came out of the water, she walked into the loving arms of Muirís, where they became one, and remained so the rest of their lives."

"Did he return her cloak?" she asked.

"No, he made love to her instead, warming her from their common passion."

"What a lovely account," murmured Áine. "What became of their union?"

"They joined forces to protect the land and create a new people. I am a direct descendent of that match—" then leaning into her, added, "As are *you*."

Deeply moved by Muirís' tale, she remarked, "It's as if we are living, or *re-living*, the experiences of our ancestors."

"Not quite," said he slowly.

"What do you mean?" she asked.

"Well, now, in our case, I was to have taken your dress, and you were to have slipped into my arms as a result, once you emerged from the sea."

"Then what?" she asked, pressing him.

"He looked down at her, and touching her chin, said

tenderly, "We were to have made passionate love and thus be intertwined forever."

A wave of excitement swelled within Áine. "That's quite a story," she murmured, as she gently leaned against him.

"'Tis no story," said he. "As I said before, I have the handwritten account passed down in my family to prove it."

"Well, maybe we shouldn't tempt Fate," her tone low and unhesitant.

He didn't need to hear any more. Gathering Áine in his arms, he asked, as he drew her face up toward his. "You are ready, so, to seal our Fate?"

She pulled back, though reluctantly, at the weight of it all. "But what about my dress and the swim?"

"We'll practice on this one stage first, so. Sure, we can always do it all again—when you feel like swimming!"

Murís gently pulled Áine back, grasping both her shoulders. He gazed deeply into her eyes, soaking up the endless waves of emotion he found there. Still no word passed between them. Minutes passed. And just as gently, Murís leaned over, and ever so softly, touched his lips to hers. They both felt themselves floating, carried off, far away.

They stopped and gazed at one another under the starlit sky. Murís leaned over and kissed her again—with a kiss as soft as the first. Together, they made the softest, most tender love that either could ever have imagined possible—with the sea breezes softly murmuring their assent about them.

CHAPTER FOURTEEN
CELTIC ROOTS

FRÉAMHACHA CIARRIGE

INSPIRED BY THE KNOWLEDGE of her cultural legacies, Áine decided to pursue her ideas to help promote
a local renaissance to bolster the economy and enhance
cultural pride. With the economic crisis threatening to
drown Irish dreams for a sovereign future, she felt there
was no better time than now to launch her Celtic Roots
campaign—her plan for encouraging a renewed commitment to all things local.

Hurrying into the kitchen for a pot of tea for the
library, she energetically set to work taking her initiative
to the next step. She started with her own contributions.
She had planted heirloom potatoes, peas, leeks, cabbages,
kale, broccoli, parsnips, and carrots—all native vegetables from seeds she had culled from her grandmother's
collection, together with some from local farms that had
preserved seeds for generations. It was gratifying to her
that she was following the old ways, which had not been
entirely lost out there along the edge of Dingle.

As she sipped some tea, she started brainstorming
about what she could do with those vegetables, beyond

selling them to others. She wanted to contribute to pre-serving historical culinary traditions, and in so doing, not only perpetuate beloved cultural practices, but serve as an economic impetus for the local area. Her memories returned to Prince Edward Island, where a significant portion of the local inhabitants had decided to find a way, through relying on traditional agricultural practices and culinary traditions, to create jobs and income for the local region. What we did there, she mused, would work equally as well here.

Áine reasoned that both places were islands teeming with plentiful, local sources for marine foods, fertile soils conducive to growing root vegetables and grasses for pas-ture-fed animals, habitats rich in wild berries and apples, and cultures featuring savoury culinary practices utiliz-ing traditional foods. She wondered how she could adapt some of the initiatives so successful back in Canada on Dingle. She spent hours making inventories of what she knew other people produced on their farms, harvested from the sea, or made from these sources. She mapped it all out graphically to create a visual of the current local economy, its limitations and potential, as well as niches for agri-preneurial initiatives. She was rather impressed with the results.

Áine knew that to make this successful both for locals and for tourists, she would need to find ways to con-nect the local food establishment with locally-grown, raised, and caught foods. Even more, however, such places needed to showcase the rich culinary heritage of local dishes and food-based products made from local sources. Such "value-added" products, she recalled, really enhanced income streams, both from locals buying from one another and from tourists who flocked to areas where such agri-tourism was favoured over the usual global fare.

She scanned the family library looking for old cookbooks where she might find some ideas from traditional recipes for her own vegetables. She came across *Irish Country Dishes*, a tome from the turn of the nineteenth century, written in English, as well as two books written in Gaelic. To her delight, she found stuck in pages here and there, hand-written recipes that offered variations to the recipe set on the page. Since many of them were written in Irish, she needed someone to translate them for her. She immediately thought of Muirís—who never strayed far from her thoughts, particularly after their night on the strand. Before going in search of him, Áine decided to skim through the cookbook in English to get a better feel for the historical dishes featuring the vegetables she grew. She poured over the book for a few hours, trying to figure out how to adapt certain recipes she thought would be popular now.

Before long, Áine was busy at work in her kitchen, creating various dishes she wanted to try out with the vegetables she had just pulled from the garden. If she could add value to each dish, that is, add an ingredient that made use of another food source from the local area, then that dish would be all the richer for it, as it would reflect the interconnectedness necessary for a local food economy to flourish.

With that in mind, she thought of the most traditional foodstuffs and assembled them on the worktable. Within minutes, she had wild salmon, scallops, haddock, potatoes, butter, cream, cheese, greens, and various roots.

While her bread was baking, she rang up Muirís to invite him to dinner the next day. Unknown to him, he was to be her guinea pig. If he liked the dishes, then she knew they would be successful in the larger area.

"Of course, Áine, I'll be there—what about tonight?"

Áine responded with a firm no. "Don't you come near me this evening, Muirís! Some of my dishes need two days' preparation. I'll see you tomorrow evening, and not a minute before."

Muirís sighed. "Right so, Áine. *Slán Leat!*"

"*Slán!*" she replied.

She hustled back to the kitchen, where she got to work mixing up batches of bread, as well as pastry dough, for the potato country loaves she would bake the next morning, together with root tarts and a fisher's pie she would prepare for supper. She worked late into the night, feeling that these were the types of foods that would help highlight the local vicinity as a centre for traditional fare.

Muirís arrived early the next evening, just as Áine finished setting the table and stoking the fire. With some traditional music playing in the background, and the delectable aroma of roasted vegetables, recently baked bread, and seafood chowder, the setting in the little cottage—now shimmering in the salmon glow of the evening sun—could not have been more inviting to Muirís. For him, seeing the energetic redhead bustling about the kitchen, occasionally glancing at him with that alluring smile of hers, cinched it for him. He was *smitten*, no doubt about that.

Having brought a bottle of his finest German *Riesling*, he poured a glass of wine for each, while he eagerly watched Áine remove some appetizers from the oven. If it tasted half as delicious as it smelled, he was sure to enter culinary heaven. "What have you here, now, Áine?" he asked, as she displayed an array of just-baked finger foods to accompany their wine. He admired the tray, wanting to know more, as his own culinary training piqued his interest.

She smiled at him, pleased by his admiration. "We're having a *traditional* night, Muirís."

He gazed in disbelief from her to the roasted leek wrapped scallops, the trout cakes, and the creamed lobster with roasted potato pastries. "Sure, my experience of traditional foods is boiled prataí, cabbage, with a bit of poached fish, and more spuds!" he said with a grin.

"Ah, I threw the boiled spuds in the bread dough, *skins and all!*" she responded, chuckling, "but that's part of the next course!"

She brought over the old cookbook from which she had taken the recipes and laid it out in front of him. "Actually, I found all these dishes more or less, in this book," she said. "Though I admit I might have assumed a culinary version of '*poetic license*' in their preparation and presentation," she added with a smile. "*Traditional* dishes for the *modern* eater, I call them. Try some," as she held out the tray to him. He rapidly filled his plate with one of each of the offerings.

They savoured the appetizers while sitting on wooden rockers outside the front door, where they watched the fading sun slowly glide down over the edge of the sea. Muirís leaned toward Áine as he reached for another appetizer. He seemed to savour each bite, saying nothing until he had consumed his miniature prataí pie.

"Well, now, Áine, these are quite savoury—lovely, indeed. I wonder would they do well in the pub."

Áine turned to him and replied in an enthusiastic voice, "Just what I was thinking, Muirís! As you had intimated before, wouldn't it be better to serve traditional foods in a pub specializing in traditional music, and in such a culturally rich region of Ireland?"

He gazed at her in silent admiration. "'Twould, 'twould, indeed, now, Áine," he said, as he rocked slowly back and forth.

She stood up and poured out a bit more wine for Muirís and herself, as she said, "Have another glass, now, Muirís, while I tell you what we did in Prince Edward Island, and how I'm thinking we could borrow from that example here."

She then launched into an account of the *Traditional Ways* campaign there, which involved resurrecting traditional Scots, Irish, Acadian French, and even Mi'kmaq dishes from local ingredients. "It became a source of pride for the islanders," beamed Áine, "but even more importantly, it put people back to work. The more entrepreneurial ones opened the restaurants, or started up the heritage farms, while those with experience in fishing, for example, started to use old-time ways of smoking the fish and preparing them."

Muirís listened intently, and when she stopped, urged her on. "Tell me more, so."

"The key to making it work was to get people to want to eat locally-prepared foods over ones imported to the island, and to entice them into eating local foods in *traditional* ways, rather than simply eating potatoes as frozen French fries, as we call them—*chips* to you—that only made the big corporations who produced the frozen pre-made fries richer." She stopped to sip her wine. "We wanted people to be enthusiastic over growing their own vegetables, and raising their own chickens, pigs, sheep, or cows, as well as make dishes from these products they could either sell to one another, or prepare for the tourist market."

"Now that's an idea," nodded Muirís in agreement. "I see a great opening here for such traditional dishes made from our own local foods and fish."

Turning to him, Áine offered an emphatic nod. "Once Government got involved, and made up tourist maps of what they called traditional culinary trails, tourists came in droves to stay in a gorgeous natural setting and consume lobster with local vegetables, done up in traditional ways." She stopped to think a few minutes before continuing. "Of course, what we need here is something more, with the current economic tidal wave engulfing us as it is."

Muirís nodded. "Right, so. We should find a way to be relatively independent of the tourist trade. What we need is to develop a market of local foods and traditional, as well as artisanal, dishes for *one another*."

Áine shook her head in agreement. "That's right. What we did Over was to create a local foods market. It became quite the social scene on Saturdays, with much of the population visiting the market to buy foods they weren't growing, catching, or raising themselves, as well as to buy interesting prepared foods."

"And did the locals, now, buy up the ready-made foods from one another?" he asked, his mind racing with ideas.

"Not only did they buy the foods, but most vendors were sold out within hours of opening," replied Áine. "In fact," she added, "We extended the market all through the year, even though most people weren't growing anything at all. What they did was make dishes from their root vegetables and fish, say, and other things, ranging from seaweed facial creams, to goat milk soaps with kelp, to wild berry jams, to chowders, and stews which they sold."

"Really, now," said Muirís. "Sounds more like a food-tasting festival than a market!"

Áine laughed. "It was a little of both, really. That was the charm of it. And it drew artisans as well—people sold sweaters and mittens they made from their sheep's wool, others painted, or did wood working, carving sea birds and fish, and the like. It was truly a successful venture, and it made people feel like small independent business owners again, instead of working for some big corporation." She leaned back against the rocker. "It became so successful, in fact, that the big French fry manufacturer left the province entirely."

Muirís thought a minute as he savoured his wine. He then shared his reflections, "So natives produced and bought largely from one another—just as they did in our 'tiger' economy. The only problem here was that the real estate economy was based on borrowed money, which few ever had the means to repay."

"Exactly," said Áine. "The idea of producing something for fellow citizens is actually a sign of a flourishing economy that promotes independence and is self-sustaining, as long as everyone doesn't go broke," she added. "However," she qualified, "One advantage that Ireland has over PEI, is the huge inventory of holiday homes located in pristine, natural areas throughout the country, but particularly here, in Kerry. Since so many of these are on the market, as the owners can no longer afford a luxury second home, maybe these could be used as holiday retreats for tourists, who would come to savour the foods, while staying in accommodations set in lovely natural settings—amid the mountains or overlooking the sea."

He chuckled, and giving her a wink and a toss of his head, said with deep admiration in his voice, "You have it all worked out, now don't you, Áine? Maybe you should run for office! You have the makings of a natural, visionary leader!"

Smiling at him, she replied, "Shall we continue our discussion indoors over dinner? I have so much more to share with you!"

He broke out in his charming, broad smile. "I'll be hanging onto your every word, I will!" He winked at her again through eyes that twinkled with delight.

Soon, they were seated around the kitchen table with the entrées proudly set out on the table. "My God, Girleen! We'll have to enter you into one of those gourmet culinary competitions!" he exclaimed with obvious approval in his voice. "Everything looks and smells just fantastic, altogether!" He rubbed his hands together. "Where will we start, so?"

Áine poured him a small bowl of cockle chowder, as she explained the origin of the dish. "Based on an old Irish recipe for grunt and cockle soups, I added—Canadian style—various fish and seafood, including Irish moss and some dulse—to round it out a bit." She added with a sly grin, "and of course, a wee dram of the *uisce bheatha*—Irish whiskey!" She smiled down at him. "I do hope you like it!"

He swallowed down a big spoonful of the soup. "It's wonderful—quite flavourful, with bits of different tastes popping out here and there as it goes down." He drank down the bowl. "Sure, that's the perfect medicine for a wet, windy day, it is!"

Áine smiled at him, utterly delighted with his response. Filling up his plate with a slice of root vegetable tart, as well as some more prataí pie, she sang out, "On to round three!"

She removed from the oven a freshly baked loaf of potato bread, from which she tore a few thick chunks, and slathering them with freshly churned herbed butter from cream from a neighbouring farm, as well as herbs from the garden, offered him several slices to accompany his meal.

"My God, Áine! You churned that butter yourself, did you?" His teeth sank into the delicious warm bread. "And the bread? 'Tis so light, yet full of flavour." He finished the bread in admiring silence. "Another food we could be serving at the pub," he mused.

"Try it with this dip," she suggested, as she offered him some garlic mussel dip.

"Now for the actual meal!" he said happily, as he tried each of the foods on his plate.

Áine explained to him how she made each from local foods, without having to resort to any ingredient beyond the vicinity.

"Absolutely astounding!" He nodded between mouthfuls. "Who would have thought to combine and prepare these vegetables in this way?"

Áine smiled. "Our ancestors, of course!" She went on to explain how she had borrowed from the trditional practices of roasting and smoking food in a peat fire, such as salmon, as well as relied on the old ways of using potatoes and leftover breads for the dough.

"Áine, these dishes are really good, astoundingly good, actually," Muirís said. "You should do this for a living."

She leaned back in her chair and said, "It's all part of the larger plan."

"What plan is that now, Áine?" he asked, then with a toss of his head, added coyly, "Would your plan, now, have any mind to be including me?"

She replied instantly, unable to restrain any longer from sharing what she had been dreaming up. "Would you let me have a go of it?"

"A go of what?" asked Muirís, not following her train of thought. "Me, is it? Sure, I thought you'd never ask!" He grinned at her.

She swatted him lightly on the arm. "We'll discuss that part of *the plan* later." She leaned over towards him. "Would you let me prepare some of these dishes for your pub, so we could try them out, on both the locals who frequent there, as well as on the tourists who come for the traditional *sesúins*," she asked in a hesitant voice, fearing he might reject her ideas.

Muirís looked at her for a moment, hoping to find in her facial expression some indication of his place in in her scheme, beyond serving merely as an outlet for her food. Finally, he said slowly, nodding, "'Tis a grand idea, surely, Áine. Would you truly like to do that, now?" He continued to gaze at her.

"I would indeed, Muirís. It's part of *the plan*." Without waiting for him to press her on the details, she launched into her thoughts about creating a local food economy that relied on traditional foods for local people. She showed him the partial list she had drawn up of food products and the like from what she knew of various locals and asked him to fill it in more.

"Grand. Grand. A grand idea," he repeated, nodding. "So you would like to host a market, then, is it, at the pub where everyone can sell their stuff?"

"Yes, something like that," she replied. "Though perhaps other business owners like yourself could also host it in their shops, or, perhaps, in the town square. But we'll need to get a list of value-added and artisanal food producers as well—you know," she added, "Get a small group of cheese makers to help other dairy farmers learn how to make artisan cheeses, for example, or others to make dishes from the dairy products." She sat back and looked over at him. "What we really need is a *school* for the traditional arts."

Muirís tossed his head. "Just like it used to be when everyone was '*someone*,'" he said.

"That's exactly the goal!" Áine leaned over towards him. "People have lost their agricultural identities, or their small businesses, by becoming consumers of the global markets, rather than continuing to develop their own product lines here at home."

"Well now, we all must eat," he said, "regardless of the state of the economy. It's much better for a host of reasons to produce our own food for our own consumption. *Sinn Féin*. Ourselves Alone." He shook his head, and added with a tinge of sarcasm in his voice, "'Tis an idea that got away from us—in our excitement over having mobile phones."

Áine gazed at him quietly for a moment. "It's interesting how much we agree on this."

He smiled over at her. "'Tis, indeed."

He took her in his arms and kissed her long, then without a moment to waste, he caught her up in his arms, and carried her off to her room upstairs, continuing where they had left off on the strand.

PART THREE
ALONE

AONARÁN

CHAPTER FIFTEEN

THE STORY OF MAEVE

SCÉAL MEDB

STILL RADIANT—even days later—from the effects of her transformational encounters with Muirís, Áine needed no excuse to return to the strand. All it took were a few wafts of salty, sea air to entice her to drop everything and head down the lane to the beach.

As she walked slowly along the water's edge, she relived, not only the deeply sensual experience she had shared with Muirís, which was enough to make her shiver, but their spell-binding exchange regarding their interwoven history and possible common fate. Until now, she had never even thought such a thing existed. "But here," she whispered, as she gazed around, "anything seems possible!"

Little did she think upon returning to the place of her birth, she would discover so many interconnections, ranging from mountaintops to fated encounters. She felt a sense of belonging—of deep connection—in ways she never thought possible. She turned back for a look at her tiny cottage nestled back up the foothills of the mountains above the strand. Was it for this reason that Maeve had left her the family homestead? Turning round again, she sat on the sand, watching the breaking waves before her. And if so, she wondered, why did it matter to Maeve that she become re-connected to her birthplace? She thought about this for some time as she continued to sit, mesmerized by the rhythmic undulations of the sea.

Though it came to her initially as a slight humming sound, she listened with all her might. The breaking waves seemed to chant:

> *I am—*
> *You,*
> *And you are—*
> *Me.*

And suddenly it hit her—like waves tossing all around her. She was here to discover her future, through returning to her past. She was meant to return to Ireland—to that rocky coast, the home of Maeve, home of her mother, and her mother before her, and all the wild salmon—to nurture, protect. To return to her place—to connect with her own ones. The thought triggered the words of the mystical Áine Críonna:

> *I am who I am, by being among my own ones—*
> *the mountains above,*
> *the waters below,*
> *and the salmon in the sea.*

The yearning to feel inextricably part of the larger something hooked her, reeling her back to the ancient place. While the death of Maeve renewed her historical place within the Ó'Suílleabháin clan, her own passion for protecting the salmon, the waters, and land around them, rooted her to them in some ethereal way. Like the wild salmon, and Maeve before her, she had returned to her original home to start a new life—and protect the lives already existing.

With such profundity flowing through her, Áine stood and slowly moved away, walking on the sand back to the cottage. Once inside the kitchen, she made a fire and a pot of tea. Gathering together a large notebook and some pens, she sat down at the kitchen table, the very one around which her ancestors had sat year after year. Taking up her pen, Áine began to write the story of Maeve.

For her story,
began Áine,
> *is the story of all women who dream for something*
> *more than that with which they had*
> *entered this world. Maeve is I, and I Maeve.*
> *She is Ireland herself—her past and her future.*
> *Her story is one of expressed passion,*
> *of innate wildness, of willful deliberateness.*
> *The story of her. The story of me.*

Some hours later, Áine was still so focussed on writing that she didn't hear the knock on the door. Suddenly, a shadow passed over the page she was writing. Looking up, she found Muirís standing over her. Her heart thundered, less from the scare of finding someone unexpectedly next to her, as from the thrill of expectation that his presence enkindled within her.

"Muirís!" she exclaimed, dropping her pen. "You startled me!"

He gazed down at her with a solemn look before gently touching her shoulder. "Sure, I hope it is not in revulsion."

She smiled up at him. "Not at all, Muirís. I'm really glad to see you."

"Are you now?" he murmured, his tone hesitant, but her warm smile told him everything. "And I am very happy to see you—so close up," he added. He squeezed her shoulder just a bit.

Leaning over her, he gently kissed her forehead, as he handed her a packet tied with a green ribbon. "'Tis long overdue," he admitted, "but I didn't think the time right—until now . . . " His voice trailed off.

With furrowed eyebrows, she took the long anticipated packet. Despite her absolute joy over seeing him, she couldn't help but retort dryly, "I had long given up hope of ever seeing this document darken these doors again, so I started my own account of Maeve's life— however fictional it may be."

"Well, that's all well and good," he said. "I am happy that you are writing, Áine, I am truly," he added, his tone sincere. "But you must put down your pen and read this," he urged her, "in its *entirety*." Áine gazed at him with questioning eyes. "You'll need to read it all to understand."

"Understand what?"

He glanced at her as he left the room. "Nothing short of everything, I should think," he said with a mysterious air. "I'll be in the kitchen making a pot of tea to go along with your reading," he added.

She studied him with a stern gaze. "What on earth are you referring to, Muirís?"

"Ah, well, it'll all become more clear as you read," he said, turning away.

With cup in hand, Áine stood up and left. "You really are perplexingly infuriating with all of your obtuse references! Right, then," she added, as she walked away, "I'll read it all, so I'll know what *you* know."

Muirís called after her. "Will we meet for supper at the Sandbar, so we won't be interrupted?"

"I'll be several hours, but sure, that's fine," she called back.

"I'll just linger awhile and see how your reading is coming along, so," he stammered.

He heard her laugh and chide him for being an old woman. "Stop fussing over me! I'm a grown woman. I can handle the story of Maeve," she called out.

"We'll see about that, now," muttered Muirís. "I only hope you are as strong as you think, so." He stood at the door of the parlour, hesitant to move, before forcing himself to walk back to the kitchen.

Áine returned to the desk. She picked up the journal and held it in her hand. Even though she hadn't much liked the genre, thinking it too invasive of another's privacy to read, she found herself magnetically drawn to this one for reasons that eluded her—beyond the obvious of wanting to know why she had been assigned by Maeve to look after the family home, as well as to write about her aunt's life.

With the first line, she stopped in sadness as she read one of the entries:

I am all alone here—with no children to comfort me in these last dark days.

Heaving a sigh, she plunged into her reading. Perhaps the answers I seek are here, she thought, somewhere in the depths of the dreams, feelings, and admissions that Maeve had consigned to the parchment pages.

Hours ticked by as Áine read. Muirís checked in on her from time to time, silently replenishing her cup of tea, with Áine barely noticing. From the shadow of the doorway, he studied her as she read. She sat slumped in her chair, only to straighten up, and bury her head down even farther into the book with a faint gasp.

"I'm here for you, Áine *mó chroí*," he said softly. "As painful as it will be, we'll get through it, you and I, if only you give me the chance." He turned and left her to her reading, knowing she would need unencumbered space to take in the truths of what she would be learning.

Áine read of Maeve's distress and disappointment over finding herself pregnant and unmarried. And she was even more surprised to discover that her own grandmother had experienced a similar fate. Just as Maeve's mother before her had done, Maeve hid herself in the home of her mother and waited out the time there.

Her father had severely lashed out at her upon hearing the news, only to have his wife, Maeve's mother, Áine, give out to him that he had no right, as he had done the same to her, stealing away her virginity and innocence. He left the home that day, never to return while his wife continued to reside there—leaving the women of the family to serve as the new proprietors of the family farm.

Áine read with mixed emotions about the birth of Maeve's first child. Her grandmother, Áine, delivered it. She stopped reading and gazed out the windows toward the sea. That's odd, she thought, wondering why her Mum hadn't ever told her that particular story about

Maeve. With a shrug, she returned to the entry in which Maeve recorded how she felt about the birth:

> *I am so desolate now that the wee child is born—I shall spend my days alone without a man to care for the child and me. If it had only been a boy, I might have more luck in persuading the father to shoulder up to his responsibilities.*
>
> *But she being a girl, I have no hopes that the father will ever marry me. Such is the fate of so many girls here in the country. I am forever lost.*

Once it was determined the babe was a girl, Maeve's mother insisted on naming her in keeping with the family tradition, particularly since she was the only one of the many grandchildren to be born in the family homestead. Áine read on, utterly surprised over the revelation that Maeve had delivered a girl as her first-born:

> *Mam made me agree to allow her to name the babe. We'll call the child Áine—Áine meaning 'brightness,' for she is the only bright star in this family now, due to your shame, said she.*

Áine sat upright in her chair, her eyes locked in shock at the name. *Áine!* Springing from her seat, she paced the room, to and fro, then round and round as her thoughts gushed with the tumult of a river in spring. Maeve had borne a daughter named Áine. But where was she? What had happened to her? Did she not survive?

My God! She suddenly gasped in horror, her thoughts in tumult. Surely, little Áine did not suffer the fate of the infamous Kerry baby scandal some years back. Surely,

Maeve would not have done away with the poor creature as one of the neighbour's daughters was thought to have done in her own despair over a similar plight.

The thought was too much. Áine reeled around as she charged for the kitchen, her apprehension racing along with her. She boiled up another pot of tea with mechanical steps, her thoughts flying. As she poured out the boiling water over the loose tea, her heart skipped a beat. Abruptly putting down the kettle, she stopped in her tracks and gazed about the room, as if to find the answers somewhere previously overlooked. She moved to the window and stared out to the sea below.

Could it be? Could it be—*me?*

The thought engulfed her so completely that she felt her heart pound through her skin. She started to breathe heavily and long sobs from the depths of her soul poured out. She stumbled to the table and slumped in the chair, burying her head in her arms. She sat like that for countless minutes, when suddenly, she sat up, stopped crying, and shook her head vehemently.

"Can't be," she asserted aloud to the walls around her. *Can't be.* She stood up and paced the kitchen. *I would have known.* Her explanation came in torrents. Surely, Maeve wouldn't have died without telling her. That would be too selfish. Of course! It's another Áine. A cousin. But where is she now?

Relieved over her conclusion, she poured herself a cup of tea, grabbed a few biscuits, and hurried back to the journal. The account moved on to chronicle a chance meeting between Maeve and Gearóid FitzGerald, whom she had been dating before she went back up to Dublin. Áine's heart skipped a beat. Muirís's father. The thought made her smile. *Small world here back on Dingle Peninsula.*

Although Gearóid had apparently come often to the house to inquire after Maeve's whereabouts, her mother would only smile and say she had gone away. Unconvinced and worried about her, the young lad had resorted to walking daily near the farm in hopes of catching a glimpse of Maeve. One day he was finally rewarded. Maeve described the encounter from the perspective he had surely taken:

As he walked along the winding river from the strand up to Maeve's farm, he saw a lass dressed in the traditional black garb with a shawl wrapped around her shoulders. Something about the way she carried herself and her manner of walking intrigued him. He trotted along until he was closer.

The lass took no notice of him, as she now stood, watching the salmon making their way upstream. Suddenly, she sat down on a large rock and started to weep. Though positioned on the other side of the field, Gearóid could hear her. Out of an innate goodness and concern, he walked in her direction to see what ailed her and offered his services.

When he was close enough to call out to her, "Dia dhuit," said he. "Are you hurt, Lass?"

Not looking up at the sound of the voice, she only hid her face more deeply within her shawl. "Ah, to be free like those salmon," said she. "Beyond all hope am I," she added, her voice forlorn. "Leave me now." She turned her head away from him lest he recognize her.

"Is there nothing I can do?" he persisted as he walked more closely, despite her reluctance to speak with him.

"All is lost. I've done everything to myself that can be done," and with that, she abruptly stood and hurried through the field, away from the enquiring eyes of Gearóid.

He felt a great sadness well up within him as he watched her walk away. Her despair touched him deeply inside. Was there no one who loved the woman who could help ease her pain? "Ah, the poor craythur," he murmured, as he shook his head.

A sharp cry suddenly rang out, and as Gearóid looked on, he saw the woman wasn't alone at all, but was carrying a baby in her shawl.

"Whist! Hush now!" He could hear the woman appealing to the wee child.

As he stood and watched the woman walk slowly away with the crying babe, he noticed something again very familiar about the way she walked that made him stop dead in his tracks. It was she! 'Twas Maeve herself! And with child!

He clapped himself on the side of the head. "Of course, you bloody eegit! It is Herself, and I have left her forlorn, with child, and she too proud to tell me a t'all." Without thinking, he sprinted after her.

"Maeve! Maeve!" he called out to her as he ran to catch up. "Don't be running away from me, love! Stop now!"

She continued resolutely on—despite his pleas.

When he caught up with her, he whirled her around to face him, and removing the shawl from around her head, he implored, "Maeve! Why have you hidden this from me?" He lifted her downturned face up towards him. "Did ye think me such a monster that I would not support you?" He took her hand in his and added, "I could—would—never forsake you."

As Gearóid gazed down into the unhappy woman's face, his heart broke when he saw her sea-green eyes filled with tears of shame. "'Tis nothing to be ashamed of Maeve."

Maeve withdrew her hands and turned away from him. "It's not as it seems, Gearóid," she said sadly and looked away.

"'Tis obvious what has happened," he responded, as he turned her around again. "Will you let me see the child?"

Without waiting, he opened the shawl enough to see a wee flock of red hair as a little girl came into view. "Ah, she's lovely!" he exclaimed. "Sure, she has your cheekbones!" he added in admiration.

Maeve quickly covered the child's head and tucked her into the protective custody of her shawl. Again, she turned away from him, before weeping silently, her body heaving waves of anguish in every direction.

"Ah there, now, love," Gearóid murmured. "No need for tears, no need a t'all."

Maeve only continued. "You don't understand," she said through increasing sobs.

Gearóid placed his hands gently on the bereft woman's shoulders, and again turning her around toward him, said softly, "Indeed, I do, Maeve. Indeed, I do." Kneeling down in front of her, he asked her solemnly, "Maeve, darlin', will you have me? Will ye and the baby have me? We'll make a fine family, I can promise you that."

Maeve turned away from his outstretched arms and responded in a despondent tone, "No, you do not, Gearóid. You don't understand at all." Her continuing *sobs told him all he needed to know of her particular feelings.*

He stood a moment, not knowing how to think. Pools of insights flooded through him, explaining her cooling off after she went up to Dublin last. She was never quite the same again, though they had spent all their time together when she finally returned home from university, even planning to be married. That summer they had spent together she had seemed distant, despite their physical communion. He didn't want to imagine the details of what came before in her life while she was away from him.

Gearóid spoke in an unfaltering voice. "Maeve," he started. When she didn't turn around, he repeated her name and beseeched her to turn around.

"Maeve, haven't I loved you me' whole life? I'll not turn away from you now in your moment of need." He put his arms around her and the babe. "Marry me, Maeve," he pleaded. "Do you not know that I would love you and the wee one?"

The only response he received was her continued sobbing. "Hush now, grá mó chroí," he urged. "You don't want to upset the wee bairn."

Although he waited for what felt like hours, she never looked up, never met his soulful gaze, never uttered the words he so longed to hear. Her silence was his penance—a long, loveless life without her.

At last, he walked slowly away, counting each step, hoping against hope that she would call out to him and ask him back. When he finally turned around to look at her, she and the babe were gone.

Áine was so choked up with remorse over the tragic tale that she closed the book. *My God. Enough for one sitting.* She decided to go out to the kitchen and let her reading sink in before continuing any farther. Refreshing her cup of tea, she went to sit outside in the sun. She gazed out over the field above the house, trying to imagine the scene she had just read being played before her. Such a strong woman was Maeve. But why didn't she marry Gearóid, she wondered. She must have loved him. He certainly loved her. Áine recalled her own encounter with old Gearóid FitzGerald in his fish shop. Just the very thought of Maeve's death—even after all the years that had passed between them—brought instant tears to his eyes.

Her thoughts ebbed and flowed with the waves below. The story just didn't make sense to her. After all, Maeve was known for always being with a man. Different explanations streamed through her. Suddenly, she stiffened. *Unless.* She thought some more. *Had there been someone else?*

Áine mulled over that question for a bit. Maeve had been rather notorious for having several men waiting out on the sidelines—in case the predominant one didn't work out. Had this been a pattern stemming back to this early period in her life?

The actions described in the journal conflicted with what Áine knew of Maeve's personality. It was not like her, after all, to choose honour over self-advancement. This latter was a trait for which she was widely known among the family for possessing—particularly having a child to look after. Why didn't she jump at the offer to be taken care of and loved? She never seemed to tire of accepting marriage proposals later when her life wasn't working out exactly as she had hoped. Certainly, the existence of a child never inhibited her from taking up with someone new, as her many children with different fathers attested. No, Maeve was not one for remaining solitary. She always had a man on her arm and pronounced proudly that she preferred it that way. The choice to remain alone seemed to Áine quite out of character for her aunt. It was all utterly perplexing. *Inexplicable.*

She returned to her reading.

> *She came and took her away today. I don't know*
> *whether to laugh or to cry.*
> *Poor wee thing. I have nothing to offer her. Is she*
> *not better without me?*
> *And now I'll start again—far, far away from here,*
> *as will she,*
> *though living different lives.*

My God! Áine gasped. *She gave her daughter away.* That's why she hadn't heard about her. She had been adopted into another family. She leaned far back in her chair and stared up at the ceiling, trying to piece together the various parts of the puzzle.

Leafing through the various entries, Áine discovered one poignant inclusion toward the end.

> *And now, as I slip inevitably into the next world,*
> *I leave behind my past and her future.*
> *She will return to her home—here—to the very*
> *house where she was born—where her fate awaits*
> *her.*

The journal slipped from Áine's hands to the floor. She sat stupefied over those last words. *Then it is me? I am the Áine here?* She shook her head and reread the entry. Then it struck her. *That's it!* She figured that Maeve was ill when she returned to Ireland that last summer. Her brain was literally deteriorating. She must have made her will when her mind was not functioning properly, and no family member around to help flush out her distorted memories and half-truths.

She realized that Muirís wouldn't have known that she was the niece—rather than the long-lost daughter. Mulling over some of their past conversations, she noted that he had referred to her several times as Maeve's daughter. Surely, Maeve in her state had mixed her up with her own daughter in those last days. Muirís, as the solicitor to the will, mistakenly assumed she was to be the recipient, since there was no other identifiable Áine in the family.

Sitting upright in her chair, she looked sadly around the sitting room that had started to feel like her home. But it isn't my home, really, she thought. It's the other Áine's. In all good conscience, she realized she would need to locate her—somehow. But where could the other Áine be living? she wondered.

She returned to the journal to discover any clues to the mystery of the vanishing child's identity and location. Instead, she discovered the truth of her own early life.

When Áine didn't turn up for dinner at the appointed hour, Muirís went up to the house to collect her. He arrived to the sound of soft sobs. Rushing in, Muirís tried to console her. "Ah, Áine, there now, 'twill be all right," he said in an as soothing a tone as he could manage, as he stroked her head and took her into his arms, where she collapsed sobbing.

"It all makes sense to me now," she cried. "If only I knew before she, she . . . " She broke down in an endless stream of tears again.

"No wonder I always felt as if I didn't belong—I *didn't*! I always felt as if I were adopted—turns out I was! Oh, why didn't anyone tell me?"

Áine realized that this new insight about her own origins explained why she never really felt part of her family in Prince Edward Island. She had always felt like an *outsider*. Instead, she harboured a deep connection to Ireland and the family home that always kept her pining to return for reasons—until *now*—had remained unfathomable to her. Had she not been told by her grandmother her entire life, that some day she would return to the family home and seek her fate as the incarnation of Áine of Old? Never had she thought it would be for this reason.

The anguished woman paced the room. "But if Maeve were my mother, then who exactly was my *father*?"

Muirís dropped his eyes to the table.

"Doesn't she identify him, Muirís? You've read the entire account. Surely she mentions him directly!" Áine stared at him, desperate for an answer that would quell the rising tide of fear within her.

Muirís turned away, unable to meet her demanding, yet wildly desperate expression. Finally, he responded. "She doesn't say, exactly."

His cagey response increased her level of anxiety. She paced the floor without answering. Suddenly, turning to him, she demanded, "Did she ever tell you, Muirís?"

He looked at the floor. "No, no, Áine, she never discussed it with me."

Suddenly a horrible thought overcame her.

"Maeve . . . my, my, my, mother . . . your father? Oh, my God! Could it be?"

She stared wildly at him with widened eyes—now brimming with horror.

"Oh, my God, Muirís! You're not, not, actually, not, my *brother*, are you?"

Muirís flushed a deep red, before abruptly turning away. "Well, the thought has crossed my mind more than once since reading the account, I must admit," he said, his tone evoking tumultuous seas of anxiety. "After reading the journal, I thought it a possibility," his deep despair flooding his voice. He turned to her and grabbed her in his arms. "Sure, Áine, isn't that the very reason I stayed away from you—when, when, I found myself falling in love with you?"

Áine turned away. "I thought it was due to Diarmuid's presence," she replied stiffly. "But you made love to me— not knowing for sure whether we were actually siblings!"

Suddenly, she clutched her stomach and announced anxiously, "I think I'm going to be sick!" Áine rushed to the restroom, where she promptly expunged all of the anguish raging inside her.

"Ah, now, Áine, don't take it so badly," Muirís urged her, as he pulled back her hair while she remained hanging over the toilet. "I'm sure there's an explanation. Surely, we cannot be siblings. Maeve would have told me." He straightened up. "For what it's worth, I read that section after, em, after."

"Don't even say it. You shouldn't be in here," she said.

"Ah, well," he sighed, with a toss of his head, "Sure, we

all have our own ways of digesting too much, whether 'tis alcohol or difficult *emotions*."

She turned to him. "Well, *are* we, or aren't we?"

Looking immeasurably sad, Muirís looked down at her as he helped her to her feet. "I really wish I knew," he said tossing his head. "I'd just like to know definitively whether the way I have been feeling about you is, is— *permissible*, so." He wiped her face gently with a cloth. "In either case, I am meant to love you."

"Oh, *God*, Muirís! Don't even mention it! And, and, and, oh God, the other night!" she cried, shoving her head back over the toilet again as tears and bile dropped to the water below.

He tried to console her. "Ah, Áine, I'm sure there's no need to take it like this. In my heart of hearts," he proclaimed, "I am sure we are only very distantly related." He gazed at her as he gently pulled her up and again dapped at her face. "You're just in shock, poor Lass. After all, we have proof—the fate in my family annals." He added more to himself than to her. "It wouldn't make sense. You and I were meant to be together—of that I am sure."

He stood still and declared in a determined voice, "I leave you with this thought." He reached out to take Áine's hand in hers. "Maeve would never have brought you here, otherwise. Sure, it was a foregone conclusion in her mind that you and I would fall in love. She told me as much." Giving her a quick hug, he left the house without another word.

CHAPTER SIXTEEN
THE STORY OF ÁINE

SCÉAL ÁINE

ALTHOUGH ÁINE PROMPTLY DECIDED TO RING up her mother, Eithne, she didn't know exactly what she wanted to say. She wasn't even sure whether to address her as her mother at all, so confusing were the latest chain of events for her.

"Em, hi Mum," she started, her tone hesitant.

"Is there an emergency, Áine? 'Tis a terrible luxury to be ringing up across the Atlantic," admonished Eithne.

"I have my reasons, Mum."

"Has something happened to you?"

"Yes, actually, something has. Something *earth-shattering*."

"Now, you're not getting married is it, Áine? Sure, you've only just landed there. Haven't I always told you, girl, to wait at least two years before plunging?" the older woman lectured. "You watch those Irish men. They'll charm the pants right off you, they will."

Deciding to avoid small talk regarding the vagaries of men—one of her mother's favourite topics—she plunged right into the depths of her personal history. "Mum, I know."

"Ah, sure, I know you know all this, but 'tis better to remind you, than have you race into something you might later regret," she pressed. She stopped a moment before sputtering anxiously, "My God, Áine! You don't *have* to get married, now do you, child?"

"Like Maeve?" asked Áine rather icily, despite her best intentions to the contrary. "Did you dole out the same advice to her?"

"Sure, she listened to no one," replied Eithne, her tone replete with scorn. She added a hasty, "God rest her soul. But what are you on about Maeve for? 'Tis you we're discussing."

"Actually, it has to do with both of us—Maeve as well as me. Mum, I know."

"You know what?" asked Eithne, her voice clipped.

"I know who I am."

"I knew this would happen with you traipsing back there. Didn't I warn you to stay here and get along like a good Canadian? So now, I suppose, you have come to identify with Ireland now, is it?" Eithne scolded.

Áine sighed. "No, Mum. I'm referring to my birth. I know. *Everything.*"

This admission was greeted by silence on the other end of the line. Áine waited for some response, some acknowledgement.

Nothing.

"Please tell me what you know," Áine pleaded.

"Never you mind *that*, now, Áine. There's nothing to talk about. It's all behind us now."

"I would really like to know more details." She waited.

"Leave the past in the *past*, Áine." It sounded as if Eithne were going to hang up.

Áine persisted. "I know you always say that, Mum, but I can't. I need to know."

More silence.

"Mum?"

"'Tis only a circumstance of birth."

Again, Áine persisted. "Yes, Mum, but it is *my* circumstance of birth I would like to discuss with you. There is no one else who can tell me about my birth mother and father."

Eithne responded, "*I* am your mother. It was all arranged before you were even born. There's nothing more to say. She didn't *want* you. *I* did. These things can't be helped. You should be grateful you have a mother at all—never mind, mourning the loss of one you never had."

The words cut a deep ravine through Áine's heart. She wiped away stinging tears, grateful only that Eithne was not physically present to see her, since she detested displays of emotion in anyone. "*Signs of weakness*," she would proclaim in disgust.

When Áine didn't answer, Eithne continued with her rant, "She gave you *away*, Áine. To me. You're *my* daughter. And I'll not lose you now to *circumstances* of history."

Áine cried silent tears as she listened to her mother/ aunt plead with her to relinquish the past.

"She's gone, Áine. There's nothing to resurrect."

Despite her instincts, Áine responded, "But I feel so bad! I was so nasty to her the last time we spoke! She was always so hard on me."

"Ah, never you mind, girl. She was a nasty piece of works herself, that one, God rest her soul. Didn't she always need to have her way? No one mattered to her as much as she did to herself." Eithne concluded as if her statement would put the matter to rest, "You're better off forgetting her. Now, how's the weather there? Rain and more rain, I suppose, is it?"

"But, Mum, I am living in her house!" retorted Áine.

Eithne didn't skip a beat. "You don't *belong* there! Pack up and leave it all behind. Come back *Home* now!"

Áine responded through more tears, now freely flowing and unrestrained. "That's the problem. I don't know where I belong—or to whom. I must stay and find out who I am, or at least, who I *was*, or might have been."

"Nonsense! Utter nonsense!" Eithne thundered. "You belong here—and to me."

Áine tried one last time before ending the heated exchange. "So will you help me, Mum, and tell me all you know?"

"No, I will *not*, Áine! I'll not raise the dead that deserve to remain dead and buried."

Eithne's tone triggered in Áine visual memories of her mother bristling as she scowled fiercely. While Áine usually shrank from pursuing her point, this one was simply too important—wrath or no wrath. "All right, Mum, I guess it's a journey of self-discovery I must embark on all alone," said Áine sadly, but firmly. "I had hoped you could help guide me in the right direction."

She shot back, "You're her daughter, all right, as *stubborn* as she was. Look where it got her! I have no more to say on this subject!" Eithne slammed down the phone on the girl's ear.

Áine ran all the way down to the beach, before bursting

into tears, where she then paced the strand amid a storm brewing from the west. The sky had transformed into a stubborn wall of impenetrable grey; white-capped waves pounded the shore, while bands of rain lashed out at everything in their path. Even so, the raging storm seemed a minor outward manifestation of the utter turmoil raging within her. She wondered whether the howling winds might offer any consolation to her own inner tempest.

Grief-stricken and overwhelmed, Áine stumbled through the now blinding rain along the shore as she made her way to her special place—the one she had shared as a girl with Maeve. *Maeve. The mother I never knew.* Her thoughts turned to her mother, Eithne—*my other mother*—she forced herself to acknowledge.

"Now I understand the reality lurking beneath her resistance," she said in a sorrowful tone to the waves lashing the shore. She felt lashed herself by a past she never knew. She couldn't figure out why they had kept the truth from her. Didn't she have the right to her own past, after all—*the right to know.*

Snippets of their heated exchange over her inheritance now pounded through her head:

"I fail to understand why you are bothering at all about this funeral of yours back there. Maeve has already been mourned, and I'm not sure there's anyone who has any extra tears to waste shedding on her, either there or here, God forgive me for saying, even if she were my sister. I certainly do not."

The exchange felt as powerful to Áine, now walking through the rain, as when it had transpired back in Prince Edward Island. She shook her head in sorrow. At last, she realized the full import behind her mother's reference to Maeve losing her heart in Ireland. Surely, a life-altering event for her—*and for me.*

As more of Eithne's response to the inheritance poured through Áine, now understood it in a new light. "No wonder," she muttered to the winds around her, "she kept referring to herself when I told her about my inheritance."

"Oh, dear God," muttered Eithne, "She's *still* interfering in my life—even from beyond the grave."

"Who is, Mum? Aunt Maeve? But how?" Áine responded.

"Damn that woman," Eithne sputtered.

"I don't understand. What does this have to do with you?"

"Nothing and everything," she snipped.

Áine again spoke aloud, addressing the raging tempest around—and within—her. "Quite a bit apparently." So now, I have my question finally answered, she thought sadly to herself. It all felt so tragic, so unnecessary—the wounded and scarred feelings all around.

The memory of Eithne's statements refueled the tears welling in Áine's eyes. She silently addressed her mother, Eithne. *I wasn't really yours, Mum. No wonder you hate to look back, as you always say. You couldn't face your own shame over participating in the complicity.*

Áine was angry enough at her mother that she found it difficult to put aside her feelings to consider how Eithne must have certainly felt over the prospects of losing Áine to her own past. No wonder she was so vehement about focussing on the future, she realized. The past to her threatened everything—and everyone—she loved, *including me.*

Áine slowly walked back along the shore. Bits of her mother's words flowed through her head as she sorted through them, making new sense of their meaning. She now understood the reasons for her insistence on identifying as Canadian, rather than Irish. With a sad shake of her head, she surmised her mother—and most likely, Maeve—were terrified that she would find out the lie they had all been living.

Suddenly, she stopped. The odd condition that Maeve stipulated about writing an account of her life assumed new meaning for Áine. *Of course! I was to discover for myself a past neither she—nor Mum—could bring themselves to tell me.* No wonder they never really spoke of their pasts in Ireland, she realized. She shook her head over her assumption that it was an Irish thing.

"Surely, you wouldn't spend time digging up the rather sordid past of Maeve, would you? Leave it buried."

Eithne's words now resonated for Áine on a completely different level than when she first had heard them. New layers of insight swirled round her thoughts, before landing sharply in a new reality. Surely, this omission was the reason for her mother's indifference to her salmon preservation work—it would re-connect her back to Maeve, her grandmother, to Ireland—to *right here.* Maybe she was even trying—in her way—thought Áine, with a tinge of sarcasm, as she perceived the irony inherent in the situation—to *protect* me.

She shook her head in wonderment as new insights poured into her, illuminating her vision. She surmised, as well, that her grandmother—most likely sworn to secrecy—relied on her mystical and obtuse predictions to prepare her for the day she would meet her past. The constant refrain—*the journey forward begins with a step back*—assumed new levels of resonance. *No bloody wonder,* she thought, as she shook her head vehemently.

Áine rushed back to the cottage, completely drenched to the skin, but oddly warm inside. Feeling a peaceful lull of calm drift through her, she tried to make sense of it. The healing power that comes with self-knowledge, she reasoned. She harboured the feeling that she had only breached the surface—much more lurked in subterranean depths.

Once she hung out her wet clothes over the blissfully warm Aga, she made a pot of tea and sat down to think by the fire. The rising feeling within, now surfaced as she realized that she simply could not expect support from someone who had no support to give. With a tinge of remorse, she concluded that her journey back—to her past—was her own, for herself only.

The formulation made her think of Muirís. She recalled his account of the *past*—a common past they shared—a fate—he called it. "*Our fate to re-live the love of our common ancestors,*" he had said. She stirred the fire, refilled her teacup, and thought some more. Her mother's reference to the FitzGerald's ancestry surfaced, as she tried to recall that bit of their conversation.

"Quite a high and mighty group altogether, so they think," she had said. "Now that's a group who lives buried in the past—imagine putting on airs because your ancestors came from France hundreds of years ago."

Áine tried to get a grip on the situation. Whatever his pedigree, and their *common past* as he called it, she decided the first step was to uncover the roots of her own.

She sighed heavily, the weight on her shoulders bowing down her spirit. She couldn't pursue her strong feelings for Muirís until she knew precisely how they were related. And she wouldn't know that—until she discovered the identity of her birth father.

Rather than wallow in self-pity, she resolved, *I must act decisively.* Through tear-rimmed eyes, she scouted through the house, looking for clues. Knowing Maeve had been fond of photos, Áine hoped there might some old ones lurking about that might reveal some clue to the fellow's identity. He figured he was the only one who might be willing to share the details surrounding her birth.

Searching through a box of old decaying photos, she found a hefty collection of ones of Maeve, each time arm in arm with a different male companion. She shook her head as she gazed from one to the other, assuming Maeve had sent them to her mother periodically through her life. *Wonder what Grandma thought about that,* she thought.

Opening a box she found under the bed, Áine sorted through its contents—until she came across a photo of Maeve in Dublin in front of the Shelburne Hotel. She looked almost regal in her elegant attire, locked arm in arm with a rather distinguished-looking man in a dark suit. Both seemed so happy. Áine stared at the man in the photo, trying to figure out if he could possibly be her father. She sighed. *It was so hard to tell.* Although the fellow seemed to have reddish hair, she really couldn't distinguish any other salient traits.

Dublin. She sat staring at the photo. Suddenly, she thought of Elizabeth. As Maeve's best friend, and someone who had only recently revealed the extent of her knowledge about Maeve's romantic past, Áine reasoned that she might know something about the matter.

In that moment, she resolved to go up to Dublin to confront Elizabeth. Standing up, she firmly crossed her arms over her chest as she stared out the window down to the sea below. *I bet she knows <u>everything</u>*.

Áine realized she had the perfect pretext. After all, her meeting with the Minister for Fisheries & the Environment had been re-scheduled, so she decided then and there to combine purposes. After confirming the new date for her meeting with the Minister, she rang up Elizabeth, announcing she would be coming to Dublin in the next few days for a meeting. Could they meet for tea?

"Why, Áine! How utterly delightful!" exclaimed the older woman.

"Shall we meet, say, at the *Shelburne*?" asked Áine, knowing it was Maeve's favourite place to be seen on a late afternoon while in Dublin.

"I would love to meet for tea, of course, Áine, but you really must come stay with me."

Áine hesitated. "I don't know." After hemming a bit, she added, "I need to keep my schedule clear in order to meet with the Minister, so I thought we should just arrange to meet for tea," she said faltering, before drumming up the courage to add, "I was hoping to talk with you about Maeve."

"We can speak of Maeve for as long as you'd like here," she said firmly, as if the matter were settled, then added, "I'll make us a lovely tea."

"Perhaps next time, Elizabeth. They've already booked me at the hotel. Tomorrow, so—teatime?" Áine had decided ahead of time that it might be easier if she met Elizabeth in a public place, in order to keep a lid on the difficult exchange that would most likely ensue between them. She was so hoping that the older woman would prove to be a friend to her as much as she had been to Maeve. She could use both some clarity and some consolation from someone who cared about her and truly understood her situation.

The next afternoon found the two women seated across from one another in the vast tearoom of the grand Shelburne. After exchanging some pleasantries, Áine launched right in. "Elizabeth, I wanted to talk with you to seek your help."

Elizabeth touched her hand. "Of course, dear. How may I help?"

"Who was my father, Elizabeth?"

Elizabeth redrew her hand, staring wildly, as if she shocked by an electrical current. "Whatever do you mean, my dear?" She attempted as hard as she could to fain ignorance over the question she understood to serve as the ineluctable opening of Pandora's box.

Áine stared at the woman. She was clearly hiding something, judging by the trembling of her hand, as she continued to take sip after sip of her tea. *I bet she wishes right now that it were a dram of something much stronger!* "You didn't know then, about the existence of the journal Maeve kept during her last year?"

Elizabeth's eyes widened. "No, not exactly," she said with obvious concern.

Áine leaned back and chuckled. "Well, she *spills the beans*, as we say in Canada."

Elizabeth decided to proceed cautiously in order to tease out the level of knowledge the girl might have of the past. "And what beans would those be, Áine? Black or green?" she added, trying to make a joke.

Áine looked at the woman with a slight tinge of disappointment. "Red, actually, as I have red hair, and Maeve did not, I think it's safe to assume that my birth father sports a flock of red hair—most likely, curly, at that."

She gazed over at Elizabeth, who was now officially trembling from head to foot. Áine pressed on. "I am her daughter, which I suspect you well knew, but didn't want to raise the dead. I can well understand, but I hope you can appreciate the fact, Elizabeth, that I need to know more."

Elizabeth gazed over at the girl. "Áine, dear, are you truly ready to face your past?" She stopped. "There's no reason for you to do so, you know. The past could lie in the past."

Áine displayed her impatient attitude. "That's what my other mother said. But I am, Elizabeth, I am more than ready," she added. "Now I realize why I was asked to write Maeve's story. For her story is *mine* as well."

Elizabeth sighed, and patted the younger woman's hand. "Ah, my dear, it is the story of many an Irish girl who grew up with dreams of perfect love, fell for the wrong man, and had her heart destroyed in the process."

But Áine was not to be diverted from her mission by anthropological analysis. She leaned over towards Elizabeth. "Who is he, Elizabeth? Surely, you know."

Elizabeth hesitated.

"Why the hesitation?" Áine pressed.

"Well, Áine," Elizabeth started, "He is a *famous* figure here in Ireland. And depending on how you handle it, you could destroy his reputation and his career."

"Like he did Maeve's?" Áine taunted. "I'm surprised that you would be so considerate of the man." Áine couldn't refrain from adding, more than aware that her tone was overly snide, "And you the anthropologist of women in Irish culture?"

"Well, now, Áine, I wish it were so simple, but it is not. I had warned your . . . your . . . Maeve, of the consequences to her of getting involved with him, as he was a man betrothed—as well as a public figure." She sighed, and leaning back in her chair, looked away into the distance. "Nothing could stop Maeve from getting what she wanted when she put her mind to it."

"Then why didn't he marry her?"

Elizabeth placed her hand over the disconcerted younger woman's. "What Maeve failed to understand, my dear, was the power of *pedigree*."

"Did he not love her, then?" Áine asked, her tone sad.

Elizabeth offered a vigorous, assenting nod. "Indeed, he did, Áine. He was *mad* about her."

"Then why?" pursued Áine.

"Ah, Áine, your mother, . . . em, that is, Maeve—" she corrected herself, not knowing exactly how the young woman was feeling about this new relation, and started again. "She was beautiful; she was beguiling; she had all of the qualities a man could want in a woman, but . . . " Her voice trailed off, not wanting to name the dreaded truth.

Áine sat upright in her chair, waiting for Elizabeth to finish. "But?" she helped the older woman along.

"She was *not* one of *us*—the Anglo-Irish, that is. She was a country woman, a *Kerry* woman of all things!" she said smiling, as if Áine would understand the contempt behind the declaration. Realizing that the young woman before her did not, she attempted to explain. "Maeve simply had no *pedigree* that he could parade in public.

If anything, she would have been an *embarrassment* to him," she added. Her involuntary gasp conveyed her regret over her impulsive statement.

The admission infuriated Áine. "An *embarrassment*, was she?" she flared. "Maeve was good enough to serve as a fantasy, meeting his sensual needs, but she wasn't polished enough to bring round in public?"

Elizabeth stammered, before blurting out the truth. "Actually, that was it." She sat back, sorting through her thoughts a moment, before clarifying. "Maeve was a highly spirited person whose passion for life and for love surpassed any sense of *tact* and social graces she might have possessed." She sipped some tea and cleared her throat, before sitting up rigidly in her seat. "Of the *latter* trait, I am sorry to say, she had *little*, if *any*, tact *whatsoever*. She said whatever came into her head—without caring about the particular rhetorical or social situation at hand."

Áine sat there, biting her lips. "Let me make sure I understand this," she said, fuming. "This socially righteous fellow, who had impregnated a woman madly in love with him, simply recused himself from any responsibility towards her and the child—me," she added with particular emphasis, "because Maeve didn't show the requisite amount of decorum?"

Elizabeth nodded. "It's more complicated than that, *certainly*, Áine, but you *are* starting to comprehend the mindset of the social elite here in Dublin," she said. "No one gets ahead here, particularly in business or politics, *without* having an *established* pedigree. In order to assume a level of social, political, or economic prominence, one simply *must* possess the social status to justify such a position. One *inherits* pedigree, or one *marries* into it. Best if one procures both."

Áine felt her cheekbones burst into uncontrollable flames as she lashed out. "Did you Dubliners learn nothing from the domination of the English over Ireland these past eight hundred years? I thought those shackles had been removed nearly one hundred years ago when we gained our political independence."

Elizabeth gazed at the woman, her look immeasurably sad. "However unfortunate for Ireland, my dear, we *are* the English, and if not them, the French before them." She gazed at Áine. "We have remained largely a *distinct* class—even to this day."

She paused before concluding, her voice genuinely sincere, "Poor Maeve, who thought her beauty and charm would gain her membership to the club." She looked over at Áine. "I tried to warn her," she recounted, as she twisted her lace handkerchief in her hand. "I was so *afraid* for her." She shook her head. "But she was so convinced that love would conquer *all!*" She looked away and mumbled, "That it did, all right. It was almost her *downfall.*"

Áine didn't know what to say with so many mixed emotions surging inside her. She sipped her tea before responding. She tried a different tack. "Tell me, Elizabeth. Did he love her?"

Elizabeth looked away, before settling her gaze back on Áine. "She liked to think he did," she said slowly, "And I do think he must have loved her—in his *own* way." She sipped her tea before elaborating. "But he was not a man to lose everything else he had in his life to surrender to the *lure* of love." She smiled at the now visibly upset girl. "Is *any* man?" she asked, almost rhetorically.

"I'd like to think so," Áine snapped.

Elizabeth looked at her as she shook her head. "Yes, *there's* that *romantic* streak that guided the actions of your mother—Maeve." She stopped, thinking she had gone too far. Resorting to her usual analytical approach to such matters, she continued, "As the case with most men, he felt that everything in his life must support his career goals." She sipped her tea before continuing. "Your mother satisfied his desire for *passion,* but when it became *complicated* . . . ," She faltered, trying to find the right words.

Áine glared at her. "Oh throw tact to the bloody wind, Elizabeth. Do tell me what you really think," she snarled, before adding, her tone bitter, "For once in your life, be utterly honest with a fellow human being—without worrying about the social implications of your opinion." She stopped a moment before continuing. "Just name the deed. No. Allow me. When Maeve got pregnant," she said, glaring at Elizabeth, who could not bring herself to even utter the word, "He dumped her." She shook her head, and turning to Elizabeth, continued in a haughty tone, "Although that is how we would say it in Canada, I should think over here, you would say that Maeve was no longer helpful in advancing his career aspirations."

Elizabeth gazed at her, and ignoring the obvious sarcasm of the younger woman, said in a tone that revealed her sense of wonderment, "Whilst I do understand your elevated level of outrage, I must say that, in this regard, you take after Maeve in saying *precisely* what you think. Despite everything we have discussed, at times, it can be a most *admirable* quality."

Áine decided to pursue her line of inquiry. "Did he love her, Elizabeth?"

The older woman looked at the younger one with sympathy. "He did, Áine. He did, indeed." She shook her head. "But as I said before, love was not enough to give up *everything* for her." She said nothing for a moment or two, before deciding to proceed. "After all, although she didn't satisfy him in ways Maeve did, his highly pedigreed and politically well-positioned fiancée opened the particular doors for him to which he had sought access."

Áine stared hard at the woman. "Who is he, Elizabeth?"

"Ah, now, Áine," she replied, looking away.

"Tell me who he is," she repeated.

Elizabeth said nothing.

"For God's sake, Elizabeth!" Áine implored. "As my mother's dear friend, tell me who my father is—please!" She stared at her with absolute agony. "Oh, why won't anyone tell me the identify of my birth father?"

Elizabeth glanced at the pleading woman, before looking away in shame. "It's more *complicated* than that," she said, averting her glance. "Even for her, I *cannot* risk—" She stopped herself from saying too much.

Áine stared at the woman, her green eyes looking more like icebergs than warm summer seas. "I see what you were trying to tell me," she said. "I see how pedigree works now. You all protect one another, and your club membership comes before friendship—before love even." She stood up. "That's quite the bond of loyalty to money and power."

Elizabeth broke down in tears. "Oh, Áine. I am so *torn*. I loved your mother so. And I *do* want to help you. But, he, he . . . " she stammered, as she daintily dabbed her eyes with her linen handkerchief.

Áine bent down over her. "He what, Elizabeth? So you know him then. Perhaps well? Whose identity are you hiding? I have a right to know!"

Elizabeth said slowly in between barely audible sobs, "He is my . . . my . . . my . . . *brother*."

"Your *brother*?" Áine repeated. She stood upright to absorb the magnitude of this new information. "No wonder you have a vested interest in protecting him."

Elizabeth wiped away tears that had filled her eyes. "Actually, it is much more complicated than that."

"My God, how can it be more complicated?"

The older woman took a sip of tea to steady herself before responding. She started slowly, "Sit down, dear. I don't suppose you read up on Irish politics."

"Politics?" asked Áine in confusion. When Elizabeth didn't continue, Áine added, "Your brother is someone in politics, then, is he? Someone in the limelight."

Elizabeth coughed. "Em, it's worse than that."

"Jesus, Elizabeth! What can be worse, as you call it, than being in the limelight?"

"Hush, girl! Do you want the entire tearoom to hear you?" Elizabeth looked around, absently smiling and nodding at various people she felt might be noticing the interaction. "He's the centre of attention."

Exasperated, Áine retorted without thinking, "For God's sake, Elizabeth, what is the man—the EU President?"

"No, no, no," she said with a dismissive wave of her hand, realizing that the girl hadn't a clue about European political structures. "That position is more ceremonial than anything."

Áine's eyes widened. "Then what, exactly, is he?"

Elizabeth leaned over and whispered. "He's much more *powerful* than that—he's the bloody *Taoiseach* of Ireland!"

"The what?" Áine almost screeched.

"The *Taoiseach,* dear—the Prime Minister of Ireland." She huffed. "Much more important than a *mere* President—whether of the EU or Ireland."

She stared at the young woman to see if she understood the gravity of the situation. "He runs *everything*. And they would do *anything*—his enemies, that is, to take him down—particularly during these economically trying times."

Áine stared blankly at her, as she felt her knees buckle down from under her. She slumped down in her seat. "Oh, my God! I had no idea!"

Neither woman said anything for several minutes. Finally, Áine reached over to the older woman, whose tears now streamed from her eyes down her cheeks, and asked kindly, "Are you *sure*, Elizabeth? Are you absolutely sure?"

Elizabeth clasped Áine's hand. "I am," she said, her expression weighed down by a sea of sadness. "There is no doubt."

Áine pursued the issue. "Did you know of a fellow back in Kerry to whom Maeve had been close? Could it have been *he*?"

Elizabeth thought for a moment. She then related the story Maeve had told her of a fellow to whom she had returned, when Edward had broken it off with her, before she even realized she was pregnant. "Whilst it is true that she . . . she . . . engaged in *relations* with that Kerry bloke," said Elizabeth, "we ruled him out as a likely suspect based on the date of your birth, as Maeve would have been twelve months pregnant had it been he."

Áine tossed the new information about in her own internally troubled sea. "That means," she said slowly, "that my, Maeve, that is, was *pregnant* when she slept with the Kerryman—Gearóid?"

Elizabeth instantly felt sorry for the girl, deeming that such information was really much too much knowledge about the antics of her mother. "I'm *afraid* so, dear," she said, gently patting the girl's hand, before coming to Maeve's defence, "But she didn't *know* she was pregnant until—*after*—hence the confusion."

Áine sat staring up at the magnificent chandelier that illuminated the room. She slowly shifted her gazed back to Elizabeth. "Well, that's a huge *relief.*"

"Why is that?" the woman asked, confused by Áine's response.

Áine turned to her and smiled. "That means I didn't have sex with my brother."

"My God!" gasped Elizabeth in horror.

"Yes," Áine replied with a chuckle, "It could have been quite messy in trying to figure out the exact nature of the relations should I have gotten pregnant!"

Elizabeth gasped again, obviously overwhelmed by what she was hearing. "I can *assure* you," she said, leaning over closer to Áine, "My brother is your father." She leaned back in her chair and gazed over at Áine. "And he does have red hair—lots of wavy, red locks—like your own."

Áine sat back at this confirmation, gazing at the woman, then leaned forward and asked, "Elizabeth, will you take me to him?"

"Oh, my *dear* girl!" she responded, completely flustered by the request.

"Please, Elizabeth, I just want to see him—just one exchange."

"That's going *too* far—" exclaimed Elizabeth in horror. "Áine, he's the bloody *Taioseach*, for *God's* sake, Girl! If it gets out, it'll *ruin* his career!"

"I don't want to ruin his career, Elizabeth," she said. "I just want to meet my birth father once in my life."

Elizabeth stared at her, saying nothing.

"Please, Elizabeth, please!" Áine pleaded.

Elizabeth stood up to leave. "I'll see what I can do," she responded primly, taking her leave without another word. She had made it almost out of the large room, before suddenly turning on her heels, she scurried back to the table. Leaning over, she whispered to Áine in a tone of genuine concern, "You *understand*, of course, my dear, that any such meeting will require the *utmost* discretion," underscoring her own anxiety through her particular emphasis.

"Of course, Auntie," said Áine, smiling, more than amused by the woman's insistence on social decorum.

"Hush, Áine! Don't be addressing me by that appellation in a public place." Elizabeth stood up abruptly and looked around, carefully scanning the neighbouring tables for any sign of recognition. Once she discovered that no one could have heard their exchange, she sat down and breathed a deep sigh of relief. She leaned over the table towards Áine, and beckoning her close, added, "Now, Áine, this is *precisely* what I mean about tact, decorum, and discretion—three *qualities*, I *must* say, that your mother did *not* possess in the *least*," and gazing out over her reading glasses at Áine, added through pursed lips, "And I'm not so *sure* about *you,* either."

"Oh, not to worry, Elizabeth, I don't plan on going round the country proclaiming my parental bonds," she replied, matching Elizabeth's acrid tone.

"Now, Áine, I think you are taking this news much too *nonchalantly.* I don't think you quite understand what is at *stake* here. My *dear* girl," she proclaimed, before moving even more closely to say in a whisper that Áine barely heard, "He's the *Taoiseach*, for God's sake! *So* much is at stake!" Elizabeth sat back and fanned herself with the menu. Once recovered, she leaned closely again and whispered over to Áine, "Do I have your solemn, your *solemn,* word, Áine, that you will not embarrass him publically in *any* way whatsoever?"

Elizabeth sat turning her napkin in her hand, twisting it ever more tightly as she waited for the girl to respond. Áine watched her a moment, realizing how torn Elizabeth must be feeling. *Poor thing. This must be very hard for her.* She leaned over, and patting the older woman's hand consolingly, whispered back, "I do understand how difficult this must be for you, and I truly appreciate your efforts in my direction." She sat back, nodding. "I will not let you down. I promise to err on the side of discretion."

Elizabeth let out another deep sigh, and with a nervous glance around the room, admitted, "I wouldn't be doing this for you had you turned out to be a *man.* After all, I have made it my life work to support the cause of Irish *women*, so I must—I really *must*—do this for you," she asserted. "You *are*, after all, an Irish woman, with a *pedigree*—albeit, unacknowledged, but nonetheless," she sipped some tea, and holding her head high, added, "one which *cannot* be ignored—despite where you were reared." She waved her hand with a dismissive flourish. "Over *there*, in the Hinterlands," she added in her stiff voice, only to purse her lips in obvious disapproval.

Áine sat upright in her seat, beaming. She smiled at her new aunt, thoroughly delighted at being acknowledged as an Irish woman, rather than as some transplanted, uncultured Canadian. She sensed a new level of connection entering her life, even if the poor woman were only trying to rationalize what must have seemed to her a transgression against her brother. At least Elizabeth didn't refuse her request for help as her own mother—Eithne—she added to herself, had done. This new family link might prove quite interesting.

Elizabeth stood up and announced primly, "I'll arrange a dinner." She thought a moment then said, "Perhaps tomorrow evening—after his talk at the economics summit at Trinity. I'll ring you on your mobile."

Áine stood up as well, and before Elizabeth could respond, she gave the older woman a big hug and kissed her on either cheek. "Thank you!" Áine gushed as Elizabeth stammered, "I see you have acquired some Continental mannerisms."

Áine winked at her and replied chuckling, "Oh, no Auntie, that is a common practice among us uncultured Canadian *Colonists!*"

Elizabeth gasped and pulled back, scolding Áine, "Now that is *precisely* what worries me about you and this impending meeting, young lady! You simply *must* have manners, tact,"

"Decorum and discretion," interjected Áine, offering a mischievous grin. "I know, Elizabeth!"

"You can *assure* me of your commitment in this regard?" asked Elizabeth, her tone haughty.

"Of *course*, Elizabeth!" Áine responded, mimicking her Aunt's tone. "You can count on me—if I can count on you!" she added smiling. "Remember, I have inherited genes from your side of the family, as well."

"*Naturally*, I am a woman of my word!" retorted Elizabeth, rather appalled at the insinuation. Picking up her handbag, she said, "Right, then! I'll ring you when I have made all of the arrangements." As she proceeded to leave, she shot a glance back at Áine and said in her highbrow manner, "I am counting on *our* shared genes for discretion, tact, and decorum to pull us through this unfortunate ordeal."

"Wait!" cried Áine. "What's his name? What's *my* name?"

Elizabeth looked down at the girl. "Pity that—not to know one's own family name. This must be very hard for you," she blurted. "Dillon. You are a *Dillon*, my dear. We go way back. And he, he is Edward. Edward Dillon." With that, she turned on her heels and left the room.

Áine sat back and sipped her tea slowly, as she watched her new aunt leave the room. She then turned her gaze to the people around her enjoying their afternoon tea at the country's most exclusive hotel. "So these are my father's people," she murmured softly to herself. "This is what the fuss is all about."

She called over the server in order to pay the bill, only to discover it had been placed on the family tab. *Imagine having a tab at the country's most prestigious hotel!* She walked slowly past the tables filled with perfectly dressed men and women. *Poor Maeve.* She felt for the poor woman who didn't stand a chance there, since the place seemed the opposite ends of the earth to primeval, Celtic Kerry. Even though I'm excited about my new family connections, I'd still choose love over privilege any day, she thought to herself. With that, she walked with her head held high out into the unadorned, fresh air.

Despite the difficult exchange with Elizabeth, Áine felt elated over discovering the identity of her biological father. *Another great life mystery solved!*

The knowledge of another blood connection to an entire family clan in Ireland—even if they were the *invaders*—she smirked, felt to her like a new set of roots of a healthy plant that continues to grow perpetually outward and down into the soil, thereby maximizing health, through the ever increasing ability to take up additional nutrients. She now had a new, deeply engrained connection, not only to family, but to community and culture, as well. She felt part of something larger, that included her in a fundamental way—*even if the man never acknowledges me in a familial way.*

As she walked through Stephen's Greene, Áine began to wonder about about the man who helped conceive her—his personality, traits, interests, and attitudes. She mulled over the possible reasons why had Maeve so loved him in particular that she had turned down the love and security offered by Muirís' father, Gearóid, whom she clearly had cared enough about to be involved with him, preferring, instead, to remain alone. It didn't make sense to Áine, particularly given what she knew of her aunt's— *mother's*—attested preference for a man constantly at her side throughout the rest of her life.

These questions piqued Áine's interest even more in the personality of this man, now known as her birth father. She felt certain that he could prove to be just the right person to whom to direct all of her questions about Maeve and his relationship with her. She stopped dead on the sidewalk as a sinking suspicion pooled within her. Had he even known about her existence? If so, had he ever followed what became of her? She shook her head, realizing the extent of their interconnections. She was to meet with a member of his own Cabinet! Was this fate playing a hand in her life, she wondered. She meant to find out, one way or the other.

She found herself leaving Stephen's Greene and instinctively heading down the road of the Dáil, home of the Irish Parliament, over which her new father presided. Recognizing the road she had taken, she started walking briskly, almost to a trot, in her eagerness to make her way to the Parliament building. She mused over whether she might even encounter him when walking by. As she stood staring through its stately wrought iron gates in front, she wondered what might happen should they haphazardly run into each other. Would he instantly recognize his own flesh and blood, perhaps augmented by the genetic legacies of the woman he claimed once to have loved beyond anyone else?

The thought so occupied her mind that she decided to spend time next door in the National Library researching the new father and the family from which he—and she—came. Finding herself a seat in the immense reading room, she began researching. She was so deeply engrossed in her reading that time sped by without Áine so much as rising from her chair. Anticipation of their intitial encounter kept her going through hours upon hours of research into the history of his family—and now hers as well. She found herself mechanicially revising her formulations and thoughts as her mind raced, while she waded through the depths of references to him and his—their—family history.

Áine read with wonder how the original family ancestor had come over on the invasion boat with the other
Normans, who had conquered the island a millennium
ago. She chuckled as she did the math, realizing that her
Gaelic Ó'Suílleabháin grandfather would turn over in his
grave if he knew that the paternal side of her ancestry
represented the very people—together with the "Bloody
Brits"—whom his Gaelic family had fought off for all
those hundreds of years. They were certainly a tenacious
bunch, those Celts, she decided. Even today, she realized
they were still resisting an oppression of sorts, though
more self-inflicted than imposed, through voluntary
coercion to the machinations of the EU. She sighed,
wondering whether Ireland would ever learn to liberate
itself from all oppression.

It was quite the family history. Besides being
"granted," *nice euphemism that,* she noted, hundreds of
thousands of acres of land—*belonging of course, to the
vanquished, native Celts*—a significant area of the country was commonly referred to as "Dillon's country,"
due to the family's vast holdings. Ambivalence poured
through her as she read with awe, mingled with disgust,
the list of successive, pedigreed generations with titles
that spanned the political spectrum, from Lords of the
Realm, Viscounts, Barons, and Captains, to Lord Mayor
of Dublin. Some ancestors were even close enough asso-
ciates of Napoleon and Marie Antoinette to have shared
a common guillotine, she noted with a sardonic chuckle.
And now Taoiseach.

A few surprising exceptions in the elite family history
gave her pause that this paternal legacy wasn't completely
antithetical to her own Celtic orientation. Although
they didn't support the French Revolution—spent too

much time partying with Marie, she thought snidely—
some of her ancestors certainly supported the Jacobite
cause in Ireland. She read how they fought alongside
the FitzGeralds—*Muirís would be impressed*—and even
the Ó'Suílleabháin clan to rid Ireland of the English
Protestant-attempted political takeover and massive land
grab. *Maybe those Normans weren't so bad after all, eh,
Granddad?*

Áine sighed as she pondered the implications. If only
Edward had considered this family legacy, he might have
chosen Maeve, viewing her Kerry heritage in a different
light—given the former historical allegiances of both
their family ancestors. She frowned over discovering that
such staunch philosophical righteousness, once exhibited among select Dillon family members, disappeared in
the next generation. When faced with the choice between
losing their lands, money, and power, or religious con-
version, the family chose to support the English and
become Protestant. *Typical.*

Áine sat back in her chair, looking around the vast
reading room. Even with the proud, Celtic legacy of High
Kings—and Queens—of Celtic Ireland in Maeve's blood,
her bloodline didn't measure up against Dillon family
history, she concluded, however reluctantly. She came
to understand her birth father in a new way. With such
imbedded ascendency, he would have gone against his
family history in choosing his passion for Maeve over an
illustrious political career. She attributed his decision to
the life force—the *raison d'être*—that must surge through
his own veins. She wondered whether one could counter
history, particularly, one's own history.

Still, she wanted to like him. She had a difficult time
concluding that the man could only be about power,

prestige, and advancement. She certainly didn't feel like that, and she had his blood running through her—however submerged the influence. She was beginning to see now why Maeve must have liked him. Queen Maeve nicely evidenced those traits herself, recounted Áine sarcastically, dedicating a large portion of her life to economic self-advancement. As much as Maeve shared those attributes with the Dillon family, she nonetheless had possessed a fiery passion that ultimately subdued her power-grabbing instincts—even if it were used often for such purposes other than *love*. They must have been quite the pair, she thought remorsefully—*if only they had been allowed to evolve as a couple*. She shook her head sadly.

Áine sat and gazed over the vast sea of dimly lit tables. People are essentially uneasy mixtures of disharmonious elements, she concluded. Her thoughts shifted to Joyce, surmising that he must have implied the very conclusion she had drawn when he spoke of the nightmare of history invading the present. With a jolt, she realized that the Master had studied right there, perhaps even articulating, at one of the reading tables, his famous assertion in his own considerations of the pervasive power of history on the Irish. Perhaps, she reasoned, it was just a matter of going back far enough, or searching carefully enough to locate hope in those rare moments of existential harmony, of transcending one's given place in the universe. If only Edward had been able to find the link between his family status and that of proud Maeve's history. Would that have made all the difference? To him? To her? *To me?*

Ah, never mind, she thought, as she dismissed the increasing melancholy she felt seeping through her. The past is, well, *passed*. She sat upright in her chair. She had to remind herself that she felt grateful for the course of her life up until that point, as well as for the new knowledge of her ancestry. She tried to subdue the rhetorical questions rising to the surface of her consciousness—no need to wonder how life would have turned out had her birth parents actually formed a family unit. They didn't—*and never would.*

Instead, she decided to focus on just which traits she might share in common with a man whom she had never met—though who helped conceive her. Particularly since she was scheduled to meet and consult with one of his Ministers, she wondered whether they shared any common political philosophies about land, local food, and even cultural preservation, or was he a raging *globalist*? Had he participated in, or actively supported the overdevelopment that resulted in the current economic demise? Since she knew next to nothing about the Irish political scene, she decided to research it. Locating back issues of the *Irish Times*, Áine read accounts of his election and what platform he represented.

To her great relief, she discovered that he had been ambivalent at best about the country's decision to join the EU. There's some hope for him, she thought—*despite his elite background.* Maybe there was more to him than a handsome face, a charming personality, and an established "pedigree"—as Elizabeth was so fond of saying, Áine recalled with a slightly caustic chuckle, that drew Maeve inexorably to him, despite her social status.

Since she still didn't quite know what he looked like, she scanned the society pages to see what the gossips had to say about him. One coloured photo particularly struck Áine. There he was perfectly outfitted in a tux, looking very slick and polished. She immediately recognized him as the same fellow as in the photo with Maeve. *No doubt about it.*

Áine was surprised to learn of his flaming red hair and freckles that hinted at some Celtic genetics, ones, which seemed counter to his "pedigree," she thought a trifle sarcastically. She wondered whether he was a *ciotógach,* as she seemed to be the only left-handed person in the entire family. She sat and stared at him, trying to memorize his every feature, wondering whether his nose, or perhaps the way his lips turned, resembled her own. At least, she now knew what he looked like, and could thus readily identify him in a group of similarly polished politicians she might chance to come across in front of the Dáil. She was determined to see his reaction upon first catching sight of her. Would he find something oddly familiar about her? Would he know her at all?

At last, Áine stood and stretched, shifting her gaze from the past to the present. In her excitement over the news, she had nearly forgotten to prepare for her meeting with her father's colleague, the Fisheries Minister. She focussed on searching for references to him and to his various addresses in Parliament over the issue of encouraging fish farms. She whistled softly, when she read of his repeated pleas to open the coastline to fish farms, claiming they would bring in much needed income to the economy. She folded the newspaper with a slight slap against the table. *I have my work cut out for me.*

She left the library feeling eager to experience the next step in the unfolding story of her identity and the fate of her salmon, as she now referred to them. Her long glance lingered over to the Dáil, in case Himself should—by chance, fate, or sheer synchronicity—be passing along the street at the same time. After a while, with no chance encounter imminent, she hurried down the road toward her hotel, looking forward to the moment when she would at last meet him face to face. But first, she had to remind herself, there was the pressing issue of the wild salmon.

CHAPTER SEVENTEEN

RECONCILIATION

REÍTIGH

PROMPTLY THE NEXT MORNING, Elizabeth rang
Áine to say that her brother would be able to come
to supper that evening, following a keynote address
he was to give at a summit over at Trinity.

"Yes, you mentioned that when we met. What kind
of summit is it, Elizabeth?" asked Áine as innocently as
she could.

"Oh, some sort of panel on the economy. A debate
over *local* vs. *global* economies, I think he said," she
responded. "I hope that doesn't mean I can't get my
Lançome imported from France anymore." She added
with a sigh, "I can't abide by those seaweed creams those
people in the West use."

Áine smiled inwardly as she assured the woman that
if they could get Lançome in the Colonies, she was sure
she would be able to continue procuring it in Brown
Thomas. Elizabeth scoffed over the very idea of buying

such a refined product in the "willywags"—as she referred to Canada. "Surely, a result of the French influence," Elizabeth concluded, her inbred sense of status shaping her attitudes.

Áine laughed and responded with gentle criticism. "Now Elizabeth, are such cultural stereotypes any way for an anthropologist to think?" It's not all ice and igloos you know, over there, and we all don't live on seal blubber." Anticipating her comment would throw the older woman off, she added slyly, "Though I do admit I crave a good seal flipper pie, occasionally—particularly when prepared the Québeçois French way."

"Good *God*! Well, you won't be eating seal pie under *my* roof!" she retorted. "Speaking of which, I must get planning the menu." With that, she rang off.

Áine couldn't believe her good fortune in finding out about the Trinity gathering, which was to occur after her own meeting with the Fisheries Minister. Knowing she had several hours before her appointment, she rushed back to the National Library to read up on the latest economic policies of the administration. She spent her time poring over the most recent report addressing recommendations for solving the country's current economic crisis. She was sure they would come up in the discussion.

She walked with measured steps into the building in which her own father spent his days, wondering whether she might meet him in the hallway, fearful that he would not recognize her. Hoping to avoid realizing her fear, she hurried into the office suite marked, Ministry of Fisheries and the Environment. Showing up ten minutes early, she sat and reviewed the notes she had taken in preparation for the meeting. So much was riding on her ability to convince the Minister to vote against the fish farms.

After a half hour of waiting, she looked up expectantly at the secretary who met her gaze. "So sorry, Dr. O'Connor," she said, "The Minister is still engaged in his meeting over the proceedings later today. Are you able to continue waiting, or will I reschedule?"

Only to happy to continue hanging out in the office, hoping to catch a glimpse of her father, she offered a brief nod. "Not to worry," she said, "I'm happy to wait." She returned to her notes while casting a furtive glance any time someone moved through the office.

After an hour, the secretary stood, and opening the door to an inner office, announced, "The Minister will see you now, Dr. O'Connor."

"Thank you," Áine said politely, as she walked past the woman to the office. The Minister had his back to her as he spoke on the phone. With a brief glance at her, followed by a wave instructing her to sit down, he turned back again to resume his conversation.

Áine took the opportunity to scan the various photographs adorning the walls, looking for Edward among the various groups of esteemed gentlemen shaking hands against different backdrops.

At last, the Minister turned toward her. "Dr. O'Connor, I presume?" He did not extend his hand.

"Yes, Minister," she said, with an unsmiling nod.

"Your own Minister has briefed me on your stance regarding our little matter of propagating fish," he said, as he leaned far back in his swivel chair, while staring at her through what Áine perceived as gleaming eyes.

Áine sat upright in her chair. "We were quite successful at repopulating the wild salmon in Prince Edward Island," she said, meeting his gaze, "a project whose results have inspired the remainder of Atlantic Canada to carry out in each of the provinces."

The Minister sat with his elbows resting on the arms of his chair, while he bounced his fingertips together as if dribbling a basketball. "Of course, your situation over there differs rather significantly from our own here," he announced.

"In which ways, Minister?" Áine arched her eyebrow, as she felt her mouth twist into an inexorable grimace.

He gave a snort. "Well, for one thing, you have almost no population, if you'll forgive me for saying—a paltry hundred thousand or so, isn't it?"

Áine nodded, as she bit the grimace from her lips.

Without waiting for her to respond, he continued. "We're trying to provide salmon, not only to our citizenry of some several million, but to supply the remainder of the EU, over a half *billion* people." Leaning forward in his chair, he took to drumming his fingers of one hand along the hand-carved mahogany desk. "I hardly think that the few wild salmon inhabiting our streams and rivers will handle those amounts, hence our need for massive fish farms." He shrugged. "Besides, we desperately need the income stream from such a venue."

She scanned his expression, knowing all too well that his features, seemingly cast into a cemented frown, would take an act of God—or *Fate*—to loosen the grip of his focus on money.

"Surely, as the Minister for the Environment, as well as of Fisheries, you must know of the research showing the detrimental effects of fish farms, not only on the immediate waters and land, but on the health of the people who consume those fish." She pulled out a folder brimming in articles. "I can leave with you some published articles of my own showing these results."

With a dismissive wave, he turned sideways, leaning back again in his chair. "No time. We have an economic crisis on our hands that must take precedence over a few paltry fish, if you'll forgive me for saying. Our immediate and only concerns are financial." Swinging back, he offered a stern look through stormy eyes. "I don't see how your project research could possibly address our issues and concerns, quite like the Norwegians, with all their oil money, most assuredly can."

She countered his menacing gaze with her own stern reproach. "Actually, Minister, my research does address a fundamental issue germane to your, our, current situation, in quite significant ways. I have been studying your economic policy documents and think I may have something to offer. Perhaps we might discuss these points."

He waved her aside before standing up. "Perhaps another time," he said, "after we have resolved our crisis." With a cursory nod, he said good day, and calling his secretary in to see her out, left the office.

Áine trembled in anger the entire way as she stomped along the long hall, down several flights of winding marble stairs through the castle-like front door, before catching her breath outside. She walked over the several blocks to Trinity College mumbling to herself. "The arrogance of that man!" she said aloud. "And the *ignorance*." She shook her head, now trembling internally for the fate of the wild salmon—as well as for the country. As she entered the magnificent iron gates of the campus, she resolved to continue her struggle against the currents of economic gain, should Ireland once again bow in servitude to yet another submissive role—this time as fish factory to Europe.

Áine's eyes were on Edward as she tried to listen attentively to his address. She felt enraptured by his presence, straining to detect any physical traits they might share. Beyond their curly red hair and freckled faces, she wondered whether his smile or eyes might resemble her own. Such a presence he has, she noted with admiration.

As she continued listening, she mumbled to herself, "Needs to work out some of those notions he is espousing, though." Judging by what he was proposing, she assumed he was unaware of her work in Prince Edward Island. She debated internally over whether she should be bold enough to mention it. She brightened at the thought that she could bring it up in the questions period that was sure to follow. "What have I got to lose?" she asked herself. She grimaced. *Only a father I never knew existed.*

At questions time, Áine raised her hand, requesting to address the Taoiseach. Here's my chance, she thought excitedly, not only to draw his attention, but also to try to present the importance of our work back Over. She realized that the Fisheries Minister would not be sharing the import of her work anytime soon. Gazing around the room, she focussed her attention on the Taoiseach, who had not, to this point, noticed that she would be speaking.

She decided to stand to centre herself in his vision and began, "Mr. Prime Minister, I have spent considerable time studying in great detail your government's report on the state of the economy and the potential for the food '*industry*,' as you refer to it, to create jobs, as well as ease the inflationary concerns over food prices."

The Taoiseach chuckled, as he glanced up from his papers to acknowledge the intrepid, new voice. "Well, that's more than I can say for a host of my colleagues, who have resorted, merely, to scanning the headings!"

The audience tittered as the moderator asked Áine, "Have you a question you would like to address to the Taoiseach?"

"Indeed, I do, though it is more of a comment than a question," she responded, before smiling sweetly at her Prime Minister father.

The moderator looked over at the Taoiseach to secure permission to allow her to continue, to which the Prime Minister waved his arm, smiled, and said in a pleasant manner, "Since the young lady has actually studied the document, I would welcome her input." His gaze registered his curiosity, surprised both by her boldness and sincerity.

Áine directed her attention solely to him, as if there were no others in the room. "If I may, Taoiseach, I would like to suggest an alternative model to the one offered in the government study, one that has worked out quite successfully—both in my former home community in Prince Edward Island, Canada, where I serve as a consultant to Government, and one that is currently taking off, if I may say so, in my new home community on Dingle Peninsula, in Kerry."

Heads turned back in surprise to view firsthand the source of what seemed such *cheeky* arrogance to some, while to others, such outrageous courage to stand up to the Taoiseach.

Quite concerned over the tenor of the woman's statement, the Minister for Fisheries interjected, "I can take this question, as I've already met with the woman."

Knowing that his Minister would never jump in like that unless he were truly worried about damage control, and eager to hear more from this spirited Canadian, the Taoiseach turned to his Minister, and said lightly, "Not at all, William. I'm happy to address the young lady's concerns." Turning his eyes back to her, he said, "We welcome your insights, my dear."

"It's Dr. O'Connor, actually, Taoiseach." She flashed her eyes at him as she smiled.

The Prime Minister stared at her over his reading glasses. She had most definitely focussed his attention. "Indeed, Dr. O'Connor," he acknowledged, returning her smile. "So what have you been doing down there in Kerry, and over in Prince Edward Island that you deem could work for all of us here in Ireland?" He continued to stare at her, wondering just who this woman was and what on earth she had to say that his Ministers could not have considered.

Áine beamed at this small victory, and smiling her most engaging smile at the Taoiseach, she began with great enthusiasm: "At the risk of sounding too dramatic, since these economic times require courageous actions, I would like to suggest an alternative to what your Cabinet has offered, which to our mind, is simply acquiescing to the big players—the global multi-nationals."

She glanced over at the Minister for Fisheries, who was now glaring at her. She hesitated. She shifted her gaze back to the Taoiseach, who noticing her fear, urged her on, "We're all ears, my dear, em, *Doctor*. Do continue."

Clearing her throat, Áine plunged in. "One of the core reasons for the unique success of the famed *Celtic Tiger* economy was recently discussed by a Trinity professor who sits in this audience." Heads turned to gaze at him, while he nodded at Áine, surprised at her acknowledgement of him.

She continued. "What he pointed out was that Ireland had enjoyed tremendous economic success, not as a result of catering to big business, but rather, because the Irish themselves created a *self-contained* economic model. In other words, the Irish bought up land, developed it with the help of other Irishmen and women, built houses, and sold them to fellow Irish consumers. Everyone involved was Irish." She smiled. "To paraphrase an infamous American sign once directed to the Irish, '*no others need apply.*'"

She stopped a moment before delving in: "Of course, the problem was that the development occurred largely with *borrowed* money, funds borrowed, in turn, from a series of lenders *outside* of Ireland." Heads nodded in agreement.

"But if the money had not been borrowed from external sources, it was a great model. Why?" She waited a few seconds before providing her response—to ensure she had the Taoiseach's full attention.

He locked eyes with her. "Yes, why was it a good model—other than the *obvious*." He smiled as the audience tittered.

Staring at him, Áine replied placing emphasis on particular words, "Because it was primarily a *local* economy—*Irish* entrepreneurs, hiring *Irish* workers, creating products marketed by *Irish* marketers, sold to *Irish* buyers, with profits invested in *Irish* banks and additional *Irish* ventures." She continued to meet the focussed gaze of Edward. To her, no one else mattered in the room.

"Continue, I'm all ears," he said. He leaned forward, locking eyes with Áine.

With a brief nod and a smile, she launched into her explanation. "Even though Irish butter and other Irish food products were sold for export to the EU, this was a subsidiary part of the economy and done at the expense of devastating economic compromises. What made it profitable, truly profitable, was the fact," and she paused to add import to the words to follow, "that the Irish themselves, *ourselves*, bought the same Irish food products."

Looking around the room, she launched the daring point, "Who needs *global*, when we have a surplus of Irish consumers, Irish workers, Irish food products, and Irish land?"

The Taoiseach nodded slowly as he contemplated the merits of Áine's analysis. Meeting Áine's gaze again, he asked intently, "And how do these thoughts relate to the models to which you previously referred, those that were adopted in Canada, and now down in Kerry?"

Áine smiled at him. "Simply put, in Prince Edward Island, we reverted back to a successful Irish model employed here before the country joined the EU. We established a *local cottage industry*—as it traditionally used to be called, pre-EU—and put every able and willing person back to work for themselves, rather than as employees of corporations or state-run government—no insult intended, Sir."

She smiled, as she waited for the import of her words to sink in, before continuing. "In other words, rather than work for the big multi-nationals, who routinely decreased salaries for their workers, the workers went back to their land and grew their own food. Some founded co-ops and farmers' markets, to sell directly to fellow consumers, while others marketed products and made them available to specialty outlets, such as restaurants, tourism, and the like. Government institutions, such as schools, hospitals, and the like, were supplied by local outlets, and consumers re-learned the lessons of their grandparents: eat in season, eat healthy unprocessed foods, rely on *local* sources for food." Murmurs were heard throughout the room. "Just like the old days."

"Indeed," he said, prodding her on. "And the outcome?"

"When Government stepped in to support the idea of a *local food* economy based on traditional practices and foods, they created an agri-tourism initiative, replete with 'flavour' trails, food maps, and pamphlets of farms, B&Bs, hotels, and restaurants, which offered traditional dishes from locally grown foods. This, in turn, brought in a flow of tourists, who enthusiastically endorsed visiting a locale that celebrated its own distinct products, resulting in more jobs for the residents."

She gazed around the room at the now visibly astonished audience. "A holistic system works because it supports and re-generates itself. Rather than be like everyone else, we decided Over just to be ourselves—'*Ourselves, Alone*'—if you'll forgive the politically resonant phrase."

"Indeed?" he uttered, not sure of what else to say. "Will you elaborate?"

"Of course," she said. "Rather than rely on fast food from God knows where, we have launched down in Kerry, a campaign, a *local foods* initiative—based on traditional practices and dishes—to grow our own food, prepare our own foods, consume our own foods, and sell our own foods to one another. We call it *Celtic Roots*."

The audience clapped in response—to Áine's utter astonishment and delight. Flustered by the enthusiastic reception of her ideas, she stole a look in the direction of the Taoiseach, who smiled and thanked her for her insights. "Young lady, you have the makings of a political leader! You should run for office!"

Someone shouted out from the audience. "Be careful, Taoiseach, lest she takes your position!" Laughter rang throughout the room.

"It apparently runs in my bloodline!" she quipped in response to more frivolity from the audience.

The Taoiseach smiled. "Well, we hope to tap into that family expertise. Someone from my office will be contacting you for more information on your great work down in Kerry. Please leave your information with one of my team."

Áine thanked him, but overwhelmed, left the room before remembering to leave her information. Outside, she panted and tried to collect her breath. Well, that was quite the first introduction to my father, she thought. If he only knew how closely aligned we really are—*and the bloodline to which I was referring!*

She hurried over the Elizabeth's house to ensure that she arrived before he did. After greeting her, Elizabeth led Áine to the library, inviting her to browse the family collection of books, while she finished a few odds and ends before supper. When the doorbell rang soon after, Áine called out that she would answer the door. She couldn't wait to see the look of surprise on the man's face when he recognized her.

Áine opened the door and stood smiling at the now visibly astonished Edward. He simply stood there dumfounded, unable to explain the presence of the beguiling young lady greeting him at his sister's residence. He soon recollected himself, and extending his hand, introduced himself, saying, "Well, well, you must be the lovely young lady, em, *Doctor*, my sister has invited to supper. Although she promised a highly intriguing evening, I hadn't quite realized that we would be re-fashioning the Irish economy!"

Áine responded in what she hoped was her most polished social voice. "Won't you come in? We're seated in the library round the fire." She turned away before he could detect the tears welling in her eyes.

They walked in silence to the appointed room, where Edward immediately made for the liquor hutch and poured out a glass of sherry, offering it to Áine. "I dare say you could do with a spot of sherry after your electrifying performance this afternoon."

After thanking him, Áine blushed. "I do hope I didn't offend. I get quite passionate over the issues you were debating."

Entering from behind, Elizabeth overheard the exchange. After greeting her brother, she glared at Áine through gritted teeth. "I take it you both have already met? Did I just overhear that Áine participated in the event today, Edward?"

Planting a kiss on his sister's cheek, he glanced over in Áine's direction before chuckling. "Participated? She *stole* the show!" Sensing his sister's disapproval, he touched her arm reassuringly. "She was just wonderful." He looked back over his shoulder at Áine who appeared flustered by the attention. He proceeded to recount how she had offered not only a sound initiative, but inspiration as well. He ended by saying, "This young woman certainly got a rise out of the Fisheries Minister! I think if he could, he would deport her back to Canada, lest she takes over his position!"

Elizabeth smiled, but did not laugh. Casting a sidelong glance at Áine, she said in a prim tone, "Whilst the girl is full of surprises, I hadn't anticipated her *pretensions* in the field of economics."

Edward smiled easily at his sister, and looking over to Áine, countered, "Oh, they're far from pretensions on this young lady's part. She's quite well informed."

Elizabeth turned away, muttering in Áine's direction, "So much for demonstrating *tact, decorum, and discretion*."

Áine offered a sheepish glance at Elizabeth, before turning to Edward, whom she was so intent on impressing. She blurted out, "Actually, I hold a doctorate in economics—a field called sustainable economics, as in conservation." She stole a sideways glance over at Elizabeth. "Before coming back to Ireland, I worked for the Ministries of Economics & Innovation in my home province in Canada, overseeing various projects, including a wild salmon conservation and re-population initiative, as well as what we called a 'traditional ways' campaign to spur a locally-based economy."

Edward chuckled. "*Innovation*, indeed! We could certainly do with a Ministry such as that. As you could see from our report, we are sadly lacking in that particular area." He toasted the two women, saying in a tone brimming in sincerity, "Cheers to new blood!"

Elizabeth and Áine exchanged knowing glances. Little did he know how close he was to saluting the truth.

Edward turned to Áine after they sat down. "So, tell me, who are you, and which family lays claim to you, young lady? There is something so *familiar* about you, but I just can't *place* you." He gazed at her for a few moments without saying anything. "Have you worked on one of my committees, perhaps? It seems from what you said that you are indeed Irish, though you have spent time in Canada?"

Through pursed lips, Elizabeth said, "Actually, dear, she's closer than you can imagine. Why don't you finish up that glass, now, Edward, and let me pour you another one."

She stood up and walked over to the bar. "I'm certainly going to refresh my glass. Perhaps we could all use with a refreshment."

Edward put up his hand. "Thank you, Elizabeth." He drained his glass as she poured him more sherry. Turning to Áine, he studied her intently for a moment. "Wait, don't tell me. I never forget a face. I am famous for it." He gazed at her, sipped some sherry, and stared some more.

"You look so familiar. If I didn't know any better," he mused," I would say you are a member of our own extended family." Turning to Elizabeth, he said, "She takes very much after our grandmother, does she not, Elizabeth?" He stared down at his glass for some minutes as if lost in thoughtful reverie before looking up to gaze at Áine again. "Yet, yet, you remind me of, of someone from long ago . . . " His voice faded—as he sank into his memories.

The room remained quiet, each sipping sherry and waiting. A few minutes later, he added, more to himself than to the others, "And the *Kerry* connection . . . " He sat up abruptly in his seat. "Does your family actually hail from Kerry?"

Enjoying his increasing discomfort as he edged toward the truth, Áine smiled at him and said playfully, "Yes, one side—my mother's side. My father's family resides here in Dublin." Edward mulled over her response. "Dublin, is it? Then surely, you must be, let me think, the daughter of one of our cousins, perhaps? Now that I look at you more, I see a distinct family *resemblance*." Turning to Elizabeth, he asked, "Isn't that right, Elizabeth? Perhaps one of Harold's daughters." He shook his head. "Though I cannot now recall any of the family residing in Kerry."

Elizabeth jumped up from the table. "I can't stand the agony any longer!" Turning to Edward, she said emphatically, "Actually, Edward, Áine is a very close family relation—much closer than you might imagine."

"Indeed, Áine," he said graciously, extending his hand. "Welcome to the family, though I really do feel as if we have met before." He gazed at her, curiosity flowing from his expression. "There is such a air of familiarity I feel about you." He then smiled easily. "I apologize for repeating that, but the feeling is quite inexplicably strong." He studied her intently. "I simply cannot for the life of me determine the precise relation." He shook his head.

Áine smiled timidly. "I wondered whether you would detect something familiar about me." She added wistfully, "Perhaps even a sense of connection."

"How very odd. Indeed, I do, though how and why exactly, I am not sure," he murmured.

She shook his hand, but before letting go, added, "And as for *knowing* a member of my family, you most certainly did—in the *Elizabethan* sense of the word, that is."

Elizabeth choked on her drink, while Edward stared at her, startled, trying to recall how the Elizabethans used the word. "How bloody *extraordinary*."

Áine smiled at him. "Actually, it gets even *more* extraordinary."

Edward looked from Áine to Elizabeth with widened eyes. Elizabeth leaned over and clasping her brother's hand with one hand, and Áine's in the other, placed them together again. "Edward, meet Dr. Áine O'Sullivan O'Connor Dillon—Your *daughter*, Edward."

"My *what*?" He stared wildly from one woman to another, as he pulled his hand from Áine's. "My *daughter*?" he sputtered. "How is that possible?"

Áine smirked noticeably, before responding with obvious sarcasm. "It's quite common, actually. Surely, you know that when you make love to a woman, chances are that you might impregnate her, *et voilà*! I appear!"

Edward stared at her with utter disbelief. "But who? And when? And how?"

Áine arched her eyebrow. "Well, I think we've covered the how question. The when part you will need to enlighten us about the particulars, but generally speaking, it was nine months before I was born."

She studied his expression before asking in a tone of unveiled disappointment, "Are you telling me that you cannot perceive in my features the answer to the *who* question?"

"You remind me of someone once deeply familiar to me, but, but it cannot be . . . " His voice trailed off as he stared at Áine. "Did you say your name was O'Sullivan?"

Áine continued, "I am an Ó'Suílleabháin from Co. Kerry. Is that familiar enough?"

Edward stared at her, taking in her various features. "Then you're . . . you're . . . *Maeve's* daughter," he sputtered, and abruptly turning on his heels, strode over to the liquor cabinet, poured himself a Jameson's, sloughed it down in one gulp, and poured another. Turning back to the women, he confronted Áine. "But how, my dear, are you *mine* as well?"

Áine emptied her glass of sherry, before responding dryly, "I thought we had already covered that aspect of the *science* of it all."

Edward gazed at her. "And what age are you, Áine?"

"I'm just 32."

"32." He mentally calculated back before continuing, "But your mother, Maeve, told me that she, she went to England to, to . . . " He couldn't finish the statement, as he looked away in shame.

Áine stared at him with steely eyes. "Apparently, she waited and waited, too long as it turned out, hoping that you might come forward to marry her. Then it was too late to do anything about me—until *after* I was born, that is."

"My *God*!" he uttered and covered his hands with his face. "I had no *idea*." He then looked up at Áine. "What did you mean by that last bit?"

Áine looked at him through infinitely sad eyes. "She gave me up." She turned away from him to hide the tears that suddenly filled her eyes. As Elizabeth silently poured her some more sherry, she said with her back to him, "I've only just found out myself in the last few weeks."

"How is that?" Edward asked tenderly, detecting the despair of the young woman.

Elizabeth gathered both of them by their arms and moving them into the dining room, said in a soothing voice, "Well, I think we can hash out the rest of the *dramatic* tale over a good meal. I think we could all use some good food, and most definitely, some wine right now."

They all seated themselves around the table as Elizabeth served each of them and poured out the wine.

She raised her glass, and smiling at both of them toasted, "Cheers! Áine, dear, welcome to the Dillon family!"

Áine smiled shyly back at Elizabeth, and stealing a glance over at Edward, said, "Sláinte! Thank you, Elizabeth."

Elizabeth glanced over at Edward. "Áine may have her mother's good looks, but she's her father's daughter, as well!"

Edward seemed pleased by the remark. Leaning over to Áine, he offered his toast, proclaiming, "How bloody extraordinary! A *daughter*! And one quite proficient at politics—like her old man!" Without further adieu, he drank down the glass of wine.

"My God, Áine! I can't get over this new development in all of our lives!" he exclaimed, then added more serious tone, "To think of how differently my life would have turned out—and *yours* as well, " he added, "had I *known*." He gazed at Áine in complete amazement. "And how is your Mum? Maeve? How is she?"

Áine glanced over at Elizabeth, mentally inquiring how much more the man could take in one evening. Just as Elizabeth decided to respond to her brother's question, Áine looked at him and said quietly, "Dead, actually. She's quite dead."

Edward's facial expression conveyed his shock. Elizabeth turned to him, placing her hand on his. "That was the funeral I attended in Kerry some weeks back. Edward, surely, you remember my telling you about my visit there."

Áine looked at the two of them. "Elizabeth stayed with me, though I didn't know at the time that she was my aunt—or *you*," she said, turning to Edward, "my *father*."

She then explained the details to Edward of how she

came to discover her past—and his. She told him all about Maeve's journal, of how she expressed in those pages her hopes, then disappointment, followed by utter despair over finding herself pregnant, unmarried, and with no means of providing for her expecting child. She even told him of how she had turned down another marriage proposal by a local man who had asked for her hand, even knowing she was carrying someone else's child.

Edward groaned, shook his head, and covered his head in his hands again, as he listened to the tale of despair. "If only I had done things differently," he said more to himself than to the others. A deafening silence hung over the dining room. Finally, Edward spoke. "And despite everything, here you are, Áine," said he, gazing at her. "What ever am I going to *do* with you, young lady?"

Áine stared at him coldly. "You are going to do nothing with me. I am not a problem, if that's what you mean. I am not a problem that needs to be solved." She turned away, hurt by his response.

He leaned over the table towards her. "Áine, I didn't mean it that way," he replied. "But this is utterly extraordinary news, and I have to think about how to present it to the world."

He took another sip of wine. "These are tough times for our people, and my enemies will use this to thwart my attempts at saving the economy." He looked away, then added slowly, "and then, of course, there's my *wife* . . . " His voice trailed off as he found it difficult to articulate the problems facing him.

Áine looked at him as a sense of tranquillity filled her. "I came here just to see if you would feel a sense of kinship with me." She leaned back. "My curiosity has been satisfied. I am not interested in making trouble for you.

I had no idea until yesterday that you were even a public figure."

She stood up. "You don't have to tell anyone about me, nor I you, if you prefer. I would understand completely if my existence is too complex to explain away— or *acknowledge*." She walked over to the cabinet and brought the bottle of wine back to the table, silently pouring more wine into both of their glasses.

Elizabeth came bustling into the room with a platter of cheeses. "I've made up the fire in the sitting room. I think it would be nice for you both to sit together and chat. I'm off to bed. I hope you'll both stay. Áine, I've put you in the green room at the top of the stairs."

Áine looked over at Edward to gauge his reaction to his sister's suggestion. She was pleasantly surprised to see that he responded positively. "What a lovely idea, Elizabeth." Turning to Áine, he offered his arm. "Shall we, Daughter?"

They both collected their wine glasses, and with platter in hand, Edward guided Áine to the sitting room. Soon they were deeply engrossed in conversation, each divulging information to the other. Áine told him all about her family in Canada, including her suspicion as a young child that she didn't quite belong. She also told him about her summers in Ireland with her mother's side of the family and with Maeve, the family encouragement to caretake the wild salmon, her subsequent career in Canada, followed by the strange inheritance, and the journey of self-discovery. He listened with a sympathetic ear to her account, interjecting every so often with a question.

As the hours went by, Edward became increasingly more taken with his new daughter. An amazing young woman, he thought. *Extraordinary, actually*. He gazed at her, studying her every feature. "Tell me more about those initiatives of yours in Canada, as well as in Kerry," he urged her, when she seemed to have finished the account of her life story. "If you're not too tired," he added, concerned that the experience might have emotionally exhausted her.

Edward stood and offered to make a pot of tea. "That would be wonderful," Áine said, as she smiled up at him. She spent the time while he was away in the kitchen staring into the fire, grateful for his interest in her. He soon returned with a tray replete with tea, scones, and some biscuits. He served her tea and asked again if she would share with him more details regarding the creation of *local economies* as an antidote to the current economic crisis plaguing Ireland.

Áine launched into an hour-long discourse about the transformational effects of the local initiatives, both on Prince Edward Island, and more recently, in Kerry. Edward listened in awe to her explanation, asking a multitude of questions. "The foundation to any thriving local economy," she said, "is to rely on the natural food products provided by the local habitat."

"What do you mean, exactly?" he asked.

"You know, native trout and wild salmon from the local rivers, vegetables from local seeds, fruits from local wild sources."

"And why are they fundamental to a local economy? What's wrong with engineered seeds that protect against the potato blight, for example?" he asked.

Áine took a sip of tea and continued. "Let's take the case of artificially created seeds—GMO seeds, and genetically engineered live foods, such as genetically manipulated salmon," she started.

"As I understand the two," interjected Edward, "They provide foolproof ways to increase the food supply."

Leaning forward, Áine responded with a vigorous rebuttal. "Quite the contrary! They actually *deplete* the natural food supply by making farmers, in the one case, and fishers, in the other, completely dependent on outside chemical sources, for the seeds, fertilizers, sprays, and insecticides, as well as on the equipment necessary to maintain a growing system for GMOs. These products are always owned by huge multi-nationals—in themselves problematic for a host of reasons not mentioned—besides the fact that they contaminate and destroy the natural native seeds and fish of a local region. This, in turn, results in farmers and fishers not being able to fend for themselves, should these companies decide to increase their prices to a point that they become unaffordable to the locals—as in the case of the GMO cotton used in India, for example, or what happened in PEI with the potato farmers who wished to choose heritage seeds over the GMO varieties. Suddenly, they could not sell any of their products, since the big companies prevented them from doing so. Not to mention the carcinogenic effects of such products on humans and livestock."

Áine stopped a moment for a breath and looked over at Edward, who seemed surprised by the information. She was shocked by his limited knowledge, particularly as the premier of a country largely agricultural in origin. "Has no one advised you about the significant environmental and economic differences between native, wild fish, such as trout and salmon, and the GE versions?"

Edward replied, "Yes, I've been told that they are larger in size, easier to raise, and more profitable both for the fish farmer and for the country as they bring in new investors, such as the Chinese."

Áine arched her eyebrow. "Do you really believe it good for Ireland to have a horde of Chinese investors buying up salmon and trout rivers here? Wouldn't we lose our independence as we have done by catering to the consumer demands of other European countries, followed by then competing with them for profits? After all, look at what happened to Kerry butter—once popular throughout Europe, it ceased being a locally owned co-op and was bought out by the multi-nationals, who took a fresh, organic product and industrialized it. Ruined it completely."

She leaned forward. "Why not base our economy on providing for fellow Irish—and be independent of those global markets, which care only about the cheapest price, rather than quality?"

Edward put down his cup of tea. "My dear, don't you see that we live in a global society?"

"Only if you wish to relinquish Irish economic independence to a small group of billionaire investors!" she retorted. She continued in a passionate voice. "Don't you see how Ireland—you—can just say *no*, as Iceland did?"

He leaned back in his chair as he gently swayed his cup in the air. "Áine, love, it is not that simple."

She gazed at him. "Actually, it is." She sipped her tea before continuing. "Remember what you learned about the American Declaration of Independence? Something about whenever a despot takes away the rights of the people, it is not only their right, but their *responsibility*, to dissolve the union—in other words," she added, "to rebel—to take back what is theirs."

She leaned over towards him. "If you don't mind my saying so, you need to take back Ireland—" Interrupting herself, she laughed and said, "To paraphrase the words of Paul McCartney, '*give Ireland back to the Irish.*' That's what the Icelanders did. And so can you. Take back the territorial waters that belonged to Ireland before the EU negotiated them away from us, give us back our fishing rights, our right to grow our own heritage food, our right to fish our wild salmon, and have neither destroyed forever by contamination from GEs, GMOs, or multi-nationals."

Edward chuckled. "You are quite the rebel. It's clear you have *Kerry* blood flowing in your veins."

She retorted, "Where would independent Ireland be today without the Kerrymen?" She leaned over to him and said, stressing her choice of words, "And now it's your *responsibility* to step up and *free* Ireland once again— this time from the bureaucrats and banksters of the EU, who insist at making money at our expense—just as the English did for hundreds of years. 'Let the Irish starve, but refund us our investments,' they insisted," she added sarcastically. "I tell you, this local economic model has incredible potential to counteract the global multi-nationals that are destroying Ireland."

Edward gazed at her in silence, absorbing the merits of her argument. He said nothing in response for a few minutes, only swirled his tea around in his cup as he thought. "You raise valid points," he said thoughtfully. "You really are quite perceptive."

Áine smiled at him, as she watched him continued swirling his teacup. "Well, I inherited my analytical and perceptive abilities. I hope they come from you."

He looked up at her, surprised by her comment, his

role in the reality of her existence sinking in. "Perhaps, perhaps," he murmured, "But in so many ways, you take after your mother," he said with admiration. "You are as strong in character as she was," he said. "I had always wished I could be as strong," he added, his tone wistful.

Áine leaned over and touched his arm, letting her hand rest there. She responded fiercely, "You can be— you are! You're the Taoiseach, for heaven's sake! You must be strong for all of us!"

She then sat back and gazed at him. "You know," she said, still unsure of how to address him directly, "We locals can do our part, but we need you, as the country's leader, to create a new paradigm that will guide our efforts and ensure their success." Áine unintentionally repeated his gesture of swirling her own teacup in the air before taking a sip as she waited for his response.

Edward gazed back and her. "This is such a remarkable exchange, Áine, for a host of reasons, some obvious—and others—not so."

Áine picked up his thoughts and responded without thinking, "I don't suppose too many people speak to you as I have done this evening."

Edward pressed his hand to the table with a vigorous slap. "Precisely so! I have to *pry* opinions and advice from those who surround me."

Áine looked at him in surprise. "Aren't they *paid* to advise you?"

He nodded. "Indeed they are, and since they would like to *continue* their highly paid salaries, they make no attempt to risk losing them by doing anything as definitive as share their actual opinions." He leaned over to her. "Tell you what, Áine! I'd like to hire you. You have no political status to risk."

"No, just the love of a newly found father," she replied dryly. "But to do what exactly?" she asked, surprised by his comment.

He gazed at her. "To advise me, of course, on such matters as *grass roots* initiatives, as well as to represent the voice of the people, who have no way outside of voting to share their thoughts with me."

Áine was quite taken aback by the idea and said as much as she looked down into her cup. "It would never do, as no one here considers me a native or a local. And should they find out that I am actually related to you, that could cause you trouble, perhaps."

Edward leaned over and placed his hand under her chin, gently lifting it until she met his gaze. "To borrow from your American example, sure, if old JFK could hire his brother Bobby to serve as his advisor, so I can hire my daughter," he said tenderly. "Besides, you're an expert with experiential knowledge sent here by your own government to advise us, your *new* government!"

Áine beamed, not only at his acknowledgment of her professional abilities, but also at his reference to her as his daughter. Her eyes filled with tears that streamed down her cheeks.

Noticing her emotional response, Edward leaned over with his napkin and wiped off the tears, saying in a soothing tone, "Now, now, I didn't mean to upset you or overwhelm you."

Áine smiled at him through watery eyes. "I'm just happy is all," she said. "I've lost a mother before I knew she was my mother, and have gained a father I never knew I had."

"Well, well," he said. "We'll have to think about how

to make up for all that lost time." Edward stood up and took the cups to the sink. "You know," he said to Áine, who was now helping him clear the table, "My mind is racing. I have many issues to think through and strategies to plan. Give me a bit of time to sort through them all, and I'll be in contact soon."

Each lost in thought, they both washed up in silence— Áine washing, while Edward dried up the dishes. Each noted with heightened emotion the life-changing nature for them of such a natural event that often occurred between father and daughter. When they finished, Edward turned to Áine and said he would be off, as he had some high-level meetings first thing the next morning. He started to walk away down the hall.

Áine watched him walk away and said softly, "Well, goodnight, then—" She found herself stifling back sobs as her eyes welled with tears. "And . . . and . . . and thank you," she said in a quiet voice.

Edward reeled around to face her. "No, Áine, thank *you* for your courage, for your honesty, and for your incredible *kindness.*"

He looked back at her and impulsively opened his arms to her. She ran to him. They hugged one another tightly as Edward whispered to her, "I won't let you down, Áine, *again.*" He kissed her forehead and turned away to leave. Suddenly, he turned around, and taking a card from his pocket, he scribbled on it before handing it to her. "Now Áine, if you *ever* need or want to speak with me, you can ring me at this number. No one but my wife and Elizabeth use this line, so it's perfectly safe to ring me. I want you to know that despite whatever happens in public, you have a direct way of reaching me. Please call before you return to Kerry and tell me where I might reach you." He patted her on the arm and vanished into the night.

Áine soon fell into a deep sleep, not waking until the sun had climbed high into the sky. She woke completely refreshed, feeling as if she had never slept as soundly in her life.

Chapter Eighteen
TRADITIONS

TRAIDISIÚN

SOMETHING ABOUT THE RECENT DISCOVERIES of her past seemed to exert a becalming influence on Áine. Knowing with certainty the identity of her biological parents, together with insights into each of their personalities, made her feel as if she had found her *place* in life. She now understood aspects of herself that had remained inexplicable to her before, such as her relentless longing for things Irish, despite being happy living as an 'Islander' on Prince Edward Island. It felt almost as if her former life there had prepared her for precisely *this* moment in time when she discovered not only her ancestry, but sources for her longings and inclinations, as well. Cultural knowledge and memories embedded within finally made sense, now that they could be connected to character traits from her lineage, as well as to a physical location—a *place* itself steeped in personal, family, and cultural history.

Áine stood outside the cottage and surveyed the landscape. She had always felt such a deep—soulful—

connection to the house and to the undulating fields, the ribbon of sand below, and the sea beyond. The mountains particularly had always drawn her, which she had assumed was due to her being named after their spiritual patroness. She had attributed this passion for *Place* to her close relationship with her grandmother, but now she realized, as she studied everything around with a new lens, she had actually originated there. Her first moments of life were interwoven with the cottage on that very site, in that particular landscape, in that part of Ireland.

The power of *Place* resonated within her more strongly than ever. She had been born in the very same house where her mothers, her aunts and uncles, and a host of grandparents had been born before her, on this ancient piece of land, protected behind by the Paps of her namesake—where, for thousands of years, her ancestors had walked, worked, dreamt, and loved. She, Áine, was inextricably linked to the place, part of its continued history. She was both an embodiment of its past, as well as now, part of its present. The gravity of her role in this history struck her deeply. She resolved to act wisely to ensure its future.

Áine knew she had to take the new initiatives in Kerry to the next stage, but the economic crisis now made it an undeniable necessity. Though a daunting task, promoting a thriving, local economy that relied on agricultural and cultural traditions of the local area, rather than upon global sources, felt right to her, and indeed, the only sustainable solution she could offer to alleviate the economic troubles plaguing the country. Such endeavours must necessarily include, she reasoned, conserving the natural resources of the area—keeping the streams wild and free from nets to ensure the perpetuation of the wild salmon; maintaining soil purity, and protecting the mountains from petro-chemically based 'alternative energy.' She knew that if she and her neighbours could pull all this off, their example could serve as a model for other local areas around the country, and perhaps lift Ireland from its economic scourge.

She decided to ring up Muirís to invite him for another meal to create a plan of action.

"Well, now, Áine, I don't know if that's such a good idea, my coming for another meal," he said, his tone immeasurably sad, before adding as an afterthought, "Though I would love nothing better, to be sure."

Intuiting his oblique reference, Áine dismissed his concern impatiently, now that she was so intent on her new local food endeavour. "Ah, Muirís, not to worry. I have some good news about the 'extent of our relations,' if that's what is keeping you at bay," she said in a soothing tone. "You can come as a friend, if not more, but you won't be coming as my long-lost *brother*, I'm happy to report!"

Muirís' tone brightened considerably at the news, as he asked in a tone of obvious relief, "Are you sure, now, Áine? I've been plagued about it since we last spoke."

"As was I, Muirís, but my trip to Dublin clarified everything. I'll tell you all about it, if you'd like, if you would come for a meal. I have some ideas I'd like to try out on you." Áine hesitated, wondering whether he had moved on to someone else, and added, "Unless you have, hmm, *other* plans."

"Nothing I wouldn't cancel to see you, Áine!" he replied, "Now that you assure me we aren't, well, *intimately* related." He hesitated. "Sure, you're certain about that, now, Áine, are you?"

"I have it from the horse's mouth," she replied, chuckling. "Besides, the horse was a green-eyed, freckled redhead like myself, so I know it to be true."

As they finished their meal, Muirís leaned over to pour her a bit more wine, and after topping off his own, put down the bottle, and lightly capped his hand over hers. "So, tell me now, you're quite certain now, is it, that we're not siblings at all, so?"

Áine left her hand entwined with his. "I'm quite certain, Muirís. I actually met my biological father, who acknowledged as much."

Muirís scowled. "The lout! Leaving Maeve to fend for herself like that! 'Tis . . . it's . . . well, 'tis bloody well cowardly, it is!"

Although admiring him for his sense of responsibility, she found herself defending her newly discovered father. Looking away, she said, "Well, I suppose circumstances were a bit complicated, and, well, I guess em, Maeve had reputedly informed him she was to have an abortion in England, so he never knew about my actual existence."

"Even so," persisted Muirís. "He should have been there for her." He shook his head and added, "And to think that me' da' offered to take over that sod's responsibility." He leaned back in his chair and gazed away out the window before speaking. "Don't I remember the expression that came over your Mum—Maeve—whenever she mentioned *Himself*—that last summer before she . . . she . . . well . . . passed on. 'Twas a look of pure *love*—for a man who had abandoned her."

Áine softly squeezed his hand. "Ah, don't be so hard on the man, Muirís. He was so good to me when he learned of my existence, and I believe he intends to become a regular presence in my life."

Muirís begrudgingly acknowledged that his response to Áine showed that he had some character.

She offered a wry grin. "You're a hard man, Muirís! You expect great things of people."

"Indeed, I do, Áine," he said, as he clapped his now fierce gaze on her. "I hope that's no crime in your eyes, so."

"Not at all, Muirís. It's one of your many admirable traits that you won't tolerate slackers!" He smiled at her, grateful that she understood his sense of exacting standards. After sipping some wine, she added, "From what I know of Maeve, I don't think she cared about having a man act *responsibly*, but rather, craved for a man to act from a deep *passion* for her. She was definitely *all* about passion, which, of course," she added, "got her into trouble over my unexpected existence."

Muirís leaned over and gripped Áine's arm, his tone emphatic. "Now, Áine, there was no regret I ever read in Maeve's eyes about your existence, only in the lack of being more connected to you."

She smiled over at him, happy to discover his high level of concern for her feelings. "I'm not sad, really, Muirís. Curious, perhaps, more than anything."

She stopped a moment to reflect, before explaining in a soft voice, "Of course, it's devastating in a way to find out about Maeve as my birth mother after she has passed. I would have so loved to have talked to her about it all." She brightened. "But I have gained a birth father, and indeed, someone who might prove to be an interesting influence in my life." She smiled at him, saying in a voice of pure happiness, "At least, no one can say I'm not Irish! And now, here I am, in my family homestead, adding another generation to a long, long line of Celts."

Muirís smiled fondly at her, and taking up her hand, said in a seductive voice, "Wouldn't I like to help you add yet another generation to this household!" He got up, and taking her hands in his, added, "Now that we're back to '*kissing cousin*' status, may I?"

Not long after their supper together, Áine, together with Muirís, whose support of and commitment to the local food project provided input critical to its success, got to work on setting up a network of food producers, vendors, and consumers. They both took up their endeavour with nearly insatiable levels of energy, soliciting the support and active participation of a cadre of people dedicated to the local food cause.

Soon farmers, cheese makers, bakers, and simply the *enthusiastic* over traditional ways joined in. One fellow designed a website for the initiative that highlighted the foods and artisanal products offered, which created a great stir throughout the area, as people took tremendous pride in showcasing their contributions to the cause. Áine created a blog component, called *Kerry Roots*, where she and others described techniques for growing heirloom native foods, as well as provided recipes for traditional dishes.

As the local economy took off among the inhabitants, Áine couldn't resist adding her own tuppence to the current national controversy regarding the economy and its direction, and after an overwhelmingly supportive response to her essays on the local as a cure for global dependence, she wrote a regular column offering advice, strategies, and solutions to the myriad of issues that had emerged as the economic crisis exploded throughout the country, based on her proven experiences back in Prince Edward Island.

Soon, the website—and particularly Áine's column, attracted the attention of government officials keen to find out just what sort of new *uprising* was brewing down in Kerry. Taking advantage of the economic crisis, the Minister of Fisheries pushed his tax revenue plan. He had lured—through offering extra-low tax rates—a multi-national corporation headquartered in Norway to set up a series of fish farms along the western coast of Ireland. The plan was to place these farms on the main rivers throughout the country, together with select harbours along the coasts of Galway, Cork, and particularly, Kerry. He was hoping to sneak this by without a vote.

If that weren't bad enough, the corporation had joined forces with what appeared to Áine as a particularly insidious enterprise, to farm genetically engineered salmon, arguing that they grew more quickly to four times the size of an average wild one. Armed with her experience from Prince Edward Island, where she had participated in campaigning against the introduction of these "*frankenfish*," as they referred to them Over, Áine wasted no time in setting up a series of blogs on the invidious nature of this endeavour—not only to the fish and consumers, but to the very *sovereignty* of Ireland itself, and the survival of its ancient Celtic culture.

Intent on selling out the last of the wild salmon, in exchange for the prospects of significant tax revenues, the Fisheries Minister had been instrumental during the negotiations over joining the EU—in selling out the fishing rights and territorial waters of Ireland, in exchange for a vision of Ireland as a corporate haven. Once Áine discovered this information, she wrote fierce invectives against the Minister's plans, and her blogs were soon reprinted on a host of websites, not only over Ireland, but over environmental and local foods movement sites around Europe—even being copied onto select sites in Canada and the States.

In a cabinet meeting in Dublin, the Minister railed against "that young pup" down in Kerry trying to undermine his efforts—and the hefty *profits* to be gained—there. He pounded the table in anger, as he tossed an overflowing file, brimming with copies of her widely reprinted missives against his initiatives. Although the Taoiseach usually listened with one ear to whatever new venture the Fisheries Minister had cooked up, when he heard the reference to the efforts down in Kerry to undermining the Minister's plans for great profits, Edward sat back in his chair, and listened intently to what he was saying. Suddenly, he smiled, realizing that his colleague was referring to none other than his newly found daughter.

"What are you chuckling at, Edward?" sputtered the Minister. "It's no joking matter what's going on down there—it could spread to the other counties, and where would we be?" He slammed his fist on the table. "What's to become of our economy—if we do not have multi-nationals invest in our resources? Sure, we'd have to fund it all *ourselves*. And from what I gather, setting up these fish farms can be quite expensive."

The Taoiseach sat up and responded in a soothing tone, "Ah, now, William, don't get your scales all ruffled.

I was just thinking that I might know your young pup. Describe her to me."

The Minister poured out a stream of invectives against the efforts of the "*Kerry crowd,*" as he called them, who were actively protesting the introduction of engineered salmon, and indeed, all farmed fish.

"She's a fiery, opinionated lass the government in Canada sent over to plague us—all passionate about her *cause* and utterly relentless in her determination to see it through. I even agreed to meet briefly with her to dissuade her—but to no avail."

He gazed at the Taoiseach and added almost instinctively, "Not so different from your own approach, actually, when you get onto something. You're like a bulldog, who latches onto the pant leg of an intruder and refuses to let go, regardless." He leaned forward and growled, "She is even *more* tenacious than you."

Edward broke out in derisive laughter. With a shake of his head and a wide grin, he declared, "She must be the very same. She accosted me at a summit talk I gave some months back. You might recall her impassioned speech. She's quite the handful." He leaned back, cherishing his memories of his encounters with the fiery Áine.

The Minister continued to vent, concluding that he needed to go down there and "handle her once and for all."

Edward leaned over to his angry Minister, and in a soothing, but firm voice, indicating that the decision was already made, said, "In having dealt with her before, I might have some advantage over you in this regard." Sitting up straight, he said on impulse, "I'll go down to Kerry myself, William. Indeed, I believe I have received an invitation to address some sort of opening festivity they are hosting, though I may arrive early *incognito* to assess the situation down there." He smiled over at the Minister. "Maybe I'll do a bit of fly fishing to see what the *fuss* is all about."

Edward cleared his throat, and before William could protest, he asked one of his staff to confirm the date of the Kerry festivities. With a re-invigorated sense of determination ringing through his tone, he stood, announcing that he would push back the next Cabinet meeting for another week until he returned, and dismissed them all. He sat for a minute or two gazing out the window with a smile on his face, before instructing his assistant to reserve a room for him at the local B&B in Dingle. He smiled inwardly, thinking about Áine. Those notions of hers regarding a locally propelled economy still resonated for him with a compelling reasonableness that his profit-hungry colleagues didn't seem to possess.

Some days later, Edward arrived in Dingle. Dressed in a large fly fisherman's hat as well as classic sixties, dark-blue sunglasses and fisher apparel, no one took any notice of him, as the town was a haven for fly fisher folk that time of year. Even the woman in the B&B smiled over his name, though not before scrutinizing his face, which he hid fairly successfully in the shadow of his hat. "Don't you have a famous name, now, but sure, we'd never be seeing your famous namesake darkening our doors here." She added with a smile, "Wouldn't some fly fishing and our lovely fresh air do him and his lot some good?"

He returned the smile. "I suppose he could surprise us all," he said in his best-sounding country accent.

Strolling down along the sidewalk, Edward noted with pleasure how locals passing by each greeted him with a "*Dia dhuit,*" with such regularity that he began to respond in the traditional way—with a "*Dia's Muire agat*" and a toss of his head. It felt good to be part of a place where people acknowledged one's existence—unlike the streets of Dublin, where they would just as soon push a fellow wayfarer out onto the road in their hurry to pass by, than exchange greetings.

Edward made his way down to the pub called *Traditions,* where a workshop was being offered for fly-fishing newbies, followed by a one-on-one guided fishing expedition. As he entered, he inhaled the enticing aroma that filled the room.

"Now that's a fine fragrance to greet a hungry gent," exclaimed Edward to the lad behind the bar. "I wouldn't be the least offended by a taste of the source of that aroma," he said with a warm smile.

With a toss of his head, Muirís laughed. "Although it leads to a fiery redhead I'm loathe to share with another man, sure, there's nothing wrong a t'all in starting with a bit of her wild salmon scones and raspberry tea, before learning to fish. It lends some *epicurean* motivation to the enterprise." He offered a nod and a broad smile.

"Indeed," said Edward, rubbing his hands with relish. "Just the very thing the doctor ordered—prior to spending the day in a cold river!"

With a warm smile, Muiris asked, "You're one of the participants in the workshop, so." He introduced himself as the instructor and guide.

Before Edward knew it, he was sitting before a large assortment of freshly baked wild salmon breakfast scones and a pot of tea. He took a bite, savouring the fresh flavour of the salmon dressed in crisp herbs, encased by an intensely buttery, flaky crust.

Muirís looked on with amusement at the expression of the stranger's face. "Well?" he asked in an expectant tone. "Is it worth standing the day out in the rain and a cold river—to catch some of that?"

Edward nodded vigorously in assent. "Indeed, it is," he exclaimed with great enthusiasm. "Utterly delectable," he announced, as he dove into the rest of the serving. "We haven't anything like this in Dublin—even at the finest hotels," he said in between bites.

Muirís shook his head with vigour. "What you're eating there, now, my man, is made from all local ingredients. *Bradáin fiáin*—wild salmon—drawn from the river a few days ago before smoked—as well as fresh butter churned, herbs picked, and a light flaky crust prepared all this morning. Sure, it doesn't get any fresher or better than that!" Muirís beamed.

Edward took another bite from his scone, savouring the flavours. "The salmon has an interesting smoky flavour to it, like nothing I have ever before encountered."

Muirís responded with great enthusiasm, "Indeed, it does. Sure, that's from smoking it with peat from the bog, as they did in the old days. We're quite proud of the *old ways* here—hence the name."

Edward nodded, grateful for an entry into the topic that prompted his visit. "Tell me, then, is it your loyalty to *traditions* down here that has fuelled the political fires about wild salmon, over, say farmed or engineered? Can you actually tell a difference amongst them?"

Muirís looked at him with a tinge of disappointment in his eyes. "'Tis a sad state of affairs in this country when a man has to pose such a question," he proclaimed. "For an Irishman not to know the difference between the taste of the *diseased* substance they call '*farmed*,' or even worse, the chemical sludge they offer as '*engineered*,' to his own historical salmon in its fresh *wild* state, well, it's a crime against our very *culture*, it is!" Muirís stared at him, his steel-blue eyes ablaze.

He gazed over at Edward with undisguised suspicion. "But then," he said pointedly, "Perhaps you haven't the Irish on you a t'all. Thought I detected a bit of a *British* accent on you." Muirís peered at him, waiting.

Edward choked on the temerity of the man to question his pedigree in what seemed like an insulting manner, but kept his temper reined in, overcoming what he sensed in the lad as reverse snobbery. After all, to the Kerryman, so he had heard, there *is* no other Ireland—but "the Kingdom of Kerry."

Edward chose his words with care, sidestepping the question of his own cultural heritage. "It's just that I've been surrounded by people in Dublin debating the issue of wild vs. 'cultivated,' as they prefer to call the caged and the test tube varieties, and I wondered what all the fuss was about."

That was the type of sentiment to set off Muirís. "*Cultivated* me' arse, if you'll excuse me' French," he sputtered. "Anyone who tells you that those others are even edible are pure eegits. They haven't a tastebud to save themselves from the toxic load of *shite* that makes up the insides of the farmed mush and the genes of the test tube imposters."

With a sheepish glance at Edward, who was now observing him with more than a bit of amusement, Muirís admitted to his own intense response to the issue.

"Ah, sure, I get agitated, I do, over the *shite* those multi-national corporate types—and now our very own government—try to foist on us, rather than our own native foods. By the end of this day, if you cannot tell the difference yourself, I'll refund your money for the course and the workshop, for I'll have failed in me' goal of saving you from your dependence on the global *chemicals*, they call food."

Edward displayed a reassuring smile, admiring the fellow's ardour. "That's the very reason why I have come all this way, you know, so I can learn all about the *wild* salmon and know the difference it makes to the palate, and from what you say, to our cultural prospects. I am more than curious about your local food movement here in Kerry—'*Celtic Roots*' you call it?"

Muirís laughed. "Ah, sure, we rely mostly on potatoes, we do, as well as carrots and onions, so the roots part of the name contains a double meaning. Rooted in tradition—in more ways than one. That's what we're all about here, my man," Muirís retorted in a proud voice. "'*Sinn Féin*'—Ourselves Alone." Who needs the global, when you can have that tart there as your local food?"

Edward looked at him with obvious amusement. "Are you Kerrymen all so *emblazoned* in your zeal for the local? You remind me of that woman who has been writing that food blog down here, *Kerry Roots*, isn't it? She makes rousing political pronouncements like that."

Thinking of Áine, Muirís smiled. "*Herself* would say that every bite is a *political* act."

"Indeed?" Edward cast a raised eyebrow in the speaker's direction. "You know her, then," he said softly.

Muirís instantly detected a change in the stranger's voice and responded with caution. "I do, indeed." Staring down Edward, he asked curtly, "And would you be know-ing *Herself* at all?" He studied the man's face, as he waited for a response.

Edward tried to remain as nonchalant as possible, responding with a shrug, "No, not really." Noting the younger man's suspicious glare, he added in as indiffer-ent a tone as he could muster, "She addressed a confer-ence I attended in Dublin."

Muirís gave a hearty laugh. "Told all of ye how ye should be doing things, did she?"

Edward grinned. "She did, indeed."

With a toss of his head, Muirís launched with great fervour into sharing a bit of his experience with *Herself.* Shaking his head, he exclaimed somewhat proudly, "Ah, I've yet to reel in a salmon that is more challenging to handle than she, and indeed, I have fought with the most fierce of them!" Then, with a toss of his head, he added, "But sure, she's well worth the effort—even if she remains forever wild and unattainable." He peered at the man. "Just like we prefer our salmon—*wild and free.*"

"I hadn't realized that our paths might cross here in Dingle," Edward said with a slight shrug. "She's so popu-lar now that I'm thinking I should ask for her autograph."

"Well, you are eating one of her *signature* dishes as we speak," Muiris announced proudly. "Sure, isn't she the very *same* who baked your scones this morning? When she's not writing her polemics, she's baking traditional dishes with local ingredients—to remind us all of how we *once* ate and *should* do again today."

"Well, well. An amazingly talented woman all round," Edward said with clear admiration in his voice.

Muirís set his solemn gaze on the man. "Sure, you don't know the half of it. She's quite the inspiration." He

looked off into the distance a few minutes before awak-
ening from his own reverie. "Right so, I'll leave you to
your last bites. I must get ready for our course, so."

Edward watched as Muirís bounded off in the direction of some men who had entered the establishment.
He held his teacup in his hand, swirling it round and
round, as he recounted his exchange with Muirís, deciding he was quite a likeable fellow, full of sincerity, and
appreciative of the quality of character.

Edward shook his head slightly, releasing a soft
sigh. He wished he had evinced even half the strength
of character of Muirís when he was his age. Looking
away through the window of the pub, he mulled over
how different his life would have turned out—had he
understood in his younger days—the level of insight
the lad had just shown him. The thought made Edward
look down at his now empty plate in sadness. He tried
to shake off the thoughts he had long kept submerged
of the utterly charming Maeve he found now swirling
through his consciousness. It was too late in that regard,
he noted sadly, but not too late to make a difference in
the life of their daughter.

He wondered whether maybe he was fated to follow
the path he did in order to be in the position in which he
now found himself, with the chance to save this country
from its rapidly spiralling dependence on the EU. As he
toyed with his tea, he couldn't help but wonder whether
Ireland had not been better off two decades ago *before*
the rise of the Celtic Tiger mentality. He hoped his time
in Dingle would offer him just the perspective he needed
to see things in a new light. Perhaps, he thought, that
light would lead him along a path away from the dark
muck into which his country had fallen.

Not long after their brief encounter, Murís gathered together the seminar participants. "*Céad Míle Fáilte, Fáilte!* Welcome, Everyone!" he called out in a hearty voice, as each person took a seat in a circle around him. "Today we'll be learning, as your man there inquired," nodding in Edward's direction, "what all the *fuss* is about, regarding one of our most beloved national assets and cultural treasures—*na bradáin fiáin,* or to you unfortunates not blessed with the Gaelic or Irish tongue, the wild salmon."

He gazed around the room, beaming. "As I said to that fella," with a nod in Edward's direction, "if ye, if ye cannot savour the difference between the true *wild* kind and the diseased *garbage* they call salmon, then I will have failed in me' mission, and that m'lads, is not going to happen, as long as old Muirís here is leading the charge!"

Muirís rubbed his hands together as he launched into his favourite subject. "Ah, the noble salmon—*na bradáin fiáin.* Sure, no other organism in the animal kingdom holds a candle to this mystical creature. I say mystical, for, sure, wasn't the noble salmon the very symbol of *wisdom* for the ancients—our ancestors?"

He glanced round the room. "But even more so, lads, the salmon represented the middle ground between this life and the next for our people, so to eat of the salmon was to gain powers of metaphysical insight into the next life and apply it to this."

He stopped and looked around at every participant before continuing. "And this is why, m'lads, we must keep *na bradáin fiáin* sacred. This is why," he repeated, his voice rising in intonation, "we must *protect* the wild salmon in its wild state from being transformed into some genetic mutation. Sure, it is only the wild salmon that dwell in our rivers and sea, which hold this cultural knowledge I spoke of . . . " His voice drifted off, as he looked off into the distance. "What would become of us as Celts if we do not continue to venerate the great symbol of ancient Ireland? Sure we'd lose our culture, altogether, we would."

He scanned the faces before him. "And this is why, I tell ye again, m'lads, why we must proclaim allegiance to the wild salmon by protecting them from those devils, who are trying to wrest away from us our own national food and symbol of our cultural heritage—all in the name of *profit!*"

Muirís abruptly stopped and changed gears. Rubbing his hands together, he spun on his heels. "Right so, lads, will we start with the traits that set the true *bradáin fiáin* apart from the bloody imposters—the farmed stuff and the frankenfish?" He opened a cold chest and brought out three salmon on ice. Gesturing to the audience, he ushered them over. "Gather round, now m'lads, and we'll take it step by step," he said, and with a wink, added, "or, if you'll forgive the pun, fish by fish."

Edward watched the presentation with increased interest, impressed with both Muirís' passion and his detailed knowledge regarding the host of issues raging over the status of the wild salmon. He hadn't quite realized how powerful a symbol the wild salmon was to the ancient Celts—as well as to their modern ancestors in Kerry.

He sat contemplating the new insights he was gaining on the matter. He found himself beginning to understand the fervour there over their local food movement. He thought of the formulation adopted by Muirís to encapsulate their mission. *Themselves alone. Ourselves Alone. Sinn Féin.* He chuckled to himself. *Now that's quite a spin on one of the country's most politically explosive expressions.* Edward pondered over its potential as an interesting new use of the term—with significant implications for the doleful set of oppressive demands mandated by the EU.

Edward leaned back in his seat, looking off into the distance. He mulled over the question of whether it could truly be economically more remunerative for the farmers and food producers to sell to fellow countrymen. He chuckled to himself over the notion that such a level of economic independence could serve as a nice kick in the balls of the EU bankers. He revelled over the idea, coming back to the present moment only when Muirís called him to attention.

Soon the participants were hands deep in touching, feeling, examining, and measuring samples of the *bradáin fiáin* alongside the imposters. "Sure, the farmed and the GE present bigger," exclaimed Muirís, "but what we want here, m'Lads, in our salmon is superior *taste.* Here the regal wild salmon reigns supreme—sure, she has no competitors. And this is where the industrialists get it wrong, thinking bigger is better." Tossing his head, he added, "Typical *Yank* notion, that."

As Muirís scanned the room, he noticed that several of the fellows nodded in agreement. He smiled. "What we'll do now is a blind taste test. Before we start, though, I'd like to introduce our *Chef.* She will be preparing our meals for the day, as well as our savouries for the taste tests we'll be having."

He called out to Áine, who emerged from the kitchen with an enormous tray of bite-size appetizers, smiling round at the workshop audience. However, when her eyes came upon Edward, she screeched to a halt and stared down at him. He immediately slumped down in his seat, pushing his hat down farther on his forehead, but not before giving her a wink and a "sshh" sign. When Áine understood Edward was acting on the *qt*, she recovered her composure by merely smiling at him, and after giving him a knowing nod in return, she moved on to the middle of the room.

"Now, Lads, you'll be needing to be especially friendly to this lovely lass, if ye'd like to eat a t'all today!"

Muirís glanced around the room, noting the appreciative looks now surfacing on the faces of the men, not only for Áine's position as *chef*, but, he surmised, for her quite extraordinary features. Bathed in the morning sunlight streaming into the room, Áine seemed to radiate light all about her as her salmon-coloured hair glistened.

"Queen of the harvest, she is, me boys!" he said, winking at the lot. "And isn't she well-named after the goddess of the land around us?" He smiled at the now blushing woman. "Áine here will be creating great treats for us throughout the day, Lads, but only," he stopped and gazed gravely around the room, shaking his finger at the sea of faces, "only if ye can learn to distinguish the Queen of Salmon from her shameful imposters."

Muirís gestured to Áine, who placed the tray down on a round table in the middle of the room, as he announced, "On to the taste test! Who'll volunteer?"

Edward was one of the first to dash up to the table, for his curiosity had now reached a crescendo. "Where will I start?" he asked, turning to Áine.

With a wide smile, she responded, "Start with whatever appeals to you." Calling out to the men gazing at various food choices, she said, "Have a good look at the colour, the texture, and the aroma that each provide.

These attributes will guide you to the real thing." Both she and Muirís stepped back to observe the participants sample the test bites.

Soon the room was filled with the mixed sounds of appreciative grunts, as well as moans of displeasure as the men smelled, prodded, tasted, spat out, and swallowed the various samples. Each recorded responses in the notebooks provided, as well as shared their opinions with one another.

While Muirís walked about encouraging the participants, Áine sat back along the wall, watching Edward as he explored the offerings. She found herself hoping against hope that he would detect the difference himself and thus come to understand fully the importance of preserving the wild salmon. "*Oh, Maeve,*" she mentally addressed her, "*I hope you're looking down on him now and sharing some of your own passion for our national relic with the man you once loved.*"

After some time had passed, and the din subsided to a hum in the room, Muirís called them all together to share the results. "Right, so, Lads, have ye become experts now on the wild salmon?" he asked, as he twirled round gazing at the men. "Tell us what you've discovered, so."

Soon they were sharing their observations on colour, texture, and taste. After listening to several of their assessments, Muirís nodded knowingly. "The thing of it 'tis," he began, "the *bradáin fiáin*, the wild salmon, is not the brightest-looking, nor even the sharpest-tasting of the lot." Heads nodded in agreement. "Sure, she's like her counterpart, the female bird, who not known for bright colours, and maybe even considered rather *bland* in appearance compared to her comely male, nevertheless reveals a *subtle* beauty that blends in with the landscape around her, and through this connection, we come to discover a *rare* beauty in the muted markings of the female over her more fiery counterpart."

He stopped in a momentary reverie before continuing. "Where was I?"

"You were waxing poetic-like on the subject of the female bird," shouted out one of the participants, while the others laughed.

Muirís turned to the man, offering a nod of his head. "Ah, sure, of course, that I was, now. Wouldn't I lose me' own head if it weren't attached?" he added, smiling at the man, "Well, then, back to the salmon from the female bird!"

Rubbing his hands with vigour, he jumped right into contextualizing his comparison. "The flavour of the wild salmon is subtle, yet infinitely more substantial, than the counterfeits who trick the taste buds by their fiercely strong flavour. The taste of the true salmon lingers on the tongue, offering an aftertaste that is pleasing and continuous, long after the bite is finished, much like the subtle flavour of a fine wine over a cheap imitation that dazzles with its sense of immediacy."

He spun around the room. "Are you following me, Lads? Are you getting the gist of what I'm trying to tell ye, now?" He picked up a savoury made from farmed salmon. "Have a look at this one, now, boys, and you'll see what I mean. This farmed salmon is brighter in colour, from the chemicals they feed the fish, while this one," gesturing to one made from genetically engineered fish, "is essentially orange in colour due to the manipulation of the colour genes by those lab *rats*, called 'food engineers.'" He scanned the room. "Do ye really want an '*engineer*' making food for you from test tubes? Sure, we're not that far gone yet, are we, as a culture?"

"Go 'way with them," shouted out one fellow, while others nodded in agreement.

Muirís then picked up a savoury featuring wild salmon. "Ah, but have a good look at this one, m'Lads, and admire the true salmon colour—the soft, subtle, yet shimmering patina of the wild salmon. A pastel pigment is what we're after, Lads."

He then launched into a succinct lecture on the nutritional merits of the wild salmon over its counterparts, going into gory detail about the complications and illnesses resulting from consuming the farmed salmon, due to their unsanitary growing conditions, as well as to the nutritionally deficient—if not directly carcinogenic—food they are fed. Upon describing the host of problems and diseases inherent in the genetically engineered salmon, Muirís smiled smugly at the moans of disgust that now filled the room.

"And, mind you," he added, "let's not forget their marketing ploys trying to make it sound as if their '*Atlantic salmon*' actually hail from the wilds of the ocean." He tossed his head with vigour. "Sure, there's nothing wild about their Atlantic salmon, unless they mean the poor things are wild from *grief* over being incarcerated in nets in our otherwise pristine Atlantic waters."

Satisfied that his audience understood the chemical, political, economic, health, and cultural implications of eating anything but the wild kind, Muirís asked them to share their experiences of the different flavours they encountered in their taste tests. Turning to Edward, he asked, with a glint of sport in his eye and a slight pitch of sarcasm to his tone, "Well, Sir, have you sorted out, now, what all the *fuss* is about, as you asked this morning, over the wild salmon?"

"I have, indeed," responded Edward, without missing a beat. "I should think that a great deal more *fuss* should be made of the true Queen of the Realm—the wild salmon."

Everyone shouted "aye!" in approval.

Rubbing his hands together, Muirís proclaimed, "Well, now, on that highly positive note of endorsement, I'd say, m'Lads, that we're ready now to take the plunge into the river!" But before they left, he added, with a level of seriousness noted by the participants, "And it is to *conserve* our cherished salmon that we must insist on extremely limited angling—only one per year. Our ancestors knew this too well, eating of the wild salmon only in highly restricted times of the year, and even then, sparingly. We would be wise to follow their example."

Once Muirís instructed the novices on the finer points of salmon fishing, and gave them each a bagged luncheon, prepared by Áine, along with a canteen of hot tea, he encouraged them to go off on their own, as he said, to experience the essence of the Kingdom of Kerry.

"I'll be checking in on each of ye throughout the day. Not to worry, the real experience of salmon fishing is to feel alone with the other great *Queen* of the land— Mother Nature *Herself*," he added with a toss of his head. Then with a wink, he added, "Who knows which spirits or *wee folk* ye might be hearing off by yourself—if ye know how to listen for them, that is!" He waved them away, each in different directions. "Whist, off with ye now! *Slán Leat*! Good luck, boys!"

Off they all went down to the place where the river meets the sea. With bucket and rod in hand, each man headed in his own direction, eager to engage in what each hoped to be an unforgettable encounter with the highly coveted, yet ever elusive salmon.

Edward chose a spot where the river tumbled down a slight waterfall, before it turned to flow in another direction. He saw it as a metaphor for his own state in life— down and about in a new way. Ah, but the waters still flow on, he noted—*even if they do take a mighty turn*. He shrugged, thinking that perhaps there was hope for him, after all.

He stood there, just holding his rod, gazing out into the river for extra layers of meaning, if not outright solutions to the myriad of concerns swarming about him, like a cloud of midges on a summer's evening. He marvelled at how closely he found the contours of Nature reflected in his thoughts, as if She offered insights into the complexity of life issues confronting him.

Yet he also discovered great solace in what Yeats had called the "*terrible beauty*" around him. The dark blue mountains shrouded in mist at their peaks, the crumbling stone walls careening down to the sea, the ancient river twisting and turning as it made its way to the sea— all seemed to signify great meaning to him. *If only I could hear their voices.* He stood perfectly still, hoping that he might hear something riding in the wind.

He felt as if Time had stopped, unaffected by the faults of man. His thoughts flowed with the current, as he wondered how long raw Nature could hold out if the wild river before him were transformed into a tamed fish farm, or if the grey waters of the Atlantic were filled with oil platforms. He realized that he must consider, before acting, how such endeavours would change the land, the flora and the fauna, the salmon—if not the very people themselves. He recalled Muirís's points, wondering whether such changes would result in destroying the core of Irish culture—in the name of economic success. He shook his head contemplatively, as he continued to gaze about him.

His concerns continued to plague him, as he stood lost in the landscape. He did not even hear the approach of Muirís, who seemed to step imperceptibly into the scene of his reverie. Yet the lad seemed not out of place as Edward's consciousness finally acknowledged the fellow's presence.

"I thought to start with you, before moving on to the others," said Muirís matter-of-factly. Upon noticing that Edward was not fishing, he asked, "Have you forgotten my lesson? Sure, your rod hasn't even touched the water yet, and you're here more than an hour." He looked at the older fellow, scanning his face. "You seem a bit dazed. Are you all right, man?"

Edward shook himself slightly, as if to remove the contemplative spell the scenery had placed upon him. Turning to the younger fellow, he responded, "*Au contraire*. I have been thinking about your lesson more than you know. I have been lost in reverie here—with your words swirling round in my head, as I gazed upon this primeval setting."

Muirís laughed. "Ah, I see," he said. "This *Place* has lured you into her lair." He studied Edward through curious eyes. "Sure, I didn't think *she* would affect you a t'all in this way. Maybe I have underestimated you, so."

Edward wagged his finger. "Never underestimate the pervasive power of your message, young man. You make a *highly* persuasive case for the *wild and the traditional.*

You just may have answered the riddle that plagues our current situation."

Muirís studied him in silence for a few moments before answering. He sensed something in the aura of the man before him. Something inside was telling him that Edward was an influential figure in the future of the country, yet one who felt undecided about which turn in the river of life to take. A small seed of insight was also germinating within Muirís that suggested this man might prove to be a powerful figure in his own future, though how, exactly, he couldn't even begin to fathom.

Muirís slowly cast out his line, exaggerating each step, so Edward could get a better feel for how to proceed. What he modelled through his actions, he mirrored in his carefully chosen words: "For those of us who feel the need to act responsibly toward our own ones, there is no other choice but endorsing the *bradáin fiáin* at all costs—for sure, although there is money to be made in the other stuff, 'twould be like selling out your very own child for the lure of a successful career."

Muirís stopped there, lost in his thoughts, as they swerved back inevitably to the story of Áine. He discovered that thoughts of her never left his consciousness, even amid a salmon fishing seminar. So engulfed was he, that he took no notice of the deadly pallor that had suddenly swept over his now grief-stricken companion.

A searing pain had shot through Edward's heart, immediately upon hearing the indirect reference to his own decision-making back then. He felt utterly overwhelmed, so churned up inside by his new experiences and insights, particularly from what he deemed an almost prophetic young man—together with this new, earth-shattering, transformational experience of meeting his daughter. My God, he moaned inwardly, *my own daughter!* It was even more daunting to discover that her mission was intertwined with the charismatic young fellow.

Muirís interrupted their joint musings by turning back to Edward. "Sure, 'twouldn't be so different from what I hear our fearful leaders are doing to us up your way in Dublin—selling out our country, our culture, our traditional ways, our salmon, our oil, and thus our very future, for a few bob and the dubious promise of a better future." He shook his head in obvious disgust.

"Indeed," Edward said in a non-committal tone. He gazed at him steadily in the eye, wondering just what the lad might know of his part in what he was, unfortunately, all too accurately describing.

"Trouble is," added Muirís, without noting Edward's penetrating gaze, "'Twould be our demise. What are we, as Irish people, if not an integral part of this wild landscape, the clear rivers soaring around us, the mist-enshrouded mountain peaks, the green fields, all which up 'til now have been pure and clean, wild and free of multi-national control and regulations? What are we, a t'all, I ask you, if we are not connected and protective of *our own ones*? Sure we'd be nothing more than nationless, cultureless pawns in a global game of domination." He turned to meet the eyes of Edward. "Is that why we fought for our independence—to give it all away?"

"You raise some essential points, there, Lad," murmured Edward, though he averted his eyes.

Muirís waved his arm around. "I would rather have all of this the way it has been for thousands of years, than a golden future that sells out an essential part of us—

like exchanging your own child for a glorious future." He gave a vigorous toss of his head. "Sure, 'tis like that altogether—what those buggers are doing up there in Dublin. They should be men and stand up for us, their children, against the EU thieving terrorists!" Muirís's expression suddenly took a sheepish turn. "Ah, now, don't get me started. Let's fish while we're still allowed. When a man can no longer provide by fishing and growing for his own ones, then the culture is lost."

Edward shot the man another look. "Tell me, Muirís, I am curious," he said, carefully choosing his words and monitoring his emotions, trying to adopt as nonchalant a tone as possible under the circumstances. "Why do you use the example of a man who sells out his children for an illustrious career?"

Muirís looked at him out of the corner of his eye in curiosity, surprised by the question. Shaking his head, he responded, "I can't get out of me' head the utterly tragic story of lost love."

Edward cast out his line out, waiting a moment before asking, "What does lost love have to do with selling out the country to big business interests?"

"No, no, not that way a t'all," admonished Muirís, as he cast out over the waters. Reeling it back in, he handed the rod back to Edward. "You go on now and try it, so."

Edward attempted again, eliciting a reluctant grunt of approval from his instructor. Edward smiled at him. "You are quite the perfectionist, aren't you, Lad?"

Muirís glanced reproachfully as he cast his own line. "If you're to do anything a t'all, you should try to do it *right*. That's what me' da' taught me, and about that, he was certainly right. Sure, it's the slipshoddy work of the politicians and their banker partners that have gotten us into the mess we're in. Had they done their jobs right, we would all be enjoying the old ways, without the luxury of a mobile phone and holiday home developments." He spat. "Such 'necessities' I can do without."

Edward gazed over at him, finding himself enjoying the austere edge to the young man's philosophy. "And how does the lost love fit into your equation, I wonder?"

Muirís' usually animated eyes suddenly clouded over, much like the skies overhead are wont to do without a moment's notice in that part of Kerry. "Ah, 'twas something I was thinking of. 'Tis never far from me thoughts, so."

Edward leaned toward him. "What is, Lad?"

Muirís gently reeled in his line, only to toss it out again in a slightly different direction. "Everything is interconnected, don't you know, in life." He stopped a moment, gazing out over the river to the mountains beyond, before casting a sly glance over at his companion. "Sure, I wouldn't be surprised a t'all if your presence weren't somehow interwoven with our mission here in Dingle."

"Is it, now?" asked Edward, not quite knowing whether the interconnections he was seeing in the exchange were the same Muirís saw, for how could he know, unless, unless, Áine *told* him. The thought made him go pale. With curiosity getting the better of him, he prodded Muirís to explain himself.

As the two men stood with their rods cast out into the river, Muirís related to his companion the tragic story of Maeve who lost the love of her life, and in turn, her daughter, to a man who chose success over love from his own ones.

"And from what I understand," said Muirís sadly, "this

bloke was somehow involved with approving the development of the experimental fish farms, which led tragically to the death of his lost love."

Edward visibly jumped at the accusation. "Whatever do you mean?"

Muirís cast a curious glance over at the man, who now seemed increasingly more upset over the tenor of the conversation. "You know that goddess who made our food this morning? Well, I'm referring to her sad tale. Sure, she doesn't actually know conclusively yet, as the results are still under examination—though she strongly *suspects*—that her Mum, whom she never knew as her mother until after her death, died from a new disease they are calling *mad salmon disease*—a version of the *mad cow*—now afflicting the farmed salmon. Sure, the woman—Maeve, was her name—" he said with a glance at Edward, "Told me herself that last summer she spent here. Not being able to get the wild kind due to the preponderance of fish farms Over, she gave in to eating the farmed stuff, euphemistically called 'Atlantic salmon,' both there and here as well—the experimental garbage they pass off as the real thing, mind you, and simply died from it. Tragic, really tragic."

Edward looked down. "I had no idea that could happen with farmed fish."

"Indeed, it does, and in increasing numbers—though they cover it up by labelling it, Alzheimer's." Muirís shook his head. "All for greed—choosing money, power, and success over our connections to one another and to our traditions. Sure, 'twas the story of Áine's birth father, Maeve's lost love, and now the same story of the current state of our country."

Muirís glanced over at Edward, only to discover a man visibly moved—if not *sickened* by the story he had just related.

"Ah, I have troubled you by my tale of woe, I see. I feel terrible, really now, so I'll leave you, so, to your salmon fishing, and wish you good luck in procuring one."

Muirís turned to go, offering as he left, "Sure, aren't you're a grand fella', altogether, for having listened to my rant and to my tale." He stopped, and directing his steady gaze on the man, placed his hand gently on Edward's shoulder. "Somehow, I think it did us both good, though, in your case, I wouldn't know, exactly, how it could have helped."

He shook his head, and casting a wary eye at the older man, who stood gazing down to the sea beyond, he added with a slight tinge of amusement in his voice, "Sure, I shouldn't be surprised a t'all to learn that you possess the authority to do something about our common plight. And in that, I wish you good luck and great *strength*." With that, Muirís disappeared over the incline.

Edward felt completely humbled by the exchange with Muirís. The wisdom evinced in the ostensibly simple fellow, a fisherman from the west of Kerry, eloquently and insightfully identified the issues resulting in the current plight of Ireland in ways that his specialist colleagues in Dublin could—or dared—not. Edward decided in that moment to look elsewhere for insight and guidance—if he were to save the country from its predators.

But it was the account of poor Maeve, and his role in the tenor of her life and death that shook him to the very core of his being. Edward stood trembling, his inner conscience pounding to the pulsating rhythm of his tremors. With his hands covering his face, he felt overwhelmed—

and terribly, terribly ashamed. He vowed then and there to make things right, as Muirís called it, whatever it would take—regardless of the consequences.

With a new sense of determination, Edward continued making resolutions. He vowed to make things right for the memory of Maeve and her tragic death, for the security of his new daughter, for the future of people like Muirís, and for their country. Imbued with an iron-clad armour of determination, Edward set himself at once to the almost insurmountable task of deciding upon a course of action, which once initiated, could not be forsaken. With such indefatigable determination, he first focussed on the task at hand—to bring back a prized catch of the wild salmon—in memory of his once proud Maeve.

He used his taut wrist to throw out his line as Muirís had instructed along the top of the water in the river's midline, proceeded by rhythmically casting the line from side to side to attract the fish. Without too much trouble, he soon achieved a beat that harmonized with the swift current of the river. As he swayed in the gentle breeze in harmony with the flowing waters and his line, Edward soaked in the raw *wildness* of the place.

A beam of sunlight emerged, bobbing along on top as the current swept through the shining water, casting its sunny spell in different directions. As the sun cast golden light on various parts of the landscape around him, shimmering on a stand of flowers here, or on the mountain above, Edward felt a soft current of tranquillity ooze through his veins, filling him with a sense of oneness with the wild, primeval place. He tried to remember how Yeats had expressed it. *Ah, yes: 'Come away—to the waters and the wild.'*

His thoughts drifted lightly through him, like puffs of clouds passing by above. He was beginning to understand what Muirís meant when he spoke of feeling *rooted* in the land about him. For those moments, he felt as an *extension*, rather than an *interloper*, of Nature—even though he was searching for a prized symbol of Celtic Nature Herself—the *bradáin fiáin*.

Edward was so lost in thought that he barely noticed the tug on his line, and when sensing it, absent-mindedly tugged back, until a sharp jolt of the line brought him back to the moment—a salmon had snapped up the bait. Now actively playing the line, he moved into the river himself, slyly closing up the space between himself and his prize. The water now thrashed as the salmon leapt into the air, still tied to the line, and crashed down again, hoping to escape. "Oh, Spirits of the Place, if you exist at all," implored Edward to the air around him, "Let me take just this one. One. Just once."

He realized that—much like the act of making passionate love—once was simply good enough for the moment. Landing this salmon would be such an exhilarating experience that he felt no need to repeat it. It was in that moment that he discovered the innate superiority of *quality* over *quantity*.

A few hours later, Edward entered the establishment to discover none of the other fellows had yet returned from their expeditions. Deciding that this was his moment for a few quiet words, he walked into the kitchen, where he found Áine alone, bent over the countertop as she rolled out some dough.

"Is that you, Muirís?" she asked, without turning away from her task.

"Actually, no. It's the other new man in your life." Surprised, Áine stood up, whirling round towards the voice. Smiling at him as she wiped off her hands on her apron, she asked, "Well, have you been found out yet?"

"Not yet," he responded. "I keep my sunglasses on, my hat down low, and my brown wig in place."

Laughing, Áine retorted, "You can lose the phony accent around me. They'll eventually figure out that you speak as if you came from a variety of locales, rather than one, you know!"

He chuckled. "I've been asked if I hail from Donegal, Galway, even Scotland! It's bound to happen, though I try not to say much or look anyone directly in the eye." He gazed at Áine. "Though it's hard work avoiding the penetrating scrutiny of that lads of yours."

Áine laughed, and changing the subject, asked, "How was your fishing experience?"

Walking over to her, and with one last furtive glance around the kitchen to make sure no one had entered, he removed his shades and quickly kissed her cheek, causing her to beam with happiness. He grasped her arm and said simply, "It was utterly *transformational*."

"Do tell!" she urged him, flushing with excitement over the pronouncement. "I'll put on some tea."

"First, I have something for you," he whispered to her, then shot out of the kitchen, leaving her guessing.

Minutes later, Áine watched Edward return with his prize—a good-sized salmon, which he presented to her. "In honour of your Mum, love."

"It's absolutely lovely," she murmured. Tears welled in her eyes as she gathered the beautiful salmon in her arms and gently walked it over to the refrigerator, where it would remain cool until ready to be cleaned. "I'll make this one up special for our supper—the way Maeve used to like it," she said in a whisper.

Turning round to Edward, she said, "You must be perished from the cold rain." She touched his jumper to see how wet it was. "Let's get you into some dry clothes while the water is heating, shall we? I'll make us a pot of tea, and you can tell me all about your transformational experience. I'm dying to hear the details." She smiled at him before bustling around preparing the tea, while he went in search of a dry jumper.

Minutes later, they sat around the island table sipping tea, as Edward related his experiences to her. Every now and then, Áine would interject with an "exactly," or "I know what you mean."

"Am I to assume," Edward said, as he twirled his tea round in his cup, "that such experiences of catching wild salmon are compromised by the presence of fish farms?"

"That's right," Áine responded. "It wouldn't be possible for the wild salmon to breed once the streams are netted for the farmed versions. The wild ones are killed off as a result." She sat twirling her tea round, as well, while she talked.

Anticipating his next question, she launched in. "The problem with allocating one river here for the wild, and that river over there for the farmed, say, is that once the farmed kind are added to the rivers, the natural food for the wild is replaced by the antibiotic-filled, chemically-laden, fattening, processed, grainy stuff they use for the farmed, which fills the rivers, infecting the wild. Even with separate rivers, the wild fish are compromised, and their numbers diminish rapidly."

She whirled her teacup round and round. "All the rivers in Ireland are interconnected."

"I see," said Edward, looking down pensively into his cup. "There is no room for compromise on this issue, if one were determined to protect the wild salmon."

"No, I'm afraid," said Áine, with a firm shake of her head. "You simply must stand up for the wild ones and the cultural traditions they represent."

He swirled away, thinking about the issues facing him. Finally, he spoke. "But how is one to feed the people, then," he asked more rhetorically, than anything else, not really expecting an answer from Áine on this mighty question that weighed him down.

"Compromise isn't always the best response to big issues," Áine began gently, "as it clouds the bigger picture."

Edward gazed at her. "Would you explain?"

She took a sip of tea. "I suppose the real question might be, given cultural, economic, and environmental reasons to protect the wild salmon, does one *need* to feed "the many" with this *particular* fish? After all," she added, "Even among the Irish, the salmon was eaten only *occasionally*, and in season—a practice which ensured its survival."

Áine then proceeded to share with him some of her recent reading into the matter, where researchers—intent on solving this very issue—have suggested that some fish, such as the Atlantic cod, as well as the wild salmon, should be allocated to a "specialty" status, while other fish, such as the Vietnamese Basa, whose unique respiratory system allows it to be raised in standing water, could be used as market fish to feed the masses.

"What an utterly fascinating idea," remarked Edward. His mind raced. "Such an approach allows the conglomerates to carry on doing what they do best—exploiting markets, but with fish that do not compromise our cultural heritage and our environmental future."

"Exactly." She smiled at him. "That was our winning argument in securing the EU trade deal, saving the wild salmon for severely restricted and highly regulated local consumption only."

He nodded. "Hmm. I like that. It makes everyone happy without compromise. *Indeed*." He smiled over at her.

"That's exactly what my work entailed on Prince Edward Island—saving the *special* for the *local*," she explained with pride. "We protected the wild salmon and exported readily abundant shellfish."

Both sat swirling their cups as each sat thinking. Unexpectedly, the door opened, and Muirís walked in, immediately noticing the two swirling round their cups in unison. "Odd behaviour, that," he remarked as he tipped his cap to Edward. "I see you have now adopted that move yourself," he said, directing his comment to Edward, who stood up, flustered by being caught off guard.

"Your young lady is very persuasive," he said, smiling at the younger man.

Muirís put his arm around Áine and brushed her head with a quick kiss. "Ah, that she is, indeed."

Edward, now covering his twinkling eyes with his sunglasses, said with a tease, "A bit like a bulldog is she, when she's onto something?"

Muirís chuckled. "She is, indeed." He squinted at him before asking, "And how would you be knowing that?"

Edward smiled at him and said easily, "Ah, many have accused me of the same. I readily recognize the trait in others." He turned away. "Thanks very much for the tea," but turning back to Áine, added, "I look forward to whatever dish you create from the salmon. I'm sure it will be utterly *delectable*," and before either could stop him, Edward abruptly left the room.

Muirís watched him leave. "A bit of a mystery, that fella." Turning to Áine and gazing at her in curiosity, he said, "You two seem to get on well. Funny, watching the two of you swirling round your teacups at the same time. Odd, that." He walked away deep in thought.

Áine got busy planning the various dishes needed for the evening supper. With the bradáin fiáin taking centre stage as the central theme, she prepared all sorts of entrées, each starring the mighty salmon, though reserving the poached salmon with hollandaise sauce for Edward and herself in memory of Maeve. She made a medley of roasted local root vegetables, and together with the sharp fragrance of freshly baked bread, the ensuing aroma emanating from Áine's kitchen rivalled any haute cuisine establishment found throughout the Continent. But the beauty of this Kerry kitchen lay in its reliance upon local ingredients and traditional dishes.

Before long, as the seminar participants filled the pub, enjoying a pint or a dram before supper, trays of appetizers arrived, each one featuring an array of traditional dishes prepared from local foods. As a tray made its way over to him, Edward marvelled at the large variety, having always assumed that "traditional" was synonymous with homogeneity.

He said as much to Áine, while tasting a particularly delicious appetizer from a tray of widely different offerings. "Now this," he said, "is absolutely *remarkable!*" Swallowing down the last bit, he added, "And I thought that traditional food meant nothing more than boiled potatoes and fish."

Áine laughed and retorted with a twinkle in her eye, "But that's exactly what you are eating—with a bit of a twist."

"Not a chance," he said, as he reached for another.

"That is based on an old recipe called 'Colcannon,'" she started to explain, when he interrupted her with a dismissive wave of his hand.

"Surely, you don't mean that old dish of mashed potatoes, with bits of left-over cabbage thrown in, do you? This bears *absolutely* no resemblance whatsoever," he declared with an adamant shake of his head.

Chuckling over his description, Áine admonished him. "You're much too dismissive of the culinary potential of the humble mashed potato. What you are consuming *is* a mix of mashed potato and sautéed kale—with smoked salmon, garlic, and artisan cheddar cheese added in a soufflé base over a potato tart," she explained, smiling.

"Extraordinary," he remarked in between bites. "I had no idea the lowly spud could taste so delectable."

"I see you're beginning to appreciate our humble cuisine," she added, arching her eyebrow.

"There's nothing humble about any of it—they are all delicious!" he proclaimed.

"Humble food can be delicious," countered Áine. "Just think of the cuisine of rural France, and you'll understand what we are trying to achieve here—by promoting and marketing our own rural food traditions."

Edward leaned over to choose another appetizer. "Tell me, what is this one?"

"Why don't you try it and tell me what you taste?" she suggested.

Edward bit into the morsel, chewing slowly to gather in the various tastes he encountered. "Something with cockles or mussels and lobster in a cheddar cheese cream sauce with seaweed." He reached over for another. "May I?"

Áine touched his arm and whispered, "I'm so delighted you are enjoying our culinary and cultural efforts here. Make sure to try at supper the poached salmon in the cream sauce I made in honour of Maeve." With that, she disappeared into the crowd with a now empty tray.

As the fishers sampled the various plates, plenty of talk ensued all round about what was needed to be done to get Dublin to protect the wild salmon and expunge all efforts at endorsing farming and genetically engineered salmon.

Edward was astounded to hear the impassioned statements of the men regarding the importance of such initiatives. He had no idea that a local economy would not only take off as it had apparently in Kerry, but that consumers would prefer it to global choices. He marvelled at the thought that they would actually prefer less choice and availability, to species purity and traditional ways. *So much for Chinese take-outs*, he chuckled to himself.

As Edward sat listening to the lively exchanges regarding their plans to take their local initiatives to other communities across Ireland, someone leaned over in his direction and peered closely at him. Suddenly, he heard directed to him, "Sure, you resemble the bloody *Taoiseach*! Surely, you wouldn't be *Himself* now, would you?"

All heads turned disbelieving eye in Edward's direction. Sinking down lower in his stool, he shrugged and said somewhat sheepishly with his best country accent, "Ah sure, don't I get that all the time? I'm just his lookalike cousin—quite distant, to be sure." With nods and tosses of various heads, the men continued on with their animated discussions. Edward exited quietly, looking forward to the market opening the next day.

By early the next morning, farmers, growers, fishers, and artisans gathered to set up their booths for the market as hundreds and hundreds of people filed into the square for the opening. An aura of pride, of *hope*, passed through the air in waves, as people shared their common passion for their great endeavour with one another.

Deciding to check out the event incognito first, Edward sauntered through the square in the early morning hours, watching the vendors set up their tables and booths. There was a bustle of enthusiasm, an air of great excitement about the place. He was surprised to see the amount of people setting up for the market. He had no idea that artisanal and local foods were in such demand, particularly in this part of Ireland. Deeply moved by the experience, Edward noted the endless stream of hopefulness he discovered in the expressions of the people, coupled with a quiet determination to take back their country, their culture, and their ways.

Before long, table after table proudly displayed a huge assortment of foods, from polished and scrubbed leeks, to fine cheeses, with every sort of combination thrown in. Edward contentedly breakfasted on an array of baked goods, including soda bread, oatcakes, and, of course, wild salmon pastries.

Amidst the throng of stands, Edward was amazed to come across a small group of older men with women actually dressed in traditional clothes as they offered their famed historical dishes, or proudly showed off hand-lined caught fish, smoked by the embers of a peat fire.

"'Tis the real ting, Laddie," asserted one old gent, as Edward passed slowly by a table laden with freshly baked pies.

"Are they now?" retorted Edward. "What are they, exactly?"

The old man rocked slightly back and forth as he deeply inhaled, then proclaimed as he waved his hand over a selection of pies, "That there is the culinary *jewel* of our wee peninsula—the famed *Dingle pie*—not to be confused with the Donegal pie, should you be so inclined," he added, as he scrutinized his prospective customer.

"Indeed," said Edward with a polite nod.

"Sure, haven't our ancestors been baking these pies for hundreds of years here, so we're quite proud of them, we are," he said, as he tossed his head to the side.

"Which ingredients make up a Dingle pie, I wonder?" asked Edward.

The man eyed Edward up and down sharply before responding in the typical Kerry manner, by answering with a question. "I don't suppose your taste buds are up to finding out on their own, now, are they now?"

Edward, now well versed in the peculiar Kerry mannerism, simply volleyed back another inquiry. "But what is it that makes a Dingle pie, well, Dingle-like, that one wouldn't find in a Cork, or the Donegal pie, shall we say?" asked Edward with a chuckle.

The old man snorted contemptuously, turned, spat, and spun round back to Edward. He pointed toward the hills that loomed up behind the town. "Will you have a look, there, Laddie, and tell me what you're seein', and if ye can see properly, ye'll know what makes a Dingle pie, from Dingle, and nowhere else!"

Edward gazed up at the hills, seeing nothing more than sheep here and there, grazing in translucent green fields—in between the stones. "Besides the sheep and the rocks, is there something more I should be seeing?"

The old man spat again, and gently rocking back and forth, sighed and said, "Aye, that's the 'ting of it, how can you *taste* what ye cannot *see*?"

He shook his head. "The subtle flavours of me' lovely pie would be lost on ye, I'm tinkin'."

"Well, I should be interested in trying one," protested Edward, taken aback at the vendor's disinterest in even selling to him.

The old man studied the confused man before him for a moment. "Sure, I'd be tinkin' that you're not much for the *poetry*, are you, now?"

Edward smiled at the question. "A smattering of Yeats, perhaps, but no, not much, no." He looked at the old man. "Is a poetic disposition required to appreciate the Dingle pie?"

The man smiled a toothless grin. "Ah, sure, the delicate flavours of me' pie—the traces of a fine, salty mist on the succulent heather, the sharp tang of chlorophyll from the early morning grasses warmed by the sun, the soft butter from the timothy flowing through the mutton fat, are the very *shtuff* of poetry itself."

Edward stifled a laugh, even as his admiration shot skyward for the old gent. "Indeed. I had never thought of a pie in that way."

He sighed again. "Sure, ye can't find that in a mutton pie from Cork, Lad, to be sure. Don't they grow different grasses, herbs, and the like in their fields, that result in a different taste, altogether."

The old man started to turn away, saying sadly, "Ah,

but ye wouldn't know about 'tings like this, now would you, Lad? 'Tis obvious ye hail from the city—Dublin, no doubt." He spat again. "God help you," he muttered.

Edward smiled. "I should think it is never too late to learn. I'd like two of your pies, please." As he pulled out some Euro notes, he asked the old man, "But tell me, what are they made from—besides heather and grass?"

The old fellow snorted again. "Ah, Lad, you're a lost soul, altogether, if ye 'tink that." He stood up straight and proclaimed, "M'lad, these pies are made from the finest mutton from up those hills, hand shredded into even finer pieces of delicate meat, surrounded in a bed of sweet carrots, delicate leeks, and fresh herbs from the fields, and covered with the most flaky crust, altogether, carved from the best cut of the mutton fat. Sure, a more delicate flavour, ye'll not find. If ye don't envision the land and sea of our *Corca Dhuibhne*—Dingle Peninsula, don't you know—as you consume your slices, I'll return your money."

Edward laughed. "No need at all. I'm sure you are right about the *visionary* experiences I am about to enjoy with these pies."

As Edward walked away, the old man tipped his cap, saying "*Slán*," to which Edward turned around and responded with a "*Slán Leat*," enjoying how easy it was for him the last few days to use the ancient farewell.

What an utterly remarkable experience! Edward thought to himself, as he sauntered through the market—to be so proud of one's food, the land, and the locality itself. He realized that the old man knew more about the nuances of flavour than the chefs up in Dublin in their fancy restaurants making foreign food. *Absolutely remarkable.*

As he continued making his way through the stalls, Edward noticed with astonishment that the vendors were not just the older generation, but many were quite young. He stopped at a young woman's table where she was selling a variety of cheeses. "Learned from me' Granny," she said somewhat shyly, "but I've also been to France to take a goat and sheep cheese-making course." She laughed and added, "No worry about running out of product. If it's one thing we have plenty of, 'tis goats and sheep!" She then went on to explain the process for making her cheese and the different wild herbs she added to some.

Edward was so impressed by the knowledge and pride of the cheese-maker. "Tell me," he said, "Where do you sell your cheeses? Do you try to sell them abroad, or up in Dublin, perhaps?"

The young woman smiled at him sweetly, as she shook her head. "Have you been to France yourself, Sir?"

"I have, indeed," he replied, somewhat mystified by the question.

"Well, then, the answer to your question lies in your tasting the cheeses themselves," she said, while raising her now twinkling eyes.

He smiled back at her and said graciously, "I'm game. Always more room for some artisan cheese!"

She offered him a wooden spoon with some thyme goat cheese. "Try this."

Swallowing down the sample, Edward proclaimed it exquisite.

"Ready, then, are you, to take it to the next culinary step?" she asked with sly curve of her mouth.

"Of course!" he responded enthusiastically, as he offered a wide grin.

She then leaned over to the table next to her, where a young fellow was selling peat-smoked hams and pork and asked for a bit of ham. She then broke open an oat farl, buttered it with bright yellow butter, added a slice of ham, and topped it with the goat cheese.

"Now try it," she urged.

Edward bit into the concoction, chewing slowly as he savoured the array of tastes. He was astonished to discover that the goat cheese had taken on a new level of flavour, enhanced, he surmised, by the rich smoky ham, the tangy butter, and the crunch of the oat farl.

"Absolutely extraordinary!" he proclaimed.

The woman smiled. "We call that culinary *synergy*! The best lesson I learned in France was not *how* to make cheese—sure me' Granny is as proficient at it as they are over there—but 'twas that flavours work best together with other flavours from ingredients from the same region."

"Indeed?" said Edward through a mouthful of food.

"Everything you are eating now comes from *here*—around Dingle. It's truly the only way to eat—local foods from a specific locale."

"How truly extraordinary!" He took another bite, trying to taste the culinary synergy of the flavours.

She laughed. "If only we could make our own wine here in Kerry as they do in France, sure, we wouldn't need any outside influence whatsoever! For what we lack in local wine, we make up for in *putcheen*!"

Edward chuckled, thoroughly enjoying the sage insights from this young woman, and soon lost himself in discussing the advantages of local foods as he sampled her other cheeses. So engrossed was he in hearing her account of the rise and initiatives of new artisan food makers among the young woman's neighbours and friends that he didn't hear himself being hailed.

"Will the Taoiseach come to the stage, please?"

"Taoiseach, are you here a t'all?" he heard bellowing out over a loudspeaker. "We're ready to begin the opening ceremony once the Taoiseach arrives."

As Edward tried to swallow down a particularly large piece of bread and cheese, he heard, "There he is!"

One by one, heads turned in his direction, as Áine emerged from behind and pulled him by the arm. "Time to fess up now, Edward, and show yourself in your true colours," she said, as she ushered him through the crowd up to the stage.

Soon Edward was standing on the stage, stilled attired in his hat and sunglasses, with a farl in one hand and his pie box in the other. Leaning over to the microphone, he said, "God help me, I'm up to my ears in delicious food! One minute, will you, while I finish my *farl* and get settled in my new function!"

The gathering crowd laughed with delight, as they watched the country's leader consume his roll.

"You'll be needing something to wash that down with!" yelled out a fellow in the crowd as a bottle of Guinness found its way to the stage.

Edward retorted quickly to a cheering crowd, "Thanks, but I eat and drink only *locally* while I'm here in *Corca Dhuibhne!*"

"Well now, we have plenty of *uisce bheatha dhuibhne*, haven't we boys? 'Tis *local!*" someone shouted out.

Edward laughed. "As long as it's not the sea water, but the 'water of life' to which you are referring!" Suddenly, an old woman came on stage and handed him a small pewter dram of *putcheen*.

Edward chuckled and asked her, "It's a bit early in the day for that, isn't it?"

The old woman smiled at him, her eyes twinkling. "'Tis for the christening of the market, so—for the *Sláinte!*"

He took the dram and laughed. "Well then, if it's for the opening," and turning to the audience, proclaimed, "Bottom's up! *Sláinte* everyone!" He drank down the drink as the crowd cheered him on and cameras flickered.

"Are you sure you're the *Taoiseach*?" shouted out a voice. "You're not looking or acting like *Himself!*"

Áine, who stood behind Edward, groaned, and going up to him, whisked off his wig, hat, and shades as he stood somewhat sheepishly in front of them all, now exposed as their political leader.

"I knew it!" exclaimed Muirís with excitement, as Áine joined his side. "I knew he was one of those fellas up in Dublin."

He tossed his head to the side. "But, sure, I didn't think he was the bloody *Taoiseach* himself!"

"You knew!" he accused Áine gently. "You've known all along, now, about the identity of that fella. Is that why you were so nice to him?" he asked, and then tossed his head to the side. "And sure, wasn't I thinking you were a bit soft on him, altogether?" he admitted, as he lightly stroked Áine's long hair.

She laughed. "I'm soft on him all right, but not in the way you think, you silly fellow!"

Muirís called out to Edward, "Speech! Speech!"

Edward retorted without missing a beat, "If the *uisce* hasn't gone to my head!"

He then launched into a highly supportive speech, saying how impressed he was with their hard work and commitment to tradition, to Dingle, to Kerry, and to Ireland. He shared his amazement over the foods he had sampled and wholeheartedly endorsed their movement. He ended his speech by announcing, much to the astonishment of everyone listening—not the least, both Áine and Muirís—that his experiences in Dingle have convinced him of the necessity for creating a new office in his administration. Effective immediately, he was appointing Dr. Áine Ó'Suílleabháin O'Connor to a special position to research traditional foods, conserve and represent local food interests, and to coordinate with *Bord Fáilte*, the Irish Tourist Board, though reporting directly to him. With that, he wished them well, telling them they all have been such a tremendous inspiration, and slipped into the crowd.

Áine walked Edward to the train station, where he was to head off back to Dublin. As they made their way in silence, each ruminating on the events of the last few days, Áine broke the silence by asking Edward if she could ask him something. He stopped, and looking down at her, smiled, "But, of course, my dear."

Rather than jumping into her question, Áine bit her lip and said nothing.

"What is it, love?" he asked her gently. "You have my full attention until I board that train, so hammer away."

She turned toward him, and gently touching his arm, said uncertainly, "It's just that I need to know something—though it's really none of my business."

"Well, then?"

"Did you," she hesitated, before continuing, "Did you *love* Maeve?" She gazed at him, as if searching for the answer in the expression on his face to her somewhat impertinent question.

There she saw everything in the look that came over him—one of anguish mixed with longing. He moaned, and then responded in a low voice, "That woman was the love of my life."

Áine looked searchingly at him and asked without thinking, "Then why—?"

Edward broke in, rather than wait for her to finish. "The trouble was, Áine, I had two loves—Maeve and my career." He then launched into his story of his life back then, of the choices before him. "And I assumed, falsely perhaps, at the time, that they were contradictory passions. All told, my dear, I chose the promise of a highly successful career over the passion of love."

They had arrived at the train station when a soft rain began to fall. Áine turned impulsively toward Edward, clutching his arm, but said nothing. He touched her chin as he noticed the expression of pain in her eyes. "What is it, Áine?"

She looked up at him, sighed deeply, gulped, and then asked, "Tell me, would you do it again? Choose the path your life took, that is."

He gazed at her for some minutes before answering. "When I look at you, I see glimpses of Maeve . . . "

He looked away, as he picked up his suitcase. "No, Áine, all things told, though it's easy to say now, I would have chosen differently. The challenge, my dear, is to find a way to *combine* your passions in life with the passion one feels for another. That, alas, I did not or was not, able to accomplish," he said, as his voice faded.

He turned back to Aine. "Until now," he added, "transformed in a new way—through the existence of you."

Áine hugged him, saying she enjoyed the time they spent together. He smiled tenderly at her. "Follow your

passions in life, Áine, whether for an individual person or a goal. If you have both, try to combine them.
Everything else will fall into place."

Áine looked at him with a queer expression on her
face, and then said to him, as he turned away, "Odd, that,
that's almost to the word what Maeve had once said to
me. Follow your passions." Looking away, she said, "If
only," but he had already boarded the train.

Part Four

At Last

Faoi Dheireadh

CHAPTER NINETEEN

TWIST OF FATE

CORA AN CINNÚINT

AFTER SEEING EDWARD OFF at the train station, Áine headed down to the strand for a good long walk to clear her head from the volley of thoughts that had taken up a match within. Various questions rolled through her—like billowing waves announcing an imminent storm at sea. What if one could return to take up life again at a specific point from which one once changed paths? Would retracing one's steps lead to a new present? Would experience and its often-painful lessons combine to offer a dramatic alternative to how life had turned out? She also wondered whether the past can re-form in the present, whether life can be re-lived in ways with the assured tranquillity of the present? What happens when the past re-awakens in the mind and heart? Or does it simply never leave—perhaps lying dormant until suddenly re-emerging with a vengeance. These questions now pounded away—like the surf on a rocky beach during a fierce storm. Wave after wave of thoughts, questions, doubts, and hopes poured into her thoughts—retreating, followed by soaking her heart again with a spray of feelings and memories.

As she walked along the water's edge, Áine thought about the account of that moment in the hospital room when her uncle—the former arch-nemesis of her aunt/mother, leaned over to kiss the very woman whom he had spent years fighting. In that moment, the time between their past and the present simply faded away. Everything else in between—their separate lives, new loves, the many, many years—disappeared. Only this new moment of re-connection and their shared past had any meaning for either of them. The old feelings—buried under layers of composted debris of pain and anger—fertilized each of their hearts.

This was obvious even in the eyes of the dying woman who could no longer control any bodily movements, but whose eyes danced and sparkled upon the kiss from the man in whom long ago she had placed her dreams for a shared future. What would have happened had she continued living? Could they have taken up where they had left off in an earlier part of their shared lives? What if Maeve were still alive now and met up again with Edward—would they be able to continue as if the past years were simply a moment in time? And could she, Áine, feel towards Edward—as a daughter to her father, even without the years they should have shared together?

Áine opened her jacket and pulled from within a chest pocket a small packet. It was filled with ashes, ones she had secretly reserved from Maeve's urn and had carried with her as she questioned Edward about his feelings for Maeve.

Turning around to take in the entire scene about her, she walked over to that part of the strand where the Bradáin River folds into the sea. Leaning over, she reached in for a small handful and chanted selected lines from a Yeats poem:

> *I am of Ireland*
> *And time runs on, cried she.*
> *Come dance with me in Ireland—*

She ran along the river's edge, casting bits of ashes into the flowing waters. She ran and ran and ran—until her run had changed to a dance. Dancing along with the waves of the sea, she continued to cast the ashes until there were no more into the now crashing waves.

"I am of Ireland," she cried aloud to the gulls ahead and to the shouting waves about her. "I am of Ireland! I am of Ireland."

Looking about her, she spied a stick, and taking it into her hands, retreated from the ocean's edge to far inland on the sandy strand where the waves wouldn't reach. With stick in hand, she wrote in looming letters the word, *Maeve*, and slowly turning around, as she gazed all about, she softly chanted:

> *I am of Ireland—and you are of Ireland—*
> *may you—and I—*
> *and all of our own ones—*
> *dance here forever—*
> *in Ireland.*

Miraculously enough, the sun emerged from behind the clouds, casting a wide rainbow over the water. Seeing it as a sign of endorsement, Áine threw off her dress, discarding it on the sand, and plunged into the waves.

As she swam around enjoying the rainbow overhead, Muirís suddenly appeared on the strand looking for Áine. Noticing only her dress that lay in a heap, he gazed out, searching for her among the rolling waves that rolled into the shoreline. Spying her as she emerged from a wave, he called out to the swimming woman, "I have your dress. Am I to see it as a *sign*?"

With the rainbow over her head, and she frolicking among the waves, Áine seemed a mermaid—a *selkie*—dashing through the waves. "Ah, that woman has stolen me' heart entirely," he muttered, with a toss of his head. "If only she'll finally have me."

"I can't hear you—come in!" she sang out, and dove down into another wave.

"You'll take me away to your subterranean lair, then!" he shouted.

"Come in, come in," she repeatedly called out to him.

"Only if you promise to marry me, so!" Muirís retorted.

"You take my dress and expect me to marry you?" she quipped, as she bobbed amid the gently rolling waves.

"Just as your namesake and mine!"

Stripping off his shirt and trousers with nothing more than his boxers, he ran out and stood amid the crashing surf. Spreading out his arms, he called out again, "So will you, now, Áine? Will you be mine, as your ancestress was to my ancestor?"

Áine's only response was to dive down under a wave that was about to turn. She was nowhere to be found.

Muirís's heart pounded as he waited for the sprite to re-appear. Suddenly, she rose from the depths of the water to stand before him with a coy smile.

"Will you have me, now?" he pressed, as he reached out to her.

Áine sprayed out water from her teeth at him and laughing, dove down again into the water away from him. Just like a seal, she re-emerged some distance away and called out, "In what way is it I should have you?"

"In all ways!" he sang out as he dove into the waves after her.

They found each other in the surf. Wrapping their bodies around one another, they rolled in the edging tide, laughing as they hugged.

"Will you?" he asked, as he kissed her cheeks repeatedly.

She rolled away and asked playfully, "Will I what?"

"Will you have me? Will you marry me?" he pursued.

Áine smiled, but said nothing, squirting water at him again through her teeth.

"Stop your antics, you *water sprite*, and answer me. I can take it no longer. I must know if we're to be together for all eternity," he pleaded.

"To be *your own one*, is it, you want, then, Muirís?" She dove into another wave and swam off some distance.

"Yes!" he shouted out to her. "To be *my own one!*"

Like a salmon jumping up into the evening sky, Áine dove through a wave and disappeared, but not before singing out,

"Yes, oh yes, oh yes, oh yes!" she exclaimed.

CHAPTER TWENTY

YOUR OWN ONES

DO MHUINTIR FÉIN

S ome months later, following the tradition of their
own ones, who had married at the site where Muirís
FitzGerald had taken the first Áine's dress, back so
many hundreds and hundreds of years ago, the new couple were to be married down along the strand where they
had sealed their love.

The guests were all seated under the tent that Muirís
had erected for the celebration. Their families, including
most of the cousins—with the exception of Diarmuid,
who couldn't break away for health reasons from his
new life on the Riviera—were seated, chatting away with
one another. Elizabeth had come down from Dublin to
attend the festivities and sat near the front. Even Eithne
had flown in from Canada—however *reluctantly*—to
attend. Muirís and his father waited up front with Father
O'Garvey.

As expected at any family function, Conor officially
commenced the ceremony in the traditional fashion.

Dressed in his family tartan, with his kilt dangling evocatively open, he started up the *uilleann* pipe and marched in his flip-flops ever so slowly down the heather-lined aisle, playing the air, "*Medb's Lament.*"

"Have you your privies this time, Conor?" called out one of the lads as his uncle walked by, to which Conor simply added a dance kick, revealing plaid boxers underneath.

Giggles and guffaws filled the air as Father O'Garvey scowled at the cheek of the bagpiper. Reaching the front, Conor ended his lament and immediately moved into a tune written by one of the eighteenth-century Ó'Suílleabháins, a noted harpist from *Corca Dhuibhne.*

Áine arrived, attired in a vintage wedding dress she had found carefully stored away in her grandmother's house. Her hair, which flowed down around her shoulders, was topped with a long veil dotted with sprigs of wildflowers.

She stood behind the curtain at the end of the aisle waiting for the right moment to enter. Her maids in waiting, her former cousins—now three newly-discovered half-sisters, Bair, Faife, and Cainder—stood by her side, one adjusting her train, while the other two fixed the veil that flowed down the bride's back.

"You look radiant!" declared Bair in awe, while Faife whispered into Áine's ear, "There now, stop your worrying—everything's perfect!"

"Well, almost everything," replied Áine with a slight sigh, as she peeked around the curtain, scanning the audience.

"It's a pity your father couldn't be with you on this day," consoled Cainder.

With a glance around, Áine muttered to more to herself than to the others, "That isn't the father I was looking for."

"Are you ready, then?" asked Faife.

"Ah, well. It's all good," said Áine in response. "I guess we'll go in once Conor finishes."

"That could be hours from now," quipped Bair. "He's in his element now, with so many eyes all giving him their undivided attention."

They laughed, as Cainder added, "I wouldn't be in the least surprised that he provided them with a solo concert—rather than a few airs as a prelude to your ceremony."

Suddenly, from behind them, a long black limo pulled up and stopped.

"Must be your limo back," said one of the girls. "Nice ride, eh?"

As the girls looked over at the auto, two men emerged from the car, one standing, looking straight at them, as the other opened the back door for another. A dignified-looking gentleman emerged, dressed in a top hat and full wedding regalia, replete with evening tails and bowtie. His serious countenance transformed into a huge smile when his gaze landed upon Áine, who upon recognizing him, immediately broke down into tears.

"My God, Áine, darling! Don't cry! You'll ruin your makeup!" Cainder screeched.

"Who is that man? Do you want me to tell him to go away? Some uninvited guest, is he?" cried Bair.

"I'll go talk with him," bristled Faife. "The nerve making you cry like that!"

Áine reached out and restrained her impetuous cousin-sister from carrying out her threat.

"No! No! Let him come! I'm delighted he is here! That's why I am crying!" she exclaimed, as she wiped away her tears.

"Who the Hell *is* he?" they all asked in unison.

"That man, my darlin' cousins, er, *sisters*, is my *father!*" she pronounced.

"Your *father?*" they repeated in unison.

"But how?" asked Cainder, as Bair and Faife, in the same breath asked, "Where did he come from?"

Smiling at both, as she dabbed her tears, Áine said simply, "I found him in the streets of Dublin."

As the two men led Edward to the bridal entourage, Áine stood beaming. Edward approached her, handing her a bouquet of the rare white heather cultivar, *Queen Medb.*

He then bowed before her, and taking her hand in his, he kissed it tenderly, saying, "Surely, you are even more lovely than your goddess namesake—and the ever tormentingly beautiful Maeve."

With tears in her eyes, Áine added the heather bouquet to her own and asked, "But Elizabeth said you were tied up in important economic deliberations with the EU."

"I flew early this morning from Brussels directly here to Kerry," he said off-handedly. "They will have to make do without me for the day."

Her sister-cousins' eyes widened in disbelief as they listened. Coming from Canada, they had not recognized Áine's father, but they certainly could surmise from the exchange that he was somebody politically important.

"Surely, you did not think I would let you down," he said, and added as Áine averted her eyes, "*Again.*"

He took her hand in his. "I had promised you never again, so here I am, to give away—but never to relinquish—my lovely daughter."

He extended his arm to hers, saying gallantly, "Shall we?"

Bair signalled to Conor, who had continued to entertain the guests with traditional tunes, to begin the wedding march. Once he began, all eyes turned to watch the bridal party as they entered the tent.

When Áine finally entered with Edward by her side, gasps of amazement filled the air, along with a hum of whispered comments from among the Irish guests.

"My God, will you have a look at who's hanging on her arm?"

"The *Taoiseach?*"

"Can't be."

"*Tá.* 'Tis indeed."

"But how?"

"Can it be he's—her *father?*"

"No. Impossible."

"Yet, there he is."

"Jaysus."

"Hand it to Maeve."

"Always had an eye for the powerful fellas."

When the bridal party reached the front of the tent, Áine turned to the utterly astonished Muirís. "Muirís, meet Edward Dillon, Taoiseach of Ireland—and my *father.*"

Muirís gazed with wide eyes from Áine to Edward. "I *knew* it. I just knew you two shared some deep secret." He tossed his head to the side and said with a wink, "Though I didn't know quite know it was *this.*"

Edward turned to Muirís, bowed low, and proclaimed solemnly for all to hear, "I release to your Knightly protection, Muirís FitzGerald, Red Knight of Corca Dhuibhne, Co. Kerry, son of Knight Gearóid, son of Knight Muirís, and back to Knight Muirís, the Earl of Desmond, the hand of my daughter, Dr. Áine Ó'Suílleabháin O'Connor Dillon. I do so, with the utmost trust that you shall cherish her as long as you live, in the manner in which this lovely, wonderful young goddess deserves."

This time, Áine gazed at Muirís in astonishment. He winked at her, as he whispered, "Sure, I had a few secrets of me' own stored up for the right moment."

"A Knight? You really are a *Knight*?" she repeated incredulously.

"Ah, sure, 'tis a long story—about eight-hundred years old, actually." He tossed his head saying, "Sure, I'll regale you with the details another time. We have a wedding to proceed with—that is, if you'll still have me."

The guests all laughed in glee over the most unusual set of circumstances emerging between the utterly astonished couple.

When Edward kissed Áine as he presented her to Muirís, the guests all clapped, and shouts of approval filled the air.

Kissing him back on the cheek, Áine, through glistening eyes, whispered, "Thank you—*Father*."

Turning to Muirís, Áine smiled sweetly up at him. "Are you ready to be my Protector, now, Knight FitzGerald?"

"I am indeed, goddess Áine, to be ever-ready at your side."

And they were married before their families—both living and dead.

PART FIVE

ALONG

LE TAOBH

CHAPTER TWENTY-ONE

WHEN WE DEAD AWAKEN

NUAIR A MUID DÚISIGH MARBH

FTER THE WEDDING, Edward experienced a radical political, as well as a personal, transformation, that some attributed to the presence of Áine in his life. He was simply *determined* to take back his country—even if it were to become the last act of his political career.

Infatigable in his explorations of the research on the wild, farmed, and genetically modified fish varieties, Edward, together with Áine as his appointed consultant, visited fish farms, research labs, and local food co-ops in Scotland, Norway, and even Prince Edward Island, where the infamous *"frankenfish"* had been developed to replace wild salmon.

At Áine's urging, he embarked on a special trip to Iceland, where he met with the Finance and Prime Ministers, as well as with citizen groups, to discuss their creation of an alternative economic model to the one being thrust upon his own country by the EU leaders.

He returned laden with solid evidence to support his burgeoning plans for saving Ireland.

Afterwards, he initiated a series of heated negotiations with the infuriated—and *fearful*—EU financial bureaucrats. Edward cleverly agreed to raise Irish corporate tax rates—a repeated EU demand—to which he had been adamantly opposed. The new rate was onerous enough that it made the other EU countries seem more hospitable to corporate cultures than Ireland. In exchange, the EU released control over managing the terms of the economic "recovery" efforts in Ireland. Edward was even able to repatriate Irish territorial waters back to Irish sovereignty from the EU—who had used to latter, to send factory ships off the Irish coast to plunder Irish fishing grounds.

It had been a terribly hard sell, but the thought of multi-nationals leaving Ireland in droves, as a result of the newly imposed Irish corporate tax rate hikes, to seek out countries such as Germany, Austria, and France, convinced the EU to back off Ireland. Behind closed doors, the finance ministers and central bank bureaucrats dismissed the country, saying they had always been difficult to *subdue*.

"Ask Great Britain, after all," they exclaimed to one another. They agreed to turn their focus on more *accommodating* countries in crisis—Spain and Greece.

As perhaps the most significant political initiative in his career, Edward launched a series of national referendums, asking the citizenry to vote on whether to ban GMO products and fish farms in Ireland, as well as whether to restructure the banks based on the Icelandic model, but not before launching a series of educational initiatives—led by Áine—to inform and educate the Irish on the issues facing them as a country.

After months of heated debates in pubs and around kitchen tables throughout the country, the Irish voted in overwhelming numbers to take back their country in ways they had never dreamed they would even wish, during the early days of accumulating holiday homes and extra family autos. It was a long road to overcoming the excesses, greed, and mismanagement that had plagued the country, but like their Northern neighbours in Iceland, the Irish remained convinced they could win their freedom—*again*. This time, however, they meant to remain true to their cultural traditions.

Before long, farmers' markets and local food systems flourished throughout the country, while the jobless took up many of the artisanal labours of their ancestors. The large supermarts closed their doors, while the previously closed small shops, once lining the villages and towns, re-opened.

Dingle, once the site of endless rows of ugly holiday home developments, became the new model for the *Celtic Roots Renaissance*. The tasteless, grey foreclosed holiday estates encircling the town were purchased by the County Council and transformed into brightly painted artisanal studios and school for the traditional arts, where both the Irish themselves and tourists flocked—to study everything from boat-building and thatching, to cheese making, heirloom seed saving, and wood-fired baking.

Áine kept busy chronicling this movement in Ireland for her blogs and website, in between growing heritage vegetables and refashioning them into sumptuous, traditional dishes for the pub. Aside from running their now renowned restaurant and pub, Muirís was appointed by the new Ministry of Fisheries to oversee the re-introduction and protection of wild salmon in the region's rivers and streams.

Their work, their love, and their common passion for nurturing and protecting the land kept them content and ever enthusiastic over their endeavours—even with a slew of their own ones, trailing about behind them.

Each evening, as the sun began its descent into the western horizon, they walked as a family along the strand, to the place where the Bradáin River meets the sea. Of all their children, little Maeve seemed the most enchanted by watching the multi-coloured salmon dance high into the evening air.

As Áine fondly watched Maeve, she thought about the journey *back* that had brought them all *forward* to this point. "Alone, at last, along the riverrun, past swerve of shore and bend of bay, brings us back . . ."

Muirís gazed over at her. "Quoting Joyce again, are you?"

She smiled at him. "It seems appropriate at this moment, somehow."

"The only difference is that you're not alone and never will be again." He wrapped his long arm around her shoulder, as they strolled down the length of the strand.

"We'll re-write it, so," she said, smiling at him, her green eyes flashing.

"'Away, among, alone, at last, along, the riverrun,' then. That about sums up our travels *back*, in our journey *forward*."

He squeezed her gently. "Like the journey of the wild salmon, so."

"My grandmother had it right. Sometimes, the journey *forward*, begins with a step *back*."

"A wise woman, she was, old Áine *Críonna*." Gently kissing his wife, he added, "And somehow, I think you'll be just like her in your old age."

After these walks, as the children snuggled in the arms of their parents for a bedtime story, they inevitably cried, "Tell us, tell us, Mammy, the tale again of *our own ones*."

And Áine would take down the book she had written about their grandmother Maeve, and her mother before her, all the way to the goddess Áine, to read to the children about their history and the family passion for the mountains, the fields—and the rivers forever teeming with wild salmon.

Now today, *na bradáin fiáin*, the wild salmon, swim upstream in that river past the rocky mountains and green vales, past the graveyard where Maeve and all of her kin lie, to the source high in the Paps of Áine, before finding their home among the stones and clear waters—to spawn and usher in another generation in a long line of now completely *wild* Irish salmon.

Some things were simply *meant* to be.

CPSIA information can be obtained at www.ICGtesting.com
Printed in the USA
LVOW12s0919260116

471958LV00004B/5/P